Keiko Suenobu

LIMIT 3

VERTICAL.

CHARACTERS & STORY

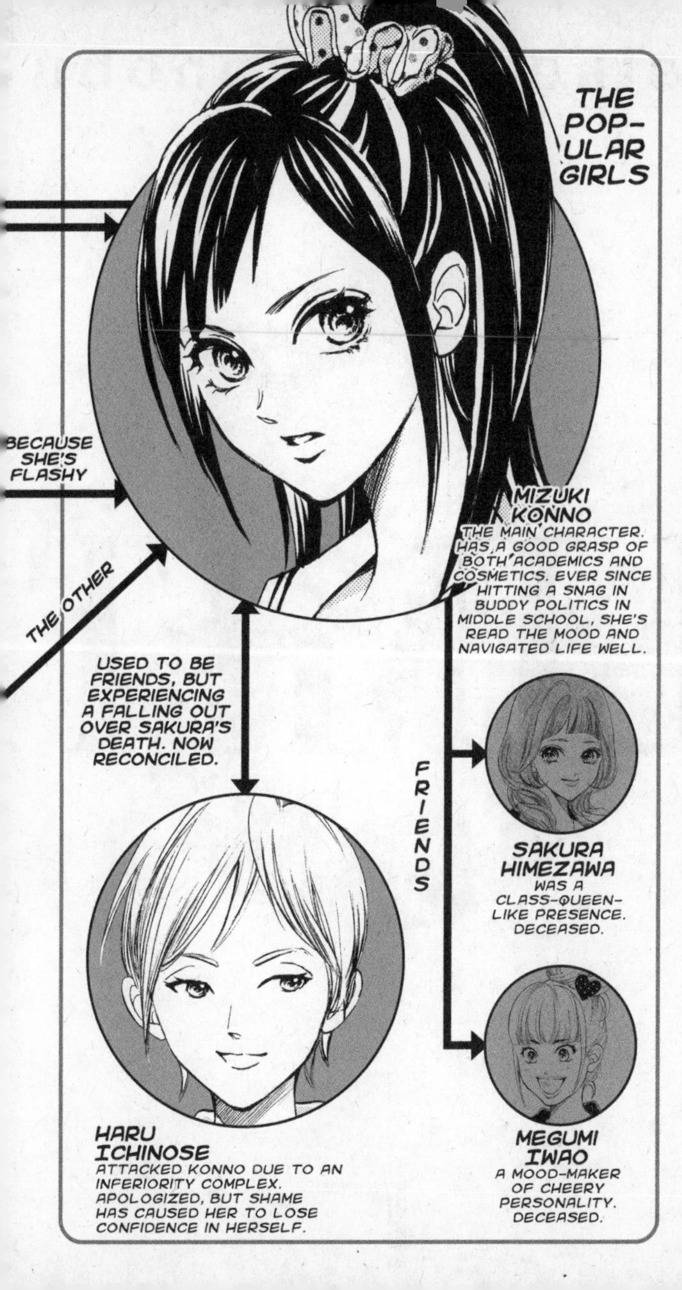
THE POP-ULAR GIRLS
MIZUKI KONNO
THE MAIN CHARACTER. HAS A GOOD GRASP OF BOTH ACADEMICS AND COSMETICS. EVER SINCE HITTING A SNAG IN BUDDY POLITICS IN MIDDLE SCHOOL, SHE'S READ THE MOOD AND NAVIGATED LIFE WELL.
BECAUSE SHE'S FLASHY
THE OTHER
FRIENDS
SAKURA HIMEZAWA
WAS A CLASS-QUEEN-LIKE PRESENCE. DECEASED.
USED TO BE FRIENDS, BUT EXPERIENCING A FALLING OUT OVER SAKURA'S DEATH. NOW RECONCILED.
MEGUMI IWAO
A MOOD-MAKER OF CHEERY PERSONALITY. DECEASED.
HARU ICHINOSE
ATTACKED KONNO DUE TO AN INFERIORITY COMPLEX. APOLOGIZED, BUT SHAME HAS CAUSED HER TO LOSE CONFIDENCE IN HERSELF.

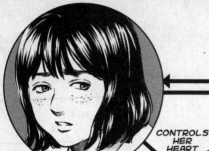

THOUGHT LITTLE OF HER

CAN'T FORGIVE HER

CONTROLS HER HEART

ARISA MORISHIGE
WAS A SUBDUED PRESENCE IN THE CLASS AND WAS BULLIED. AFTER THE ACCIDENT, SHE GETS AHOLD OF THE ONE WEAPON, THE "SCYTHE," AND VENTS HER ANGER.

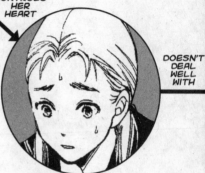

DOESN'T DEAL WELL WITH

CHIKAGE USUI
HAS A DOCILE PERSONALITY AND IS EASILY INFLUENCED BY OTHERS. HAS A LEG INJURY.

NEITHER CAN UNDERSTAND

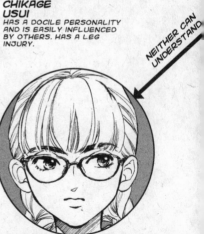

CHIEKO KAMIYA
A CALM, COOL, AND COLLECTED PERSONALITY. HAS AN ABUNDANCE OF KNOWLEDGE REGARDING NATURE AND RESCUE, BUT ALSO HAS A CALLOUS SIDE.

A SUDDEN BUS ACCIDENT THAT OCCURRED ON THE WAY TO AN EXCHANGE CAMP CHANGES EVERYTHING. THERE ARE ONLY A MERE FIVE SURVIVORS, ALL GIRLS. KONNO'S PERFECT, ORDINARY LIFE THAT WASN'T EVER SUPPOSED TO CHANGE COMPLETELY CRUMBLES AWAY.

MORISHIGE RULES THE FIELD THROUGH FEAR, AND HARU REVEALS HER JEALOUSY. KONNO, WHO STOPS BEING ABLE TO TRUST BOTH HERSELF AND OTHERS, HARBORS A DEEP SENSE OF DESPAIR, BUT DRAWS COURAGE FROM KAMIYA'S STRONG FIGURE AND REGAINS HER FOOTING.

MEANWHILE, HER SENSE OF ISOLATION HEIGHTENING FROM THE ANXIETY THAT SHE IS GOING TO BE ABANDONED, USUI FINALLY GRABS MORISHIGE'S "SCYTHE" AND TAKES OFF. EVERYONE'S SPIRITS FALL APART ONCE MORE. AND WHO IS IT THAT IS GAZING UPON THEM FROM AFAR?!

contents

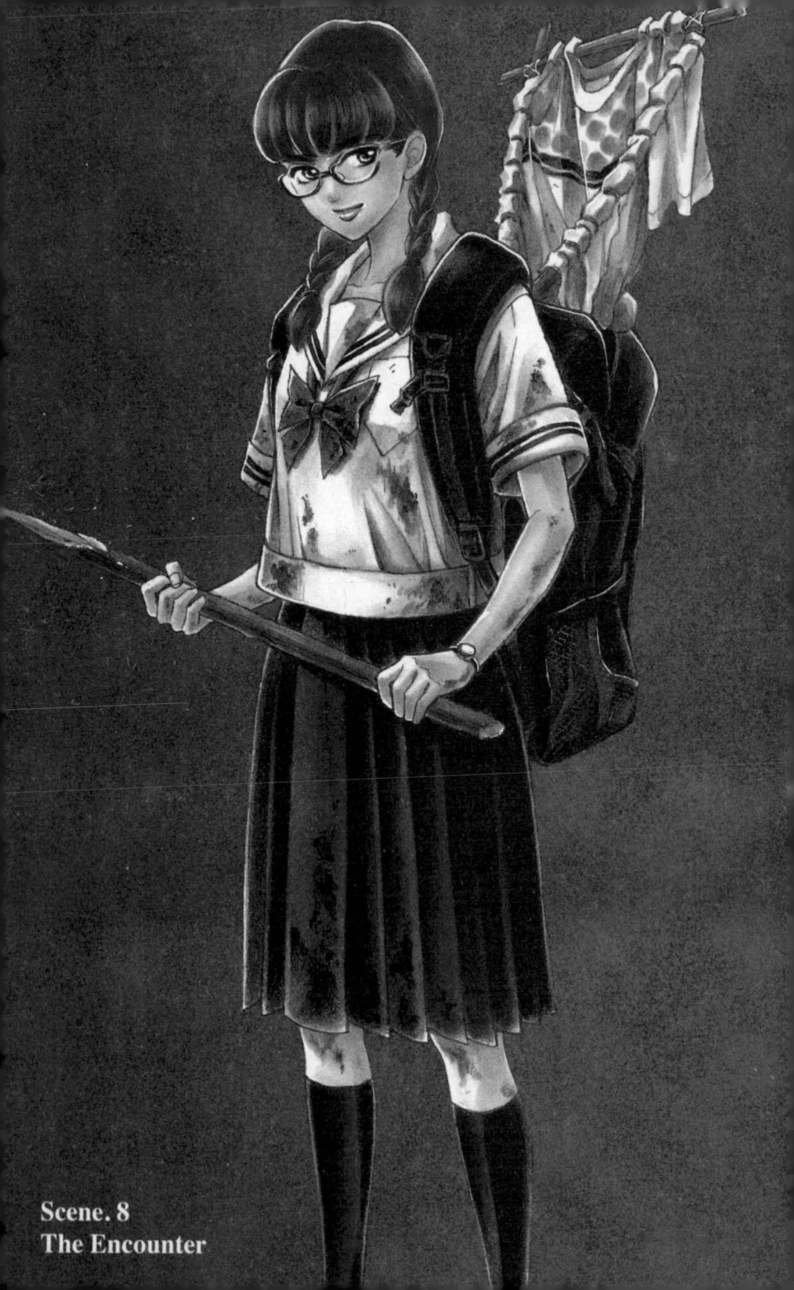

Scene. 8
The Encounter

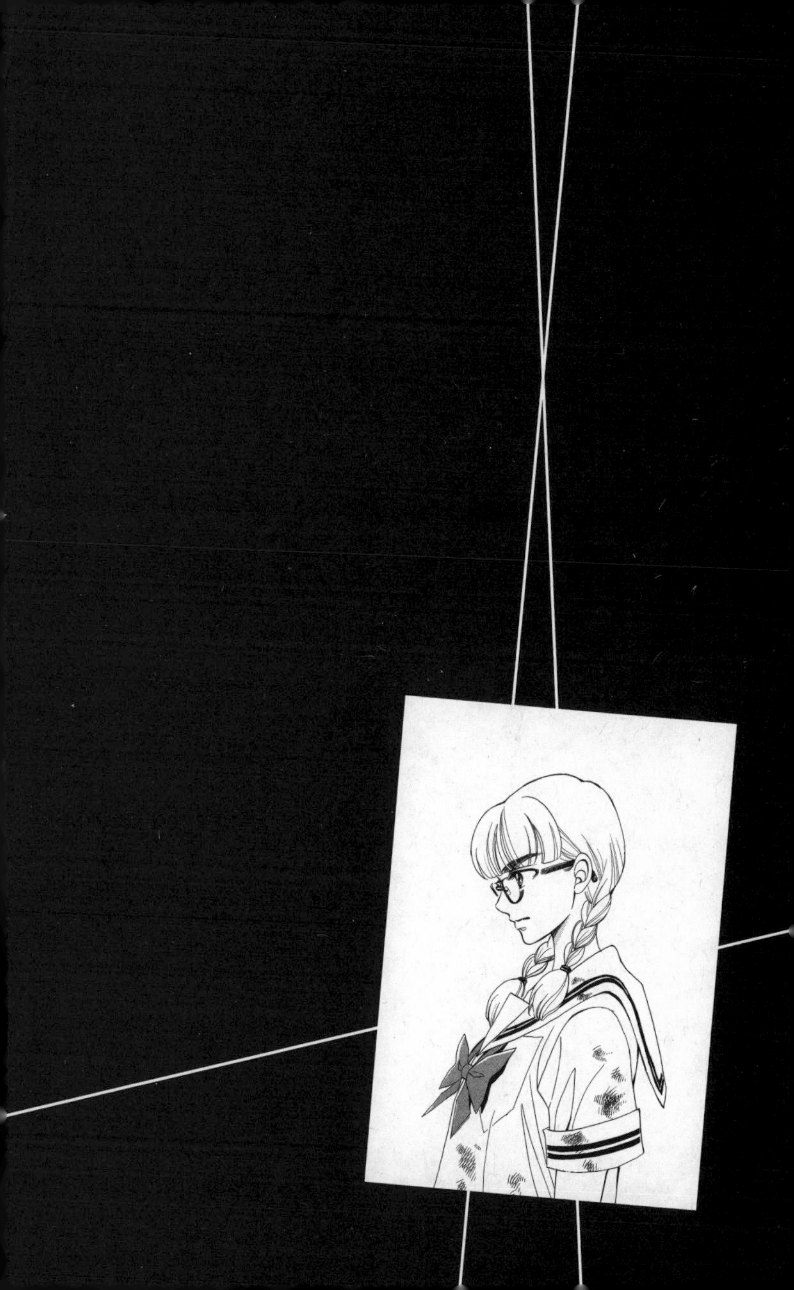

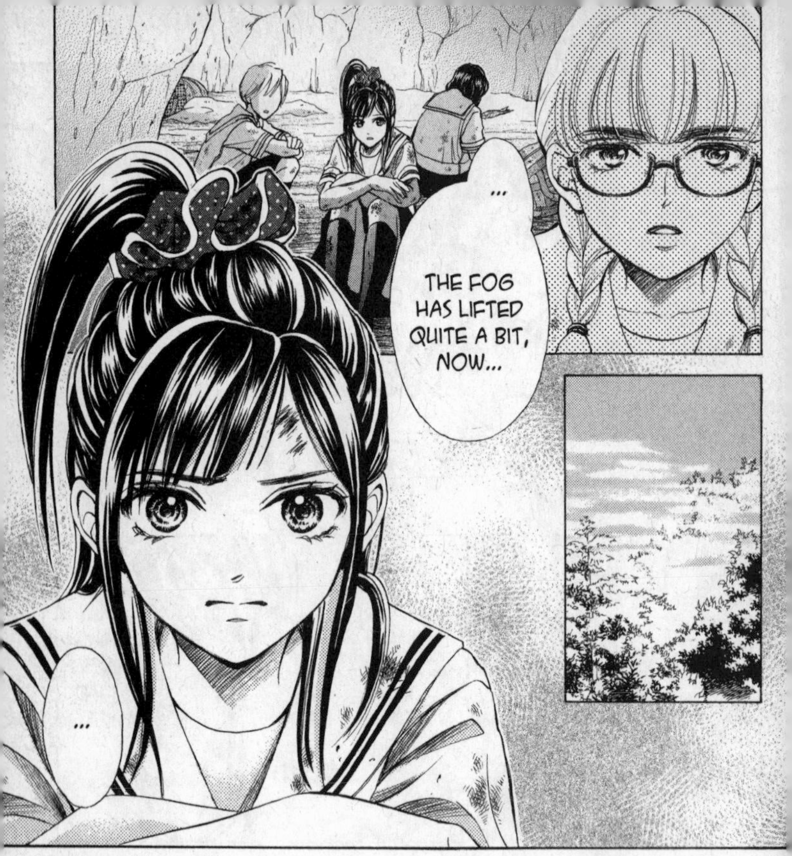
...
THE FOG HAS LIFTED QUITE A BIT, NOW...
...

LIMIT

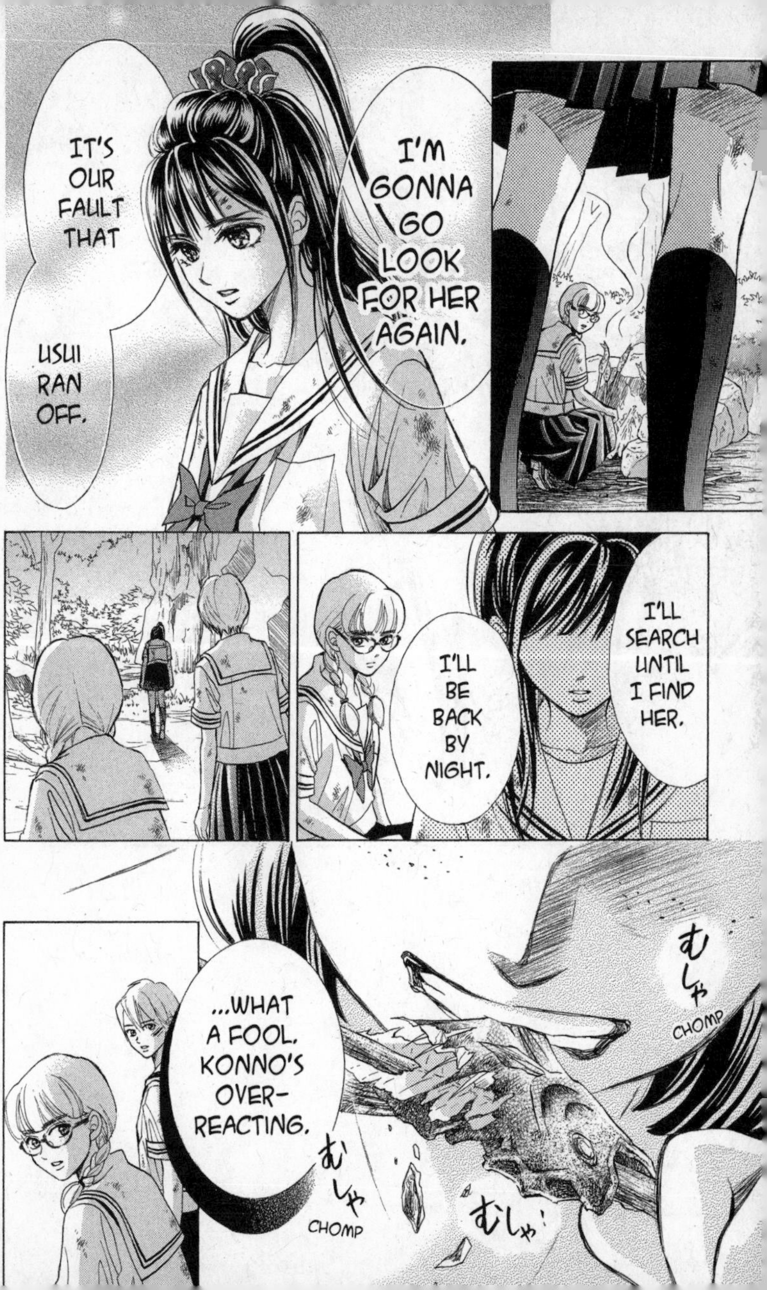
I'M GONNA GO LOOK FOR HER AGAIN.
IT'S OUR FAULT THAT USUI RAN OFF.
I'LL SEARCH UNTIL I FIND HER.
I'LL BE BACK BY NIGHT.
むしゃ
CHOMP
...WHAT A FOOL. KONNO'S OVER-REACTING.
むしゃ
CHOMP
むしゃ!

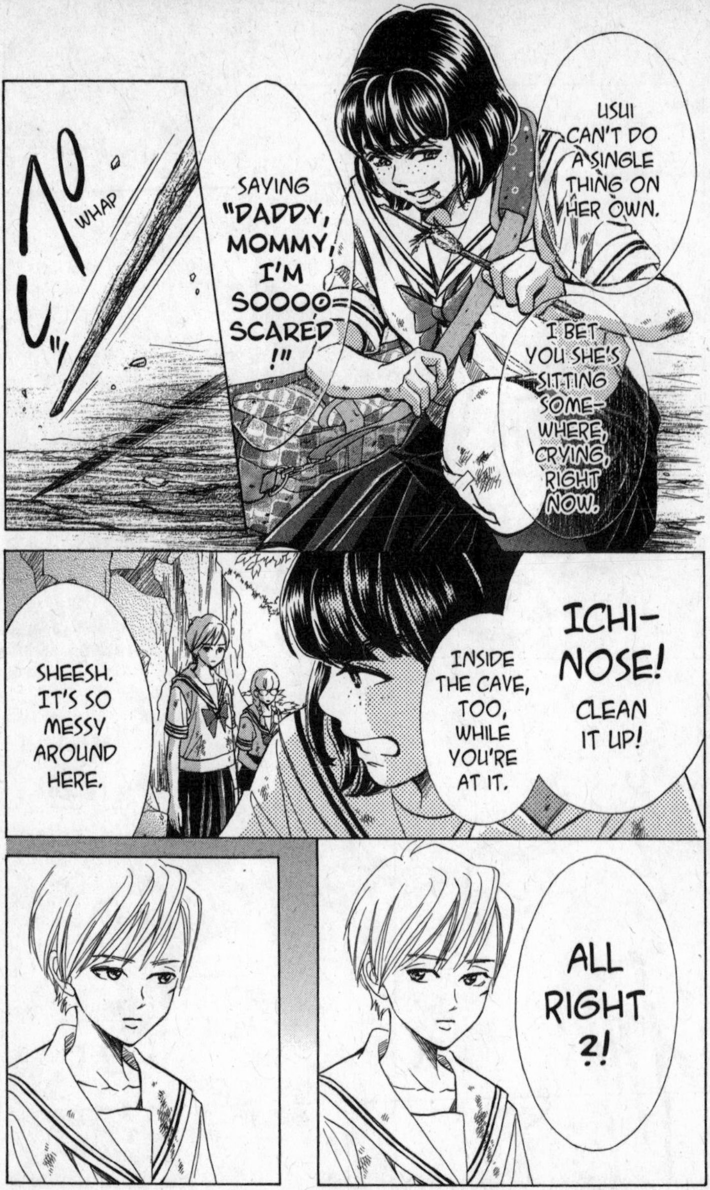
USUI CAN'T DO A SINGLE THING ON HER OWN.
I BET YOU SHE'S SITTING SOMEWHERE, CRYING, RIGHT NOW.
SAYING "DADDY, MOMMY, I'M SOOOO= SCARED!"
WHAP
ICHI-NOSE! CLEAN IT UP!
INSIDE THE CAVE, TOO, WHILE YOU'RE AT IT.
SHEESH. IT'S SO MESSY AROUND HERE.
ALL RIGHT?!

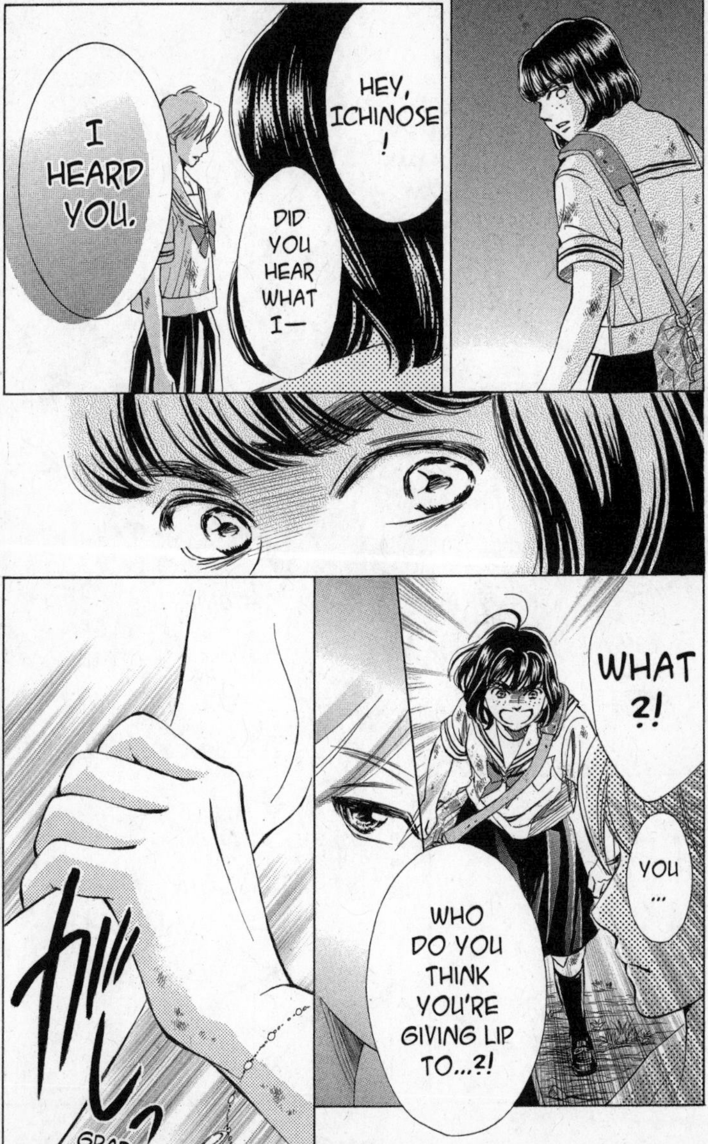
HEY, ICHINOSE!
DID YOU HEAR WHAT I—
I HEARD YOU.
WHAT?!
YOU...
WHO DO YOU THINK YOU'RE GIVING LIP TO...?!
ガしっ
GRAB

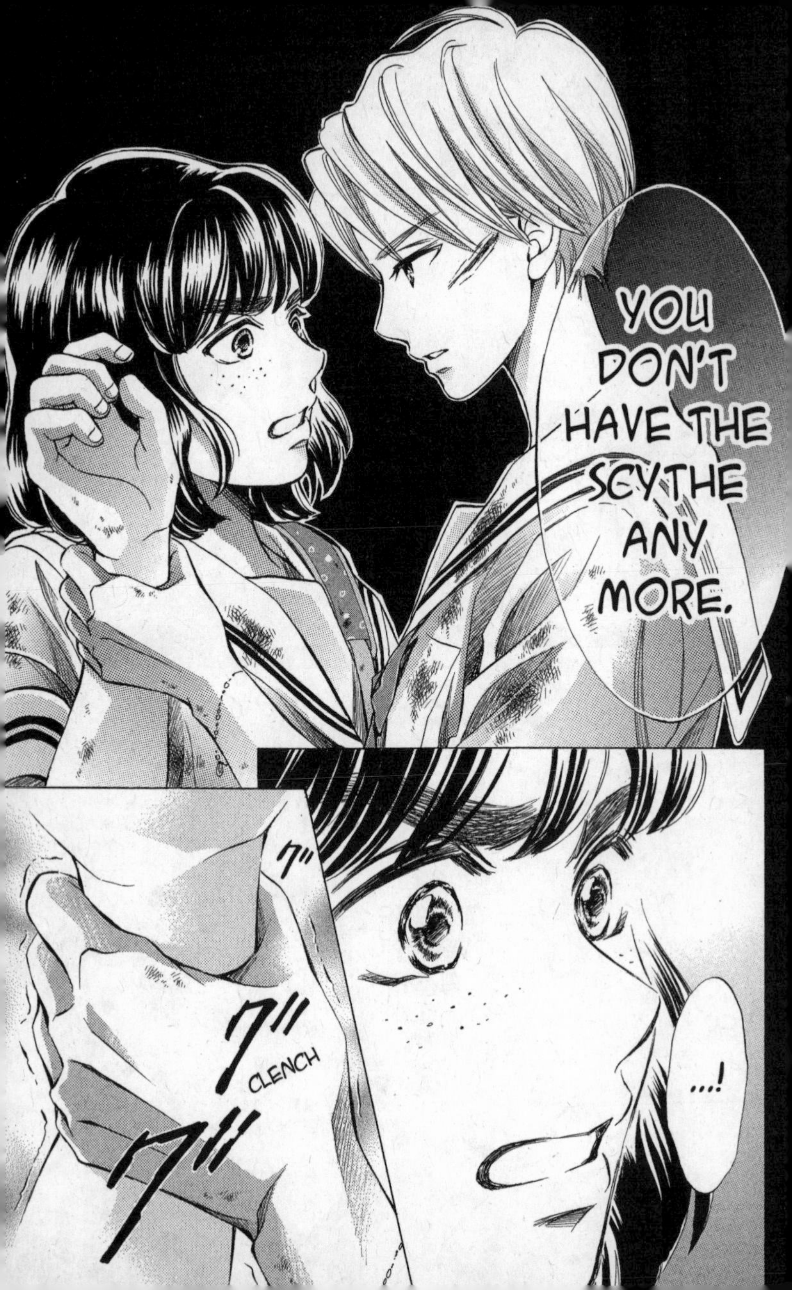
YOU DON'T HAVE THE SCYTHE ANY MORE.
...!
グッ
グッ
CLENCH

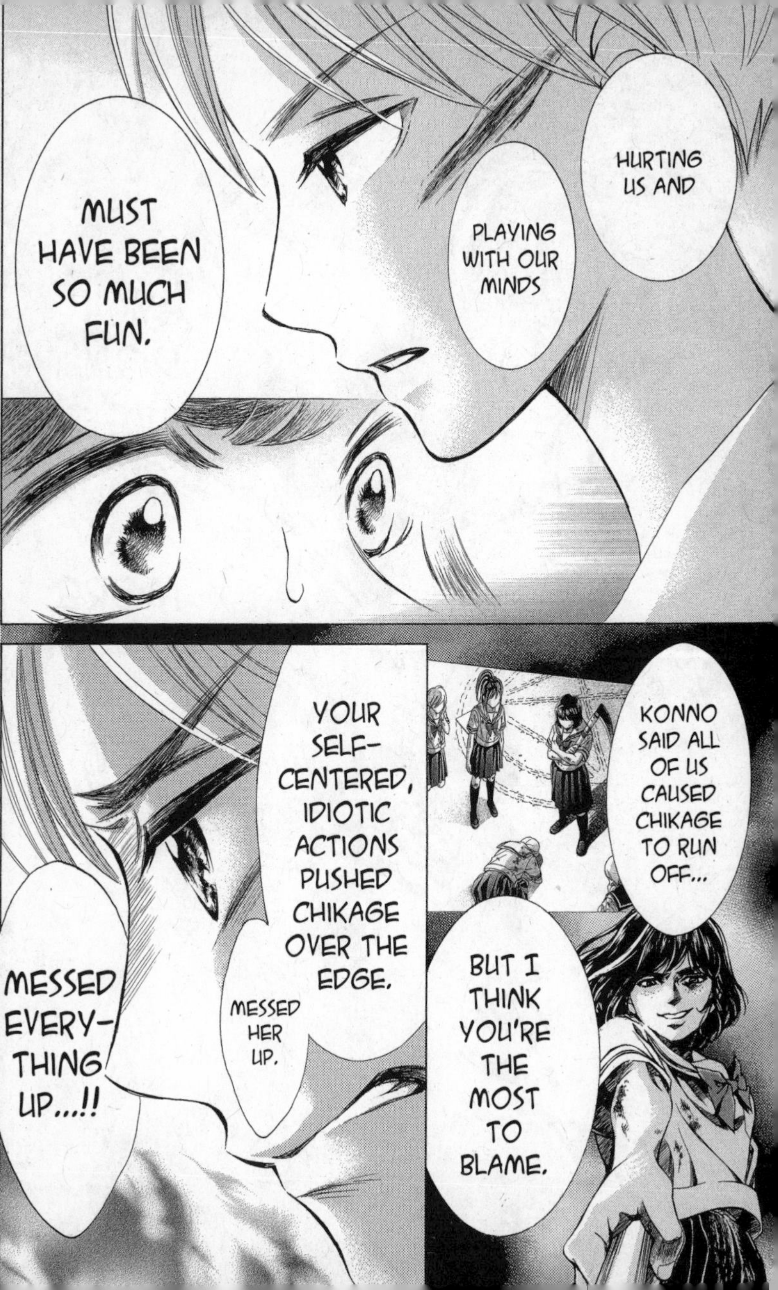
HURTING US AND
PLAYING WITH OUR MINDS
MUST HAVE BEEN SO MUCH FUN.
KONNO SAID ALL OF US CAUSED CHIKAGE TO RUN OFF...
BUT I THINK YOU'RE THE MOST TO BLAME.
YOUR SELF-CENTERED, IDIOTIC ACTIONS PUSHED CHIKAGE OVER THE EDGE.
MESSED HER UP.
MESSED EVERY-THING UP...!!

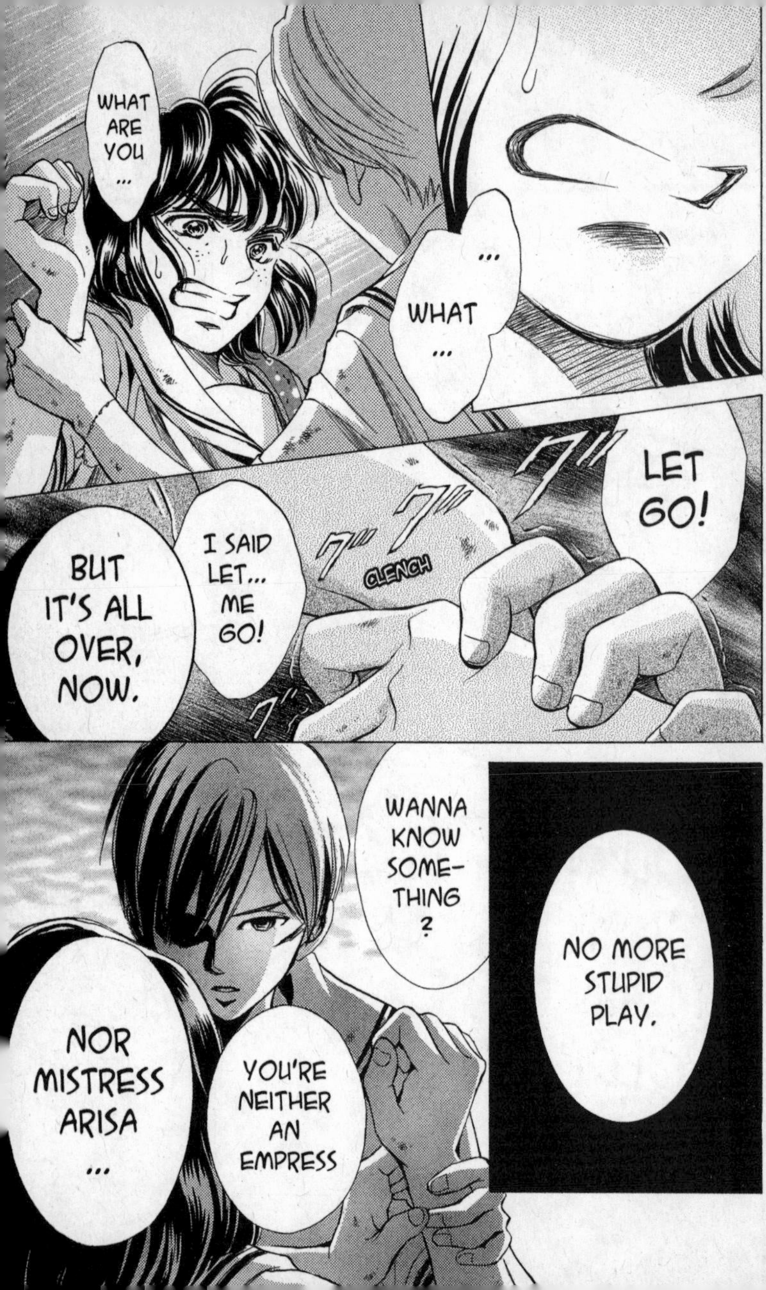

... WHAT ...
WHAT ARE YOU ...
LET GO!
CLENCH
I SAID LET... ME GO!
BUT IT'S ALL OVER, NOW.
NO MORE STUPID PLAY.
WANNA KNOW SOME-THING?
YOU'RE NEITHER AN EMPRESS
NOR MISTRESS ARISA ...

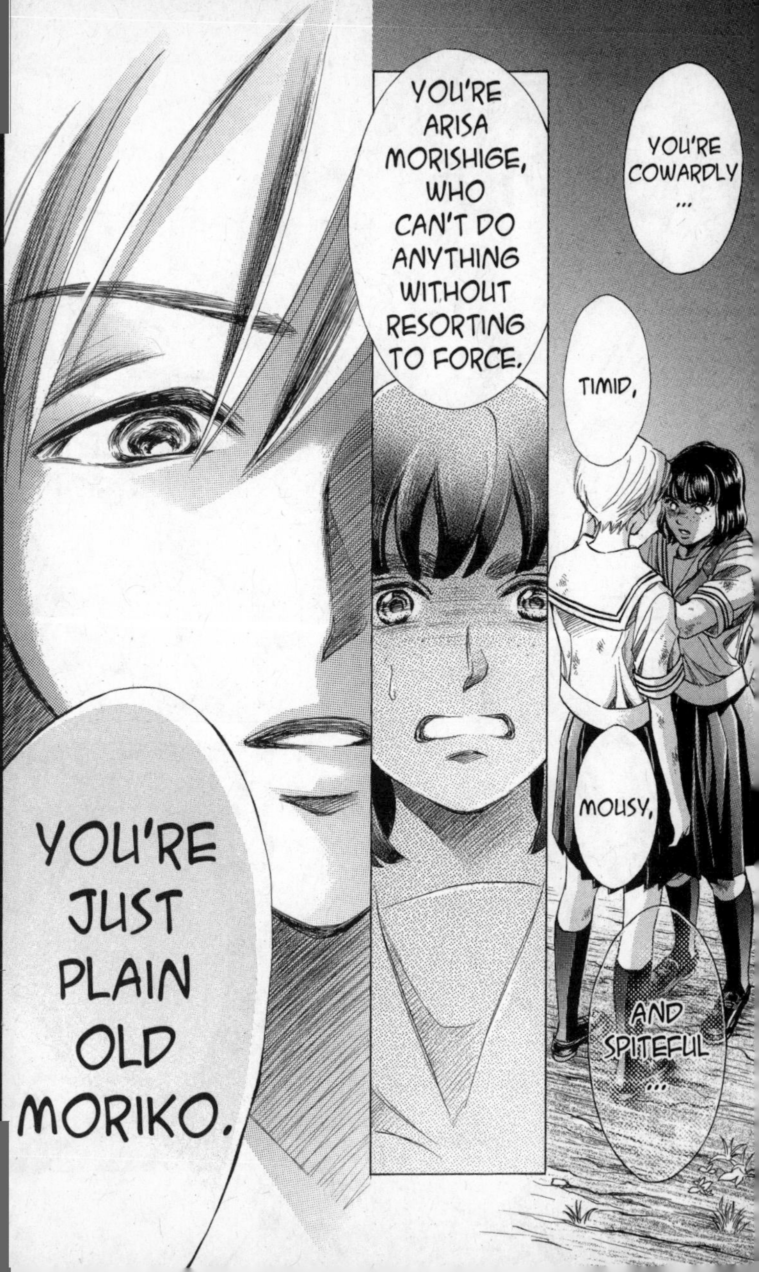
YOU'RE COWARDLY ...
TIMID,
MOUSY,
AND SPITEFUL ...
YOU'RE ARISA MORISHIGE, WHO CAN'T DO ANYTHING WITHOUT RESORTING TO FORCE.
YOU'RE JUST PLAIN OLD MORIKO.

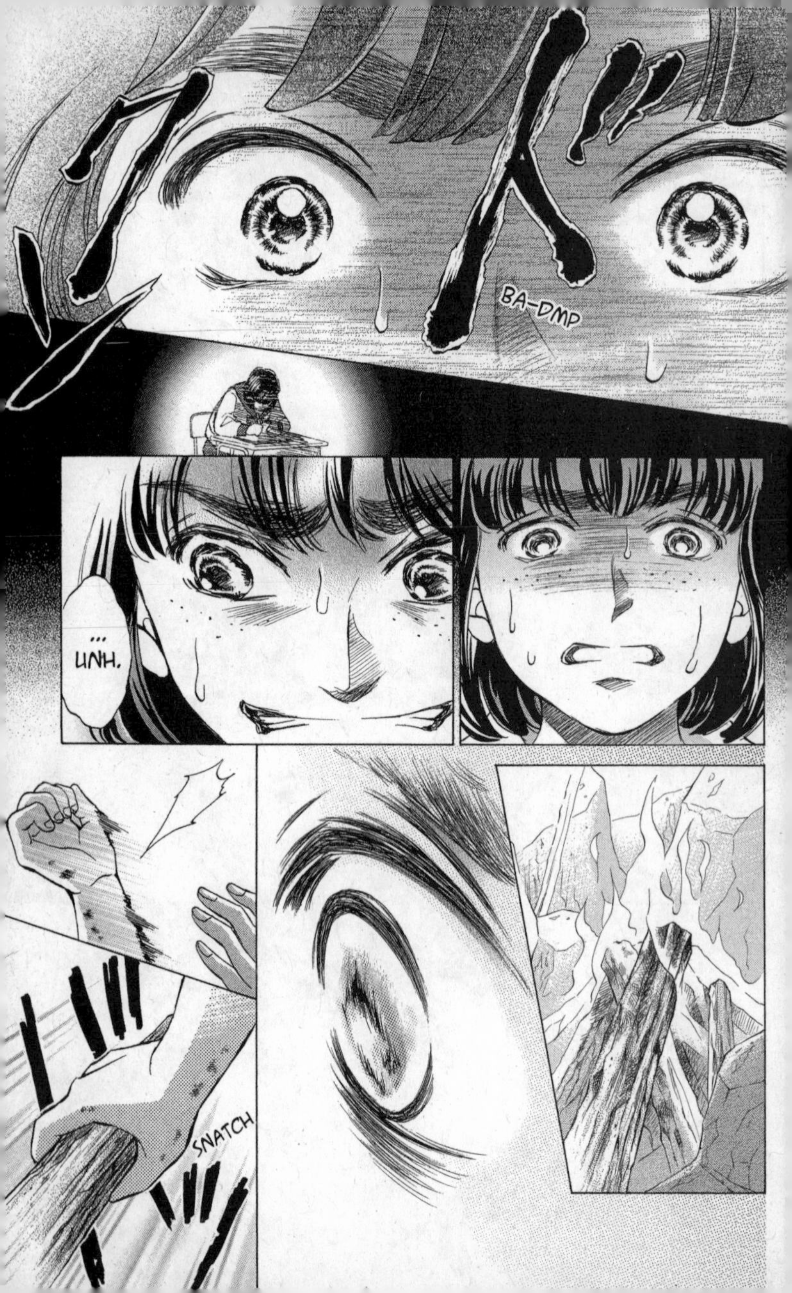
BA-DMP
... UNH.
SNATCH

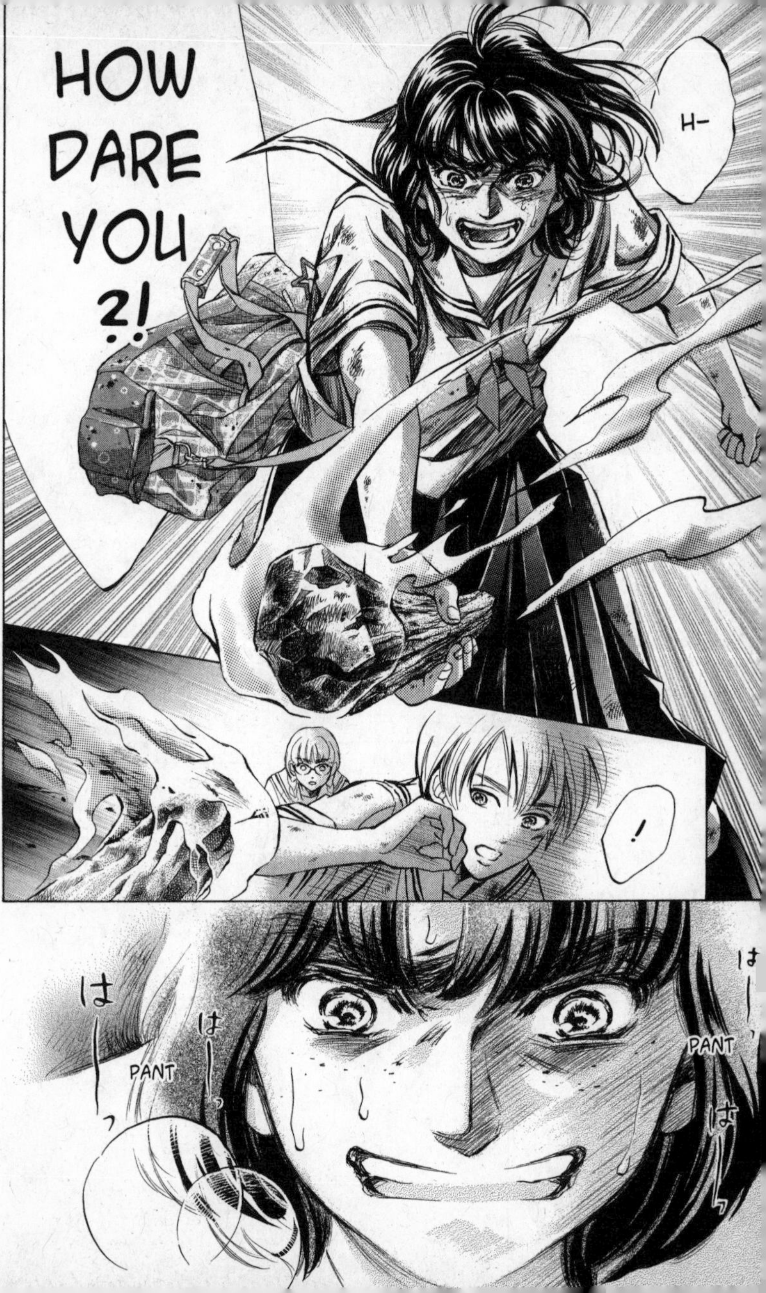
H-
HOW DARE YOU ?!
!
はー、
PANT
はーっ
はーっ
PANT
はーっ

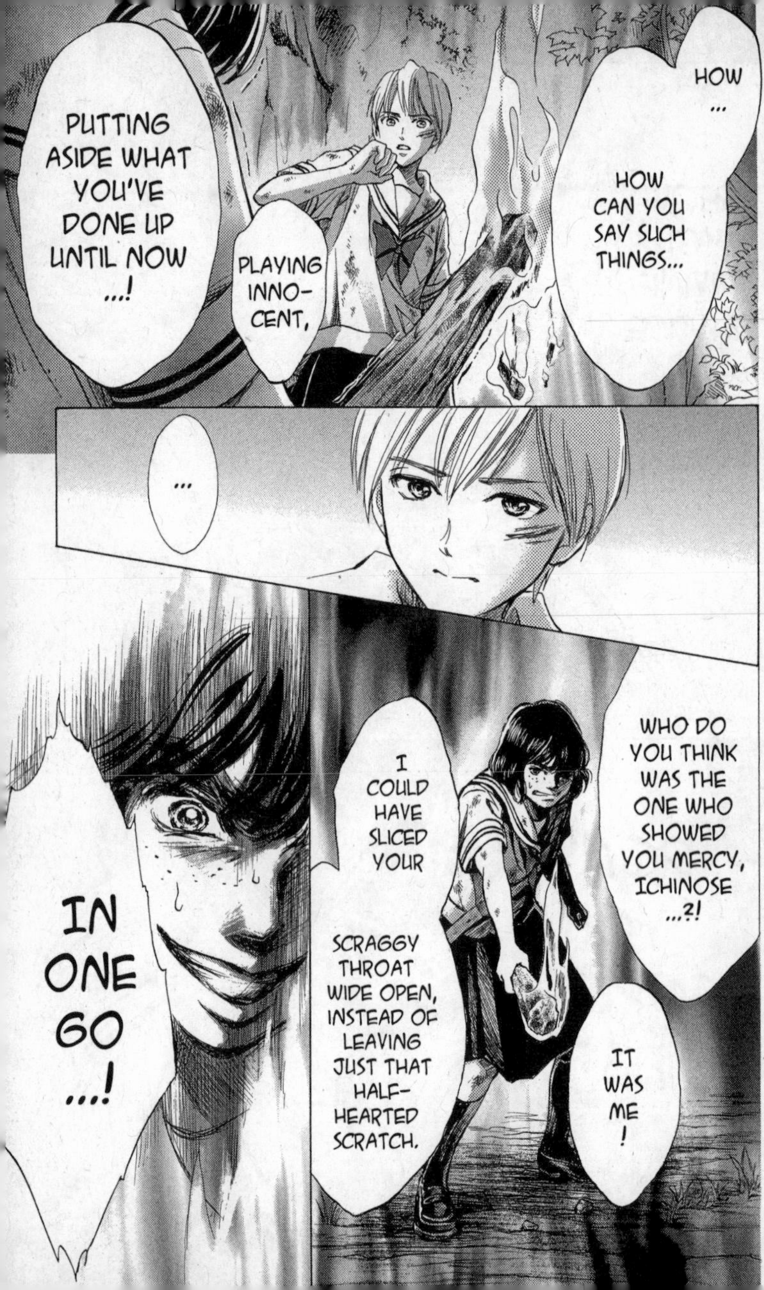
HOW ... HOW CAN YOU SAY SUCH THINGS...
PLAYING INNO-CENT,
PUTTING ASIDE WHAT YOU'VE DONE UP UNTIL NOW ...!
...
WHO DO YOU THINK WAS THE ONE WHO SHOWED YOU MERCY, ICHINOSE ...?!
IT WAS ME!
I COULD HAVE SLICED YOUR
SCRAGGY THROAT WIDE OPEN, INSTEAD OF LEAVING JUST THAT HALF-HEARTED SCRATCH.
IN ONE GO ...!

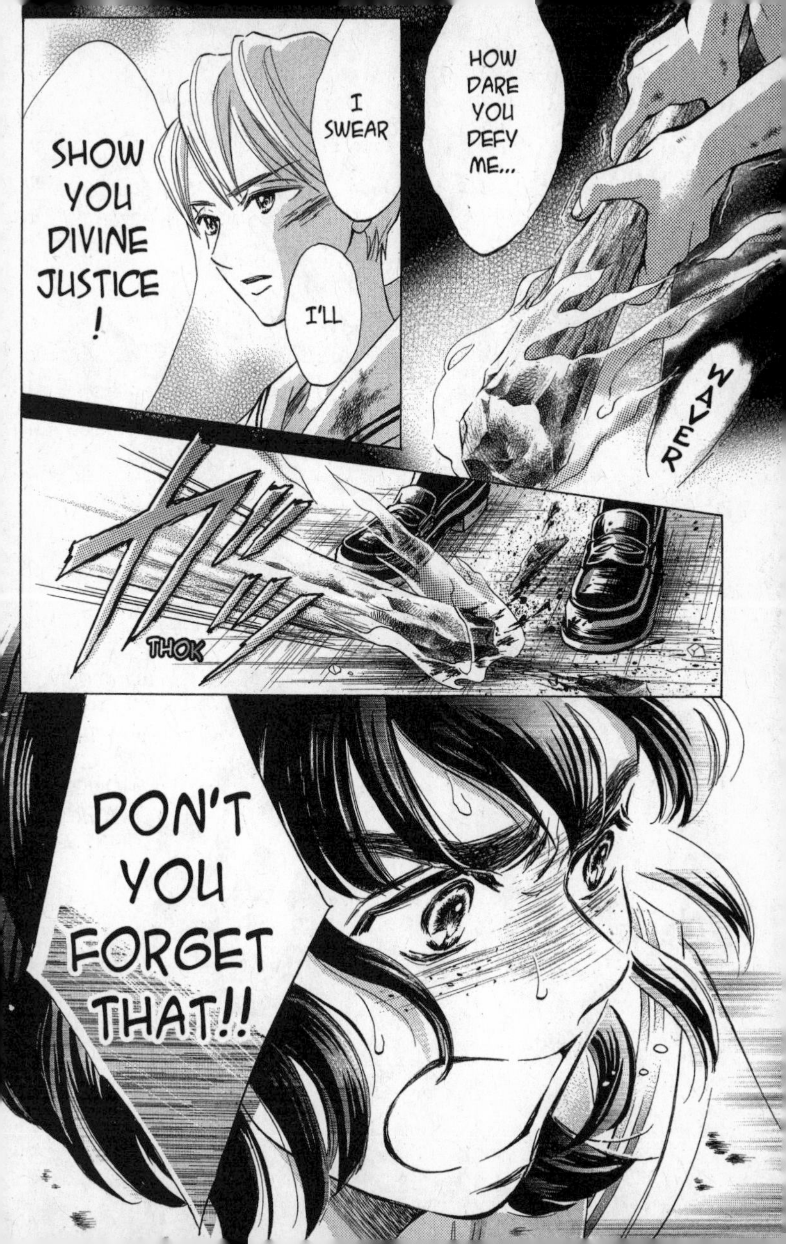
HOW DARE YOU DEFY ME...
WAVER
I SWEAR
I'LL
SHOW YOU DIVINE JUSTICE!
THOK
DON'T YOU FORGET THAT!!

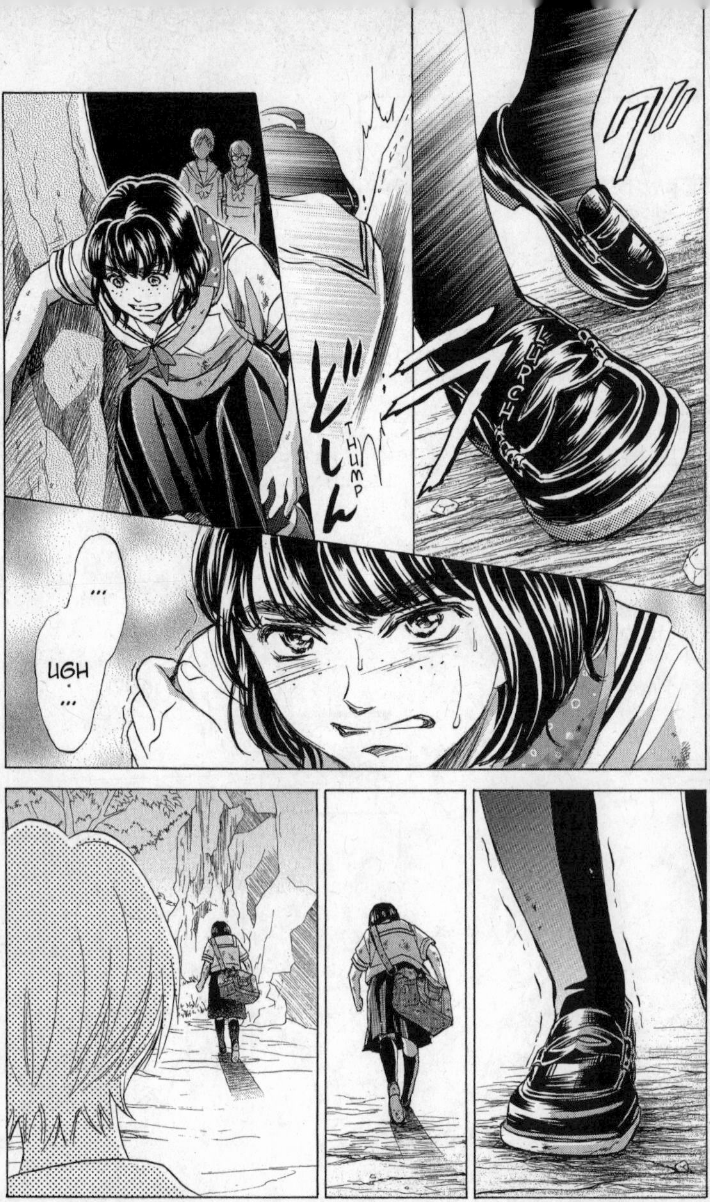
LURCH
どしん
THUMP
...
UGH
...

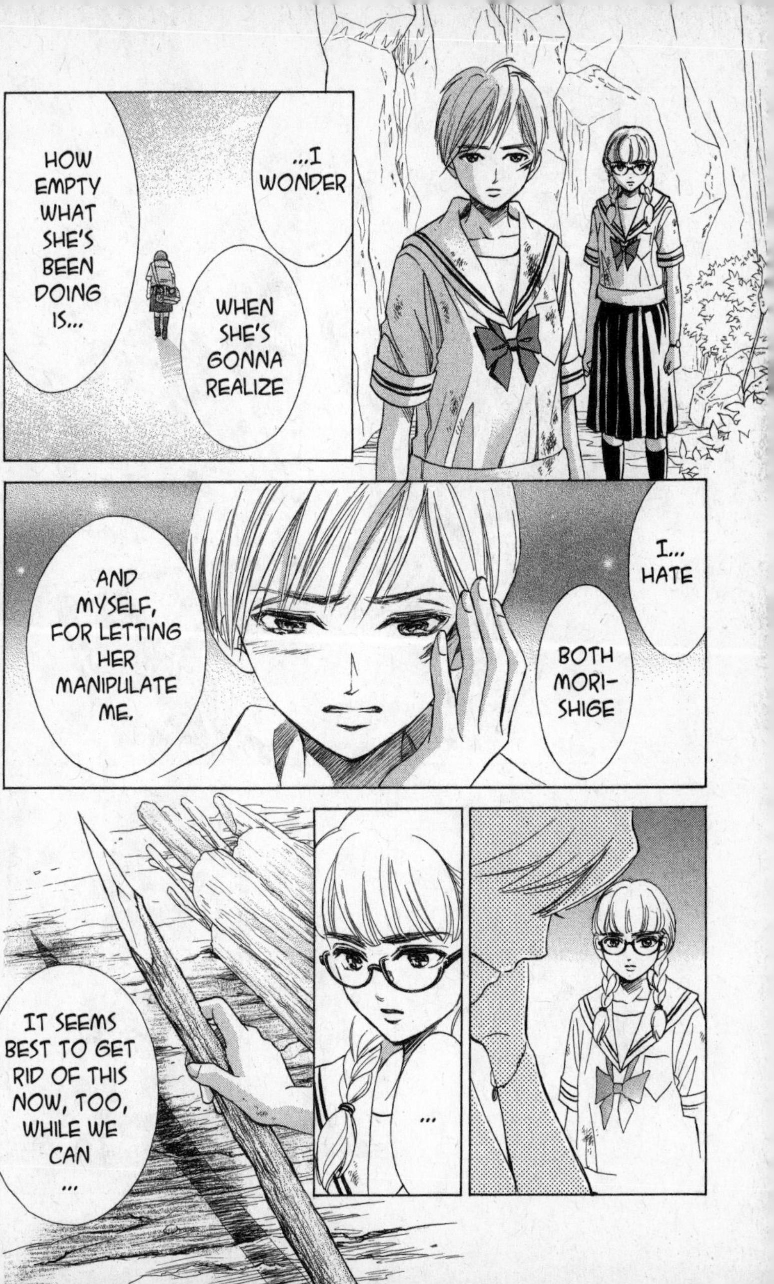
...I WONDER
WHEN SHE'S GONNA REALIZE
HOW EMPTY WHAT SHE'S BEEN DOING IS...
I... HATE
BOTH MORI-SHIGE
AND MYSELF, FOR LETTING HER MANIPULATE ME.
...
IT SEEMS BEST TO GET RID OF THIS NOW, TOO, WHILE WE CAN ...

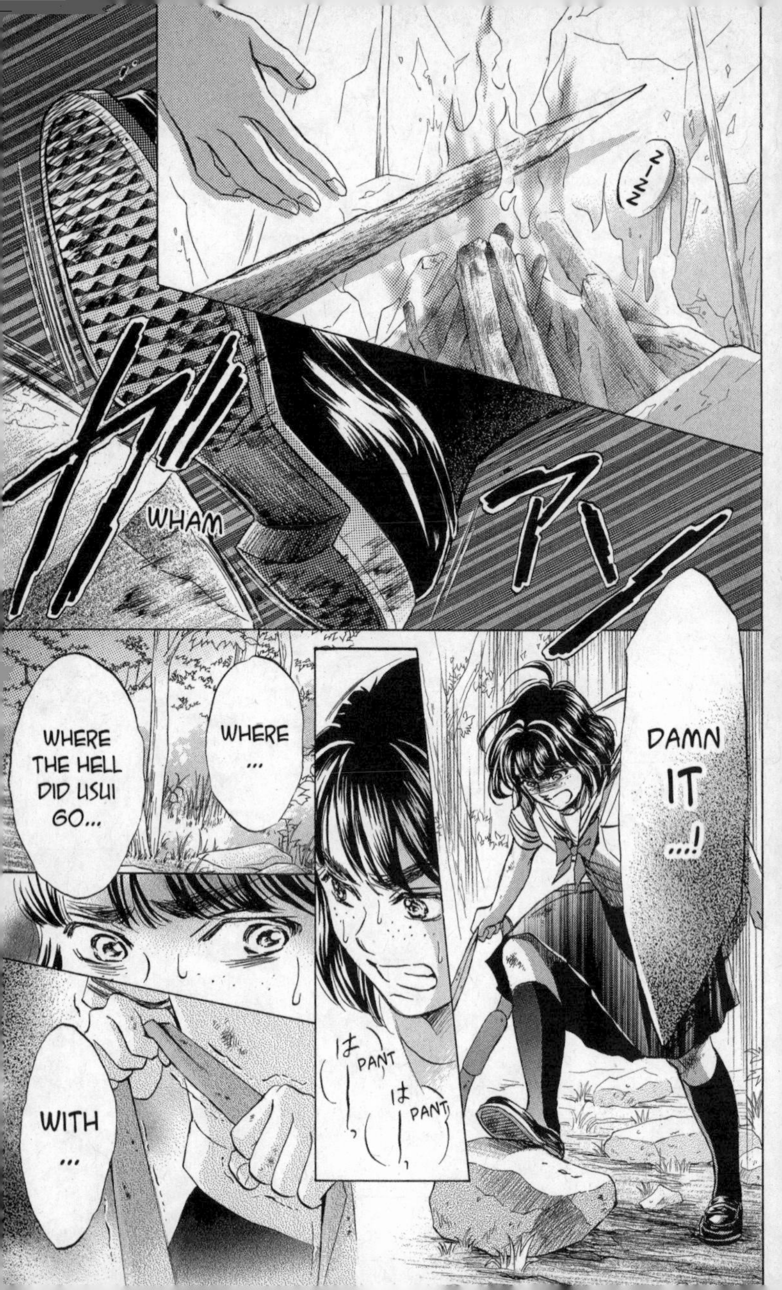

ZINN
WHAM
DAMN IT ...!
は PANT
は PANT
WHERE ...
WHERE THE HELL DID USUI GO...
WITH ...

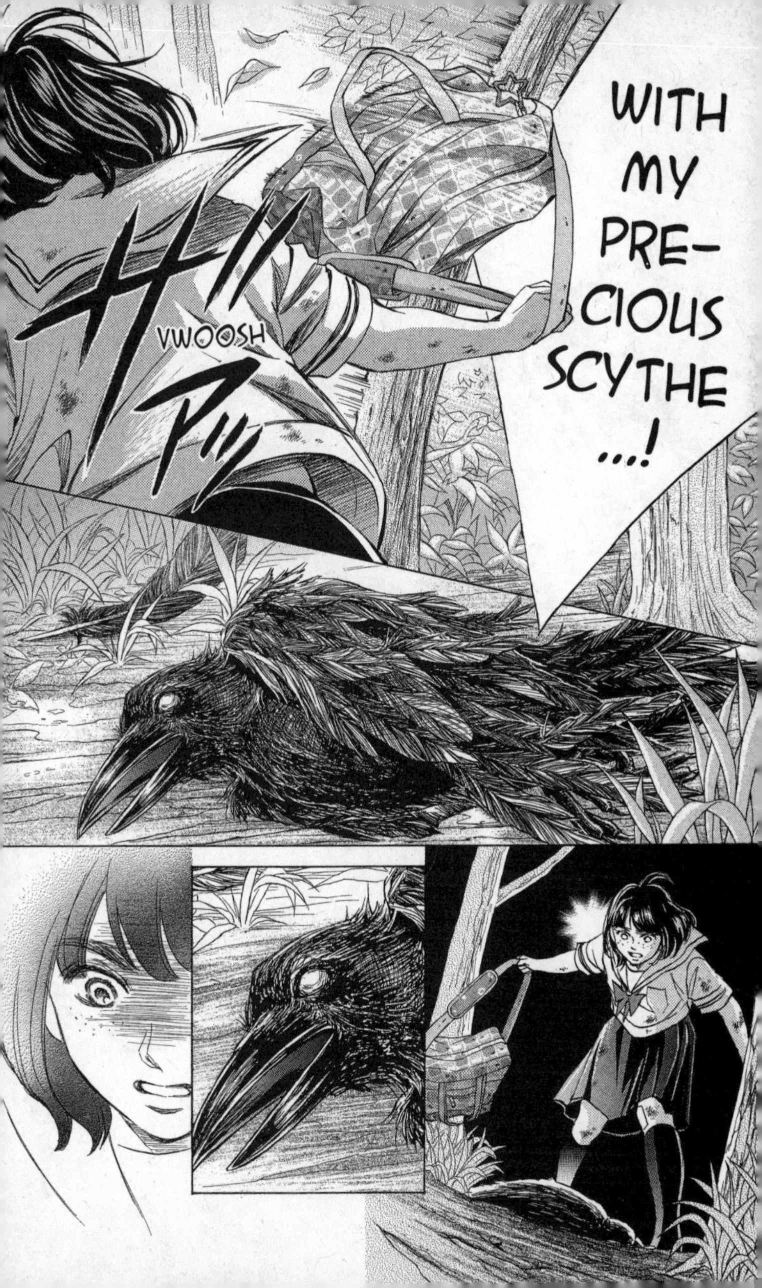
WITH MY PRE-CIOUS SCYTHE ...!
VWOOSH

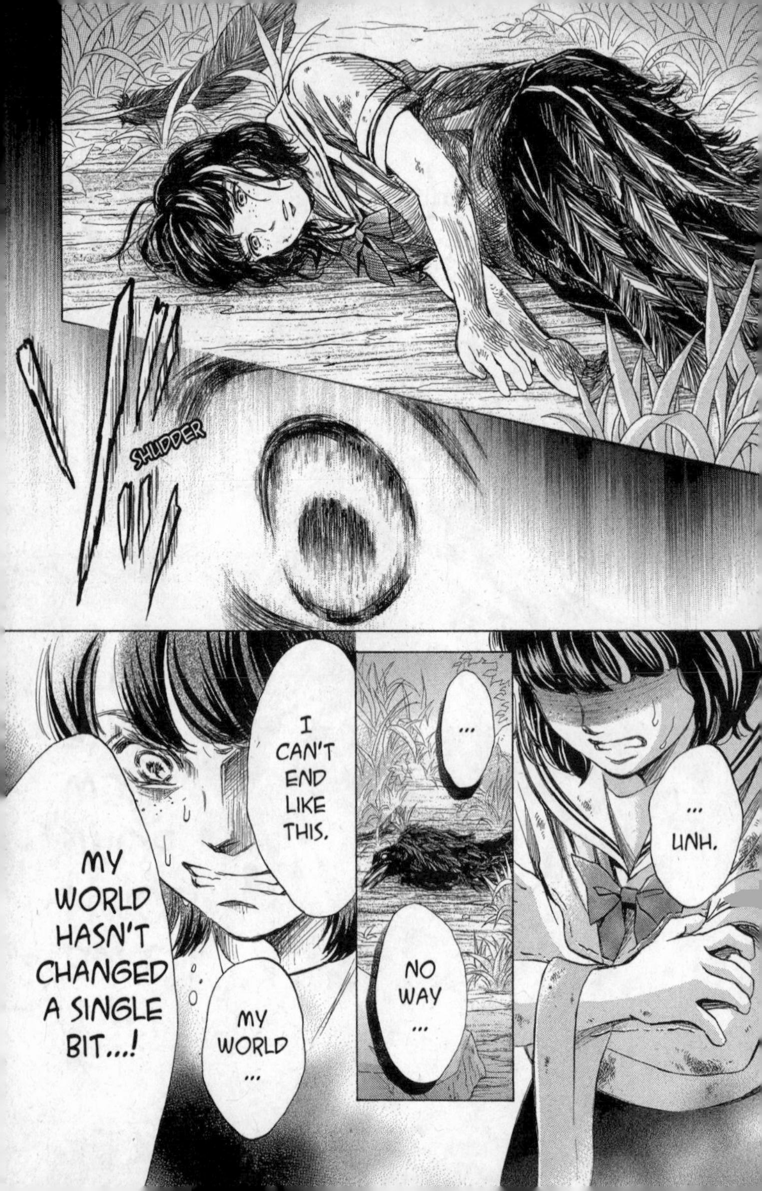
SHUDDER
... UNH.
...
NO WAY ...
I CAN'T END LIKE THIS.
MY WORLD HASN'T CHANGED A SINGLE BIT...!
MY WORLD ...

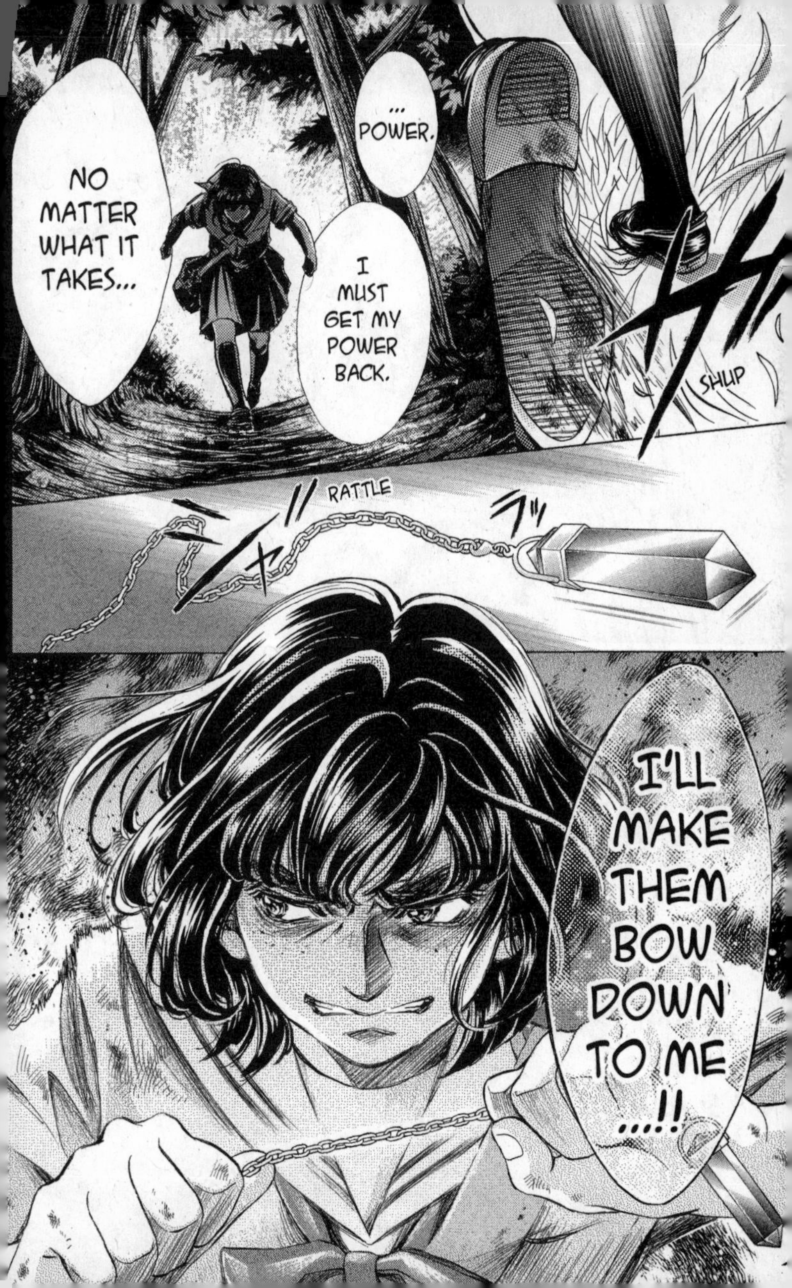

... POWER.
I MUST GET MY POWER BACK.
NO MATTER WHAT IT TAKES...
SHUP
RATTLE
I'LL MAKE THEM BOW DOWN TO ME ...!!

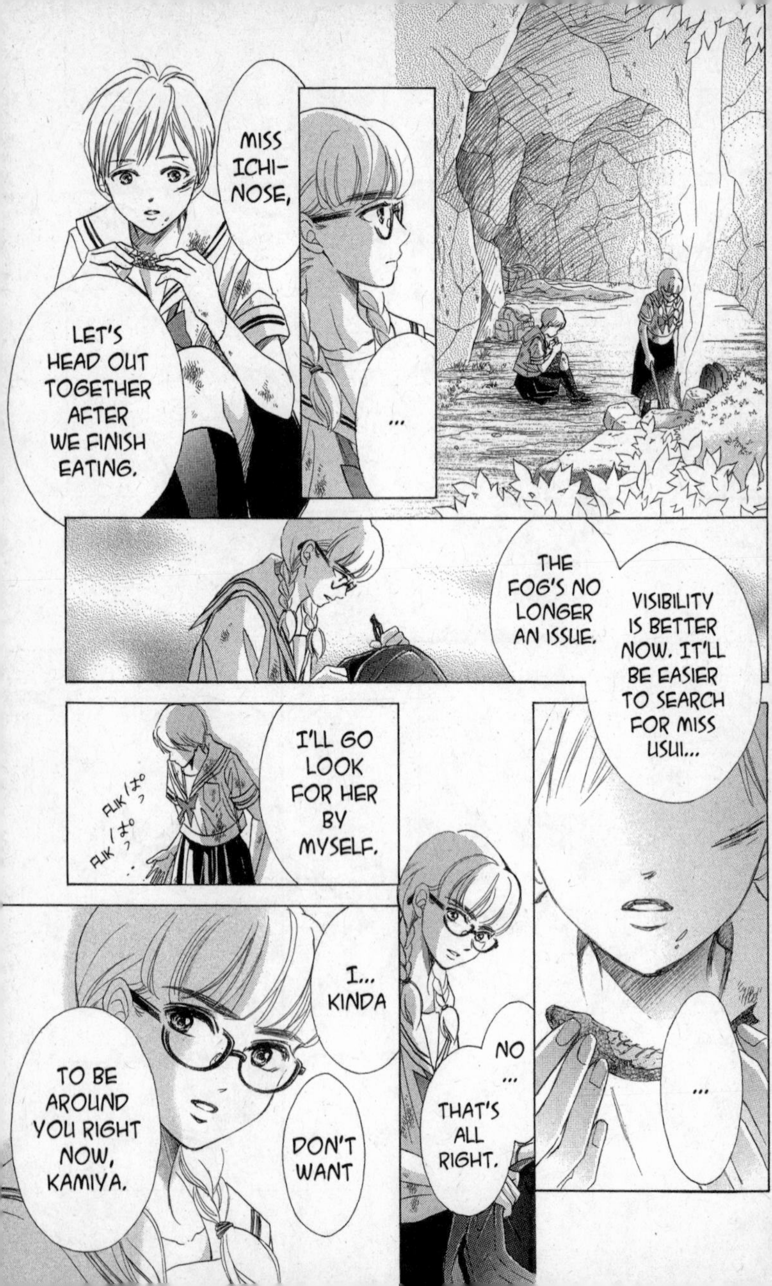
MISS ICHI-NOSE,
...
LET'S HEAD OUT TOGETHER AFTER WE FINISH EATING.
THE FOG'S NO LONGER AN ISSUE.
VISIBILITY IS BETTER NOW. IT'LL BE EASIER TO SEARCH FOR MISS USUI...
...
FLIK ぱっ
FLIK ぱっ
I'LL GO LOOK FOR HER BY MYSELF.
NO ...
THAT'S ALL RIGHT.
I... KINDA
DON'T WANT
TO BE AROUND YOU RIGHT NOW, KAMIYA.

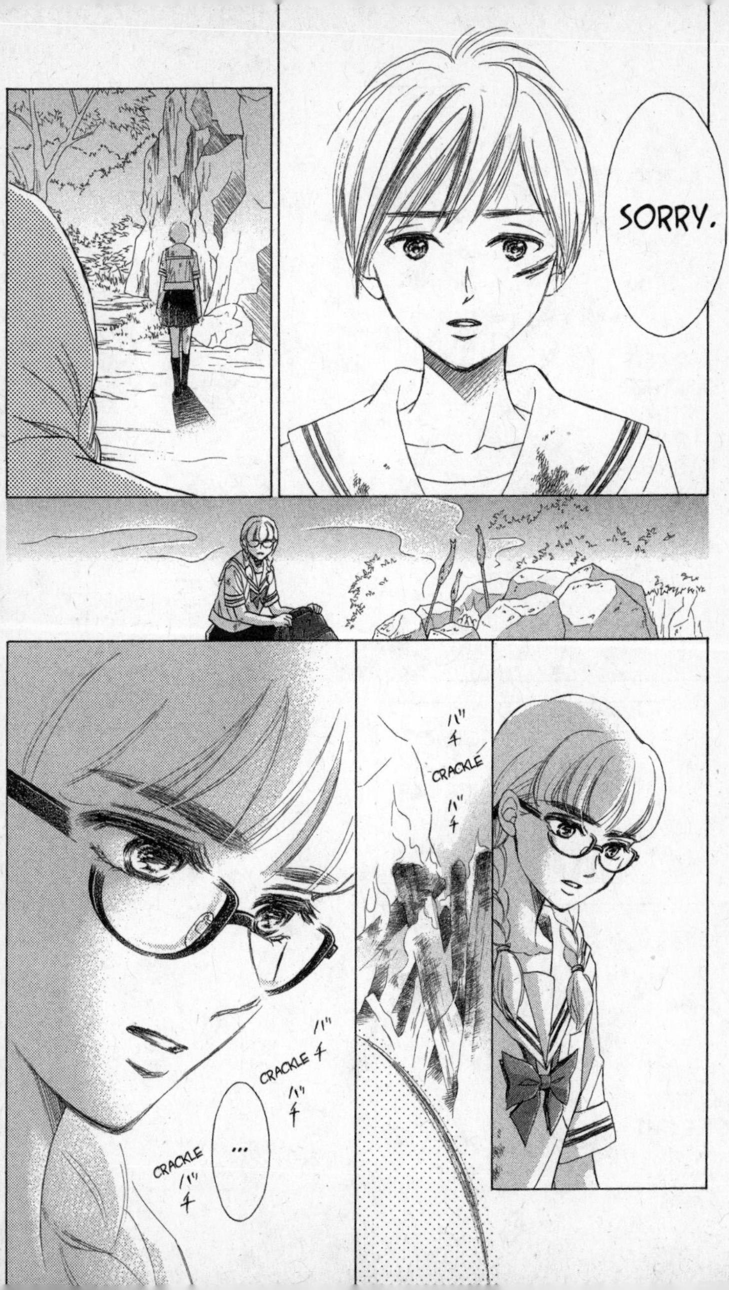

SORRY.
バチ
CRACKLE
バチ
バチ
CRACKLE
バチ
...
CRACKLE
バチ

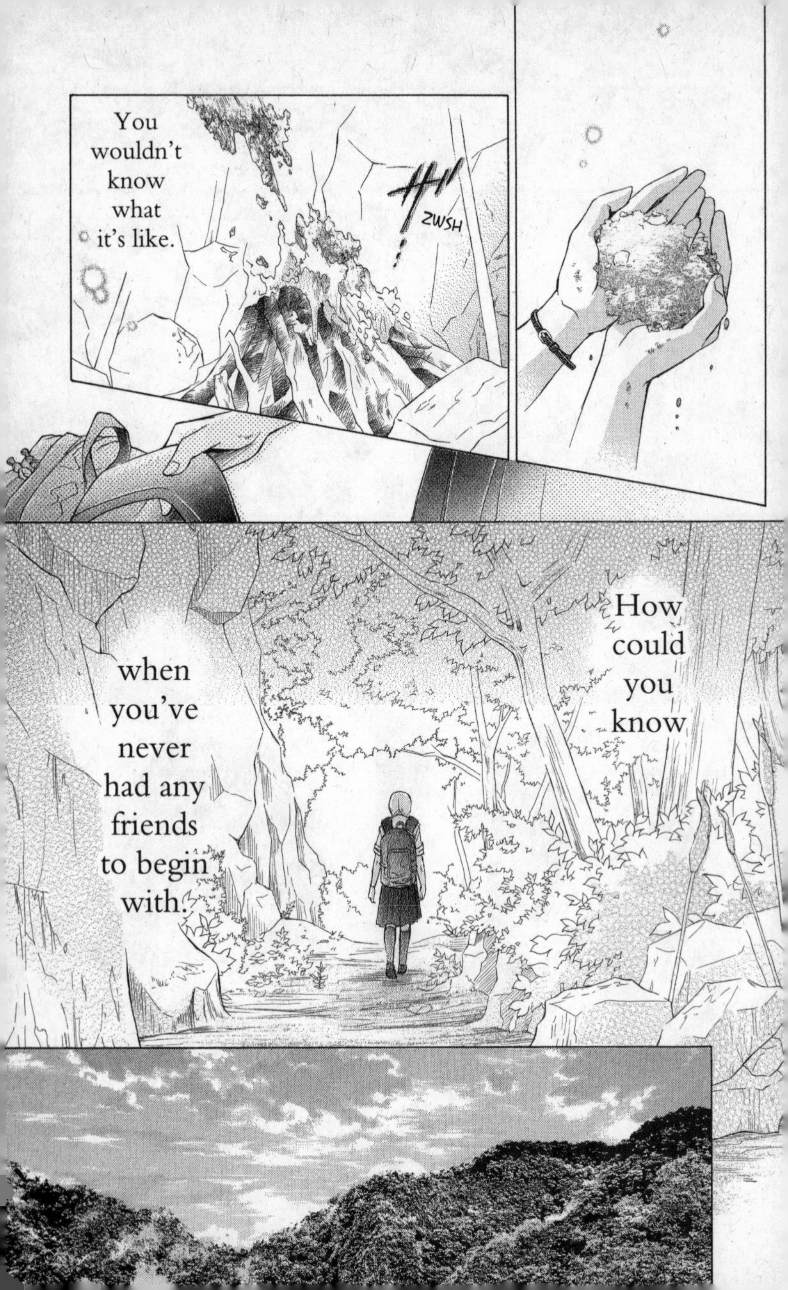
You wouldn't know what it's like.
ZWSH
How could you know
when you've never had any friends to begin with.

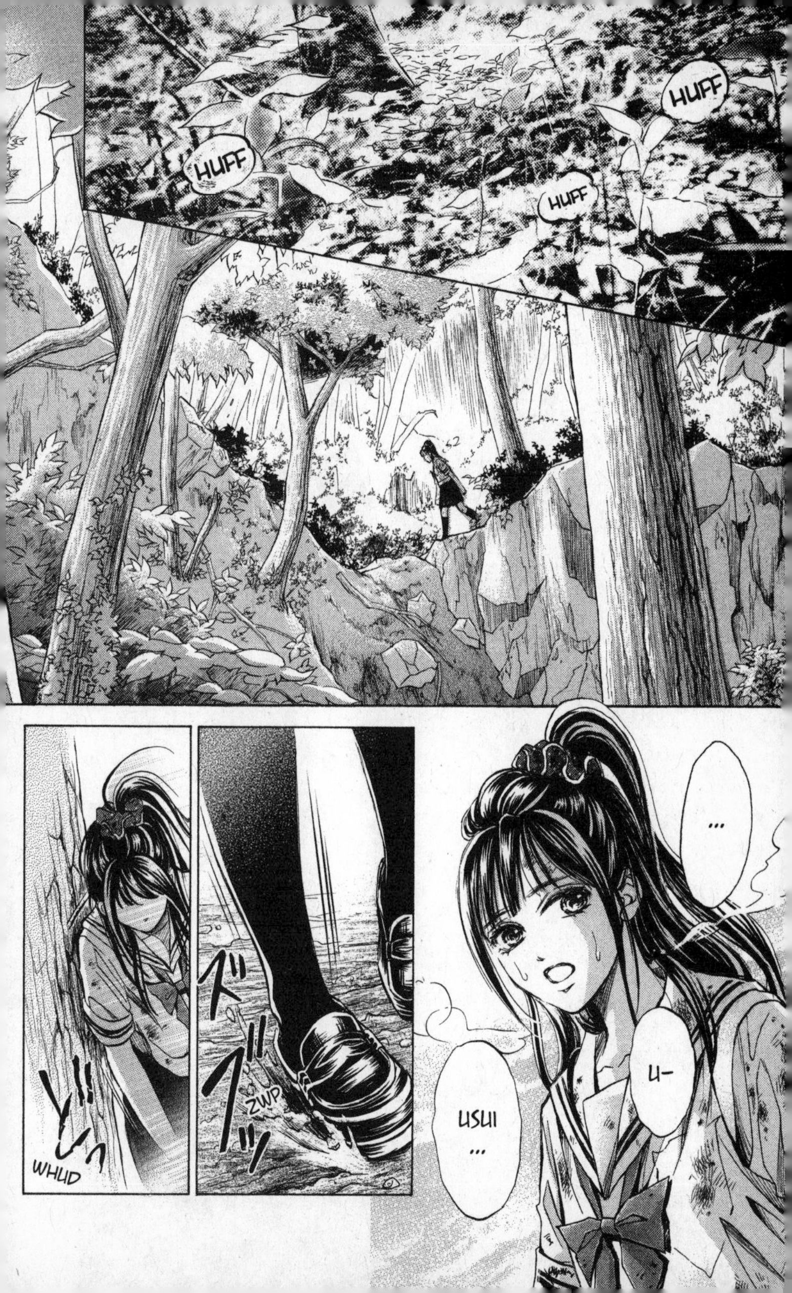
HUFF
HUFF
HUFF
...
U-
USUI ...
ZWP
WHUD

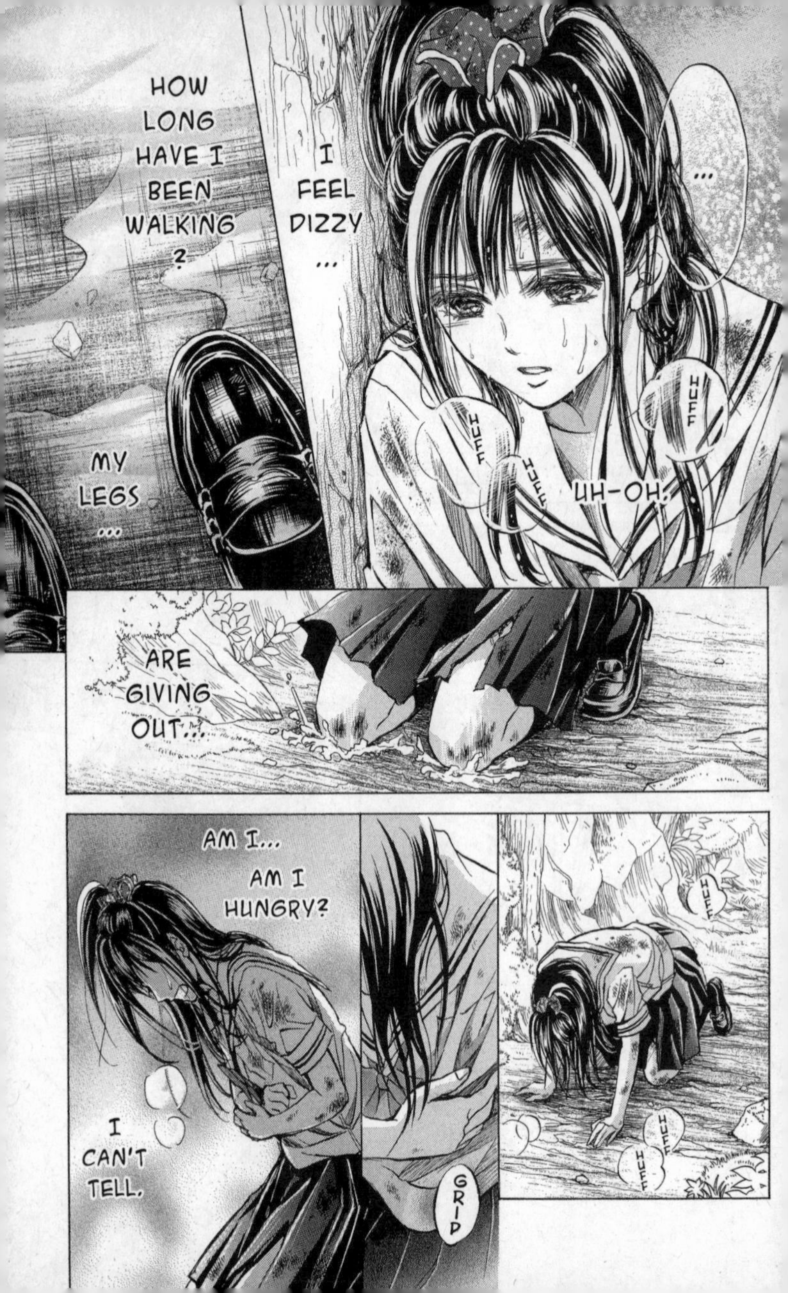
...
I FEEL DIZZY...
HOW LONG HAVE I BEEN WALKING?
HUFF
HUFF
HUFF
UH-OH.
MY LEGS...
ARE GIVING OUT...
HUFF
HUFF
HUFF
GRID
AM I... AM I HUNGRY?
I CAN'T TELL.

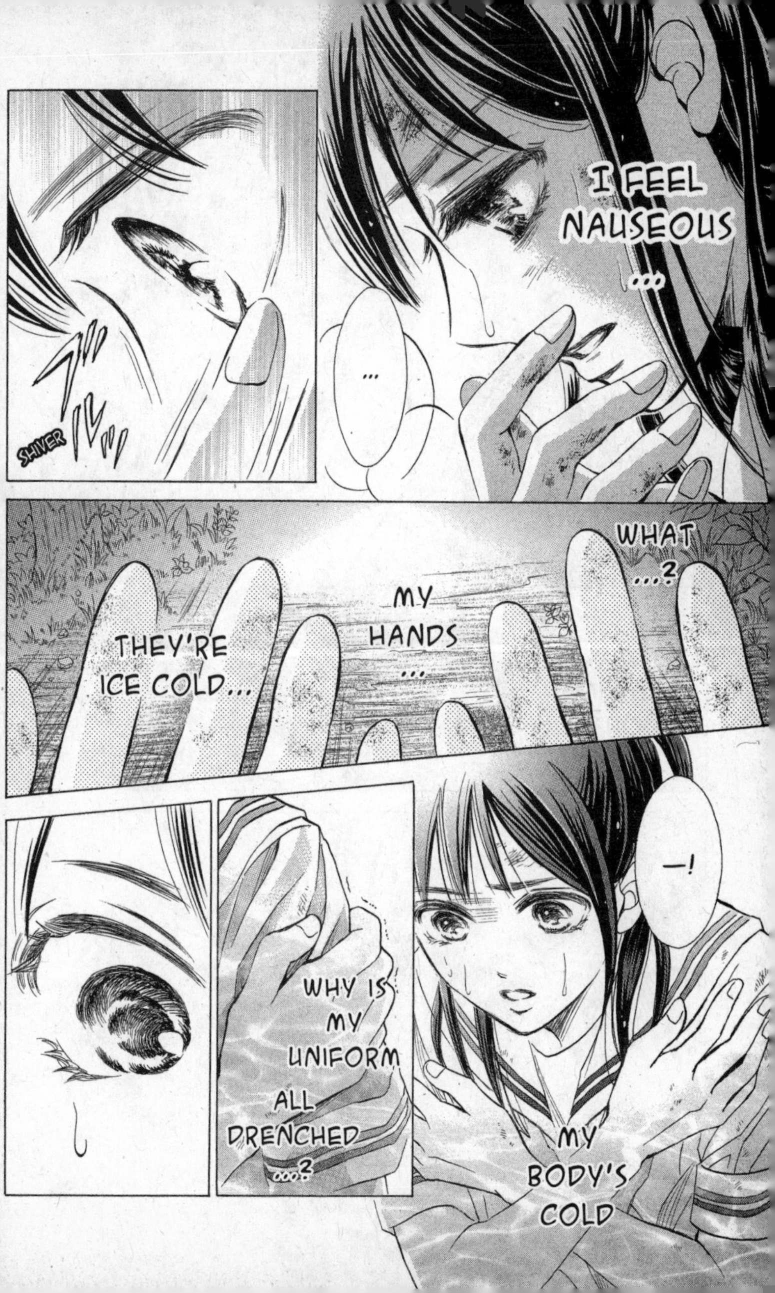
I FEEL NAUSEOUS ...
...
SHIVER
WHAT ...?
MY HANDS ...
THEY'RE ICE COLD...
—!
MY BODY'S COLD
WHY IS MY UNIFORM
ALL DRENCHED ...?

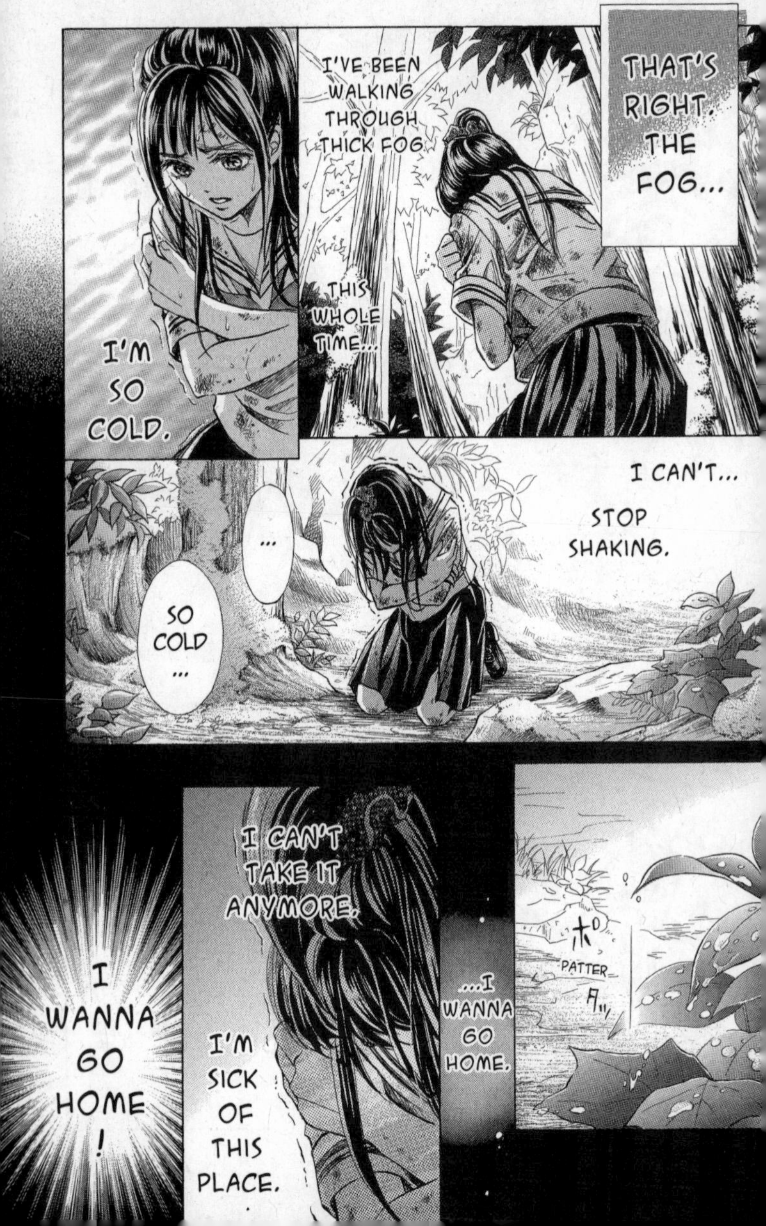
THAT'S RIGHT. THE FOG...
I'VE BEEN WALKING THROUGH THICK FOG
THIS WHOLE TIME...
I'M SO COLD.
I CAN'T...
STOP SHAKING.
...
SO COLD ...
PATTER
...I WANNA GO HOME.
I CAN'T TAKE IT ANYMORE.
I'M SICK OF THIS PLACE.
I WANNA GO HOME!

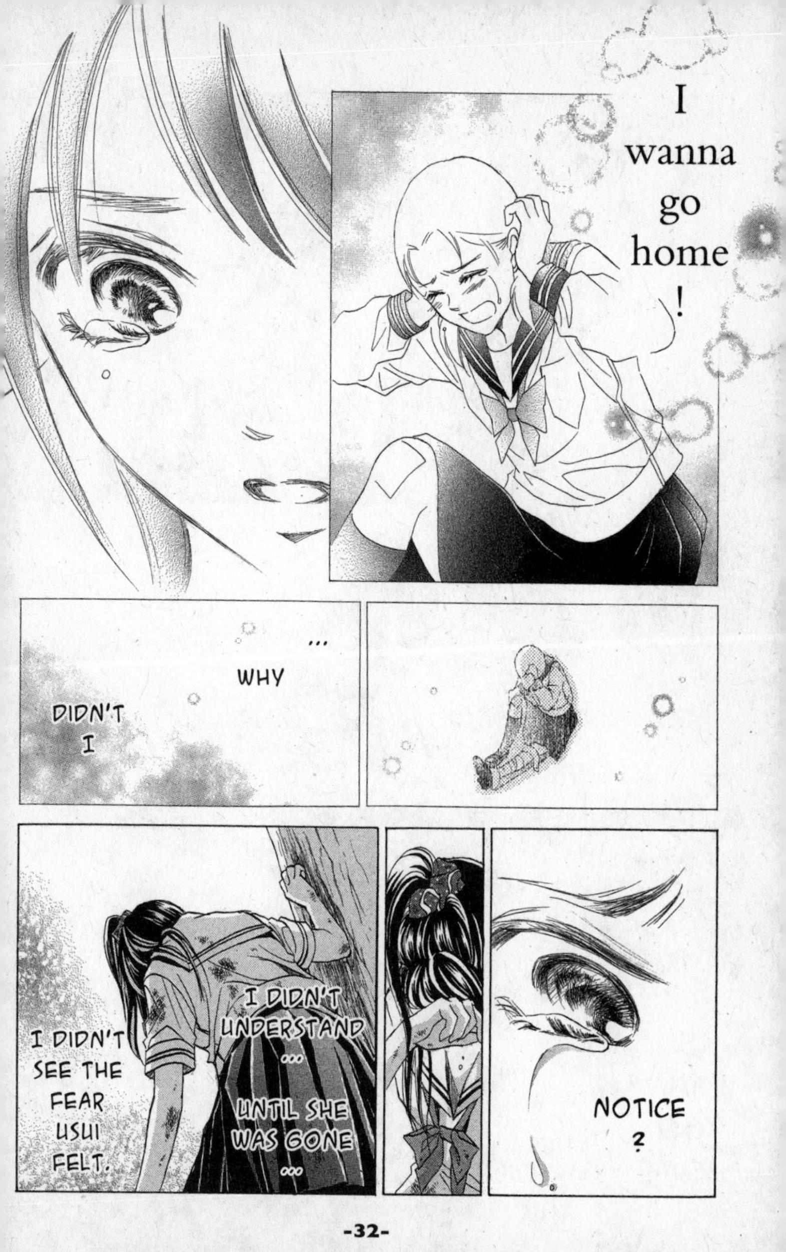
I wanna go home!
... WHY
DIDN'T I
NOTICE ?
I DIDN'T UNDERSTAND ... UNTIL SHE WAS GONE ...
I DIDN'T SEE THE FEAR USUI FELT.

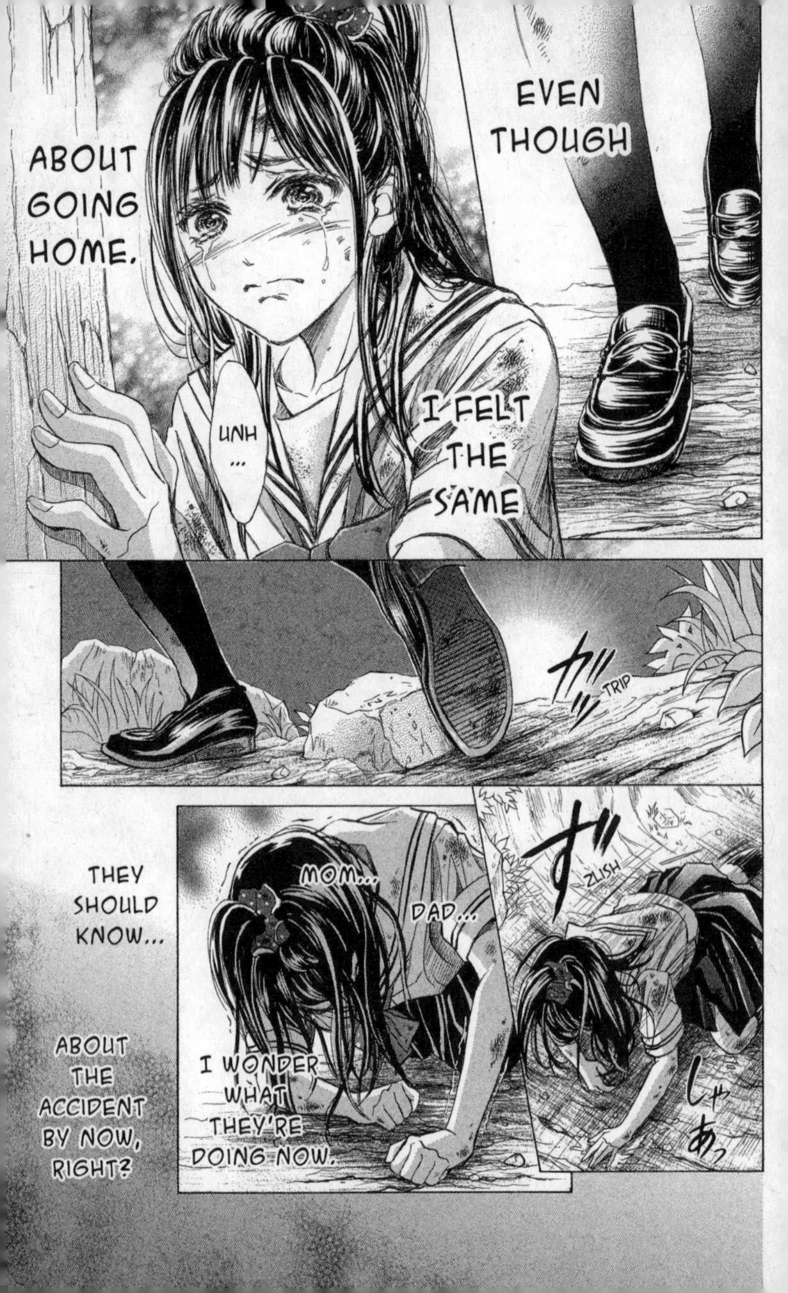
EVEN THOUGH
I FELT THE SAME
ABOUT GOING HOME.
UNH ...
ガッ
TRIP
ずっ
ZLISH
しゃあっ
MOM...
DAD...
I WONDER WHAT THEY'RE DOING NOW.
THEY SHOULD KNOW...
ABOUT THE ACCIDENT BY NOW, RIGHT?

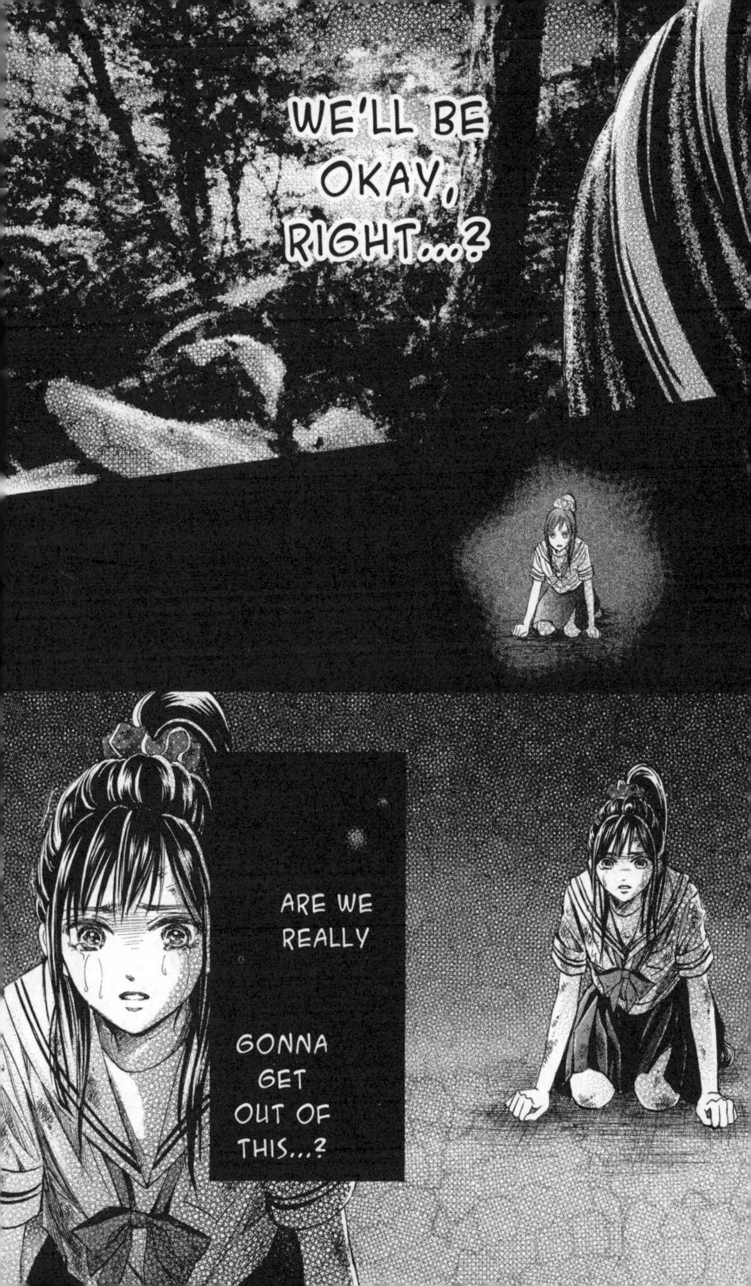
WE'LL BE OKAY, RIGHT...?
ARE WE REALLY
GONNA GET OUT OF THIS...?

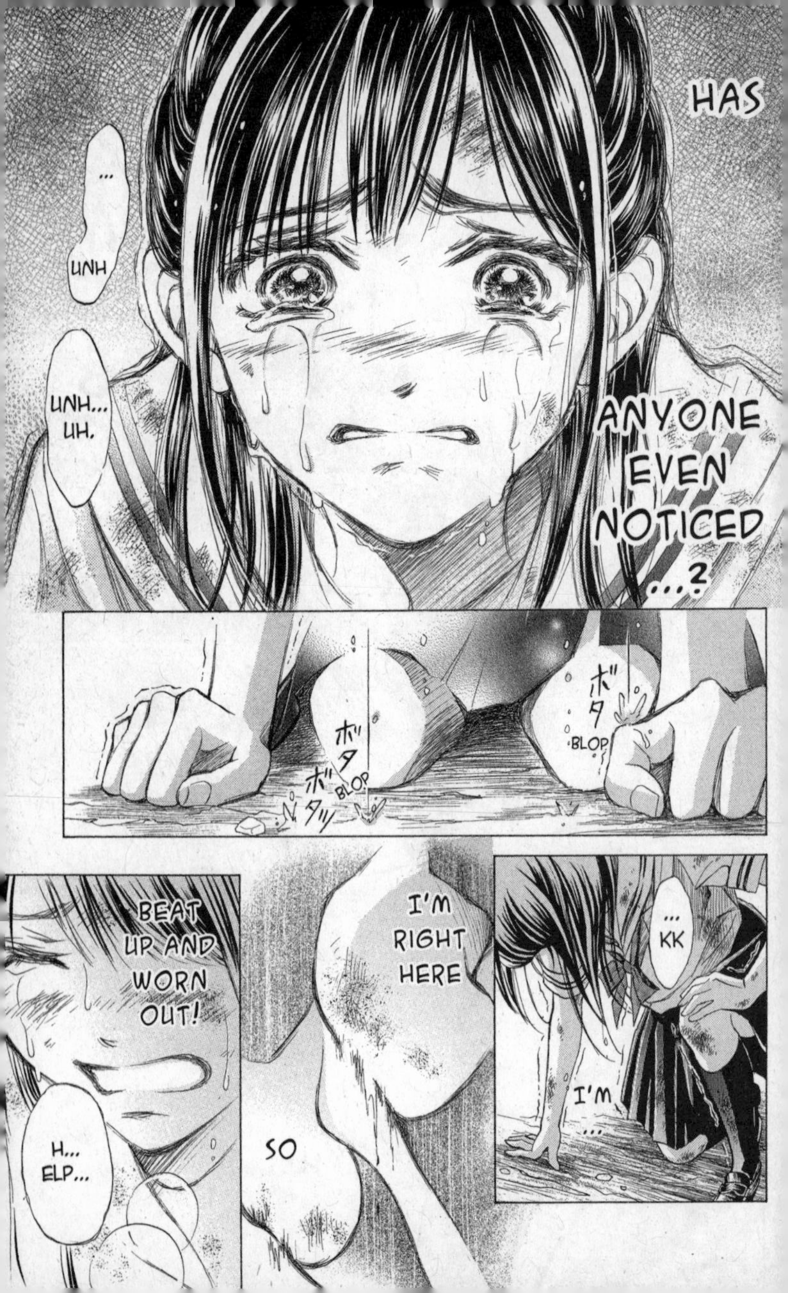
HAS
... UNH
UNH... UH.
ANYONE EVEN NOTICED ...?
ボタ BLOP
ボタ ボタッ BLOP
... KK
I'M ...
I'M RIGHT HERE
SO
BEAT UP AND WORN OUT!
H... ELP...

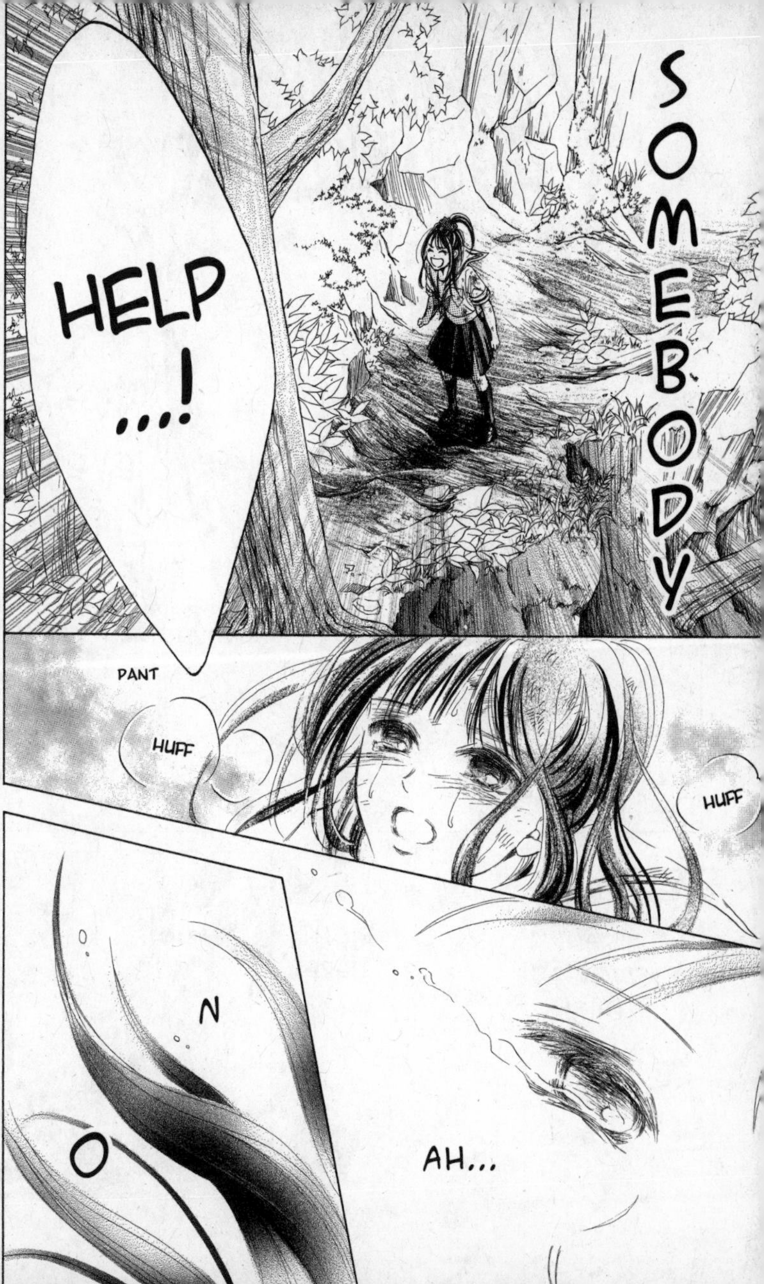
SOMEBODY
HELP...!
HUFF
PANT
HUFF
AH...
NO

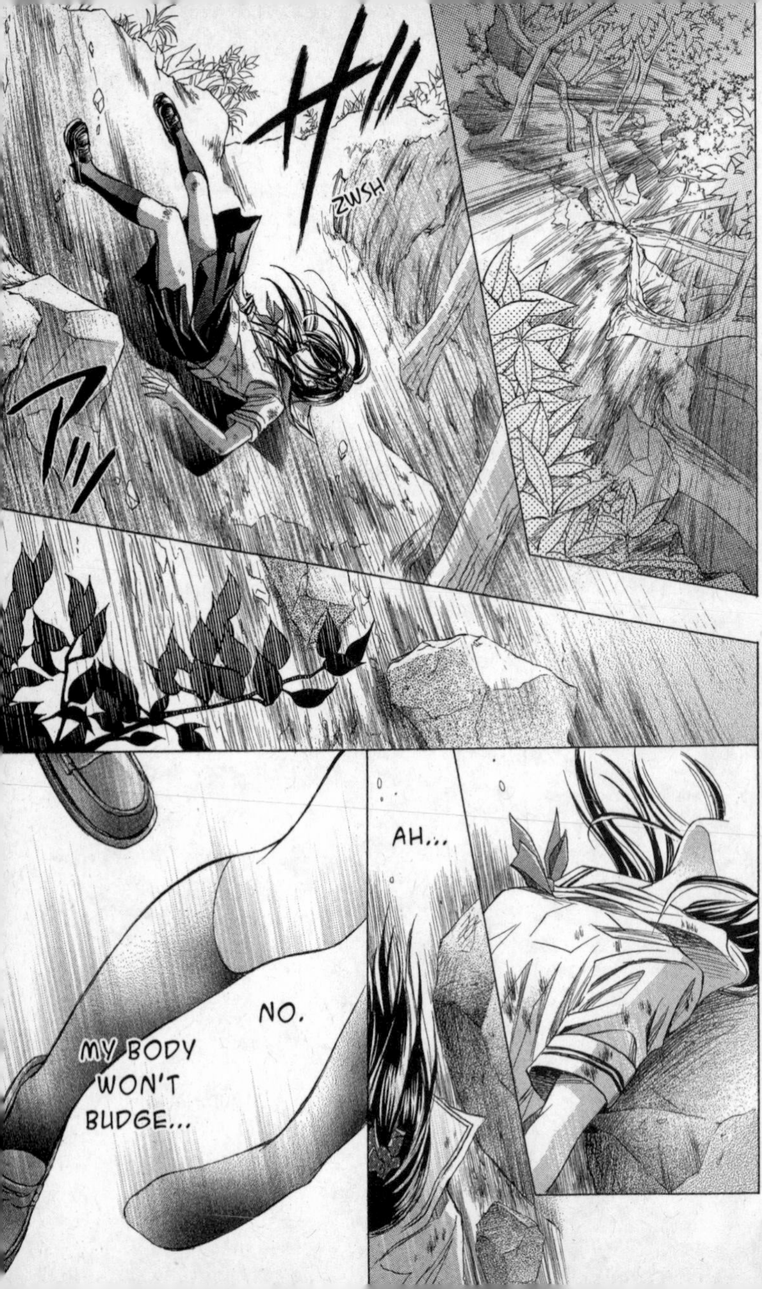
ZWSH
AH...
NO.
MY BODY WON'T BUDGE...

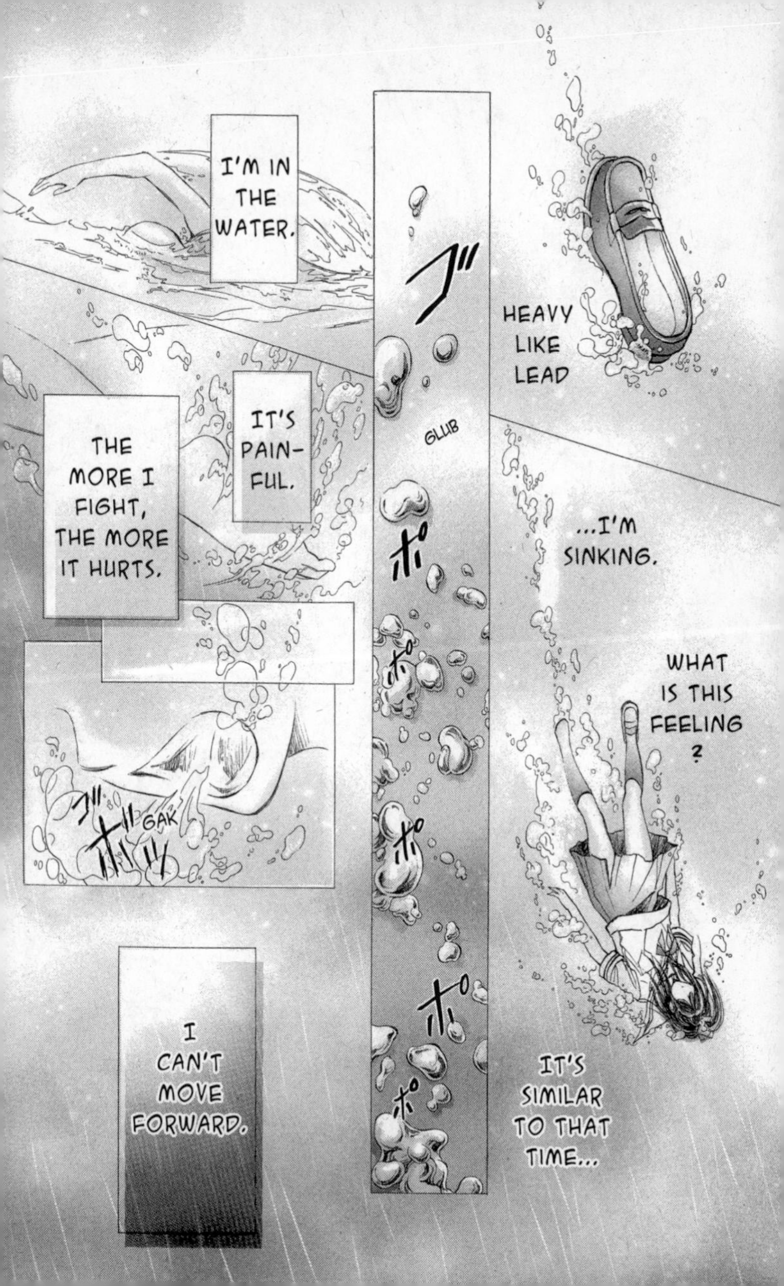
HEAVY LIKE LEAD
...I'M SINKING.
WHAT IS THIS FEELING ?
IT'S SIMILAR TO THAT TIME...
GLUB
I'M IN THE WATER.
IT'S PAIN-FUL.
THE MORE I FIGHT, THE MORE IT HURTS.
GAK
I CAN'T MOVE FORWARD.

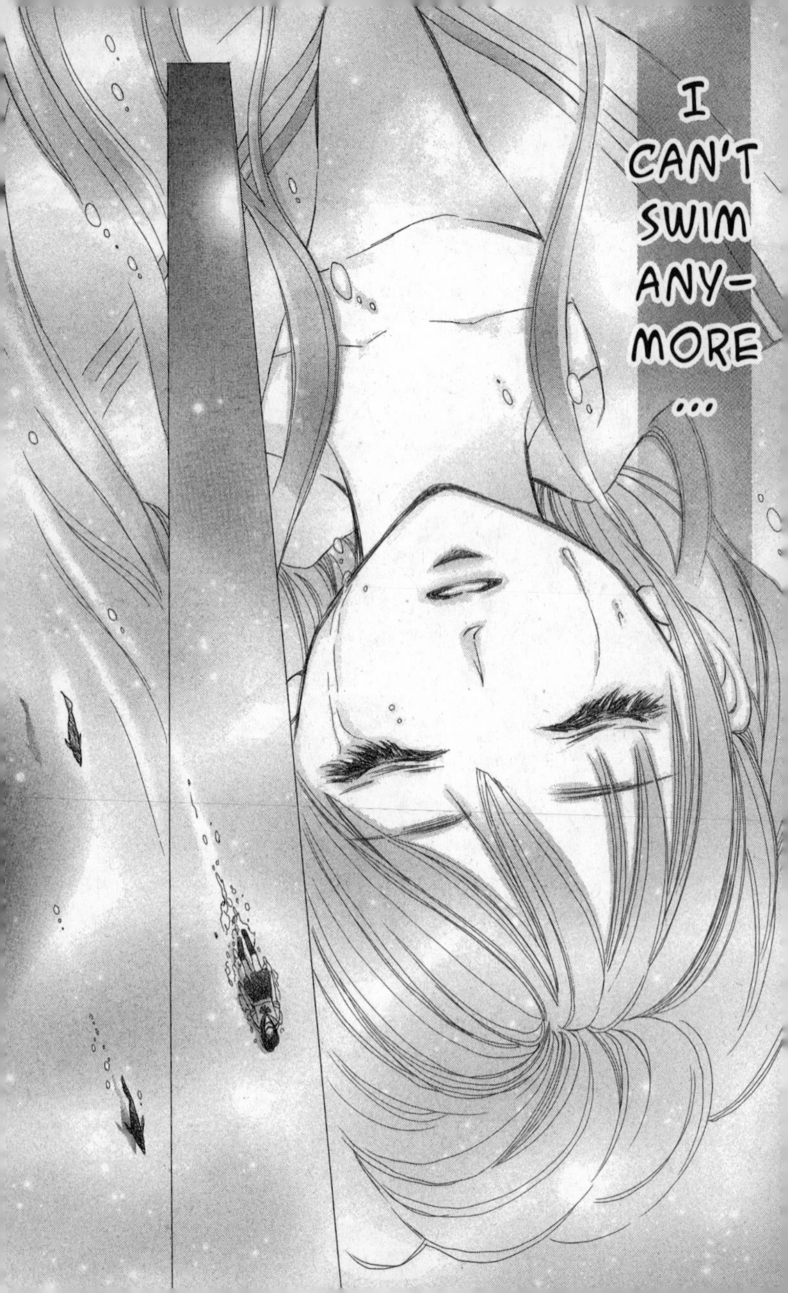
I CAN'T SWIM ANY-MORE ...

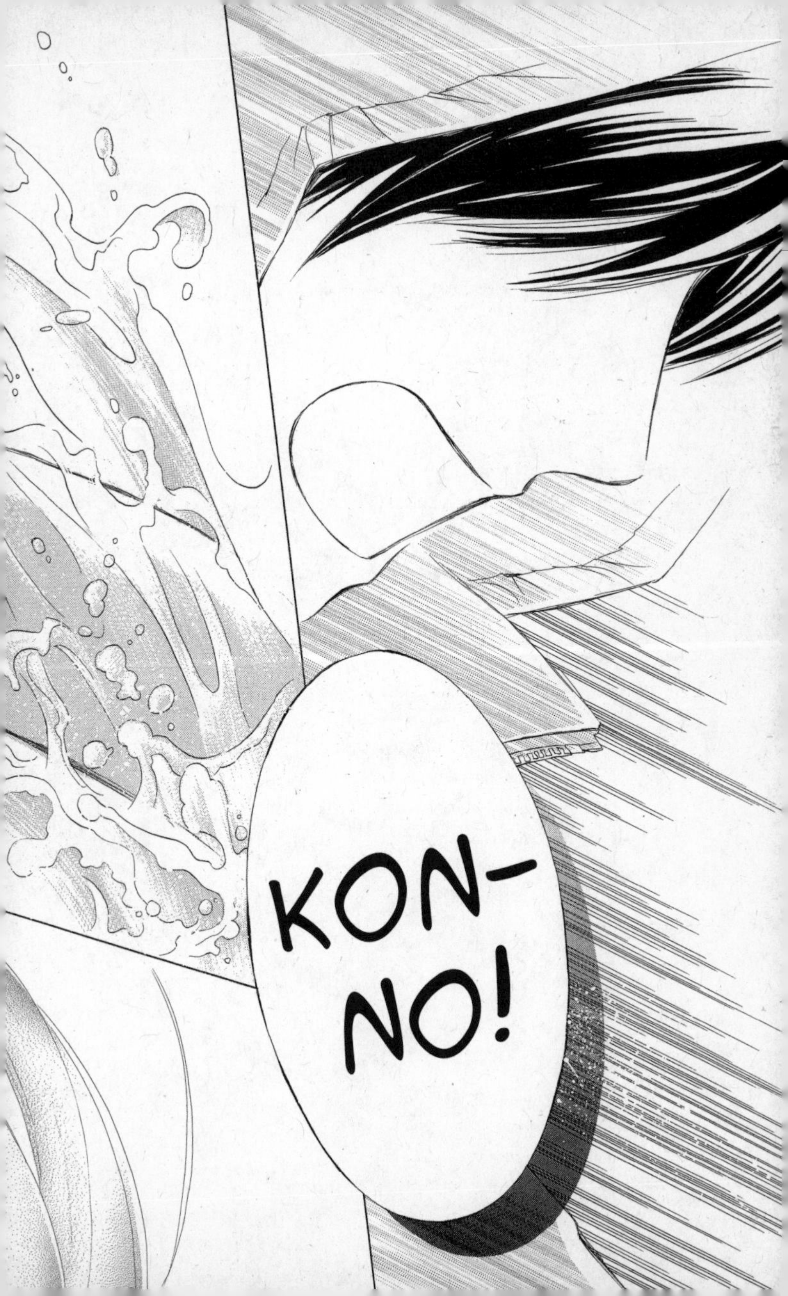
KON-NO!

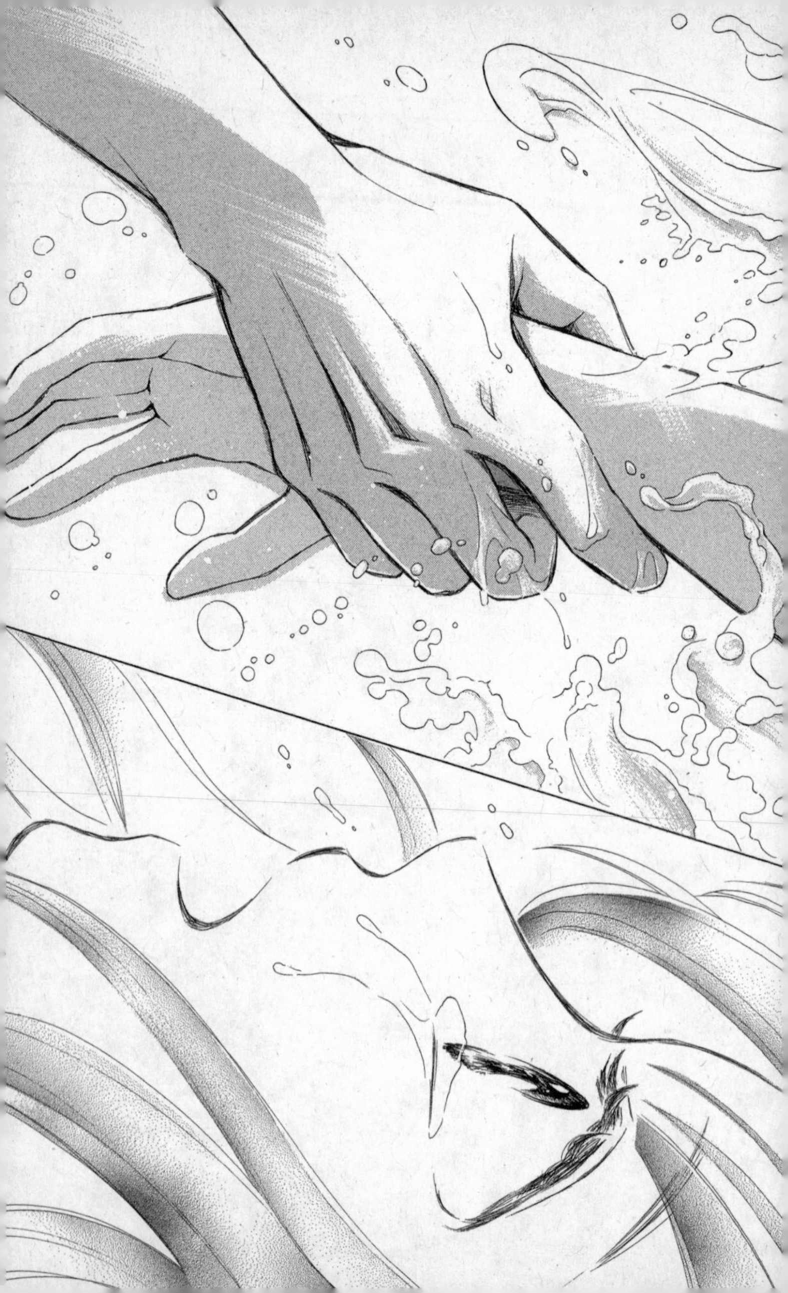

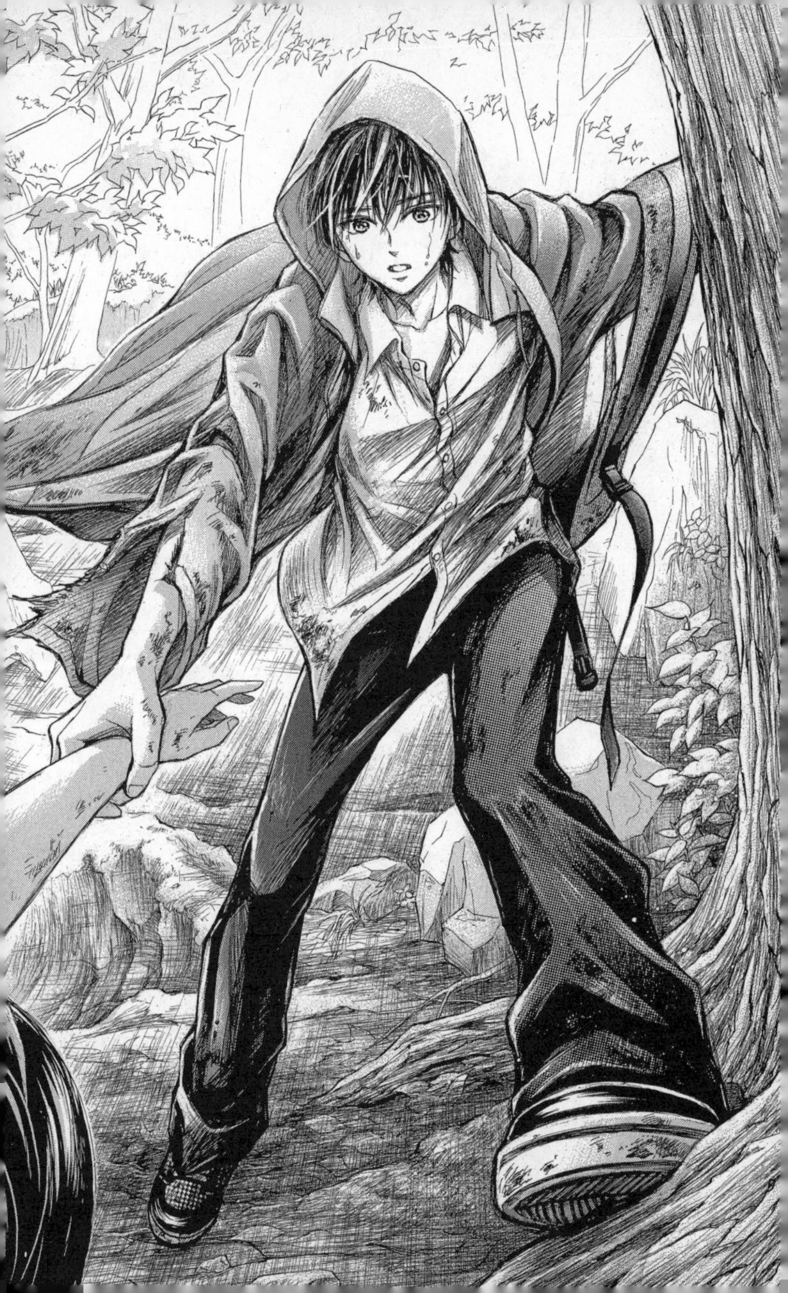

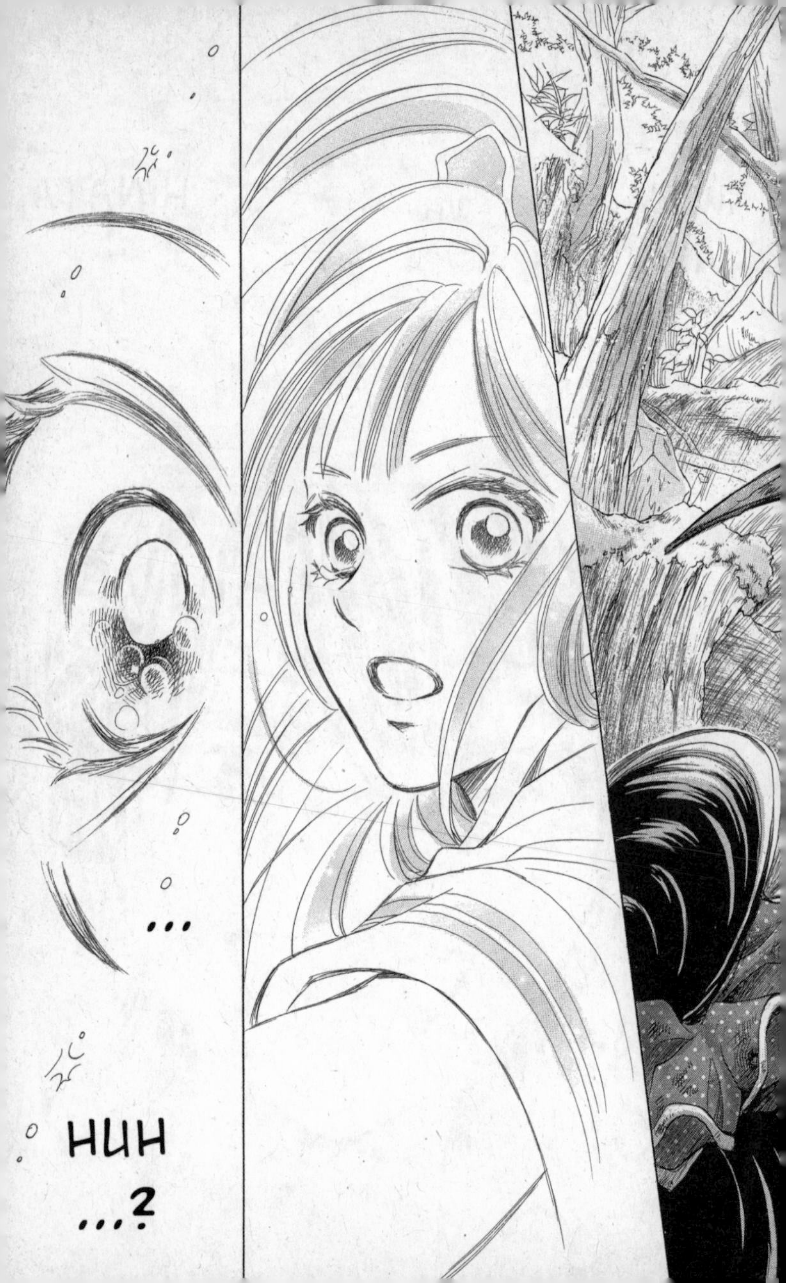
...
HUH ...?

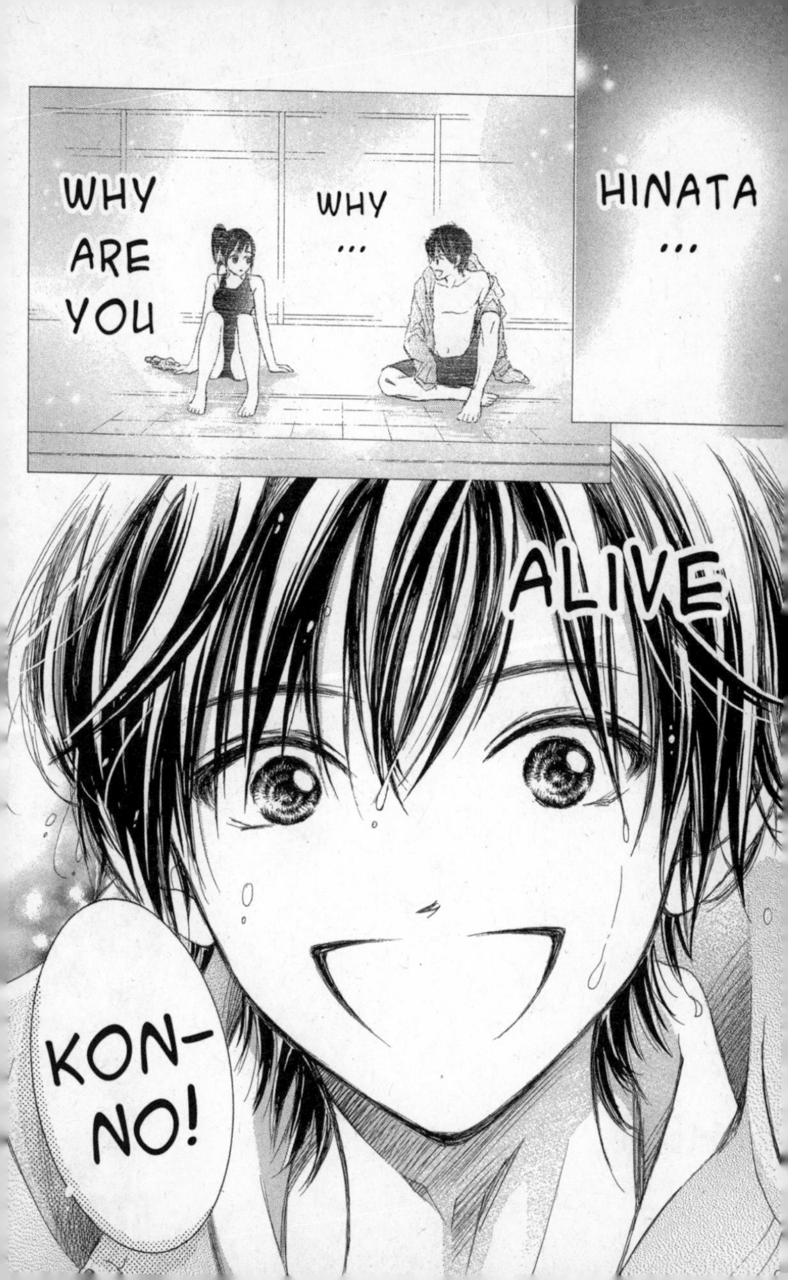
HINATA ...
WHY ...
WHY ARE YOU
ALIVE
KON-NO!

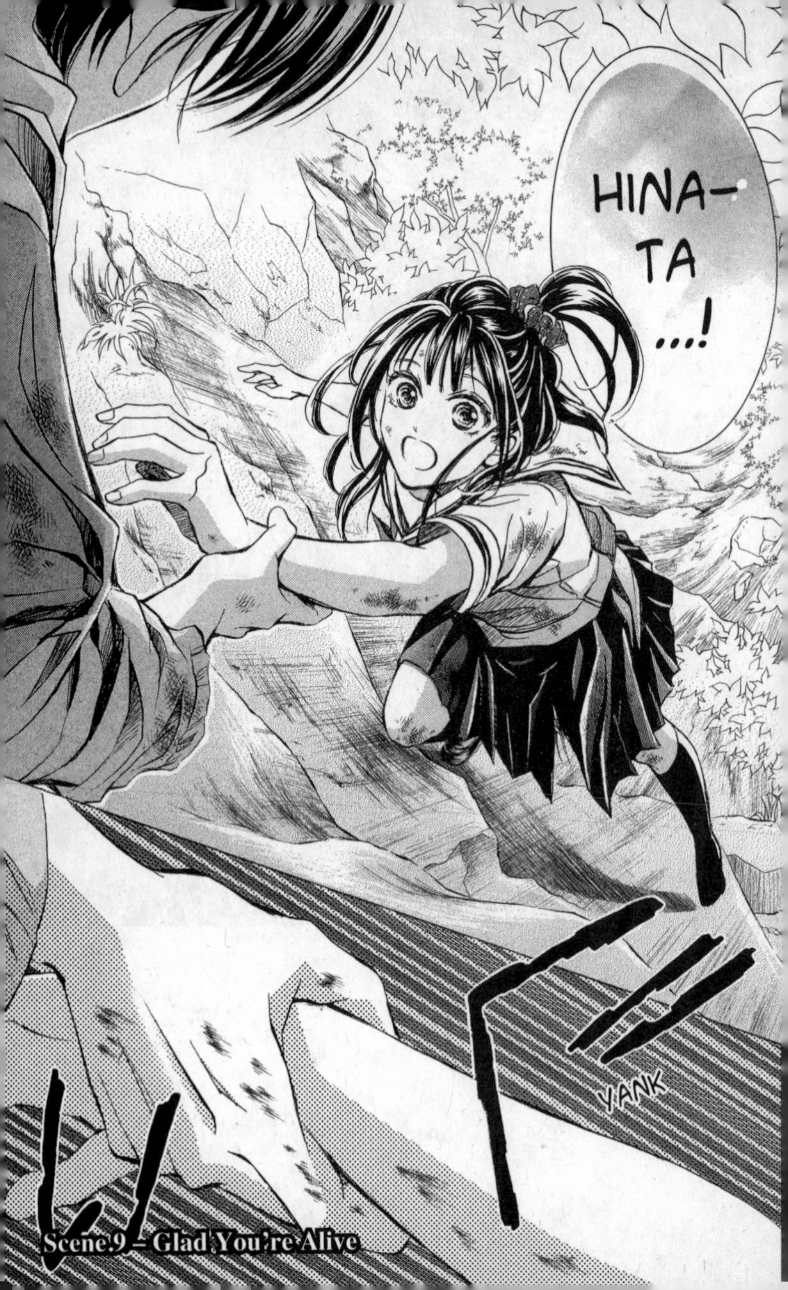
HINA-TA ...!
YANK
Scene.9 – Glad You're Alive

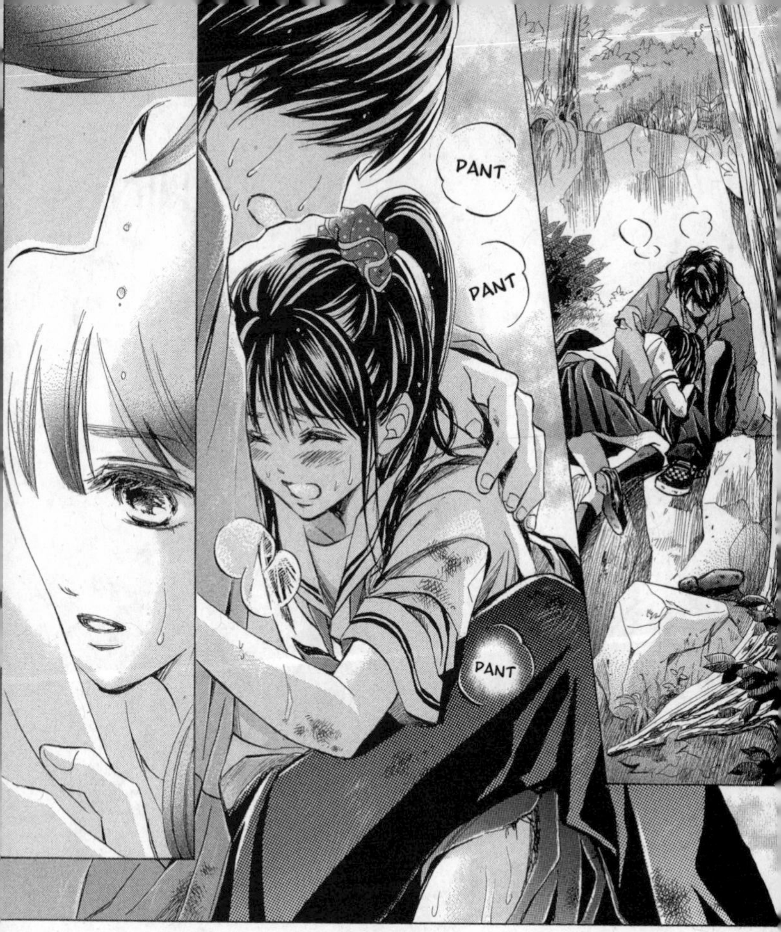
PANT
PANT
PANT

LIMIT

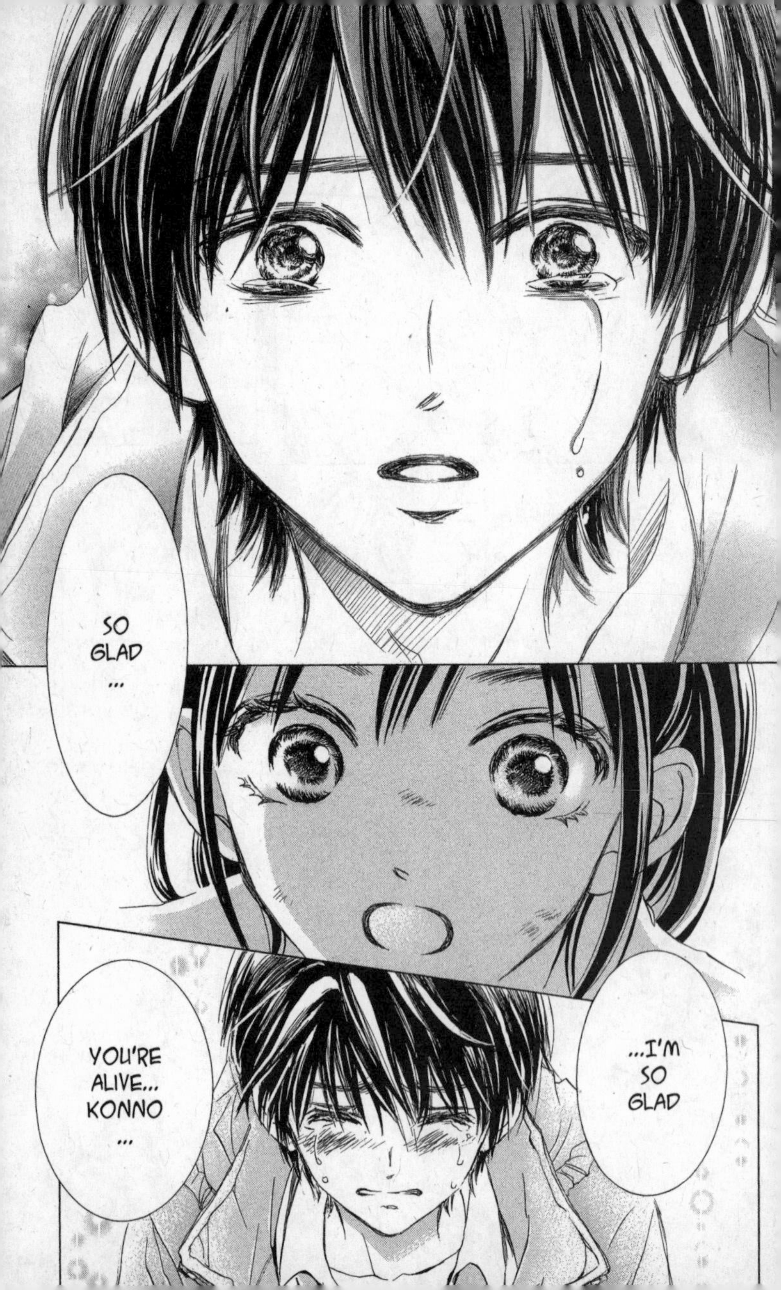
SO GLAD ...
...I'M SO GLAD
YOU'RE ALIVE... KONNO ...

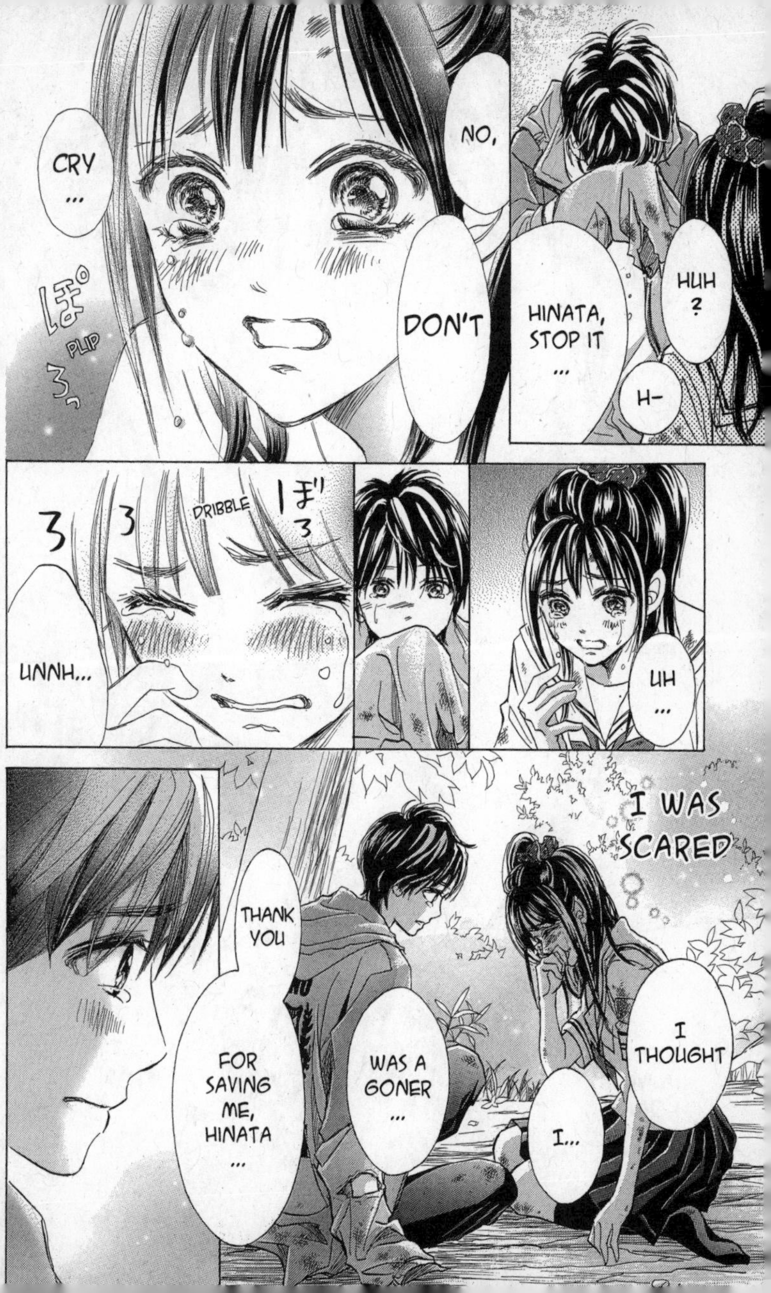
HUH ?
H-
HINATA, STOP IT ...
NO,
DON'T
CRY ...
ぽろっ
PLIP
UH ...
UNNH...
ぼろ
ろ
ろ
DRIBBLE
I WAS SCARED
I THOUGHT
I...
WAS A GONER ...
THANK YOU
FOR SAVING ME, HINATA ...

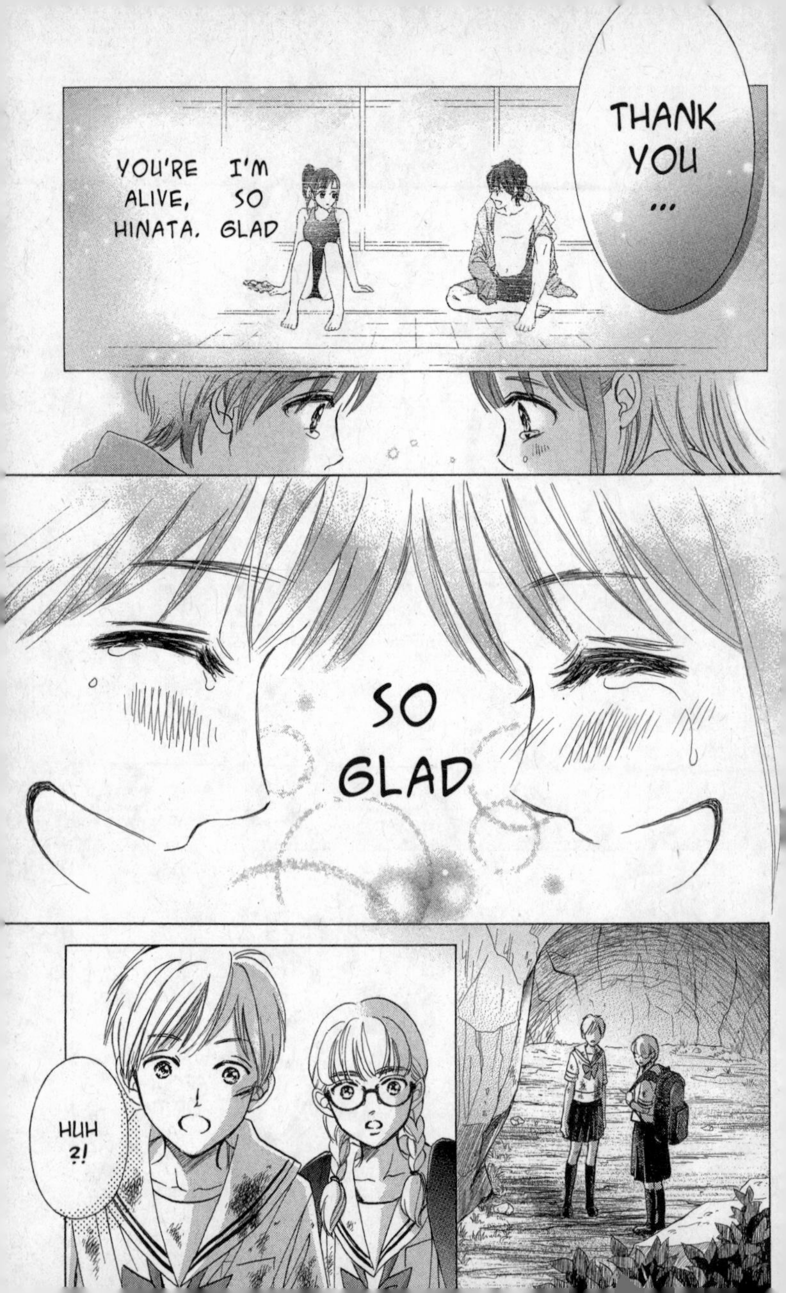
THANK YOU ...
I'M SO GLAD
YOU'RE ALIVE, HINATA.
SO GLAD
HUH ?!

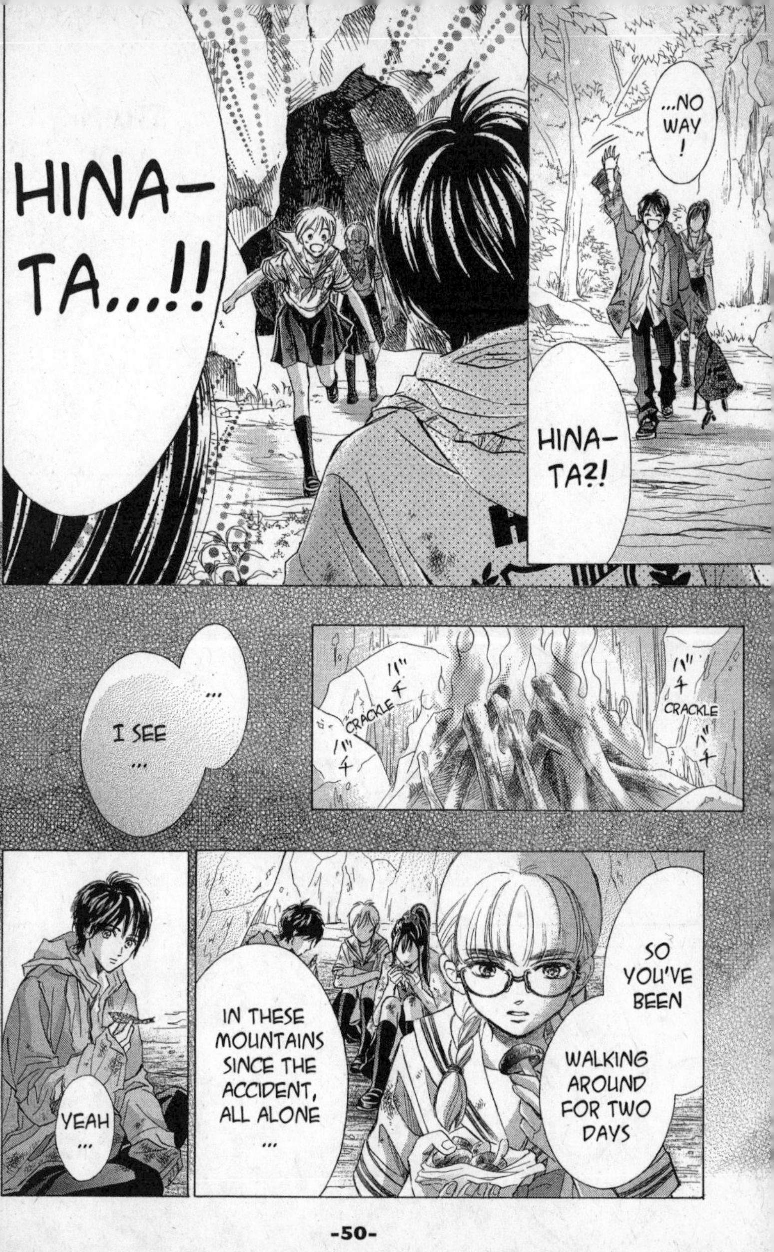

...NO WAY!
HINA-TA?!
HINA-TA...!!
バチ CRACKLE バチ
バチ CRACKLE バチ
... I SEE ...
SO YOU'VE BEEN WALKING AROUND FOR TWO DAYS
IN THESE MOUNTAINS SINCE THE ACCIDENT, ALL ALONE ...
YEAH ...

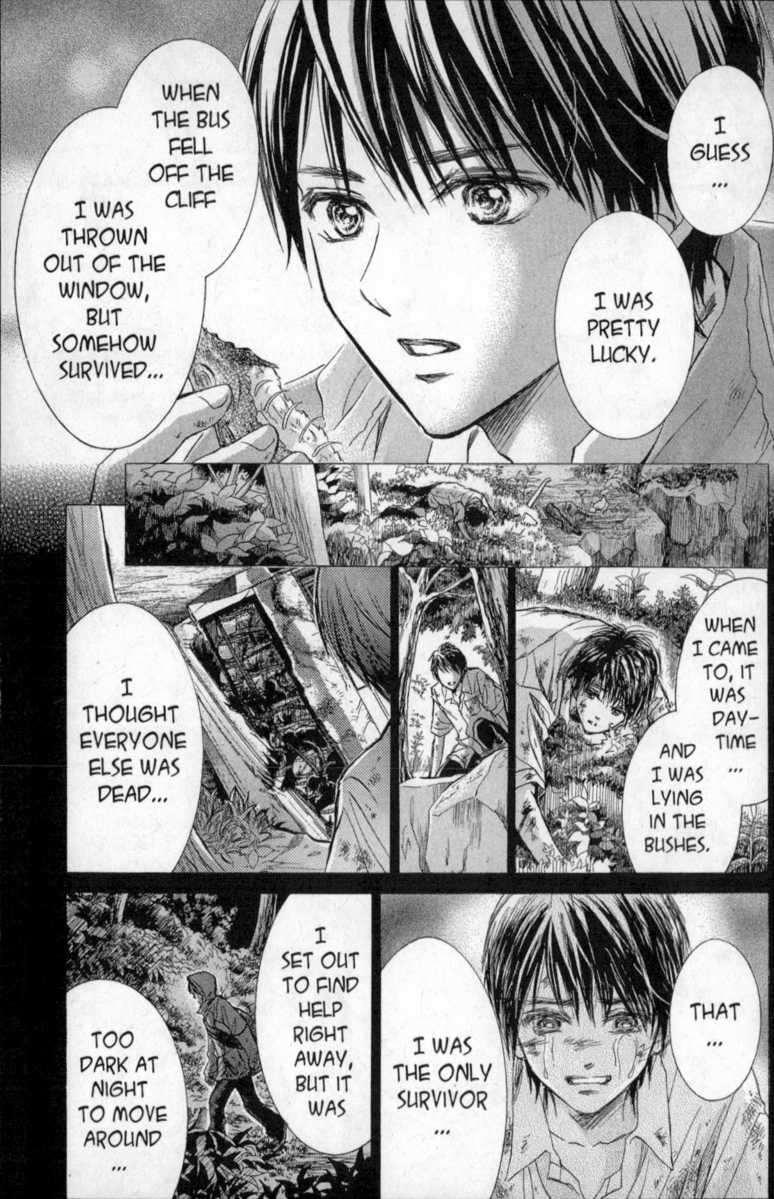

I GUESS ...
I WAS PRETTY LUCKY.
WHEN THE BUS FELL OFF THE CLIFF
I WAS THROWN OUT OF THE WINDOW, BUT SOMEHOW SURVIVED...
WHEN I CAME TO, IT WAS DAY-TIME ...
AND I WAS LYING IN THE BUSHES.
I THOUGHT EVERYONE ELSE WAS DEAD...
THAT ...
I WAS THE ONLY SURVIVOR ...
I SET OUT TO FIND HELP RIGHT AWAY, BUT IT WAS
TOO DARK AT NIGHT TO MOVE AROUND ...

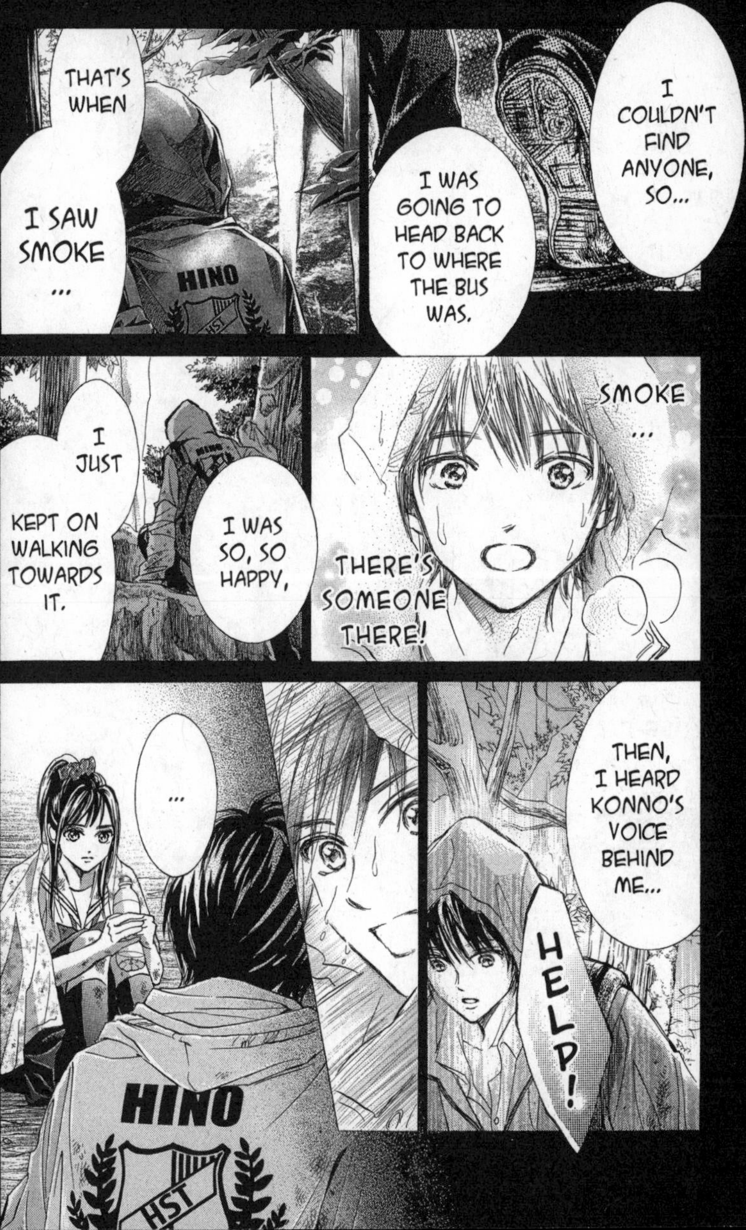
I COULDN'T FIND ANYONE, SO...
I WAS GOING TO HEAD BACK TO WHERE THE BUS WAS.
THAT'S WHEN
I SAW SMOKE ...
SMOKE ...
THERE'S SOMEONE THERE!
I WAS SO, SO HAPPY,
I JUST
KEPT ON WALKING TOWARDS IT.
THEN, I HEARD KONNO'S VOICE BEHIND ME...
HELP!
...

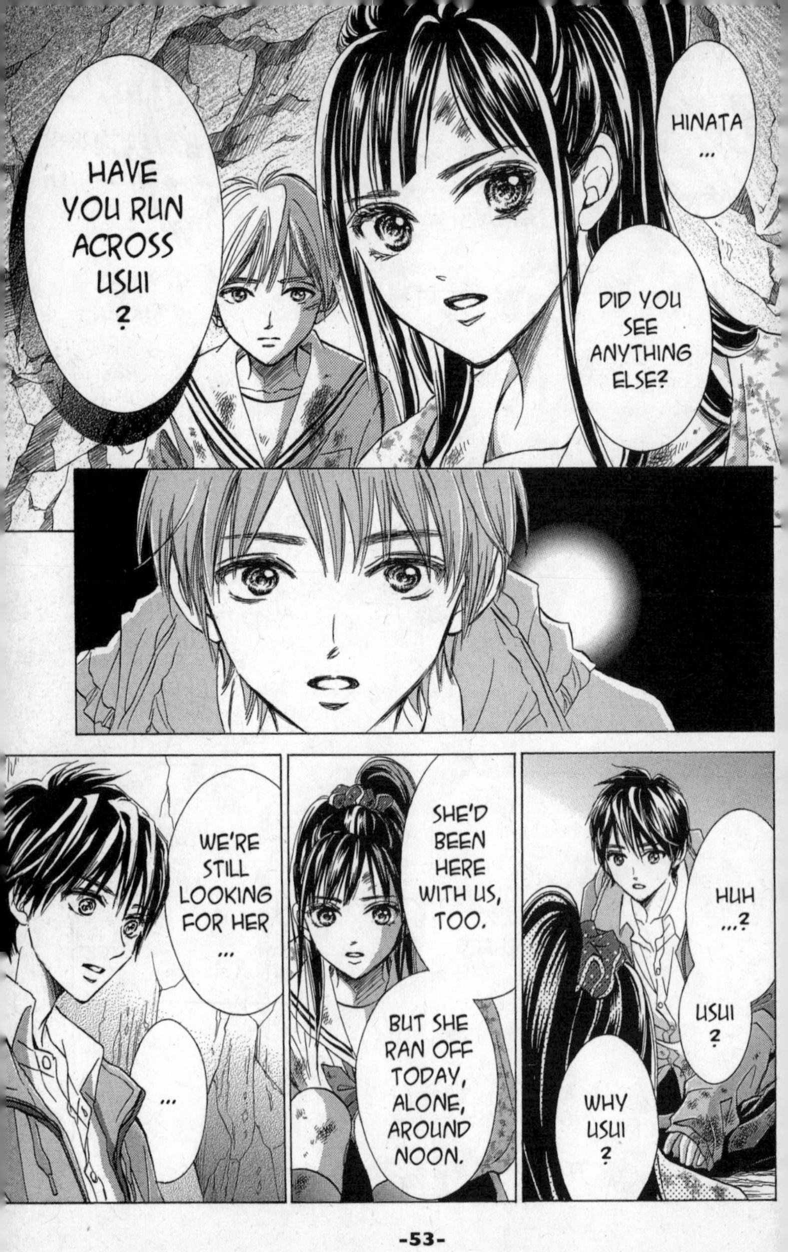
HINATA ...
DID YOU SEE ANYTHING ELSE?
HAVE YOU RUN ACROSS USUI ?
HUH ...?
USUI ?
WHY USUI ?
SHE'D BEEN HERE WITH US, TOO.
BUT SHE RAN OFF TODAY, ALONE, AROUND NOON.
WE'RE STILL LOOKING FOR HER ...
...

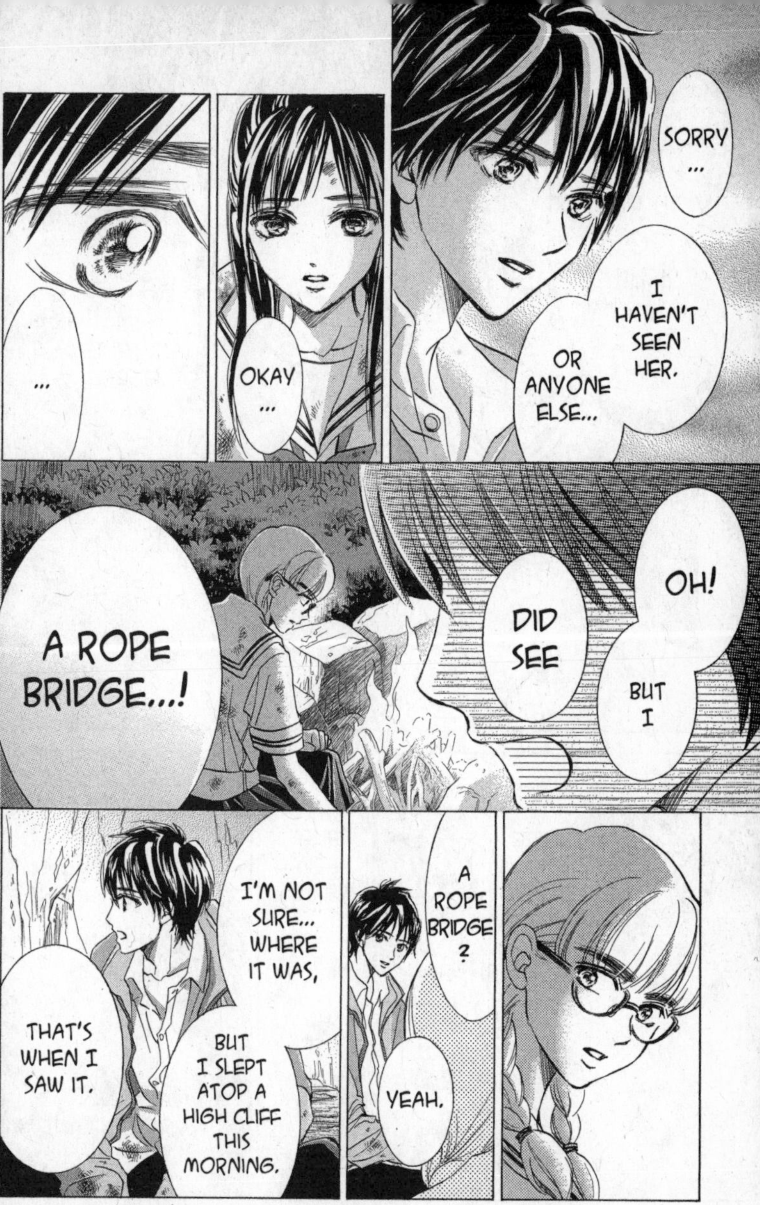

SORRY...
I HAVEN'T SEEN HER.
OR ANYONE ELSE...
OKAY...
...
OH!
BUT I
DID SEE
A ROPE BRIDGE...!
A ROPE BRIDGE?
YEAH.
I'M NOT SURE... WHERE IT WAS,
BUT I SLEPT ATOP A HIGH CLIFF THIS MORNING.
THAT'S WHEN I SAW IT.

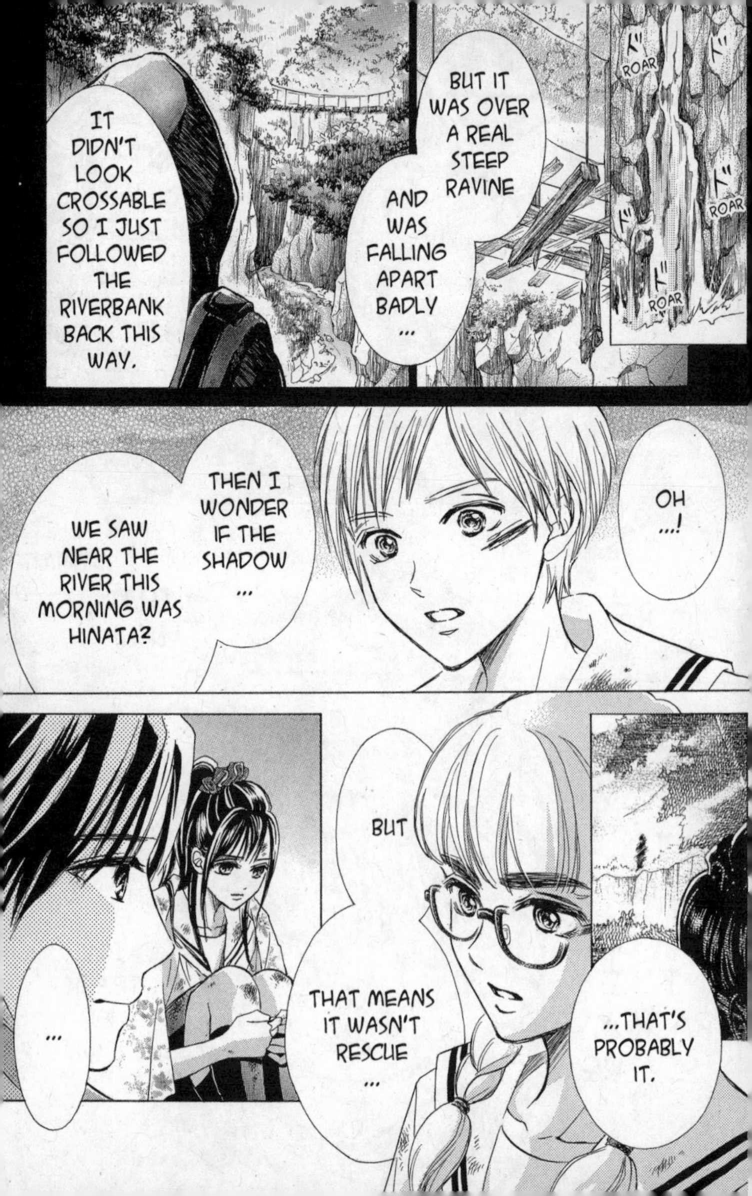
ROAR
ROAR
ROAR
BUT IT WAS OVER A REAL STEEP RAVINE
AND WAS FALLING APART BADLY ...
IT DIDN'T LOOK CROSSABLE SO I JUST FOLLOWED THE RIVERBANK BACK THIS WAY.
OH ...!
THEN I WONDER IF THE SHADOW ...
WE SAW NEAR THE RIVER THIS MORNING WAS HINATA?
...THAT'S PROBABLY IT.
BUT
THAT MEANS IT WASN'T RESCUE ...
...

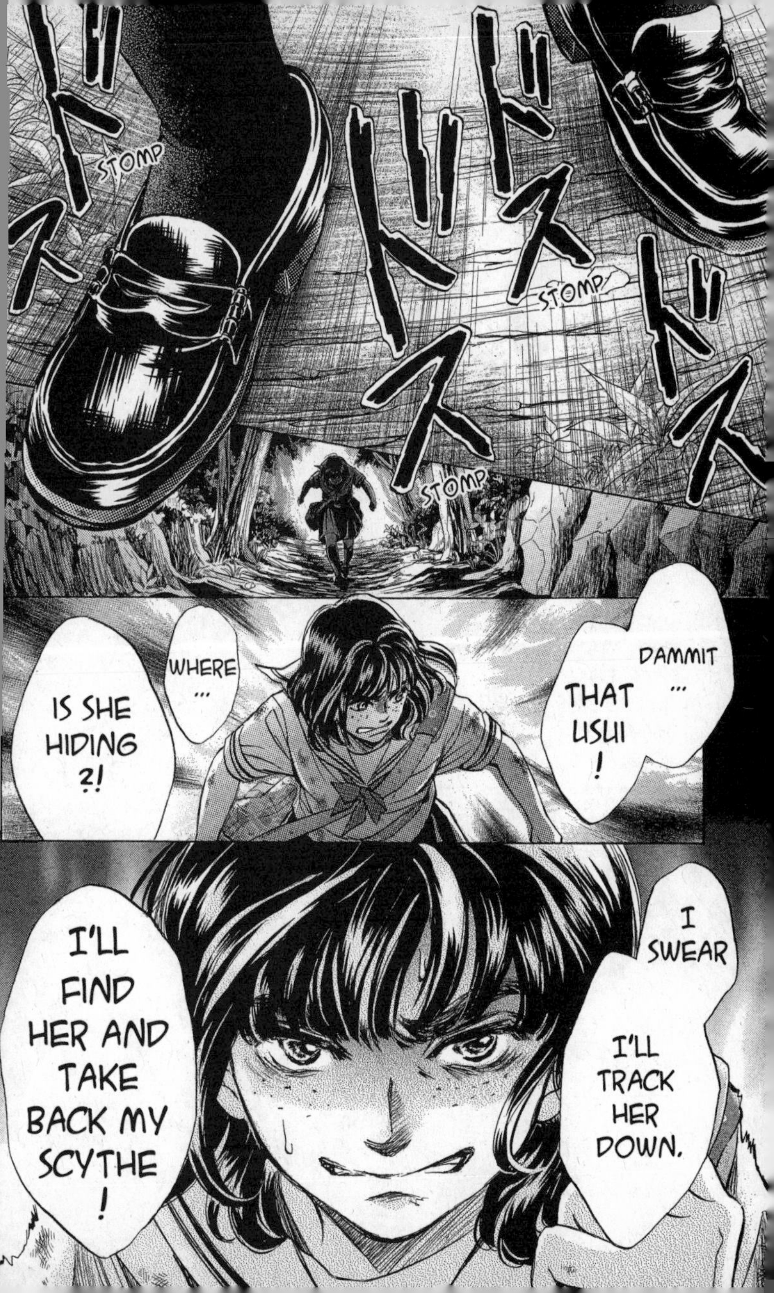
STOMP
STOMP
STOMP
DAMMIT ... THAT USUI!
WHERE ... IS SHE HIDING?!
I SWEAR I'LL TRACK HER DOWN.
I'LL FIND HER AND TAKE BACK MY SCYTHE!

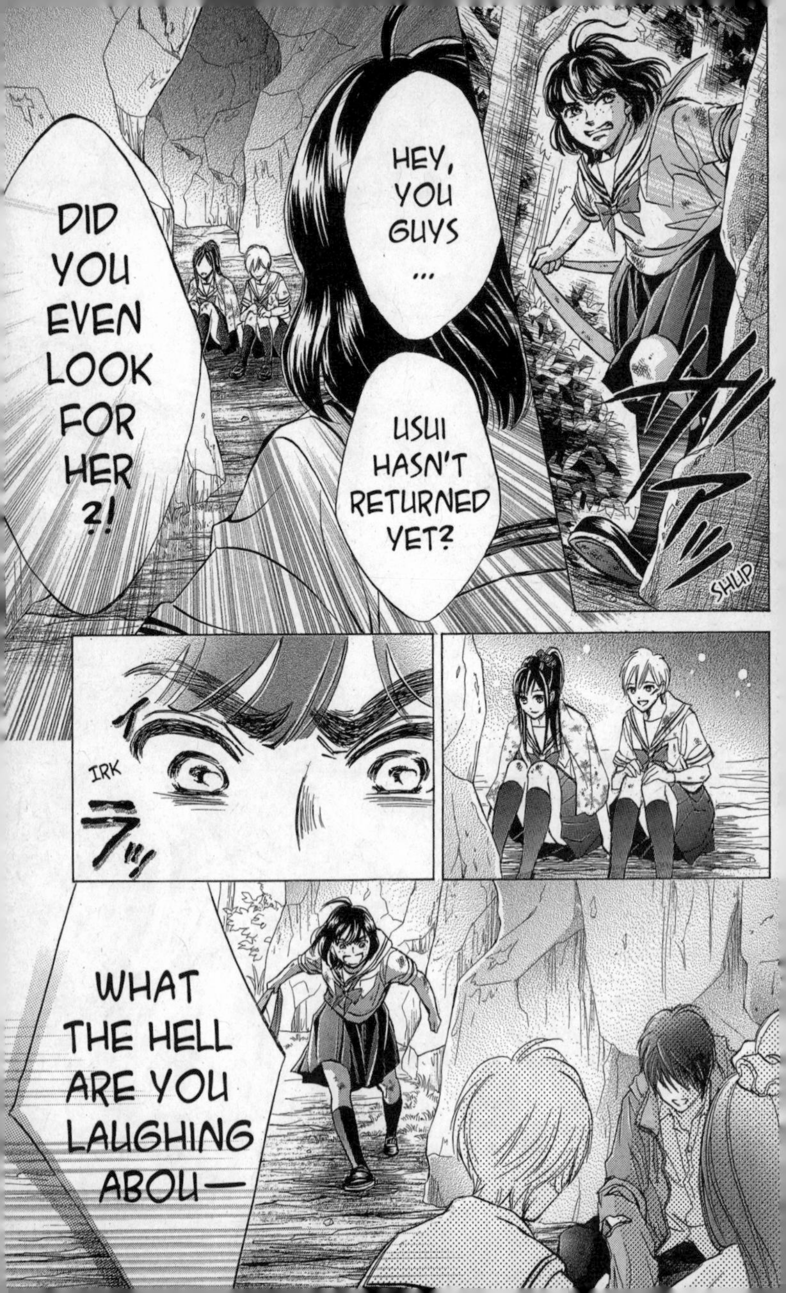
SHLUP
HEY, YOU GUYS ...
USUI HASN'T RETURNED YET?
DID YOU EVEN LOOK FOR HER ?!
IRK
WHAT THE HELL ARE YOU LAUGHING ABOU—

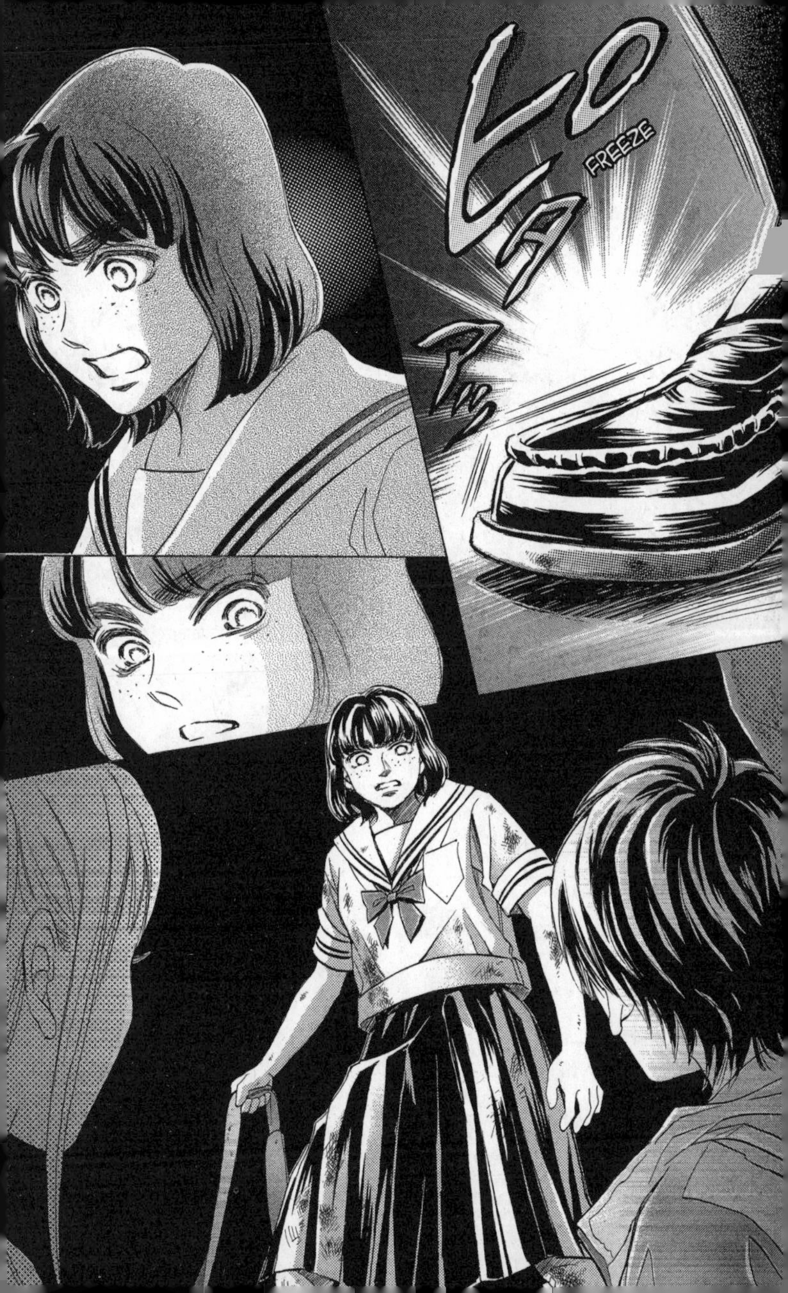
FREEZE

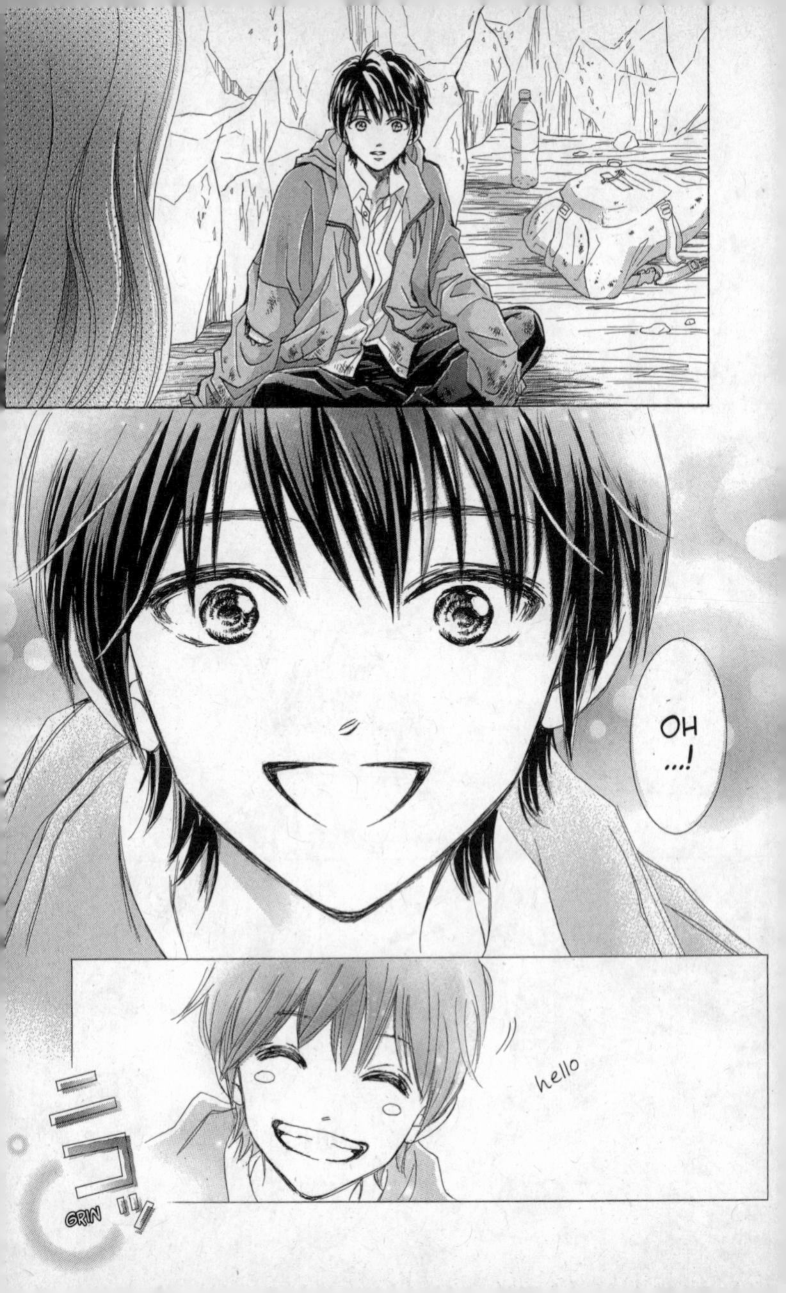
OH ...!
hello
GRIN

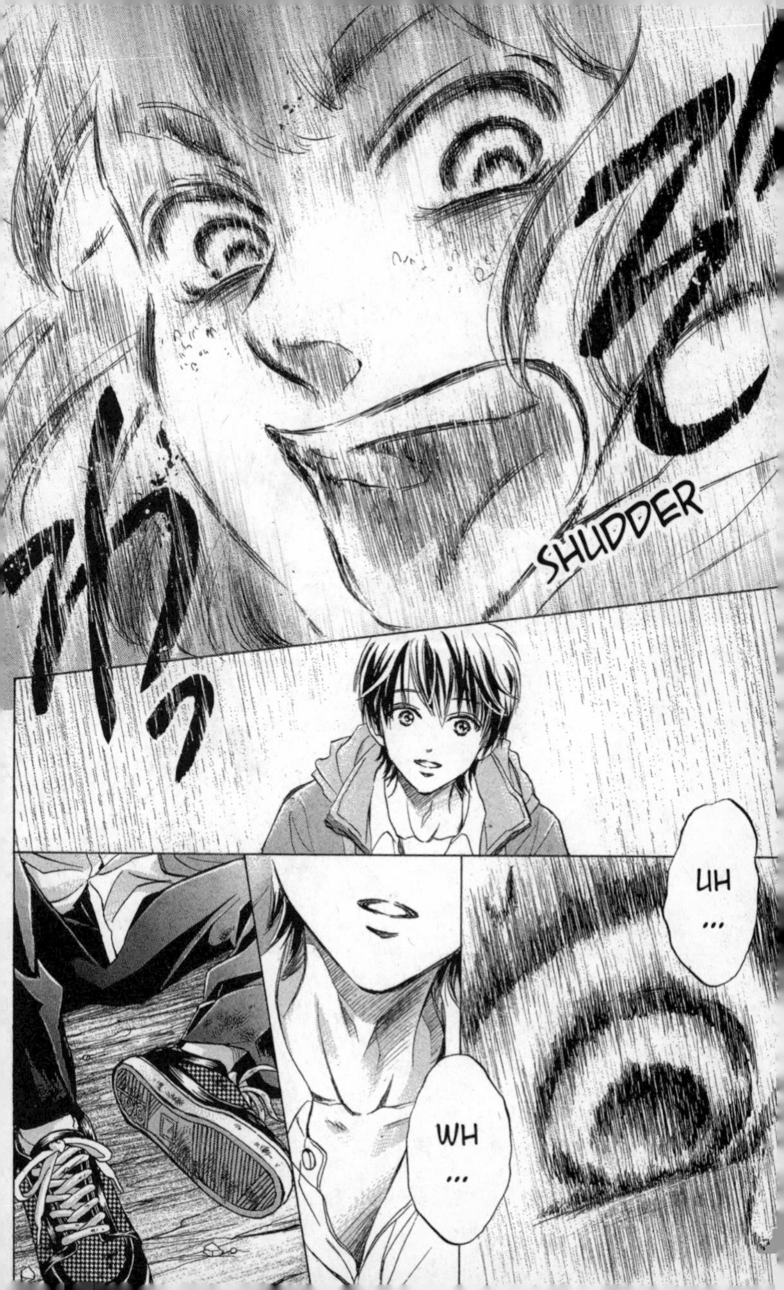
SHUDDER
UH ...
WH ...

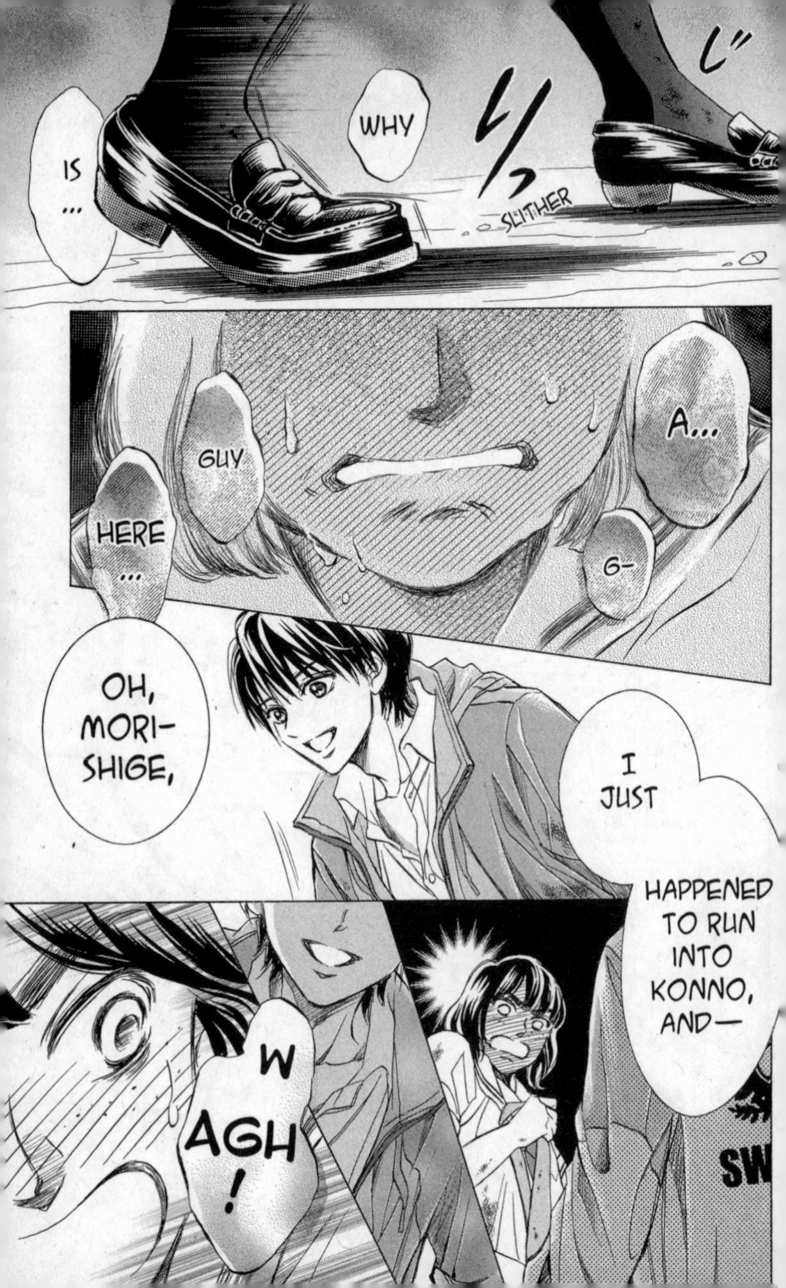
SLITHER
WHY
IS ...
A...
G-
GUY
HERE ...
OH, MORI-SHIGE,
I JUST HAPPENED TO RUN INTO KONNO, AND—
W AGH!
SW

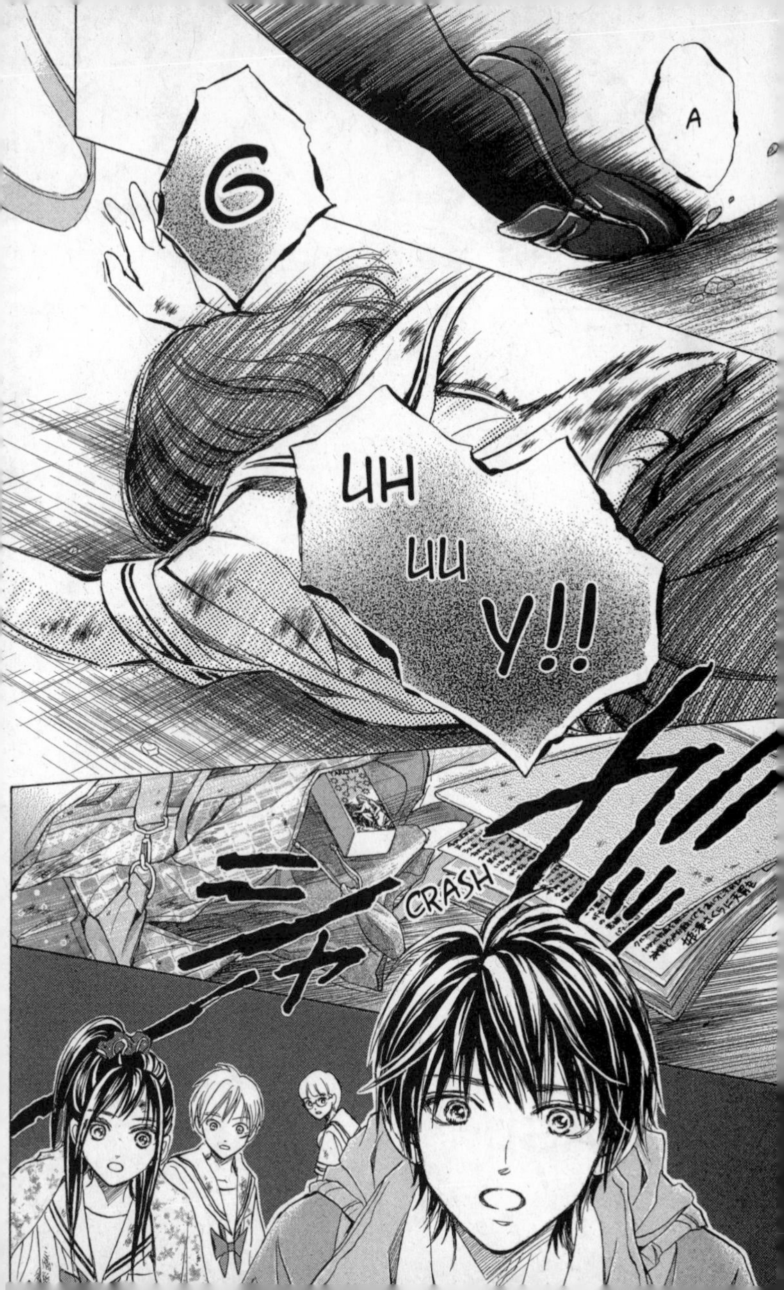
A
G
UH UU Y!!
CRASH

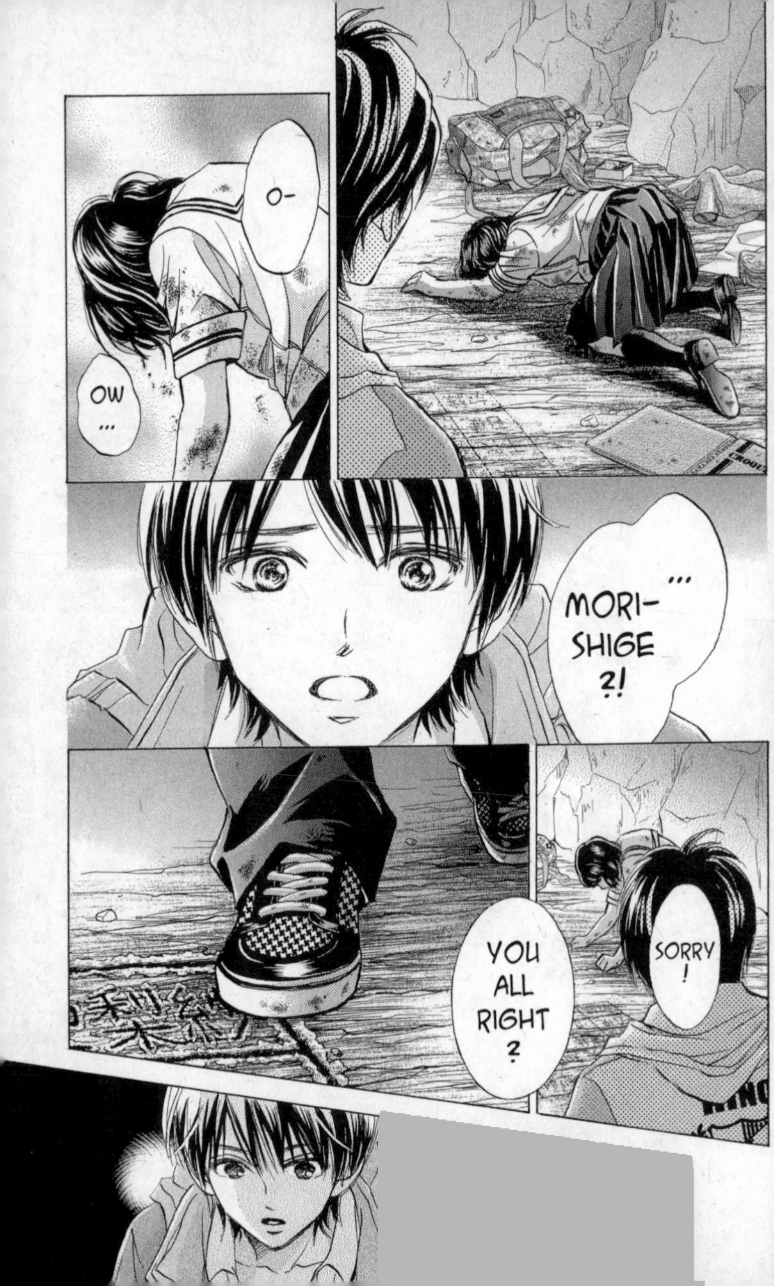
O-
OW ...
... MORI-SHIGE ?!
SORRY!
YOU ALL RIGHT?

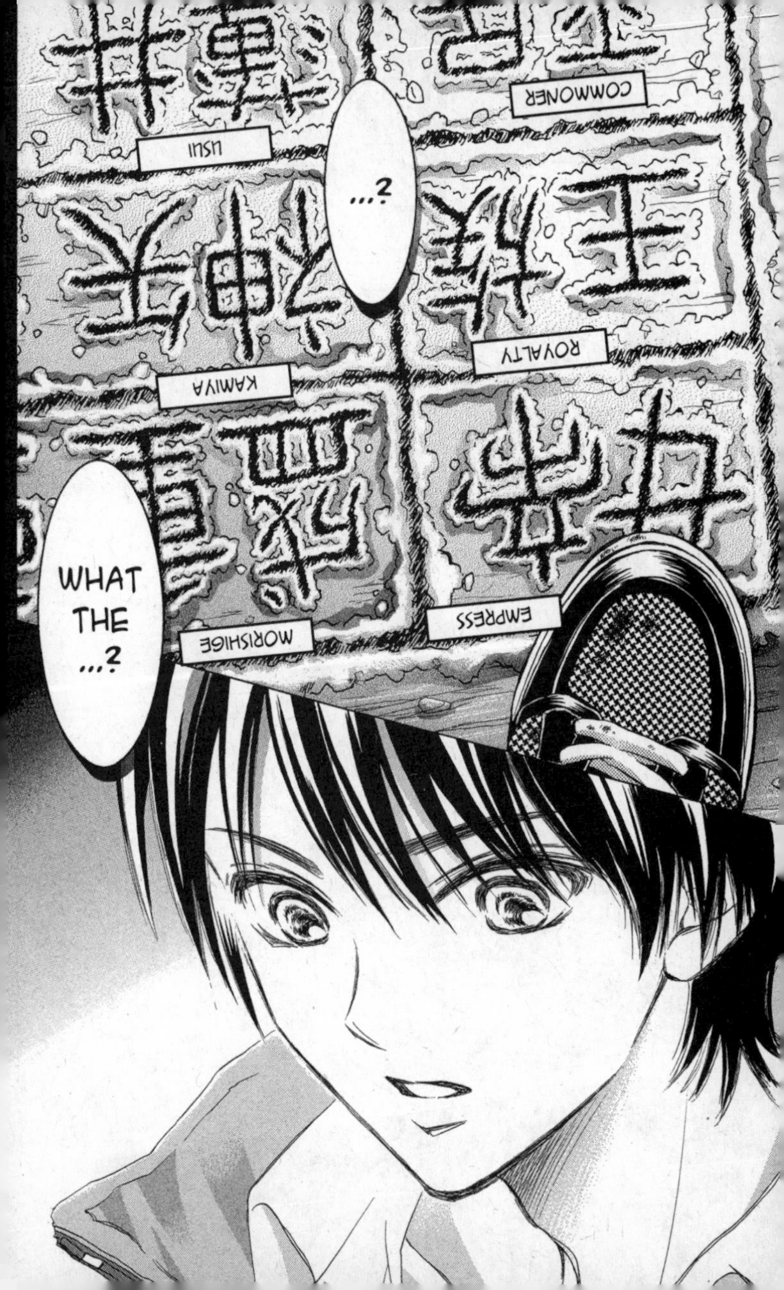
COMMONER
USUI
...?
ROYALTY
KAMIYA
EMPRESS
MORISHIGE
WHAT THE ...?

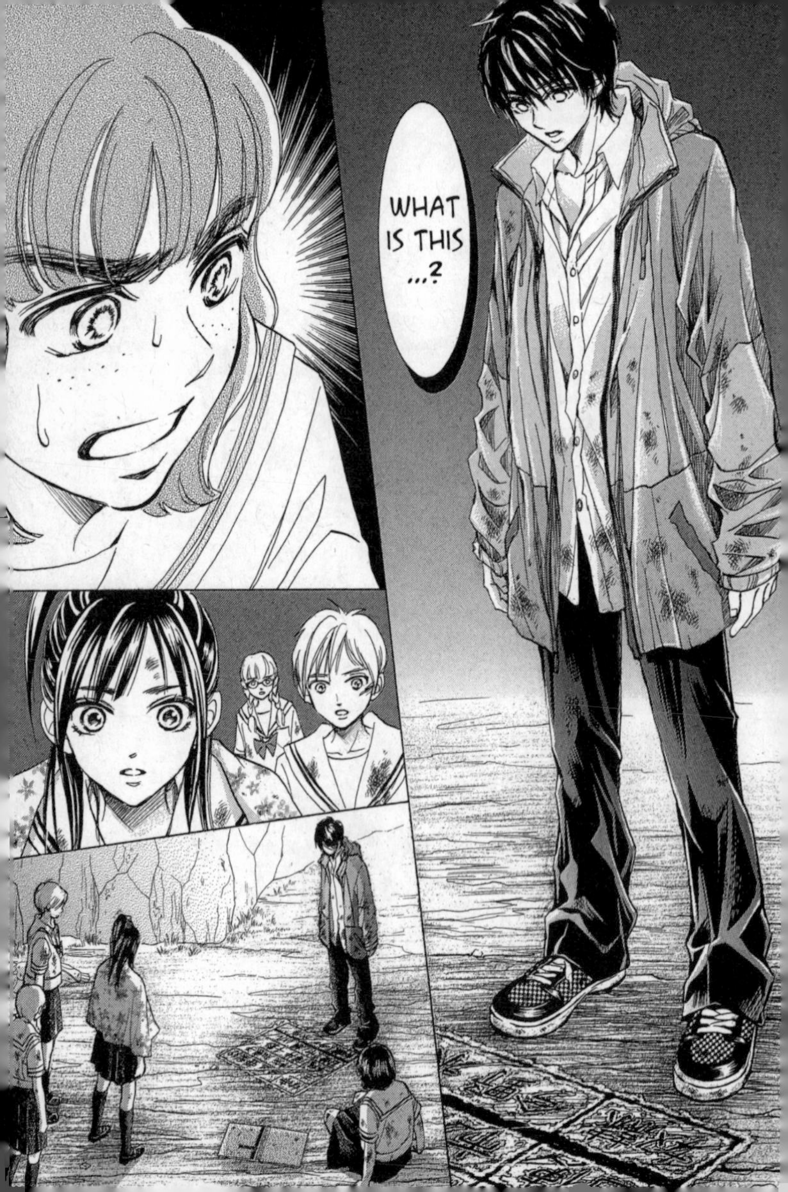
WHAT IS THIS ...?

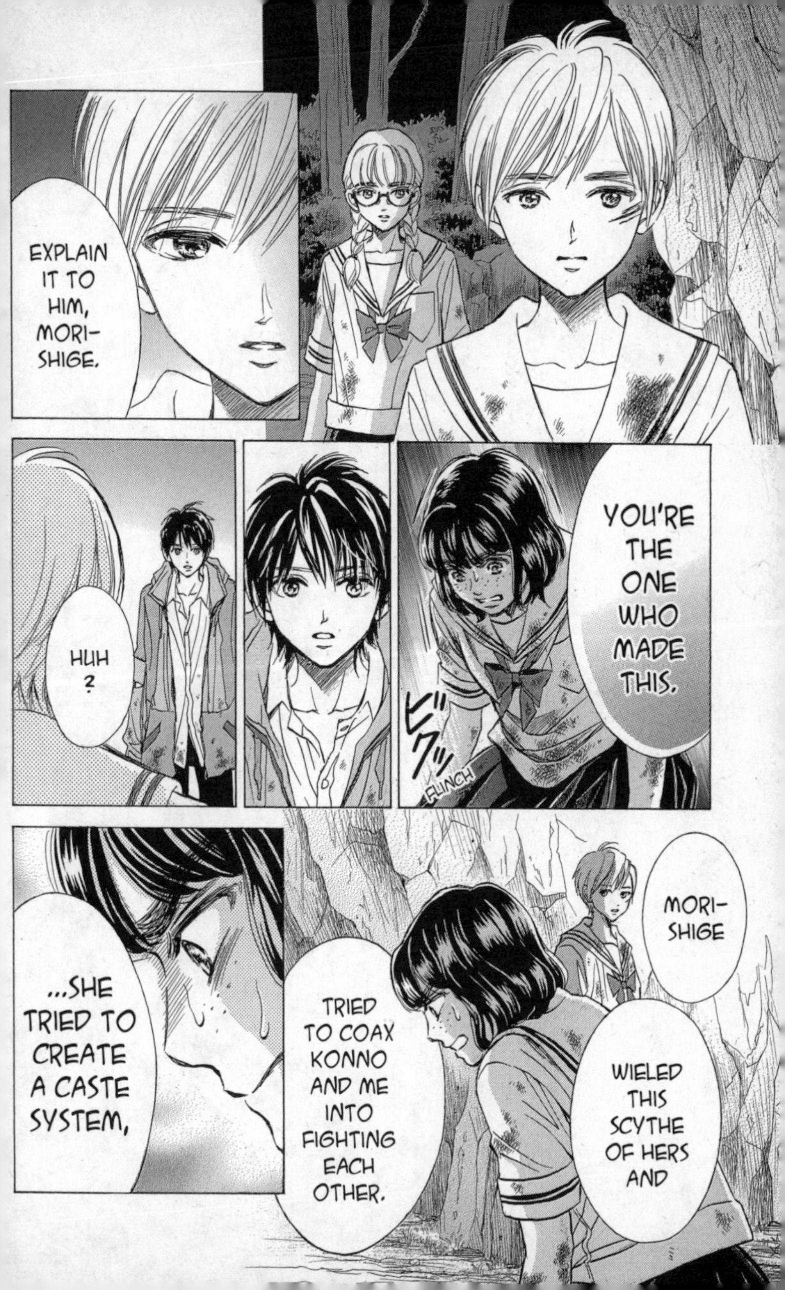
EXPLAIN IT TO HIM, MORI-SHIGE.
YOU'RE THE ONE WHO MADE THIS.
ビクッ
FLINCH
HUH ?
MORI-SHIGE
WIELED THIS SCYTHE OF HERS AND
TRIED TO COAX KONNO AND ME INTO FIGHTING EACH OTHER.
...SHE TRIED TO CREATE A CASTE SYSTEM,

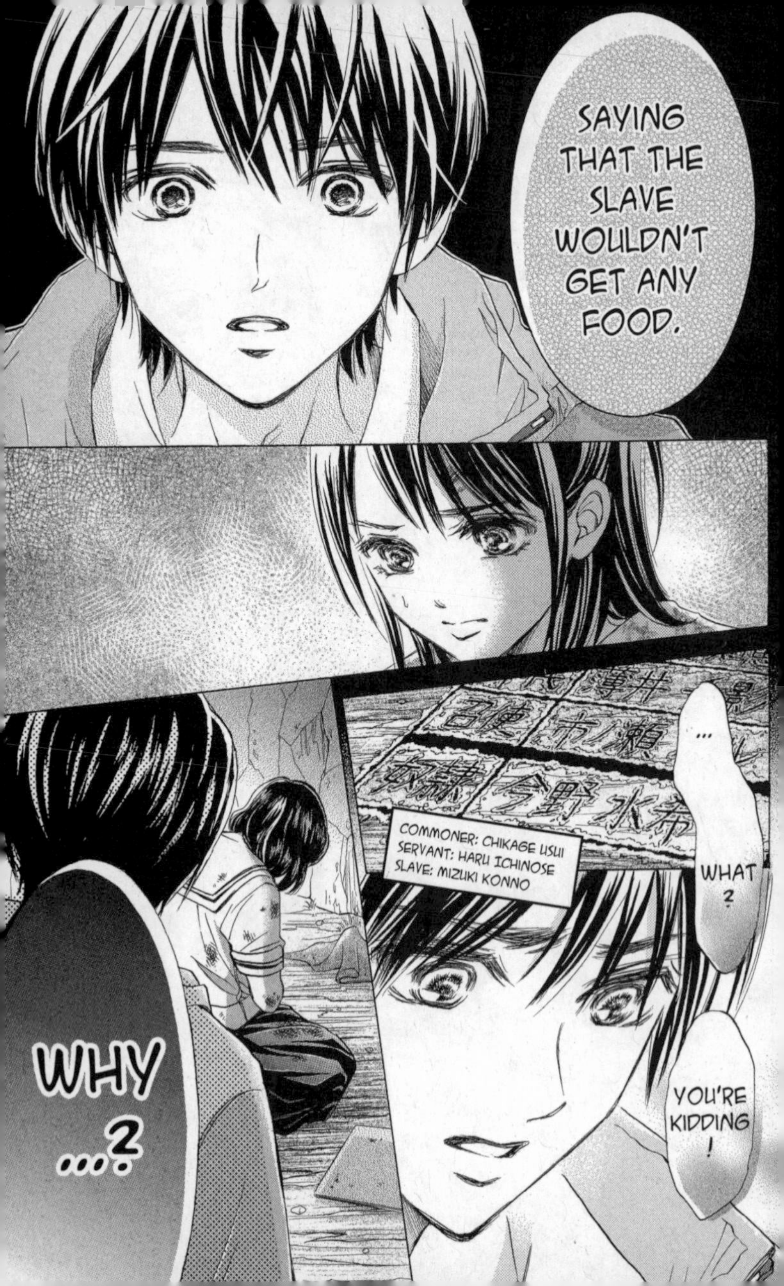
SAYING THAT THE SLAVE WOULDN'T GET ANY FOOD.
...
COMMONER: CHIKAGE USUI
SERVANT: HARU ICHINOSE
SLAVE: MIZUKI KONNO
WHAT?
YOU'RE KIDDING!
WHY...?

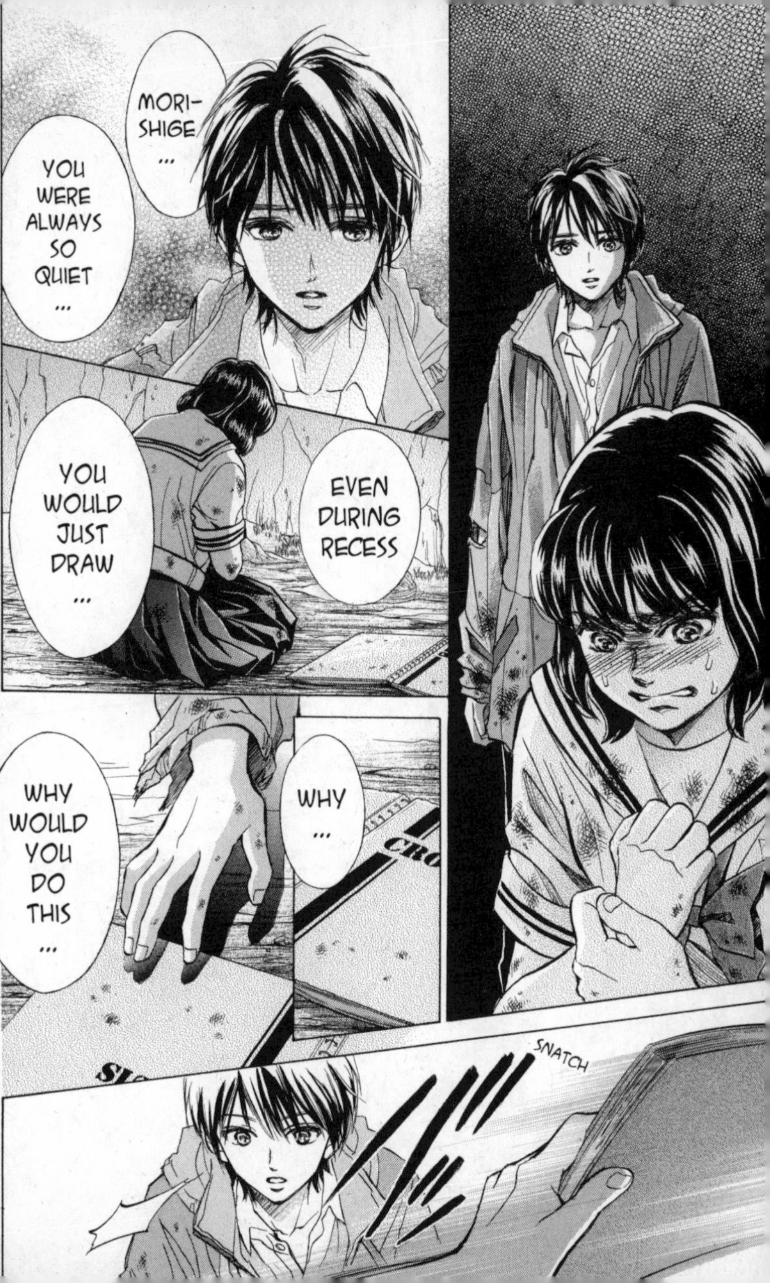
MORI-SHIGE ...
YOU WERE ALWAYS SO QUIET ...
EVEN DURING RECESS
YOU WOULD JUST DRAW ...
WHY ...
WHY WOULD YOU DO THIS ...
SNATCH

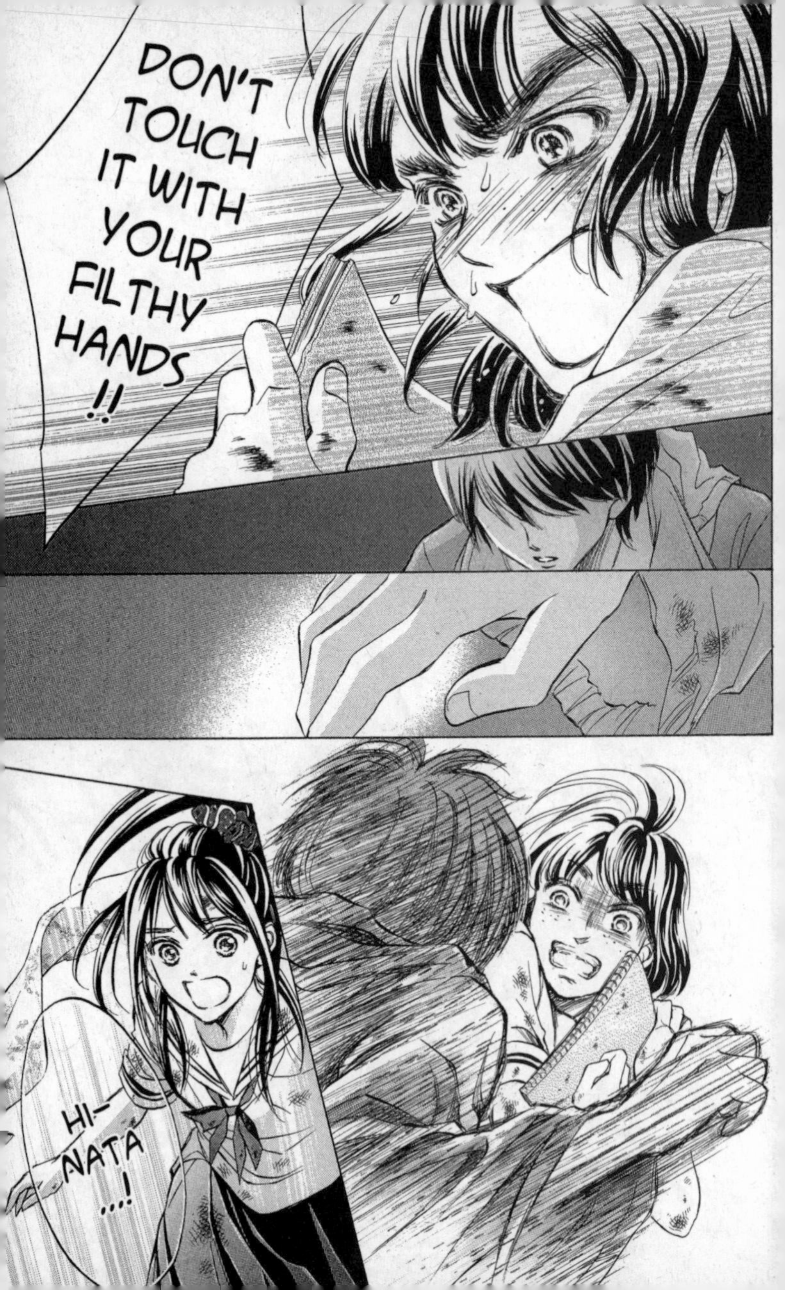
DON'T TOUCH IT WITH YOUR FILTHY HANDS !!
HI-NATA ...!

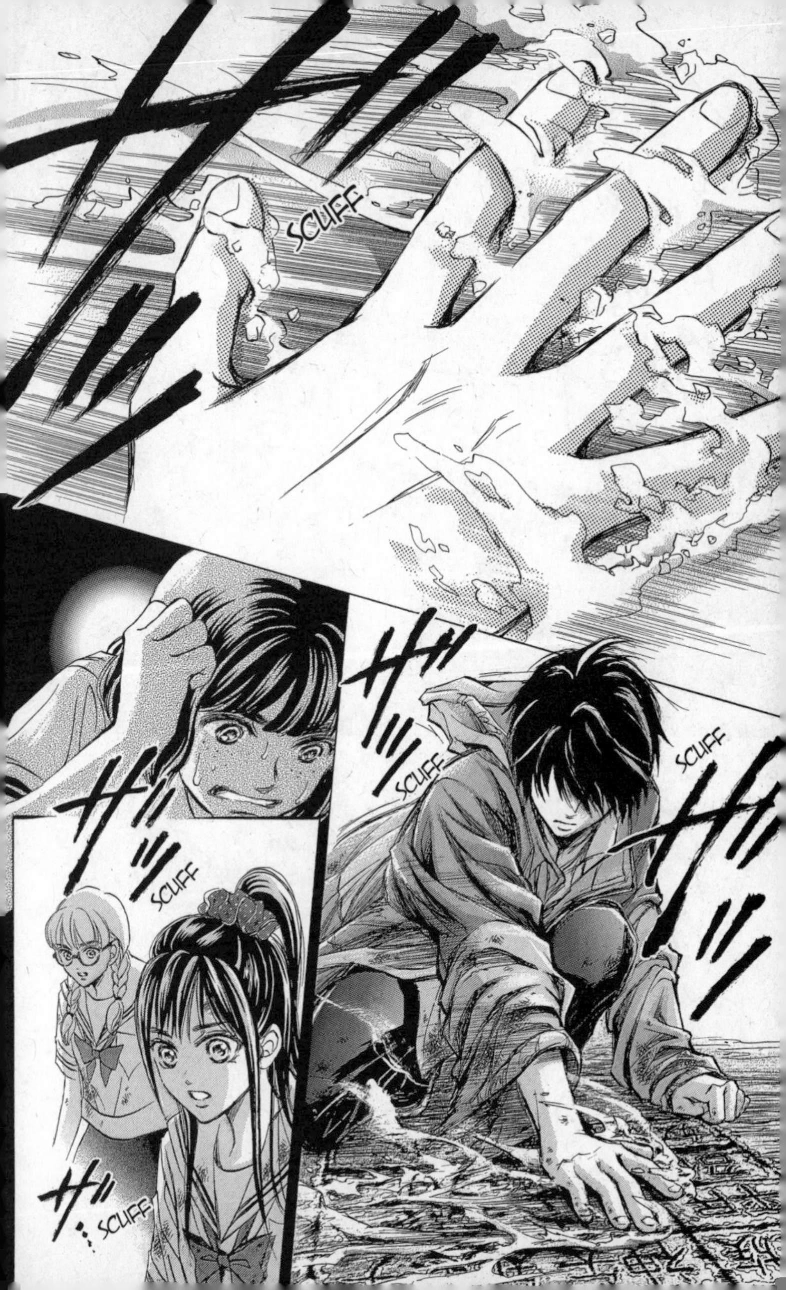
SCUFF
SCUFF
SCUFF
SCUFF
...SCUFF

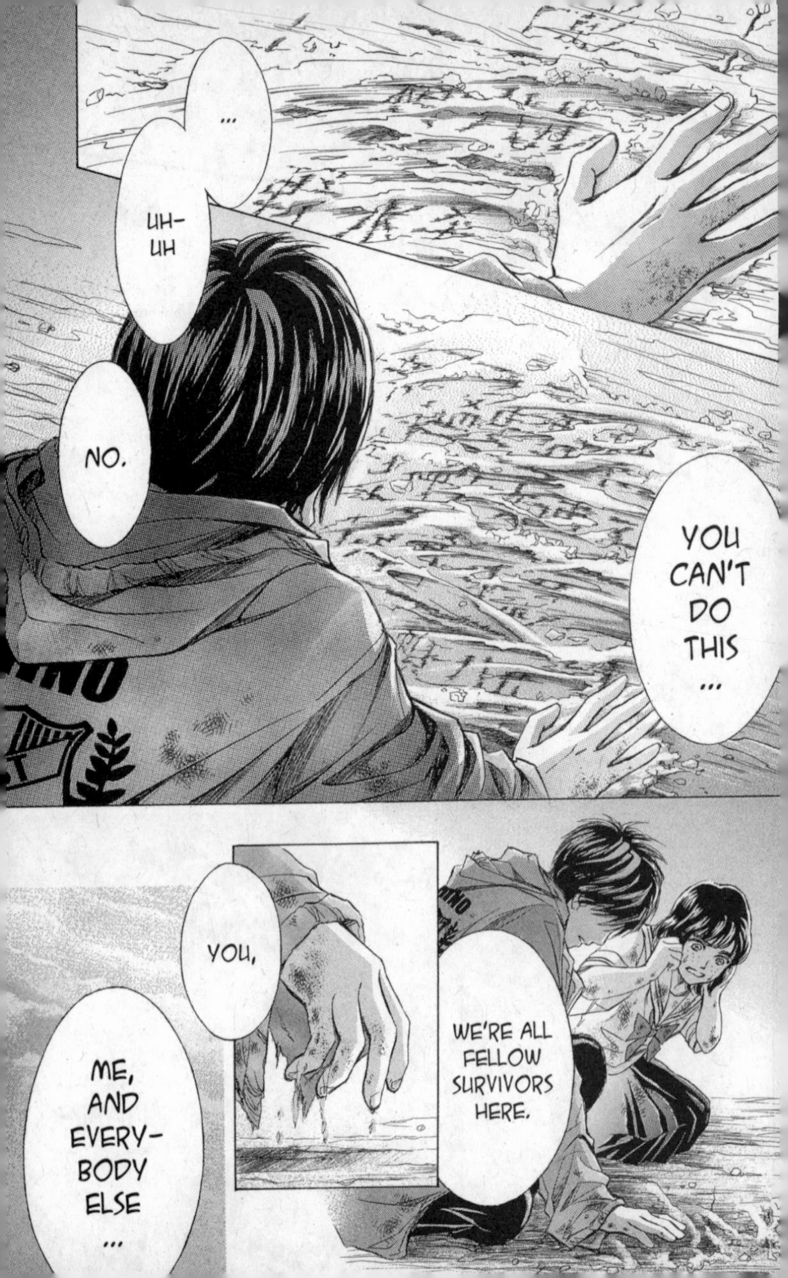
YOU CAN'T DO THIS ...
...
UH-UH
NO.
YOU,
ME, AND EVERY-BODY ELSE ...
WE'RE ALL FELLOW SURVIVORS HERE.

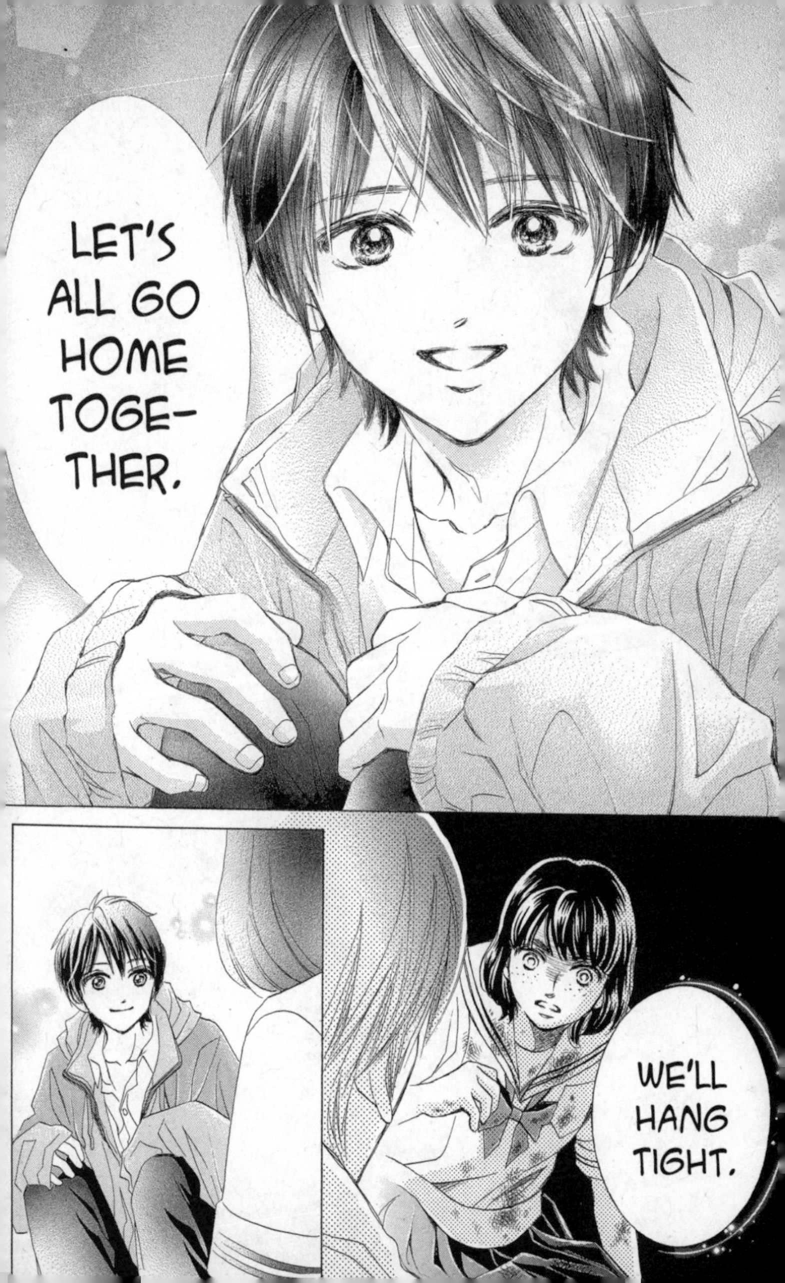
LET'S ALL GO HOME TOGE-THER.
WE'LL HANG TIGHT.

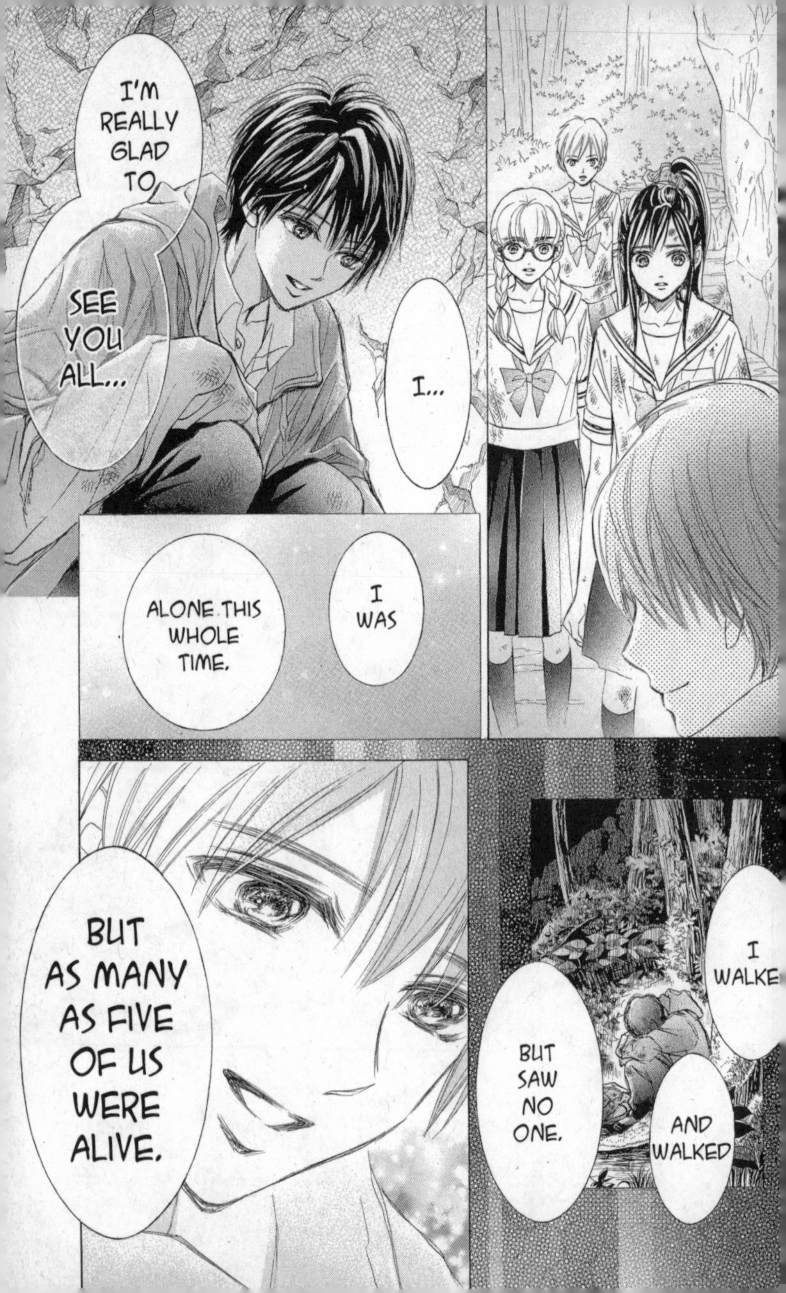
I'M REALLY GLAD TO
SEE YOU ALL...
I...
I WAS
ALONE THIS WHOLE TIME.
I WALKE
AND WALKED
BUT SAW NO ONE.
BUT AS MANY AS FIVE OF US WERE ALIVE.

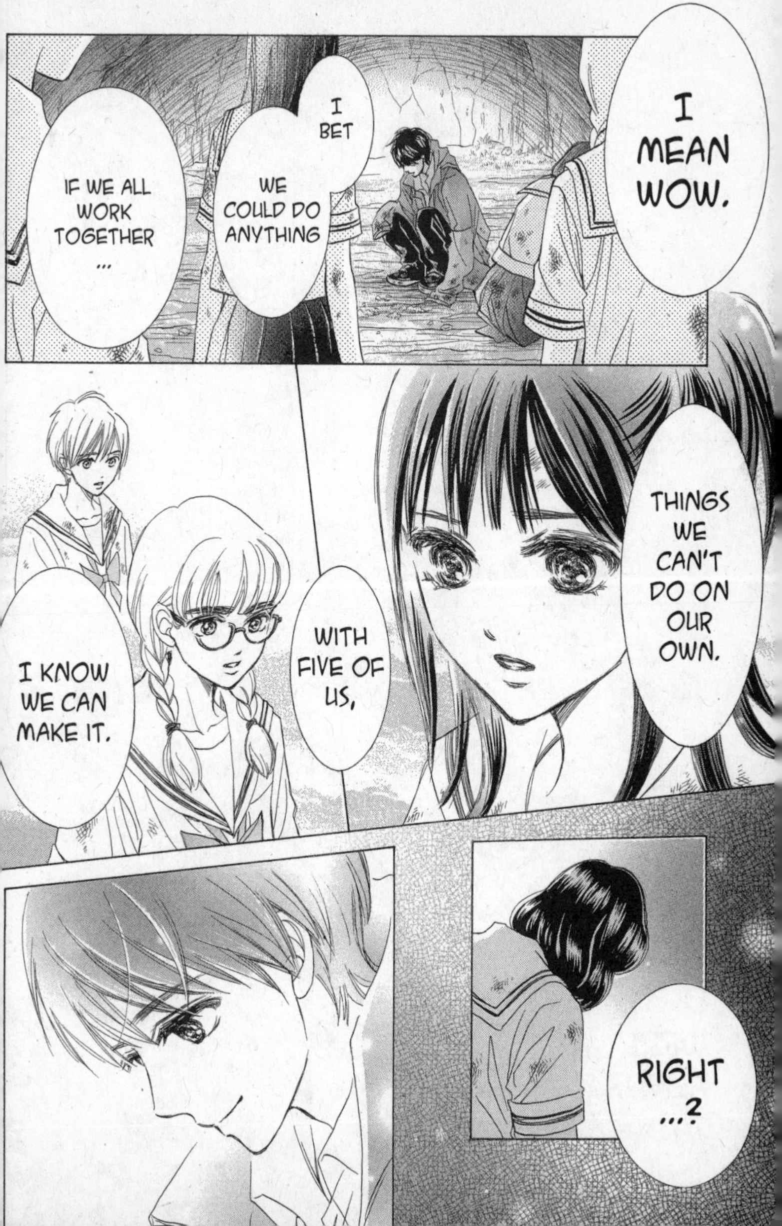
I MEAN WOW.
I BET
WE COULD DO ANYTHING
IF WE ALL WORK TOGETHER ...
THINGS WE CAN'T DO ON OUR OWN.
WITH FIVE OF US,
I KNOW WE CAN MAKE IT.
RIGHT ...?

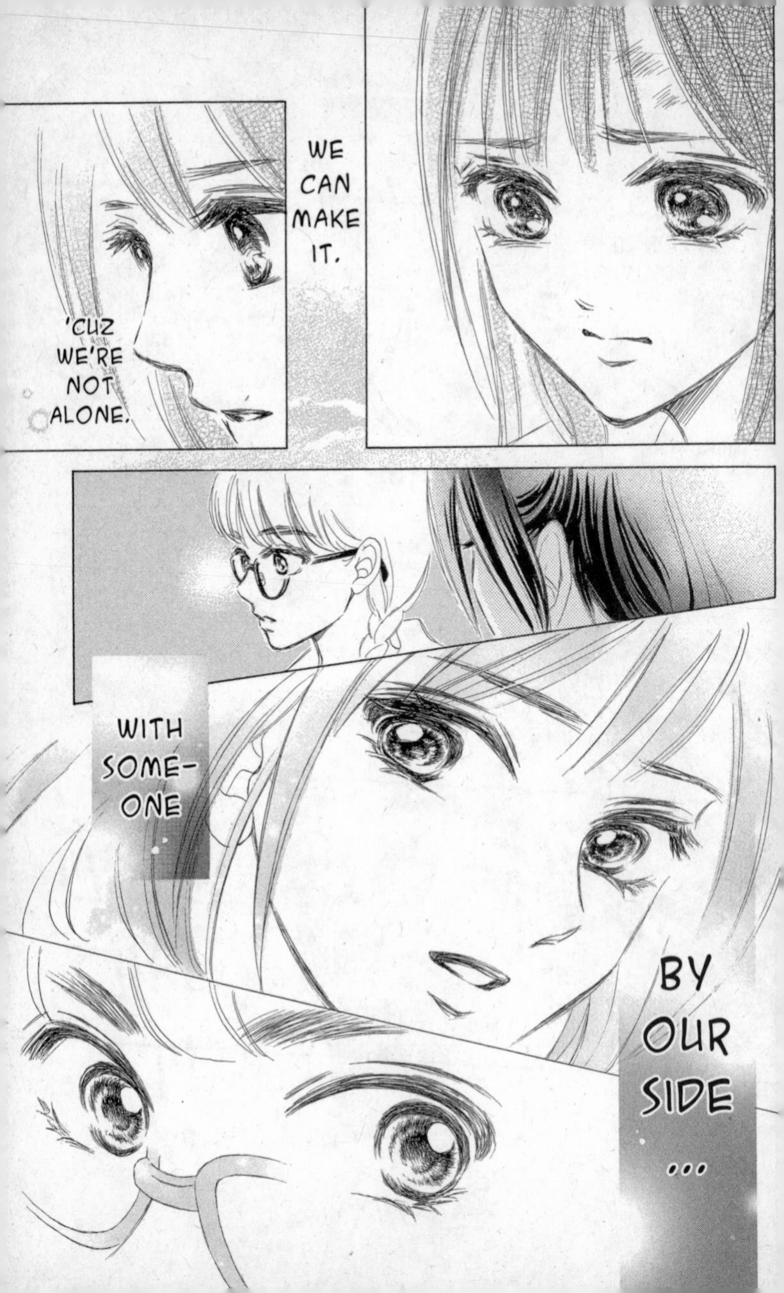
WE CAN MAKE IT.
'CUZ WE'RE NOT ALONE.
WITH SOME-ONE
BY OUR SIDE ...

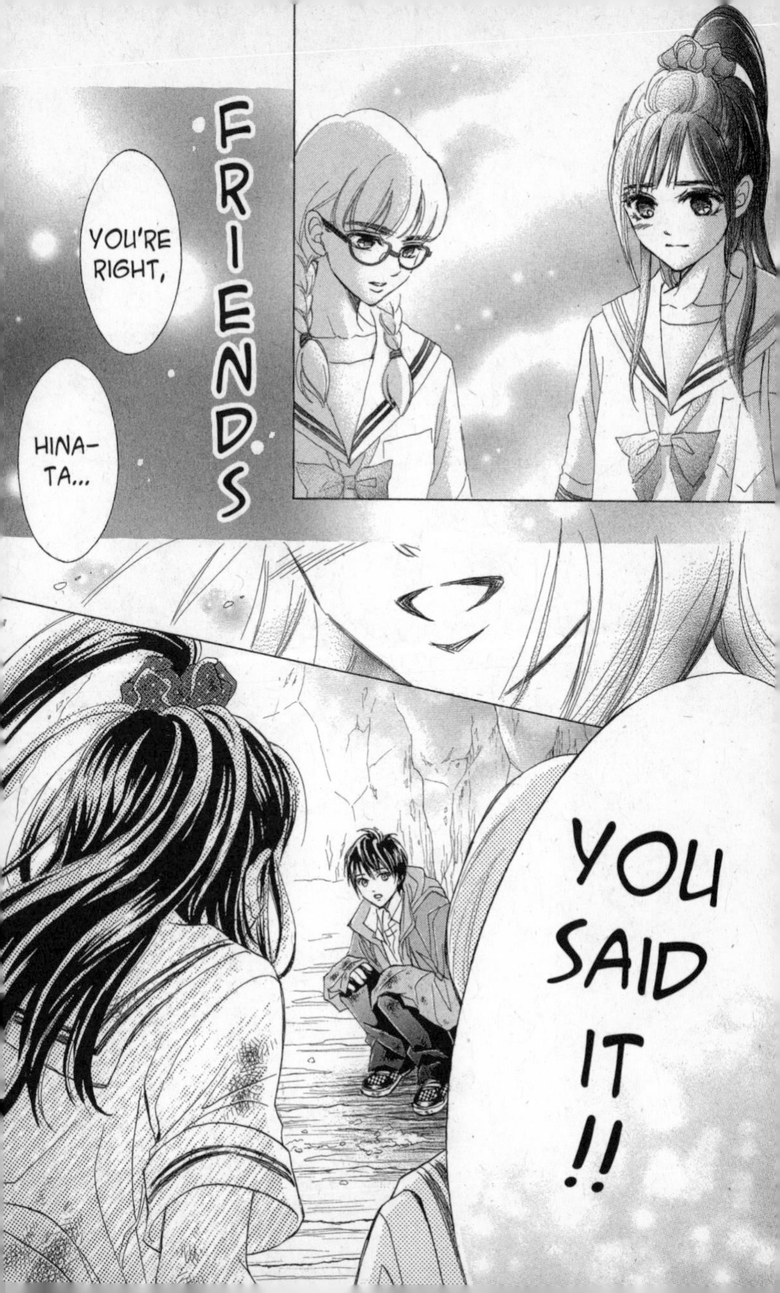

FRIENDS
YOU'RE RIGHT,
HINA-TA...
YOU SAID IT!!

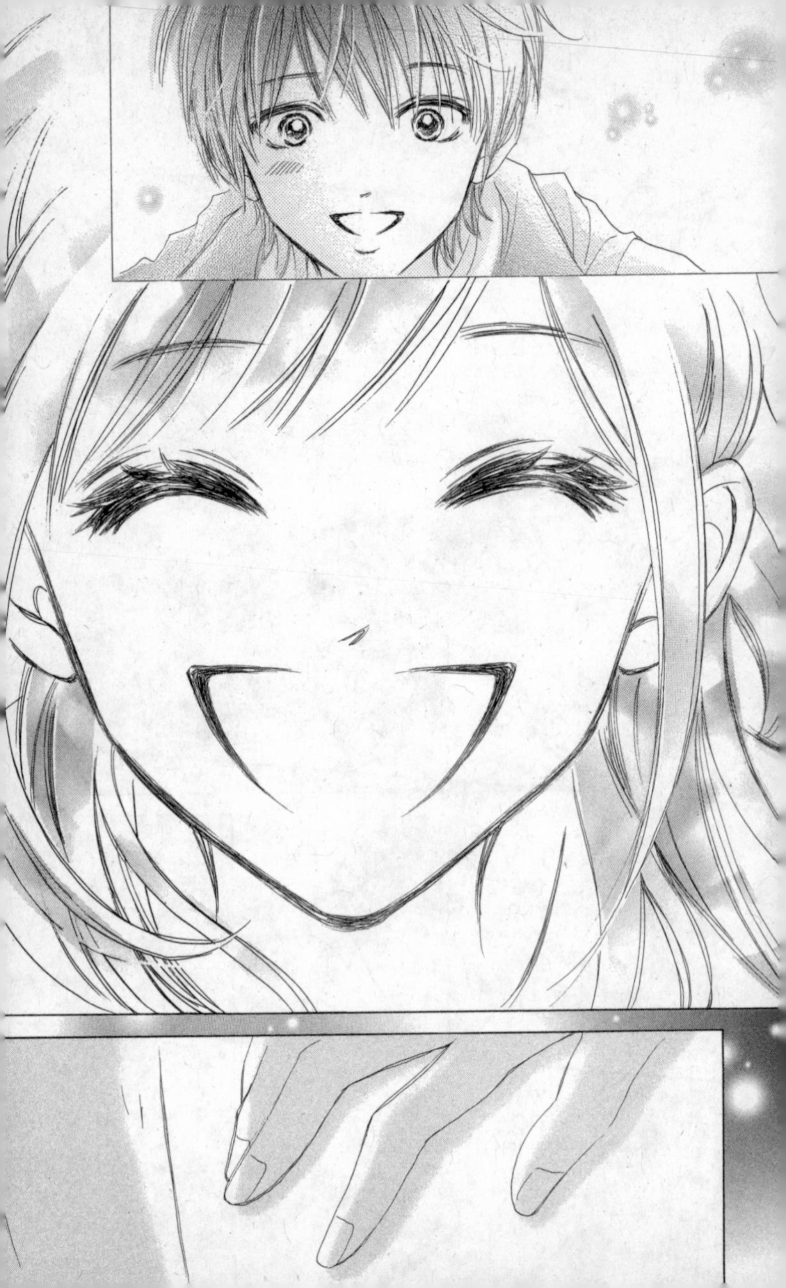

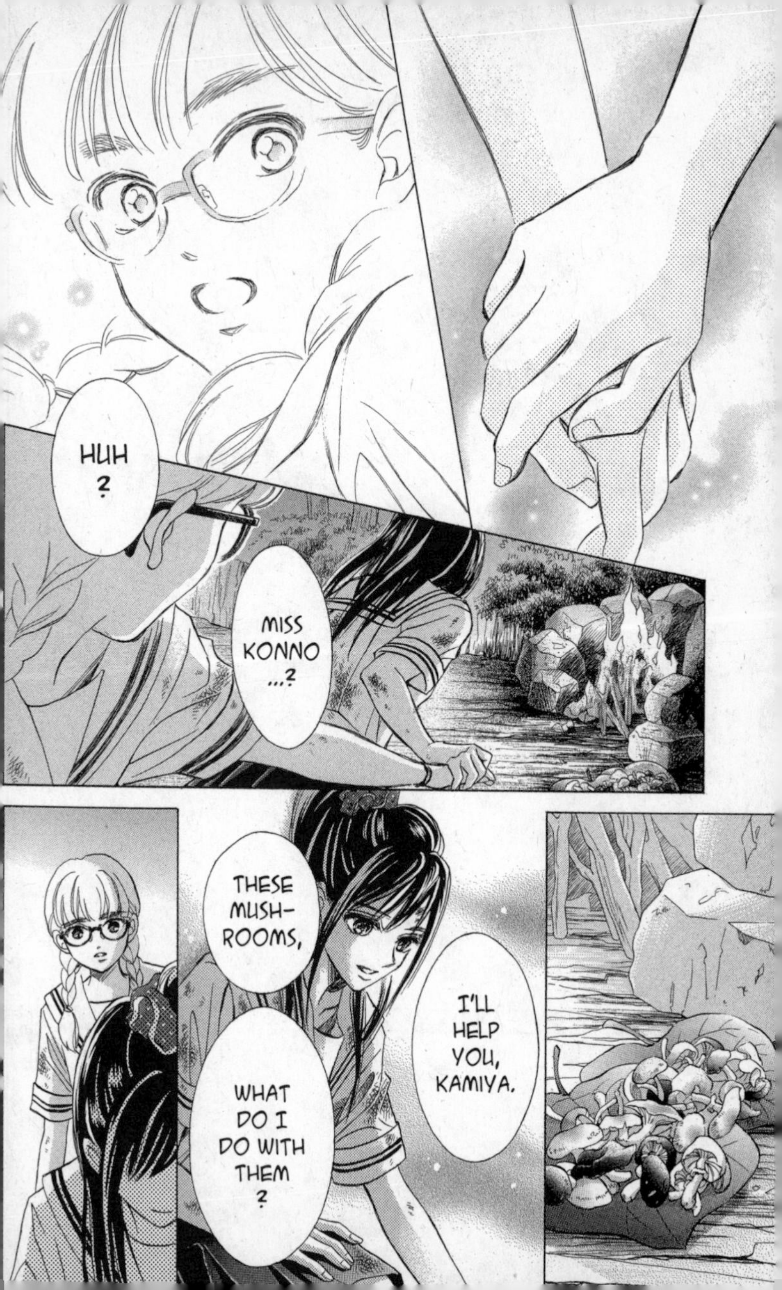
HUH?
MISS KONNO...?
I'LL HELP YOU, KAMIYA.
THESE MUSH-ROOMS,
WHAT DO I DO WITH THEM?

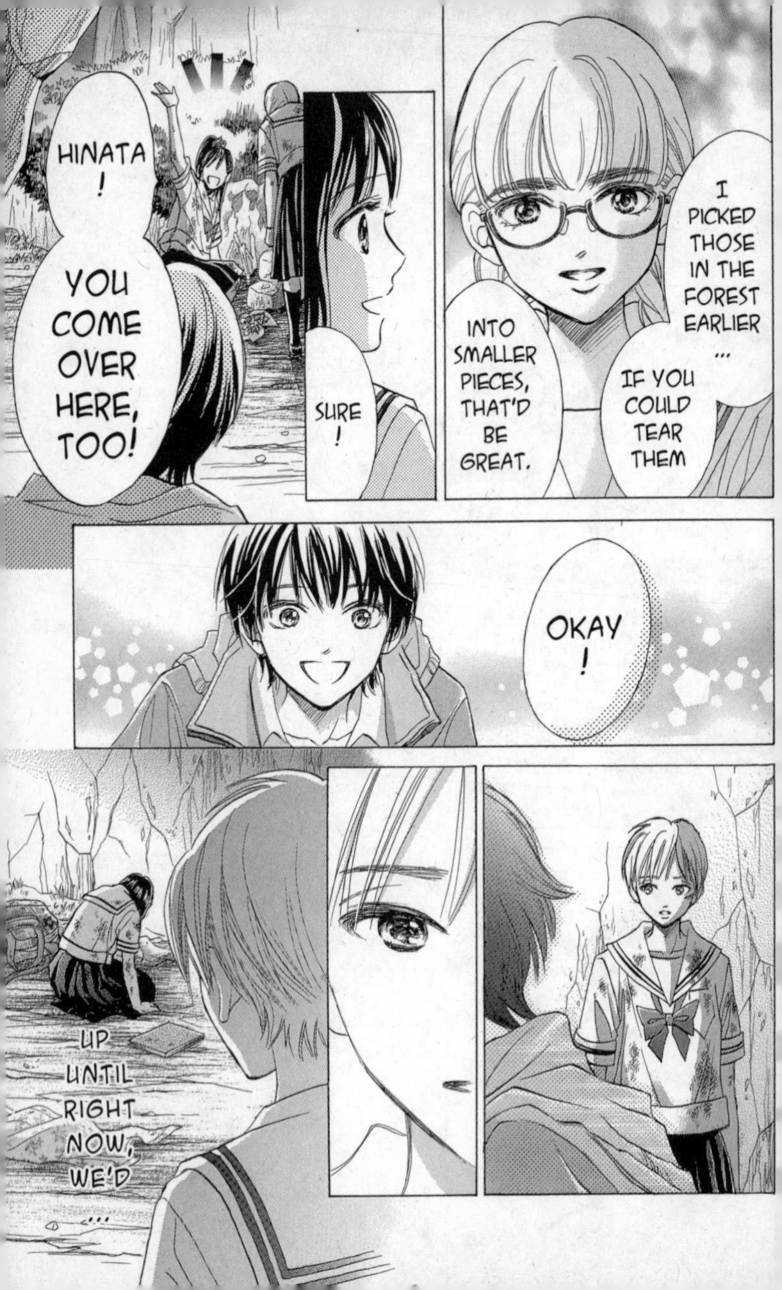
I PICKED THOSE IN THE FOREST EARLIER...
IF YOU COULD TEAR THEM
INTO SMALLER PIECES, THAT'D BE GREAT.
SURE!
HINATA!
YOU COME OVER HERE, TOO!
OKAY!
UP UNTIL RIGHT NOW, WE'D ...

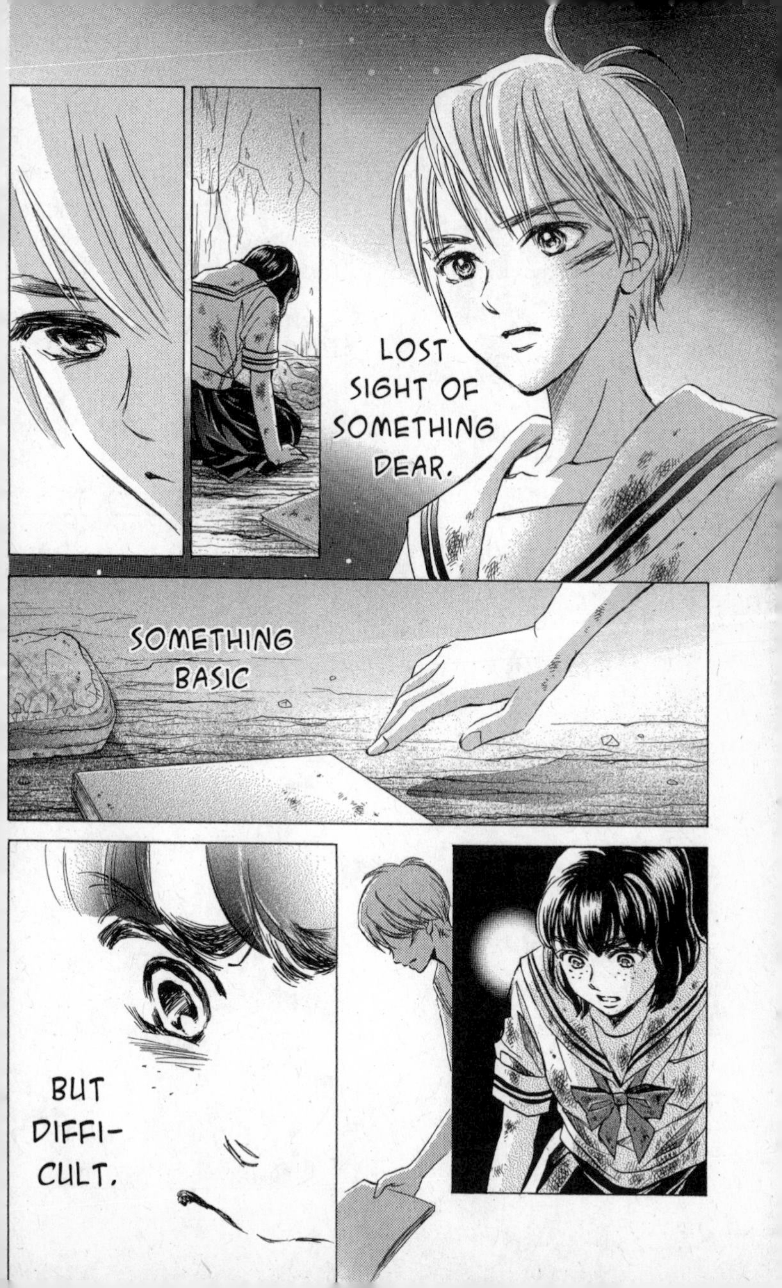
LOST SIGHT OF SOMETHING DEAR.
SOMETHING BASIC
BUT DIFFI-CULT.

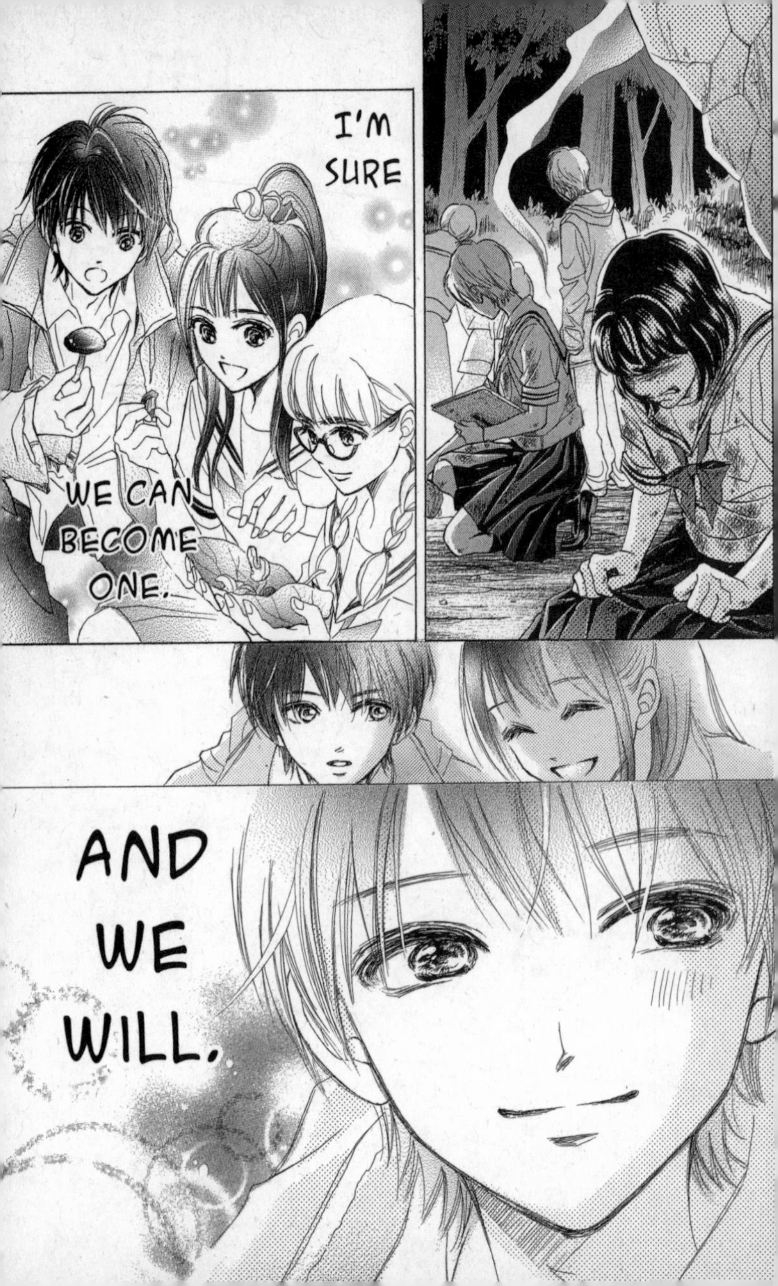
I'M SURE
WE CAN BECOME ONE.
AND WE WILL.

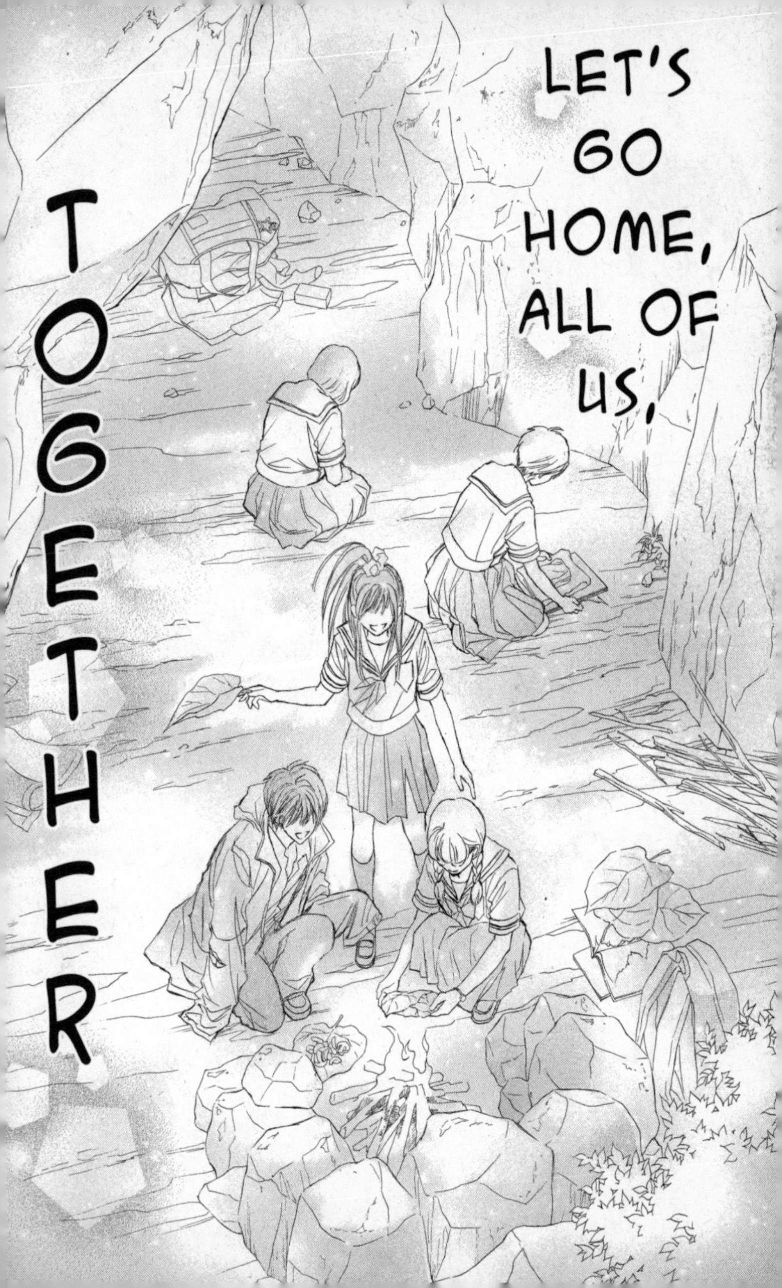
LET'S GO HOME, ALL OF US,
TOGETHER

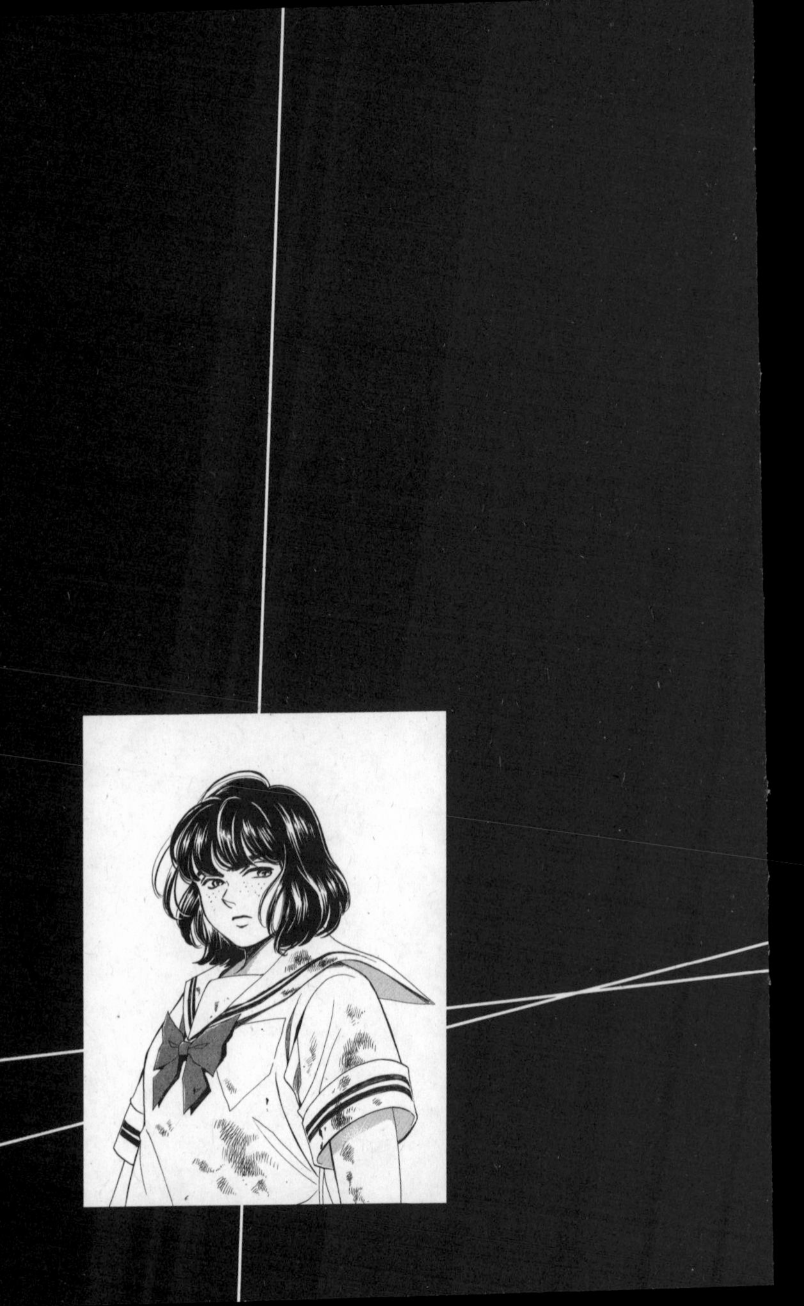

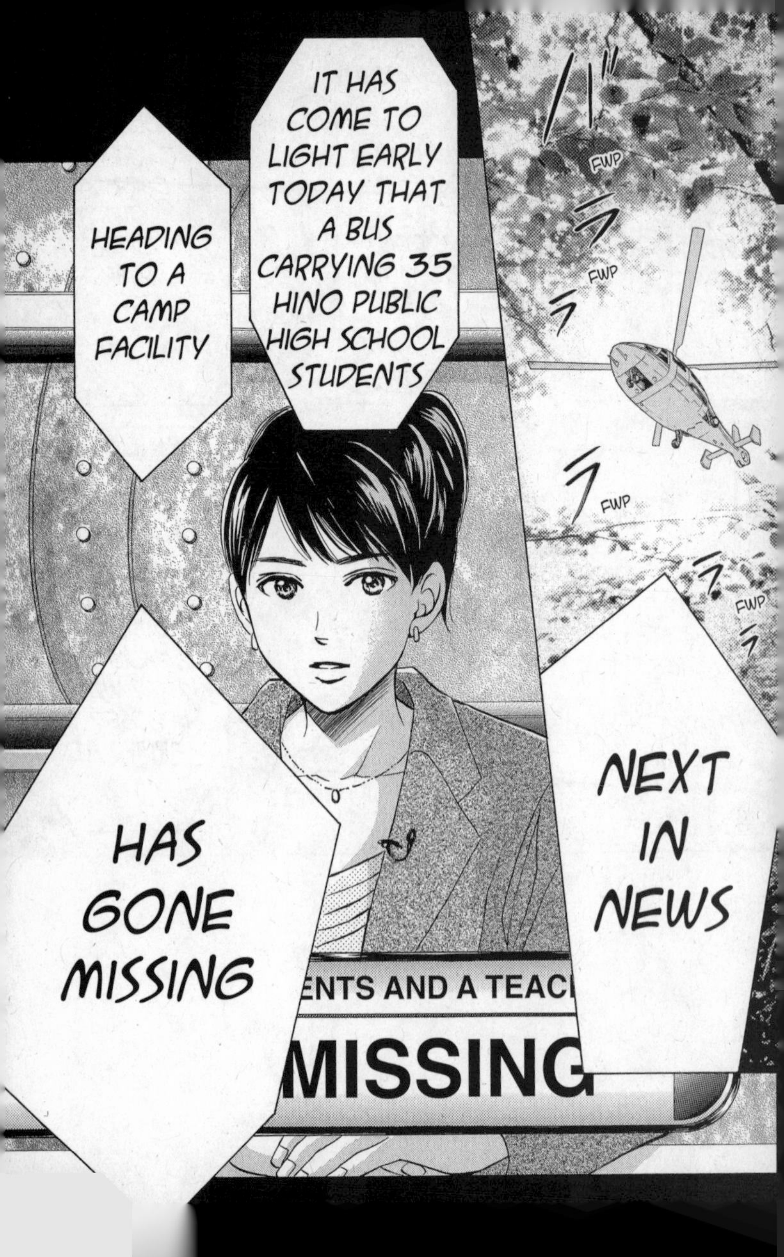
FWP
FWP
FWP
FWP
NEXT IN NEWS
IT HAS COME TO LIGHT EARLY TODAY THAT A BUS CARRYING 35 HINO PUBLIC HIGH SCHOOL STUDENTS
HEADING TO A CAMP FACILITY
HAS GONE MISSING
ENTS AND A TEAC
MISSING

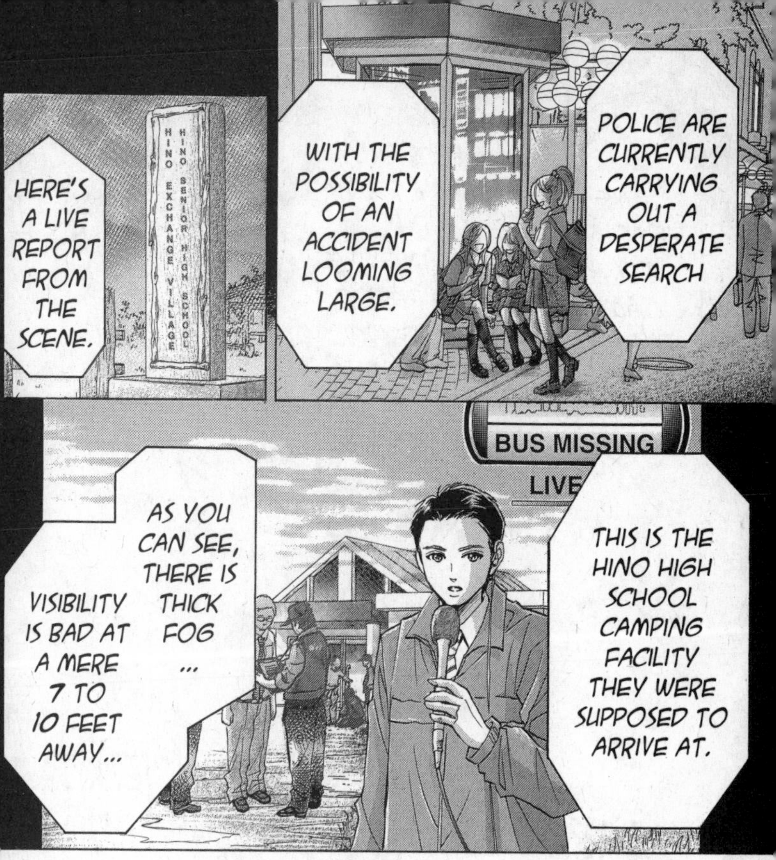
POLICE ARE CURRENTLY CARRYING OUT A DESPERATE SEARCH
WITH THE POSSIBILITY OF AN ACCIDENT LOOMING LARGE.
HINO SENIOR HIGH SCHOOL
HINO EXCHANGE VILLAGE
HERE'S A LIVE REPORT FROM THE SCENE.
BUS MISSING
LIVE
THIS IS THE HINO HIGH SCHOOL CAMPING FACILITY THEY WERE SUPPOSED TO ARRIVE AT.
AS YOU CAN SEE, THERE IS THICK FOG ...
VISIBILITY IS BAD AT A MERE 7 TO 10 FEET AWAY...

LIMIT

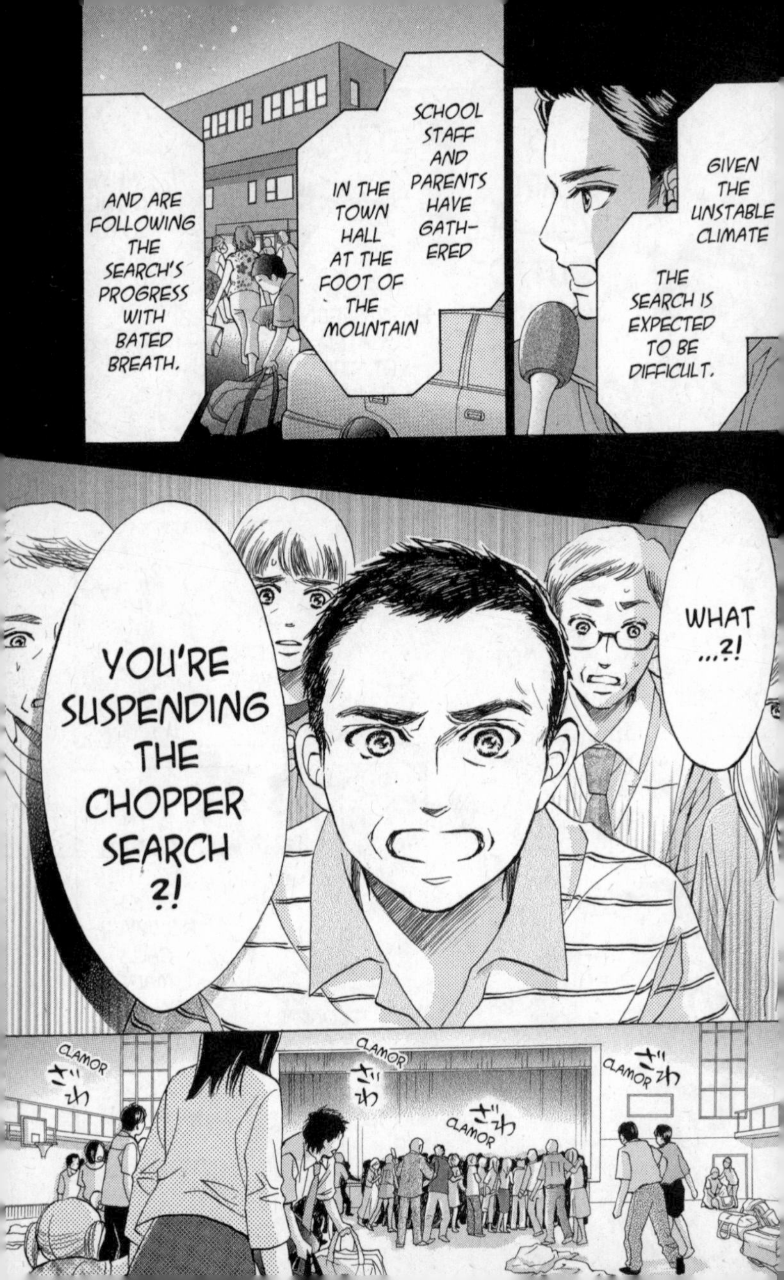
GIVEN THE UNSTABLE CLIMATE
THE SEARCH IS EXPECTED TO BE DIFFICULT.
SCHOOL STAFF AND PARENTS HAVE GATH-ERED
IN THE TOWN HALL AT THE FOOT OF THE MOUNTAIN
AND ARE FOLLOWING THE SEARCH'S PROGRESS WITH BATED BREATH.
WHAT ...?!
YOU'RE SUSPENDING THE CHOPPER SEARCH ?!
ざわ CLAMOR
ざわ CLAMOR
ざわ CLAMOR
ざわ CLAMOR

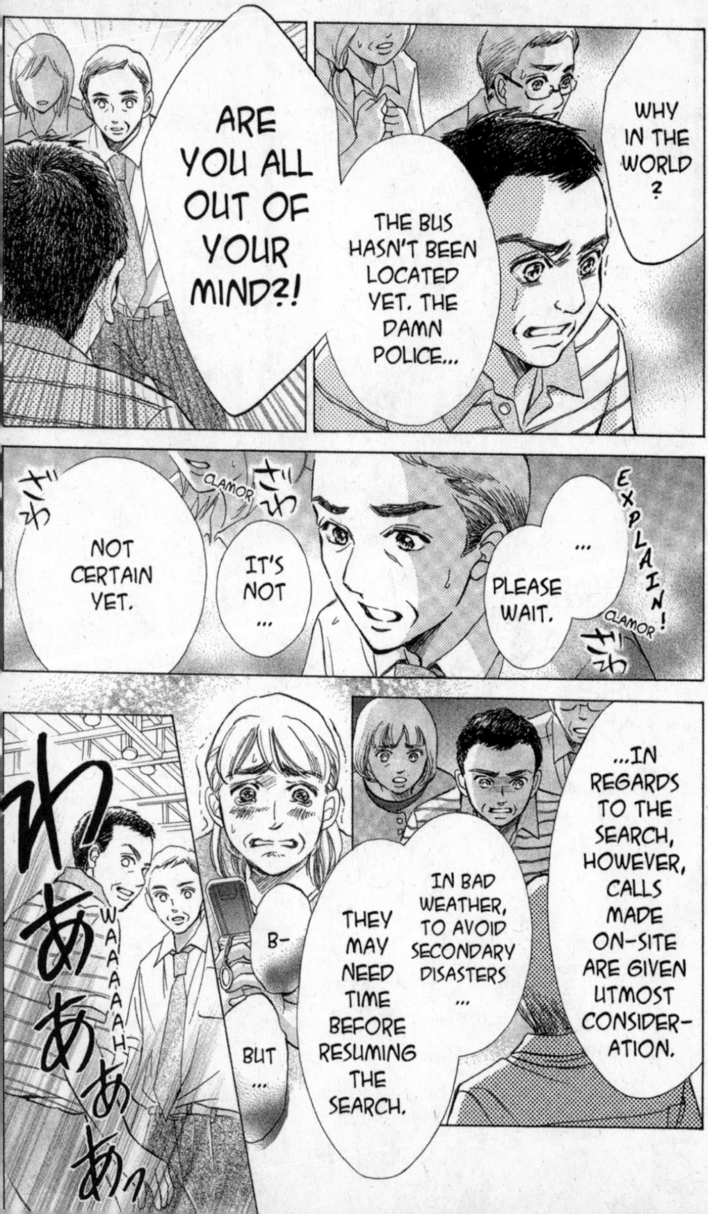
WHY IN THE WORLD?
THE BUS HASN'T BEEN LOCATED YET. THE DAMN POLICE...
ARE YOU ALL OUT OF YOUR MIND?!
EXPLAIN!
CLAMOR
ざわ
...
PLEASE WAIT.
CLAMOR
ざわ
IT'S NOT ...
ざわ
NOT CERTAIN YET.
...IN REGARDS TO THE SEARCH, HOWEVER, CALLS MADE ON-SITE ARE GIVEN UTMOST CONSIDERATION.
IN BAD WEATHER, TO AVOID SECONDARY DISASTERS ...
THEY MAY NEED TIME BEFORE RESUMING THE SEARCH.
B- BUT ...
WAAAAAAH
わあああっ

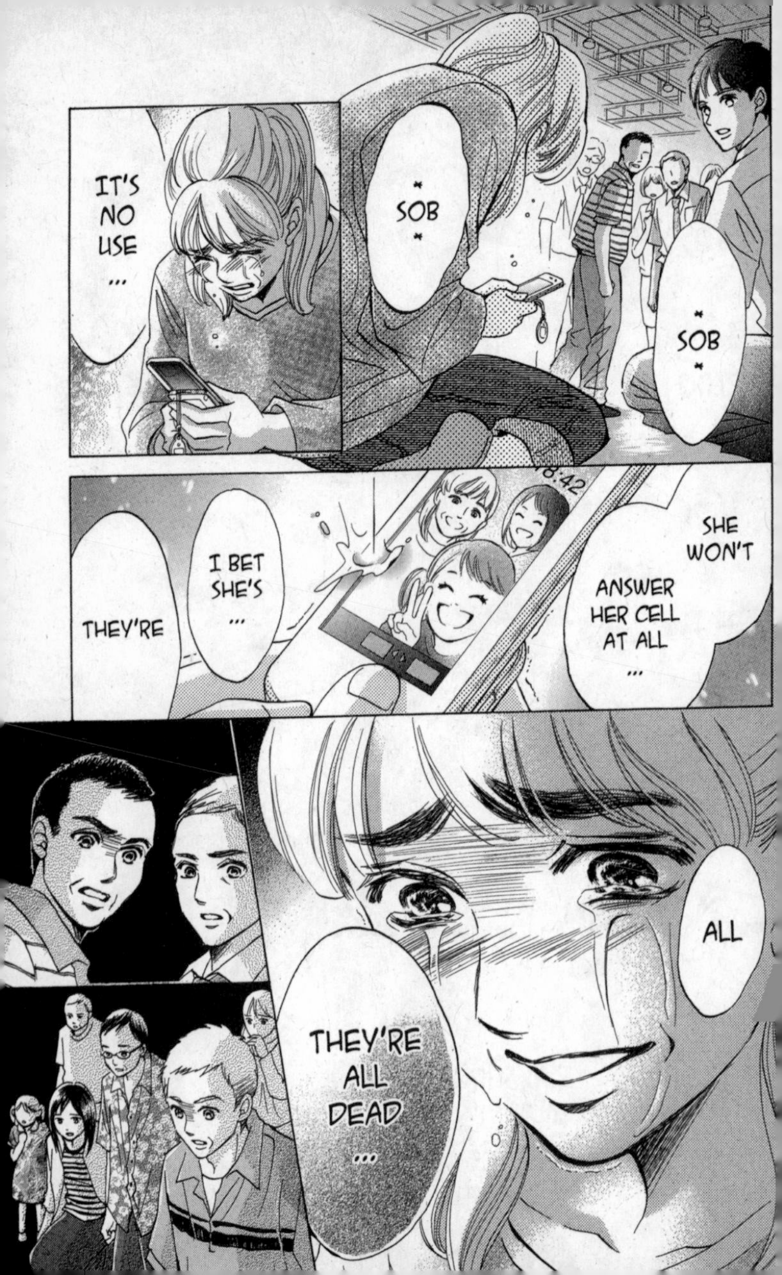
SOB
SOB
IT'S NO USE ...
SHE WON'T ANSWER HER CELL AT ALL ...
8:42
I BET SHE'S ...
THEY'RE
ALL
THEY'RE ALL DEAD ...

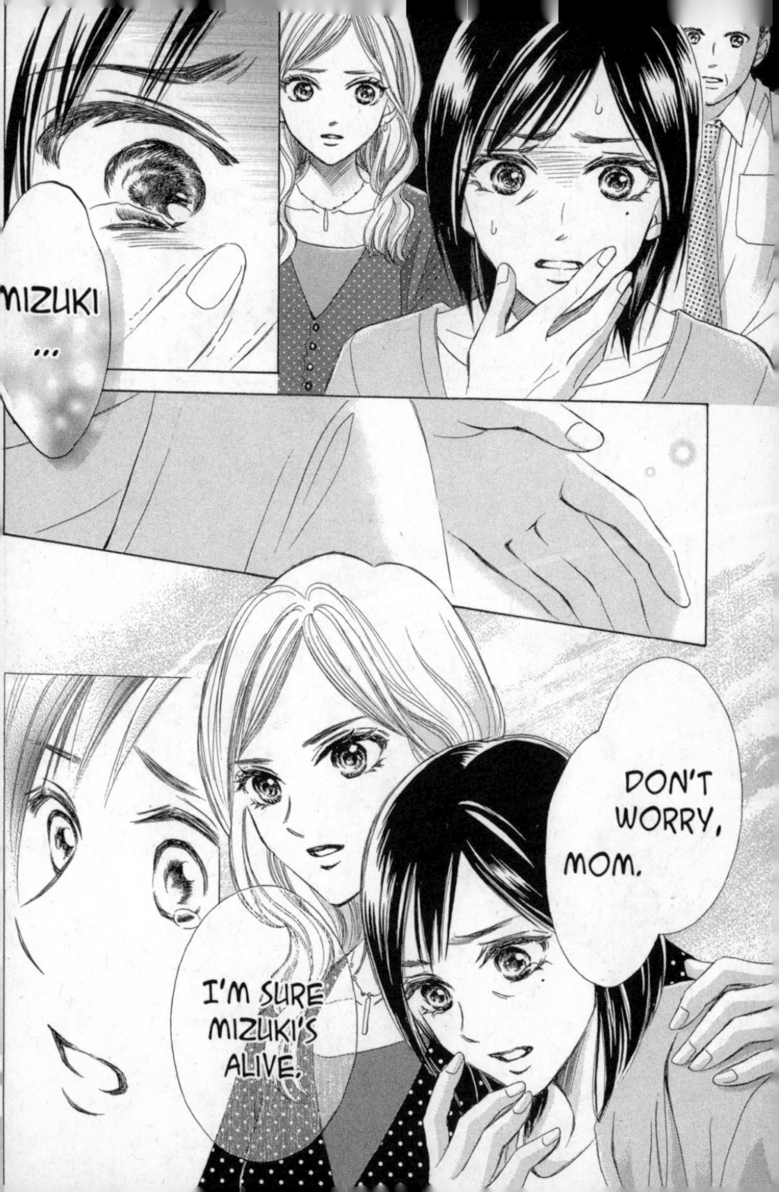
MIZUKI ...
DON'T WORRY, MOM.
I'M SURE MIZUKI'S ALIVE.

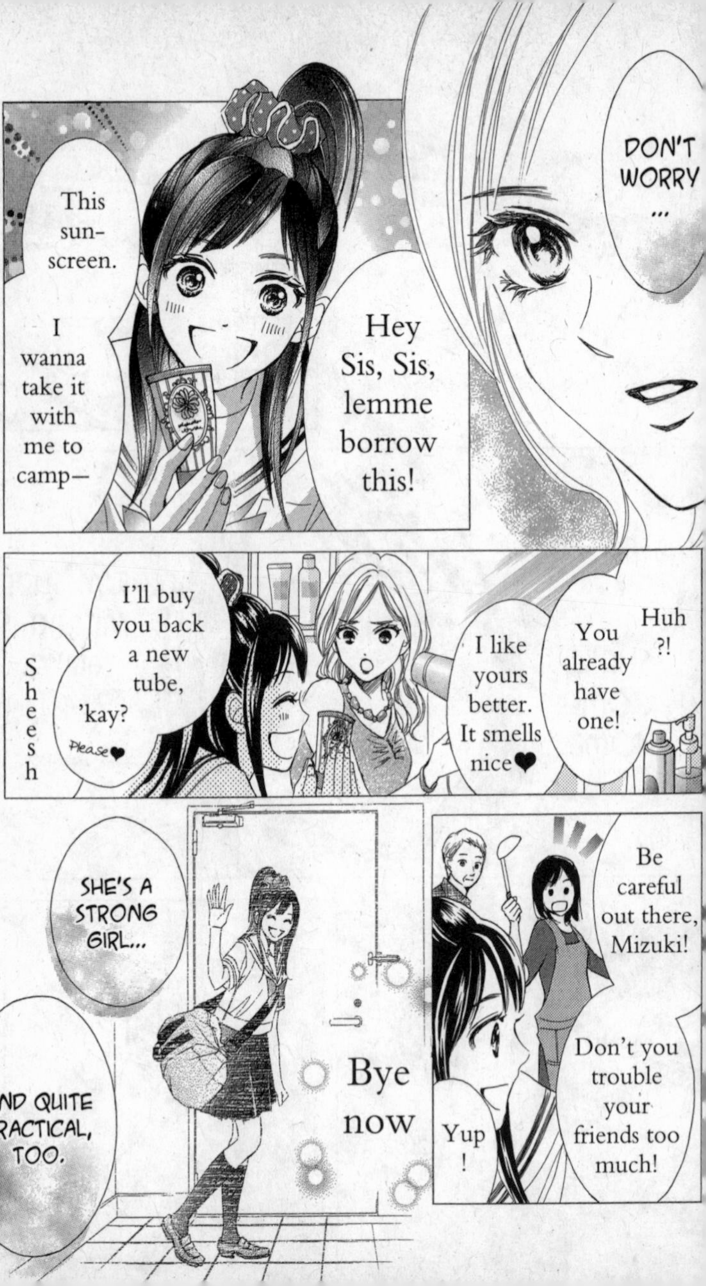
DON'T WORRY ...
Hey Sis, Sis, lemme borrow this!
This sun-screen.
I wanna take it with me to camp—
Huh ?!
You already have one!
I like yours better. It smells nice❤
I'll buy you back a new tube, 'kay?
Please❤
Sheesh
Be careful out there, Mizuki!
Don't you trouble your friends too much!
Yup!
Bye now
SHE'S A STRONG GIRL...
AND QUITE PRACTICAL, TOO.

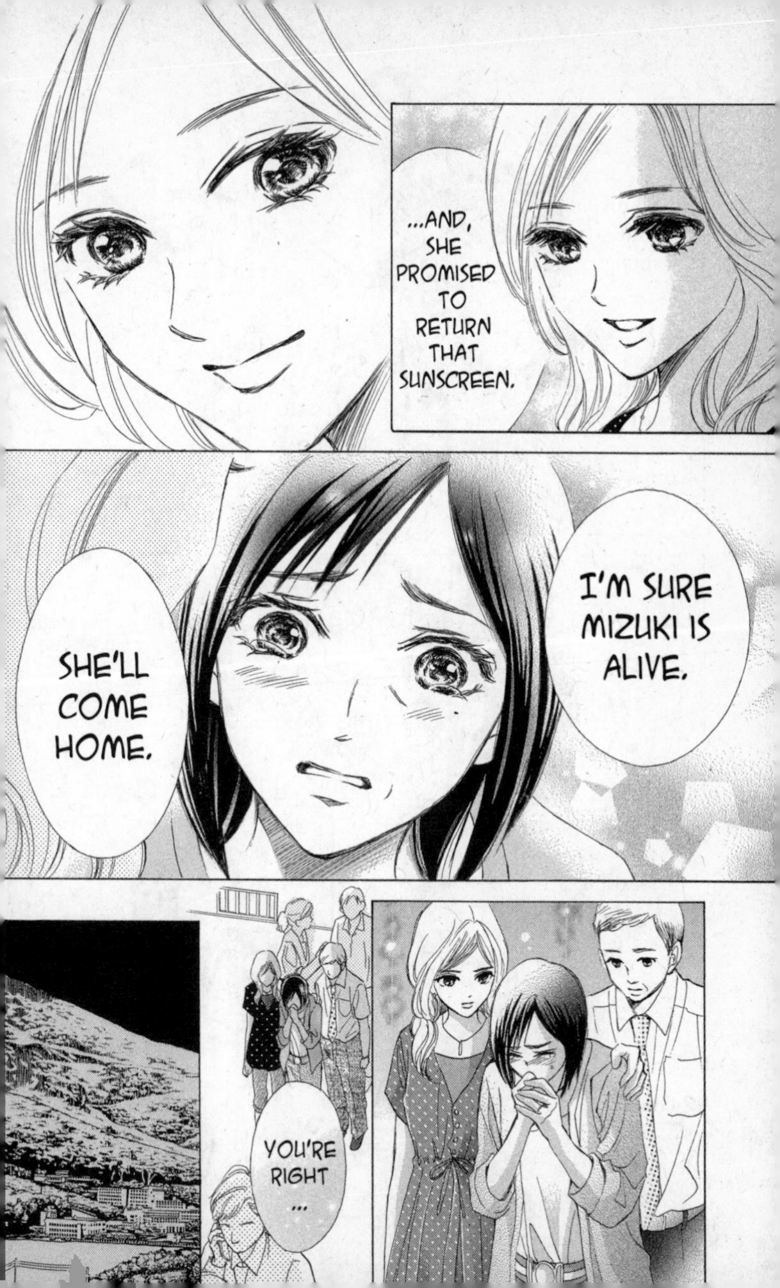
...AND, SHE PROMISED TO RETURN THAT SUNSCREEN.
I'M SURE MIZUKI IS ALIVE.
SHE'LL COME HOME.
YOU'RE RIGHT ...

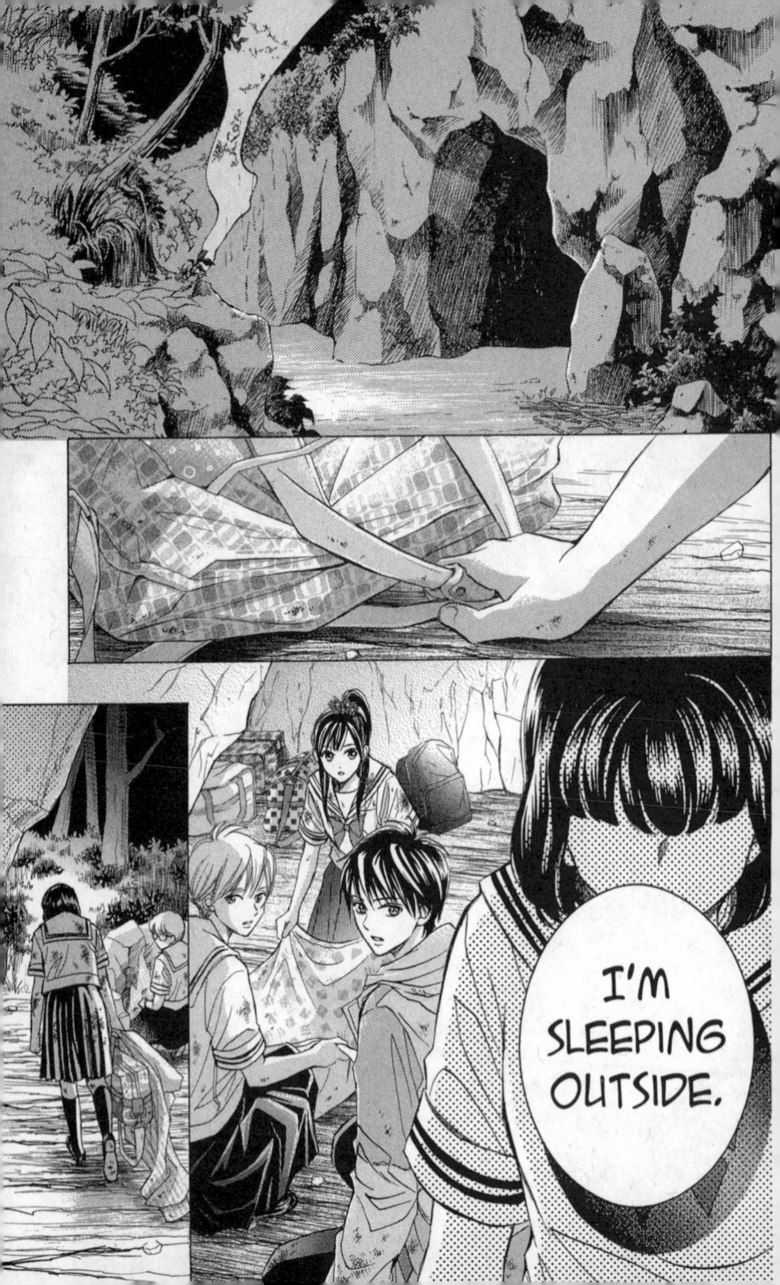
I'M SLEEPING OUTSIDE.

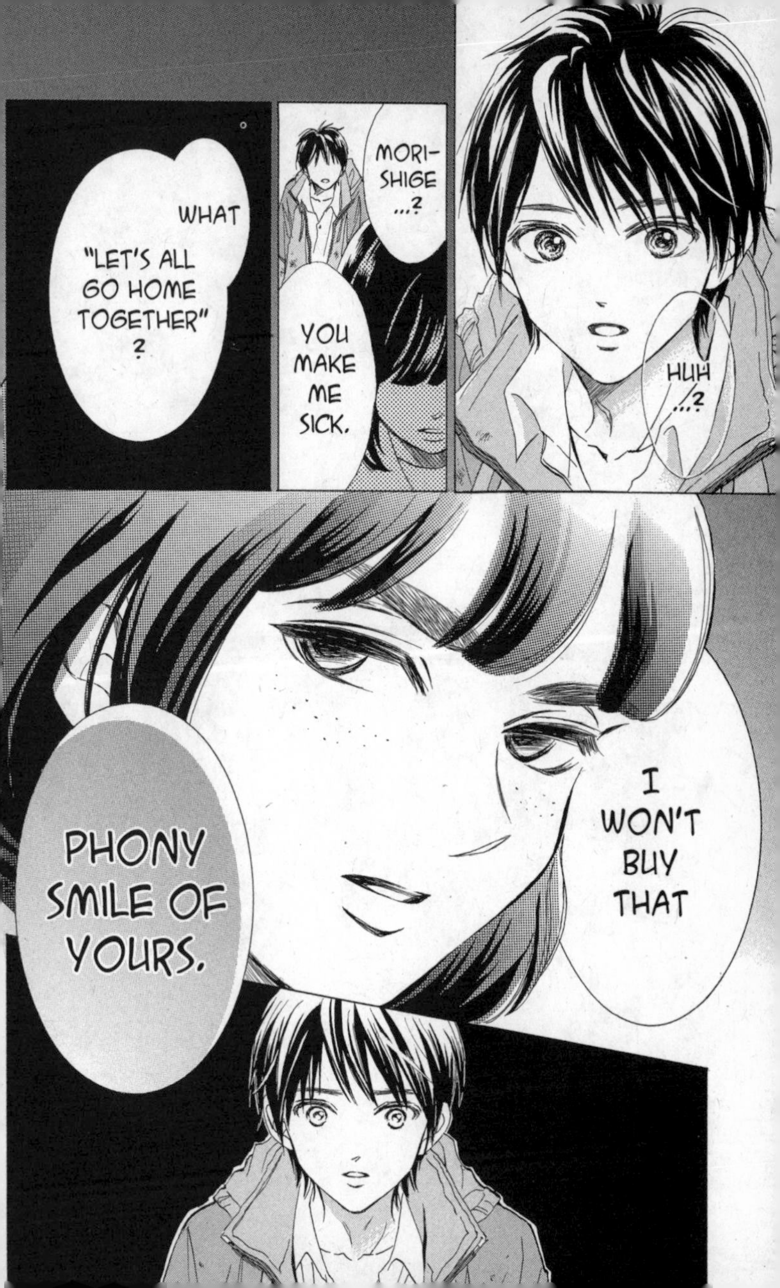
HUH ...?
MORI-SHIGE ...?
YOU MAKE ME SICK.
WHAT "LET'S ALL GO HOME TOGETHER"?
I WON'T BUY THAT
PHONY SMILE OF YOURS.

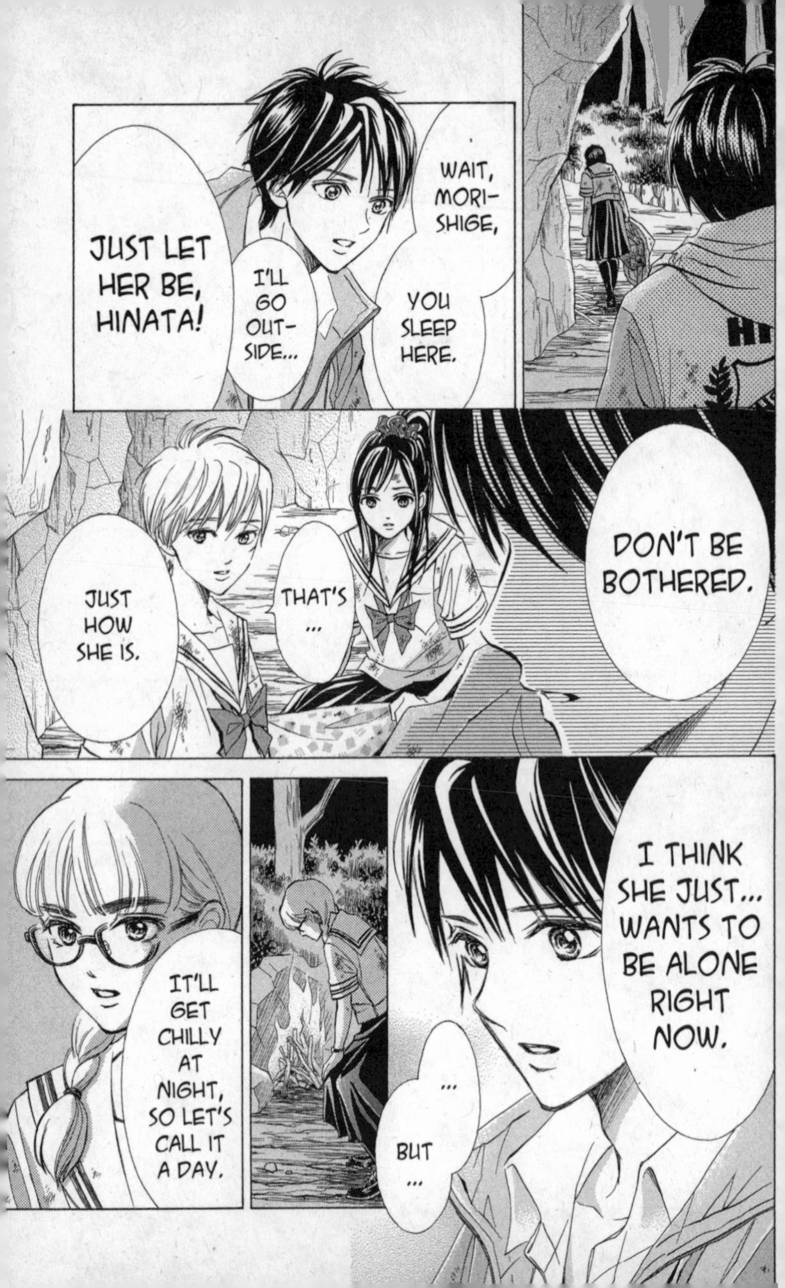
WAIT, MORI-SHIGE, YOU SLEEP HERE.
I'LL GO OUT-SIDE...
JUST LET HER BE, HINATA!
DON'T BE BOTHERED.
THAT'S ...
JUST HOW SHE IS.
I THINK SHE JUST... WANTS TO BE ALONE RIGHT NOW.
... BUT ...
IT'LL GET CHILLY AT NIGHT, SO LET'S CALL IT A DAY.

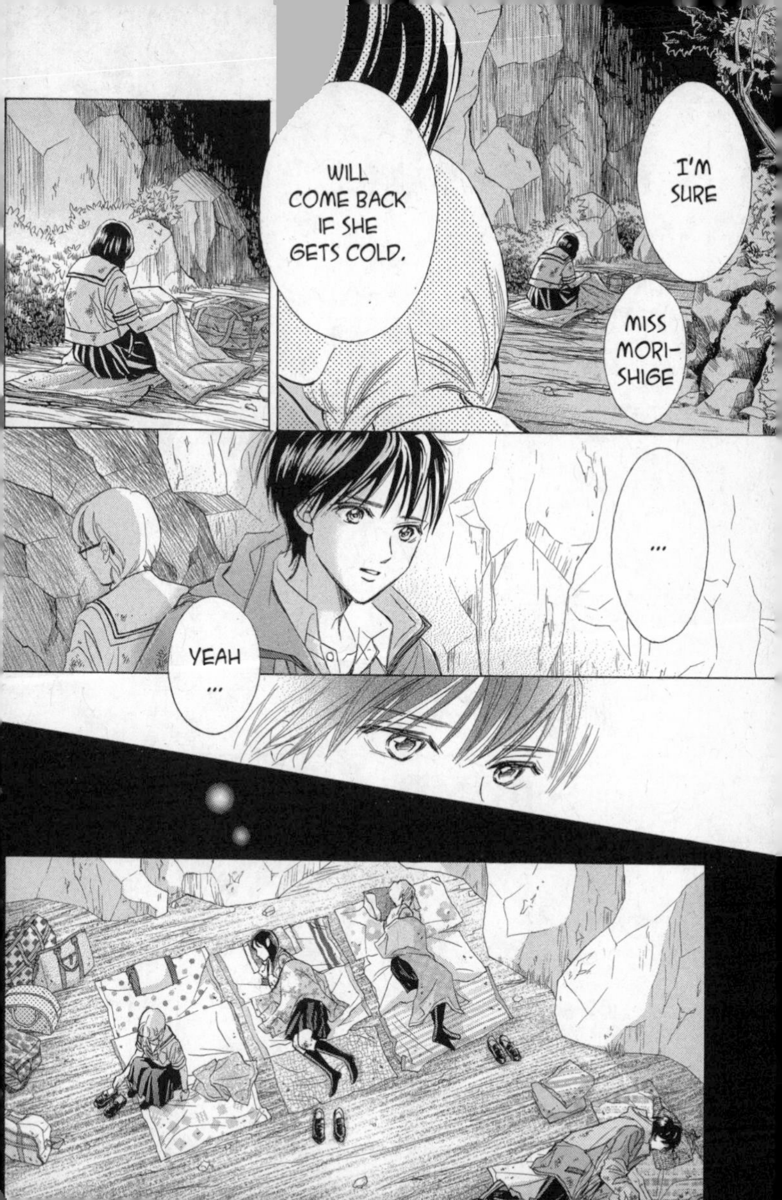
I'M SURE
MISS MORI-SHIGE
WILL COME BACK IF SHE GETS COLD.
...
YEAH ...

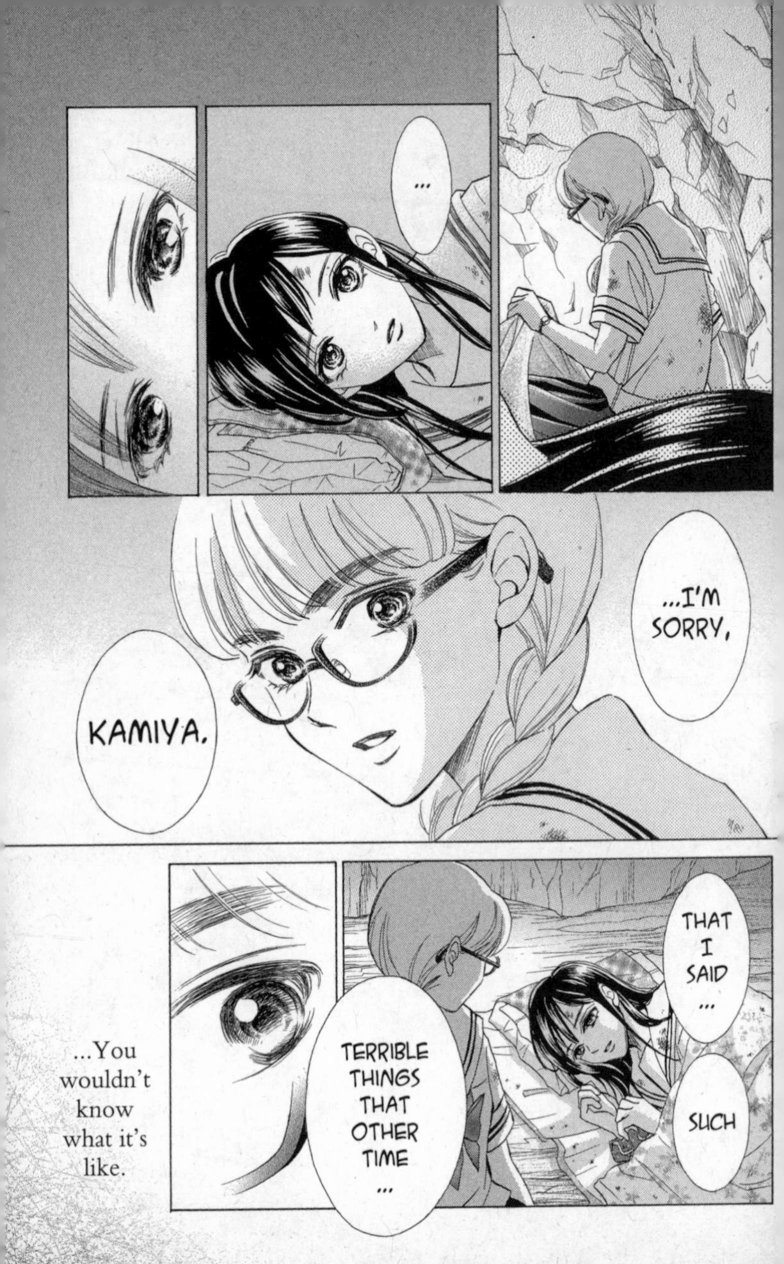
...
...I'M SORRY,
KAMIYA.
THAT I SAID ...
SUCH
TERRIBLE THINGS THAT OTHER TIME ...
...You wouldn't know what it's like.

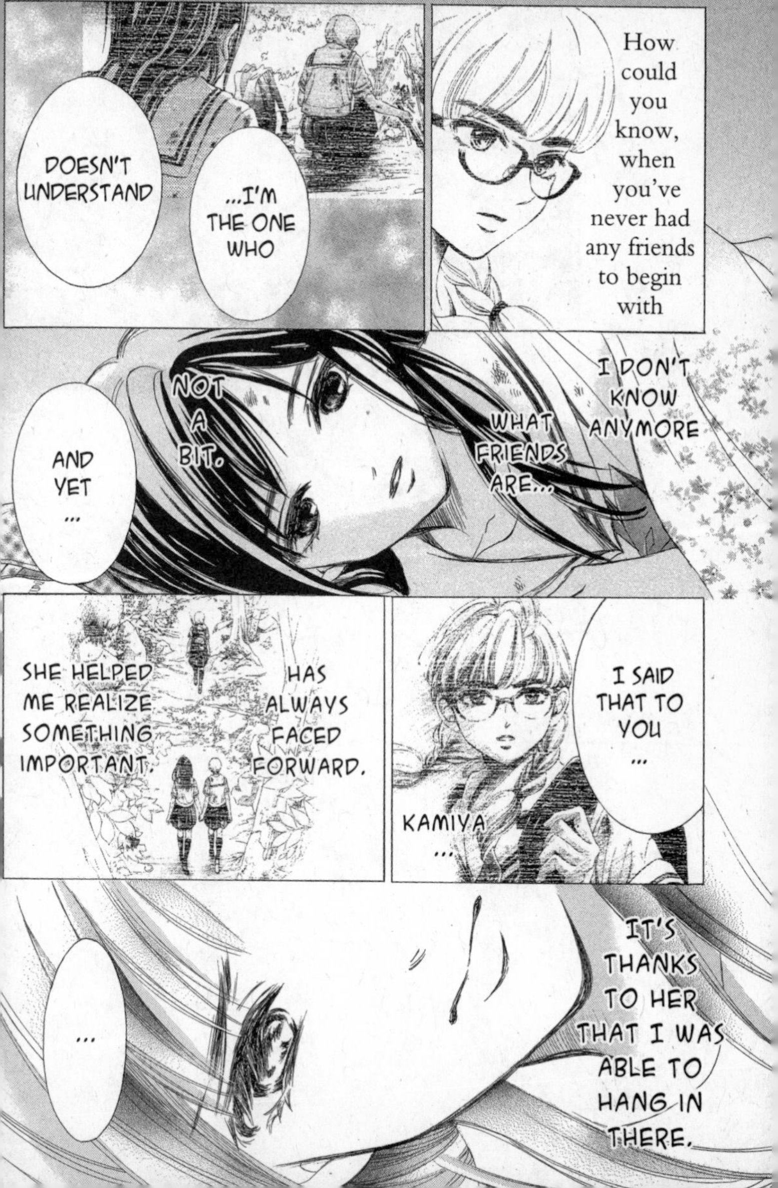
How could you know, when you've never had any friends to begin with
...I'M THE ONE WHO
DOESN'T UNDERSTAND
I DON'T KNOW ANYMORE
WHAT FRIENDS ARE...
NOT A BIT.
AND YET ...
I SAID THAT TO YOU ...
KAMIYA ...
HAS ALWAYS FACED FORWARD.
SHE HELPED ME REALIZE SOMETHING IMPORTANT.
IT'S THANKS TO HER THAT I WAS ABLE TO HANG IN THERE.
...

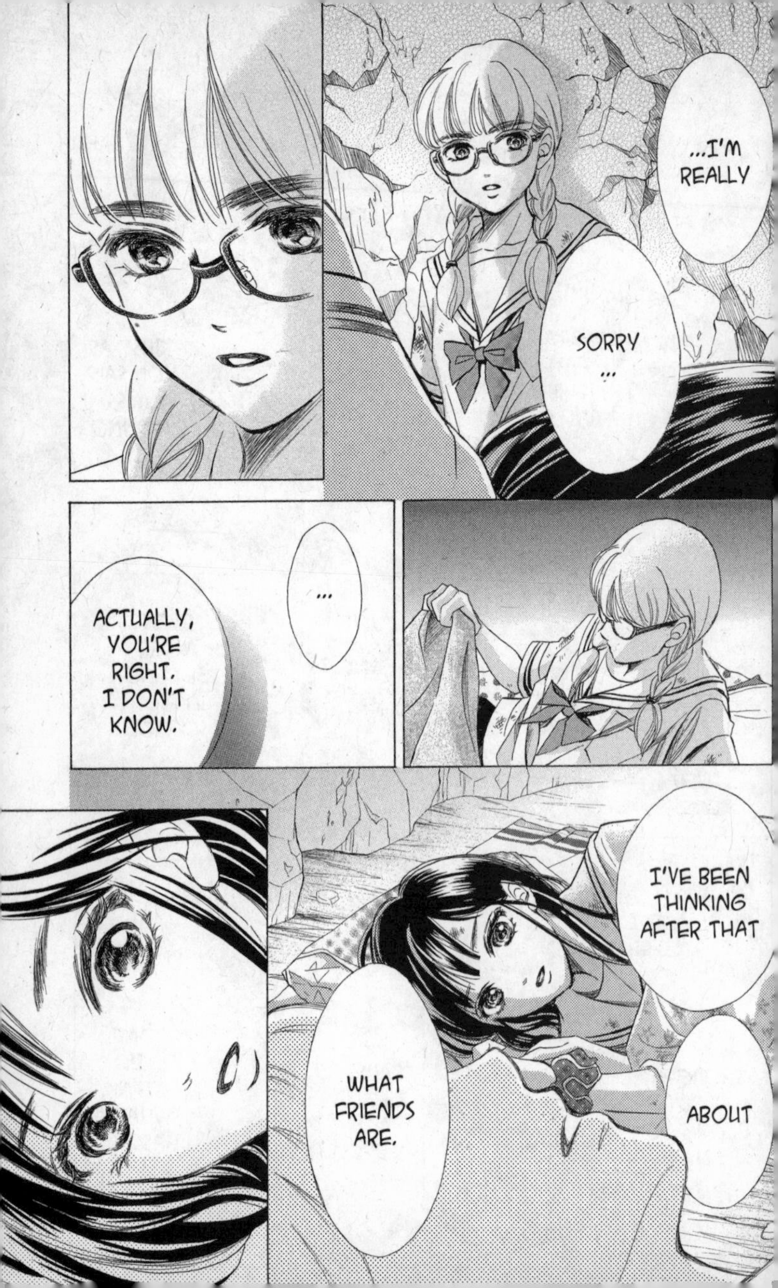
...I'M REALLY
SORRY ...
...
ACTUALLY, YOU'RE RIGHT. I DON'T KNOW.
I'VE BEEN THINKING AFTER THAT
ABOUT
WHAT FRIENDS ARE.

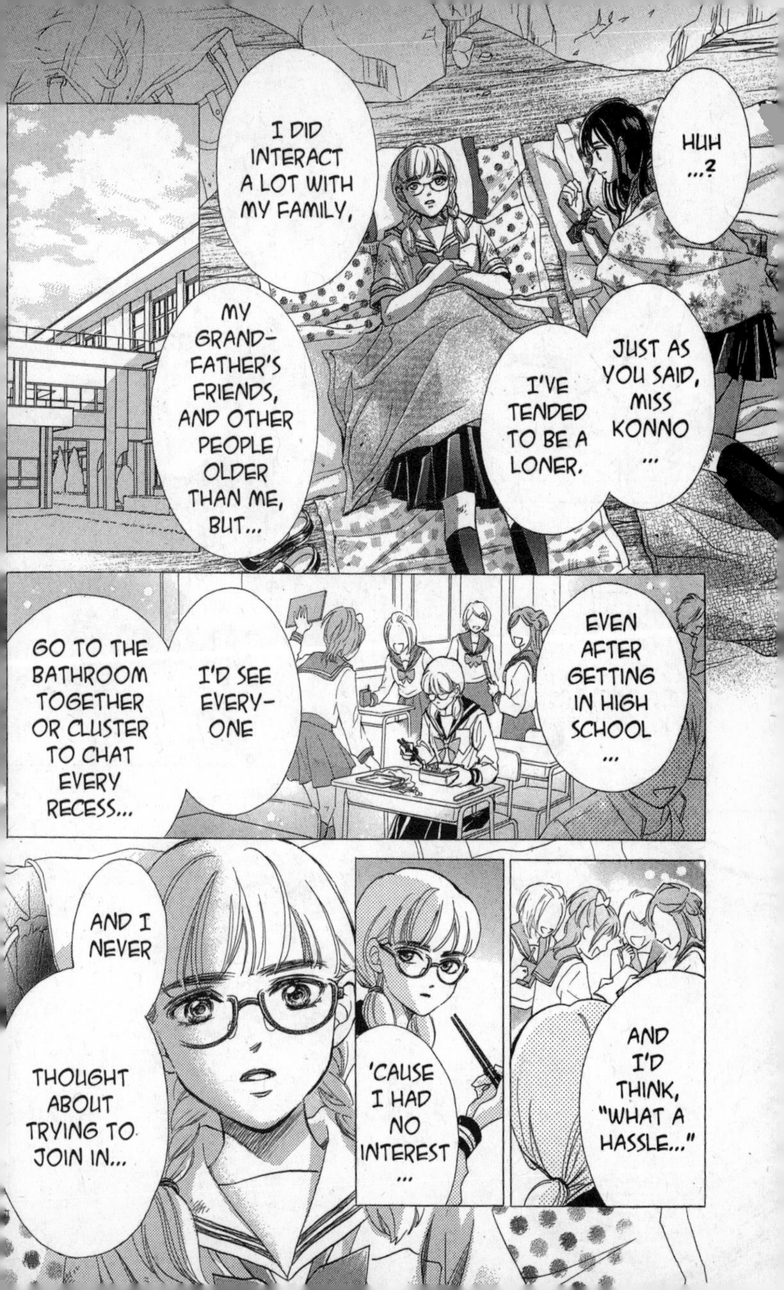

HUH ...?
JUST AS YOU SAID, MISS KONNO ...
I'VE TENDED TO BE A LONER.
I DID INTERACT A LOT WITH MY FAMILY,
MY GRAND-FATHER'S FRIENDS, AND OTHER PEOPLE OLDER THAN ME, BUT...
EVEN AFTER GETTING IN HIGH SCHOOL ...
I'D SEE EVERY-ONE
GO TO THE BATHROOM TOGETHER OR CLUSTER TO CHAT EVERY RECESS...
AND I'D THINK, "WHAT A HASSLE..."
'CAUSE I HAD NO INTEREST ...
AND I NEVER
THOUGHT ABOUT TRYING TO JOIN IN...

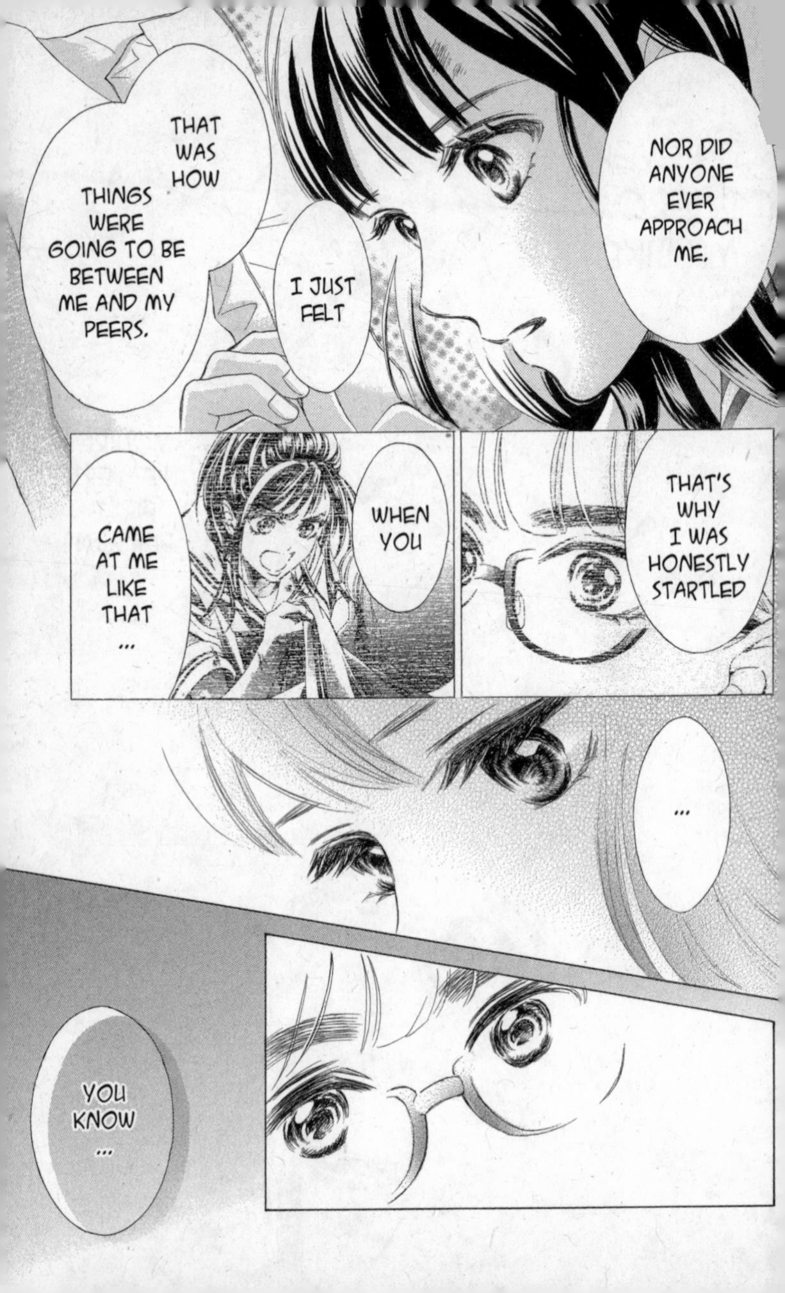
NOR DID ANYONE EVER APPROACH ME.
I JUST FELT
THAT WAS HOW THINGS WERE GOING TO BE BETWEEN ME AND MY PEERS.
THAT'S WHY I WAS HONESTLY STARTLED
WHEN YOU
CAME AT ME LIKE THAT ...
...
YOU KNOW ...

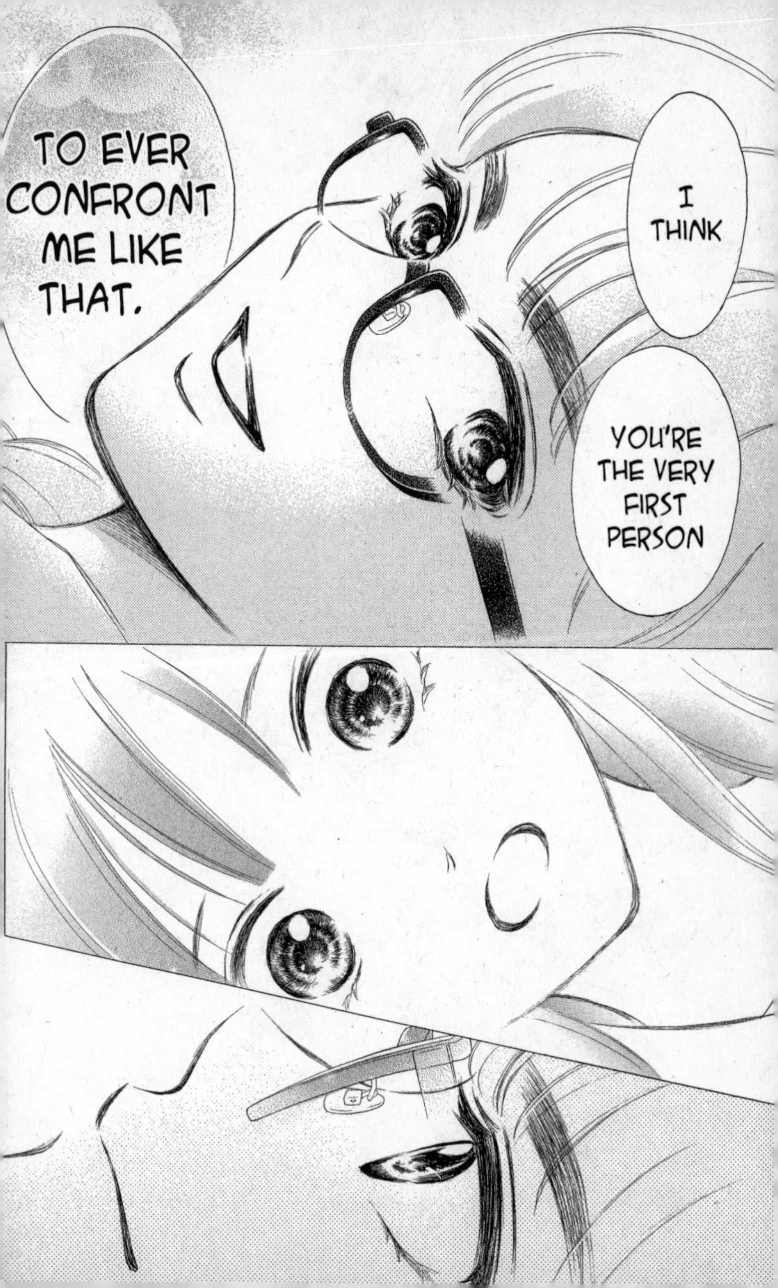
I THINK
YOU'RE THE VERY FIRST PERSON
TO EVER CONFRONT ME LIKE THAT.

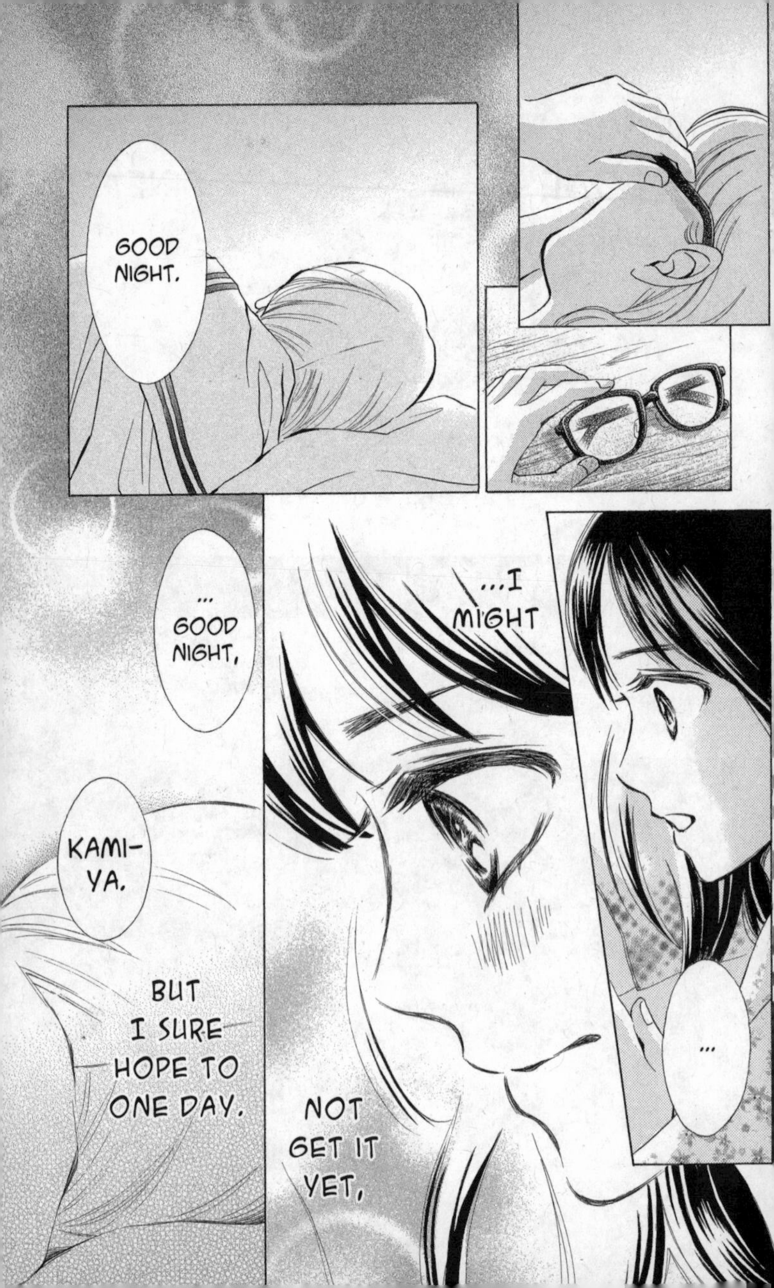
GOOD NIGHT.
...
...I MIGHT
NOT GET IT YET,
... GOOD NIGHT,
KAMI-YA.
BUT I SURE HOPE TO ONE DAY.

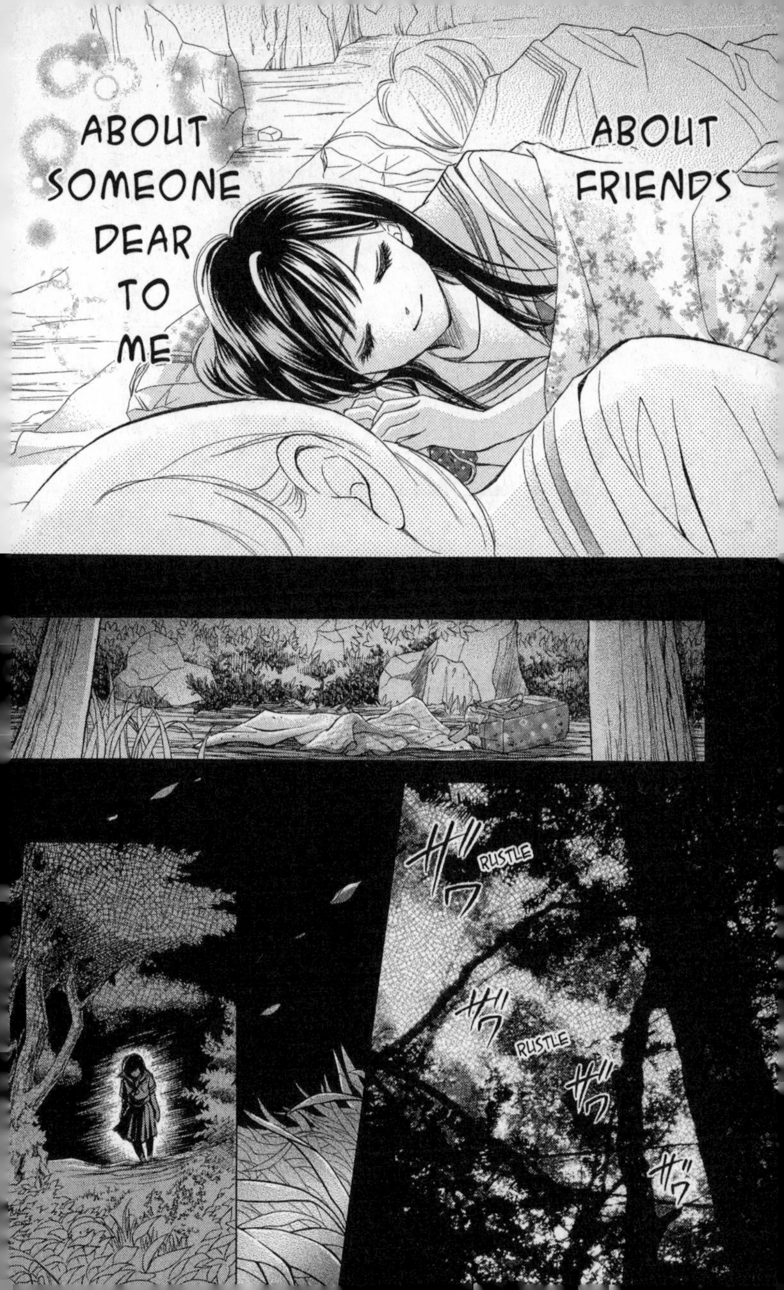
ABOUT FRIENDS
ABOUT SOMEONE DEAR TO ME
ザワ
RUSTLE
ザワ
RUSTLE
ザワ
ザワ

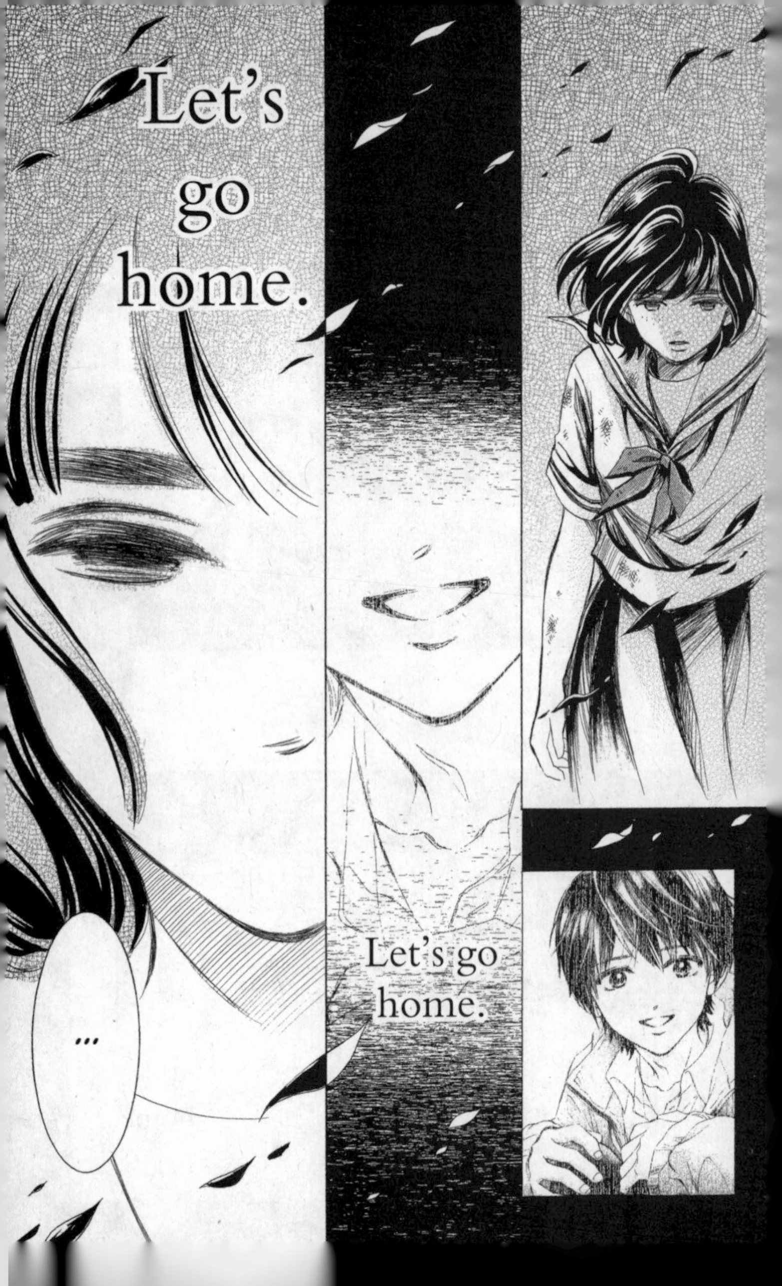
Let's go home.
Let's go home.
...

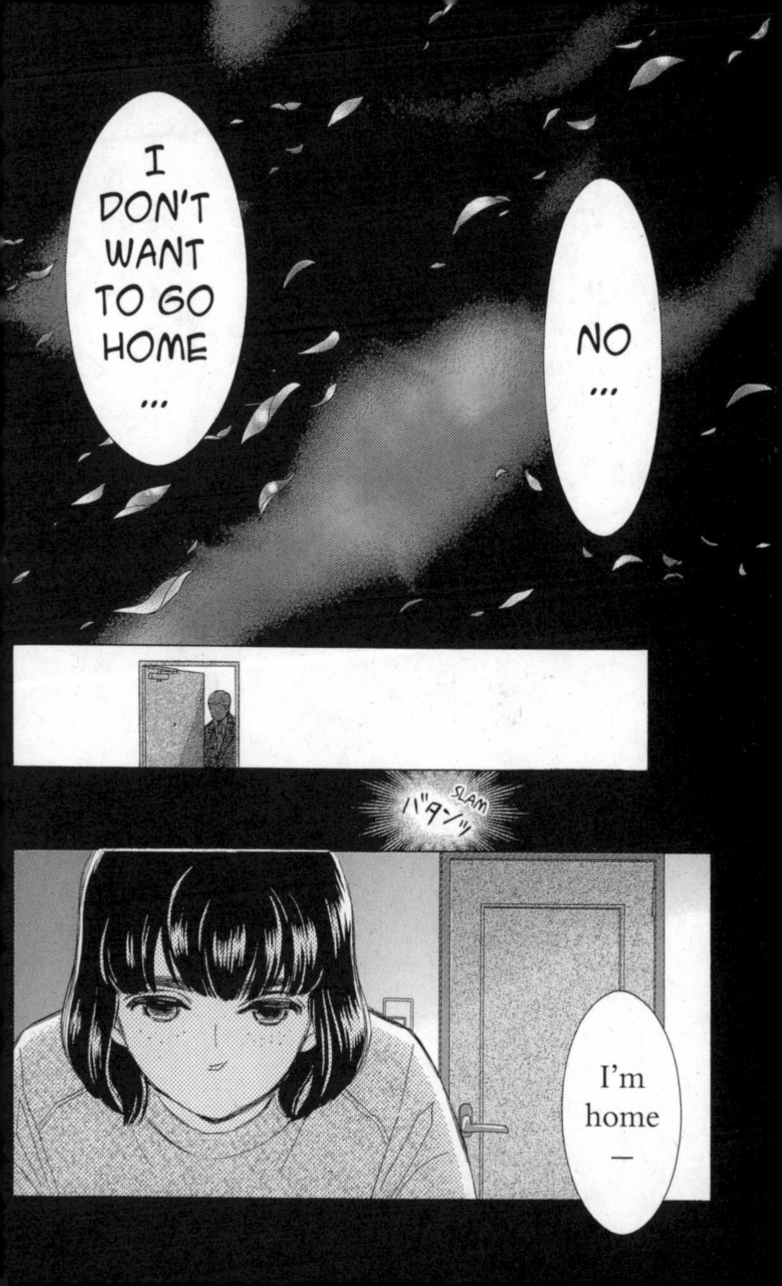
I DON'T WANT TO GO HOME ...
NO ...
SLAM
バタンッ
I'm home —

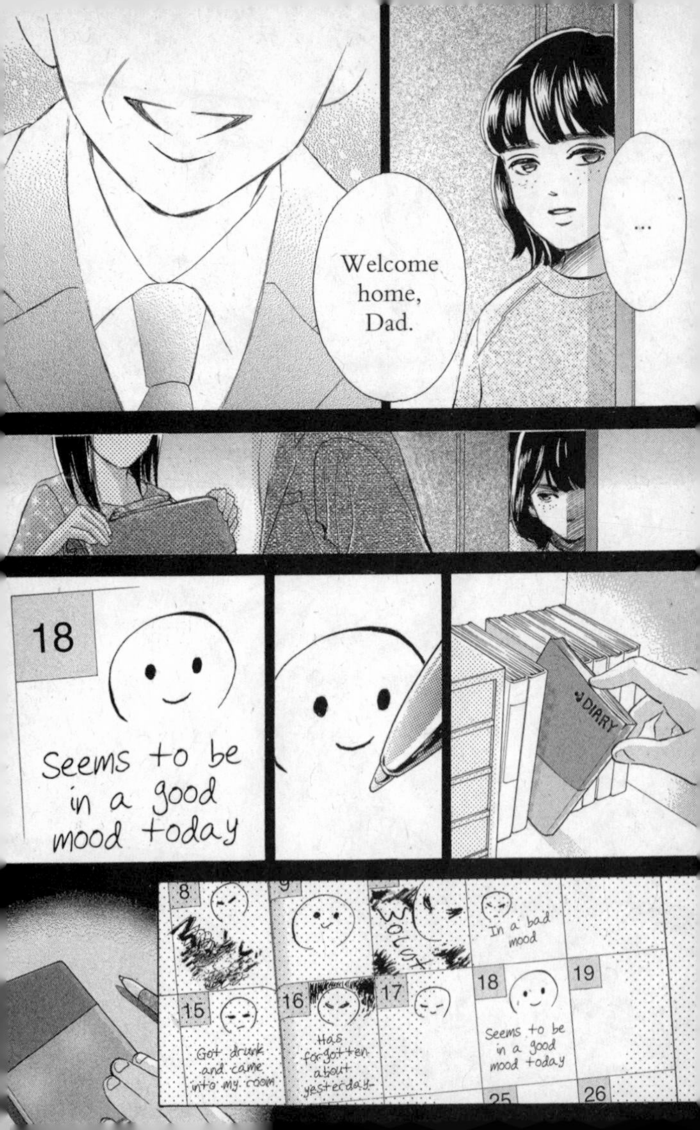
...
Welcome home, Dad.
DIARY
18
Seems to be in a good mood today
In a bad mood
15
Got drunk and came into my room
16
Has forgotten about yesterday
17
18
Seems to be in a good mood today
19
26

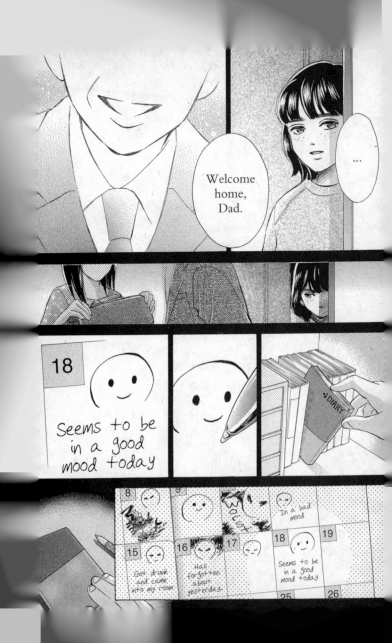

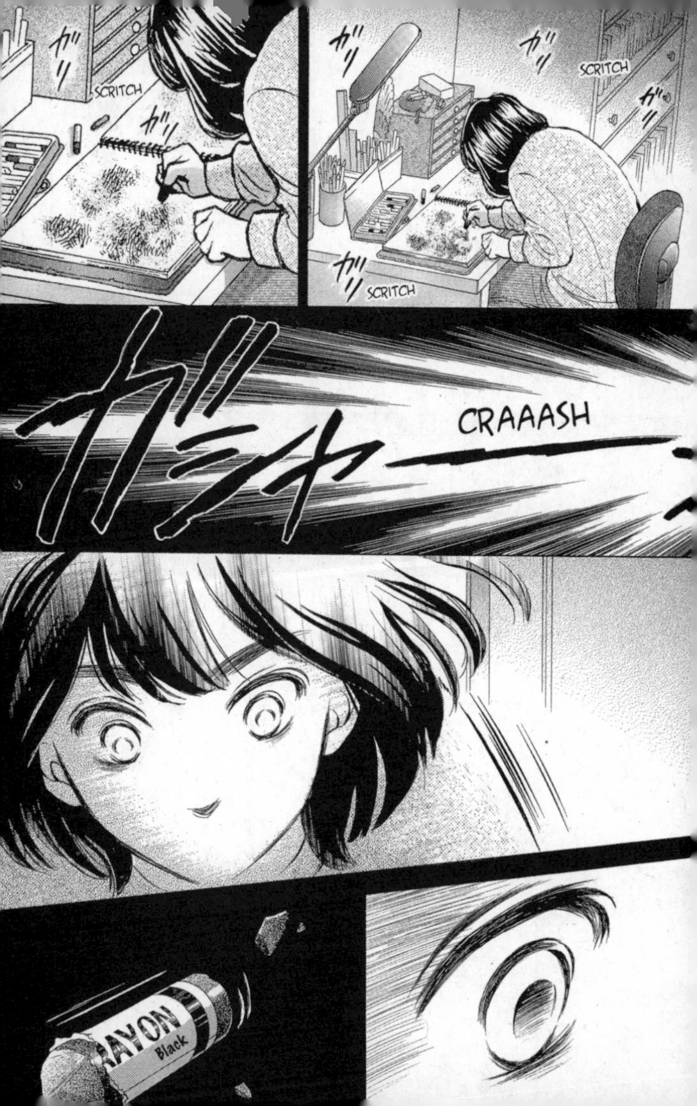
ガリ
ガリ
SCRITCH
ガリ
ガリ
SCRITCH
ガリ
SCRITCH
ガリ
ガシャー
CRAAASH
RAYON
Black

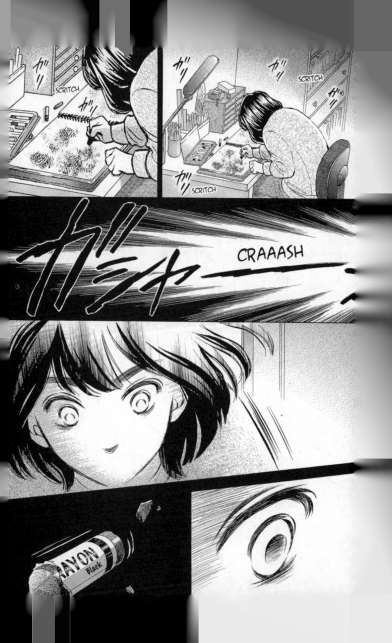

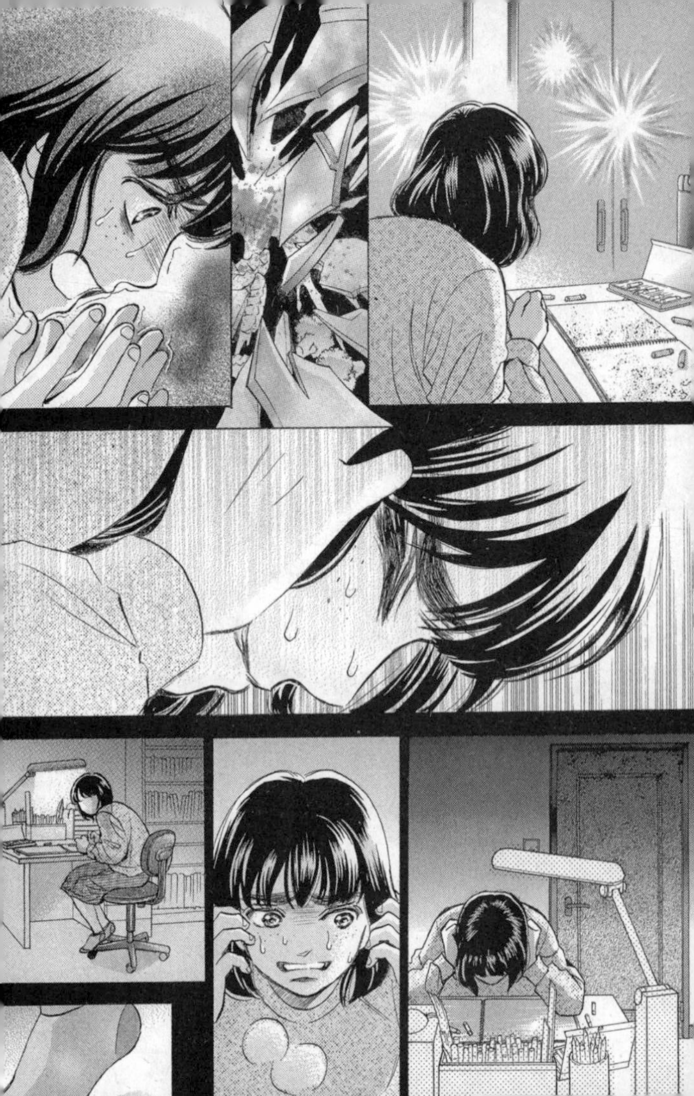

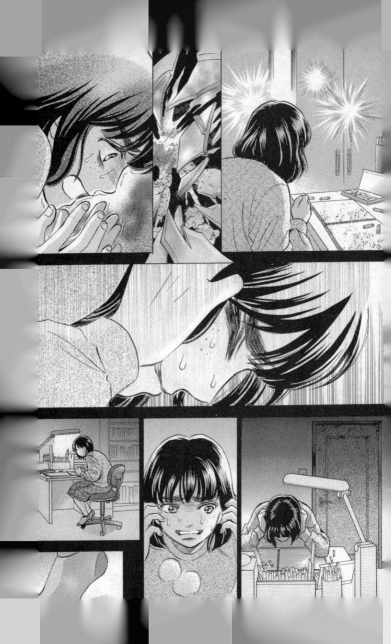

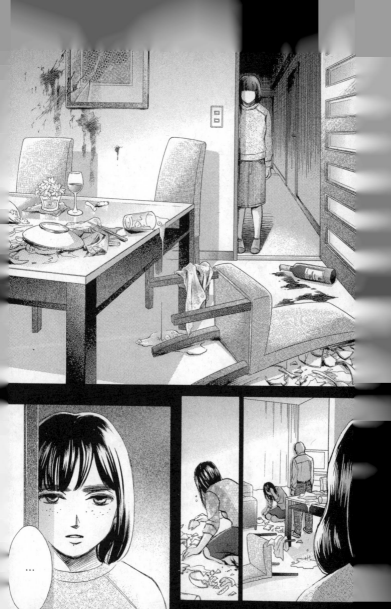

...

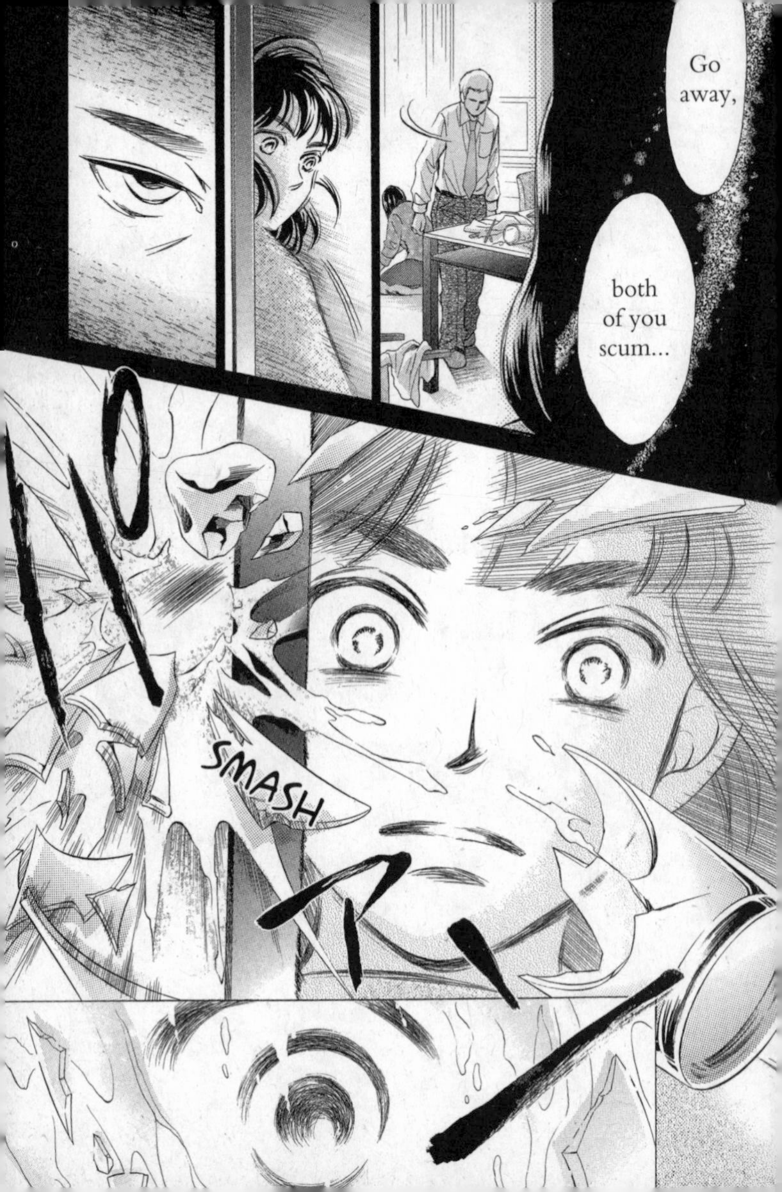
Go away,
both of you scum...
SMASH

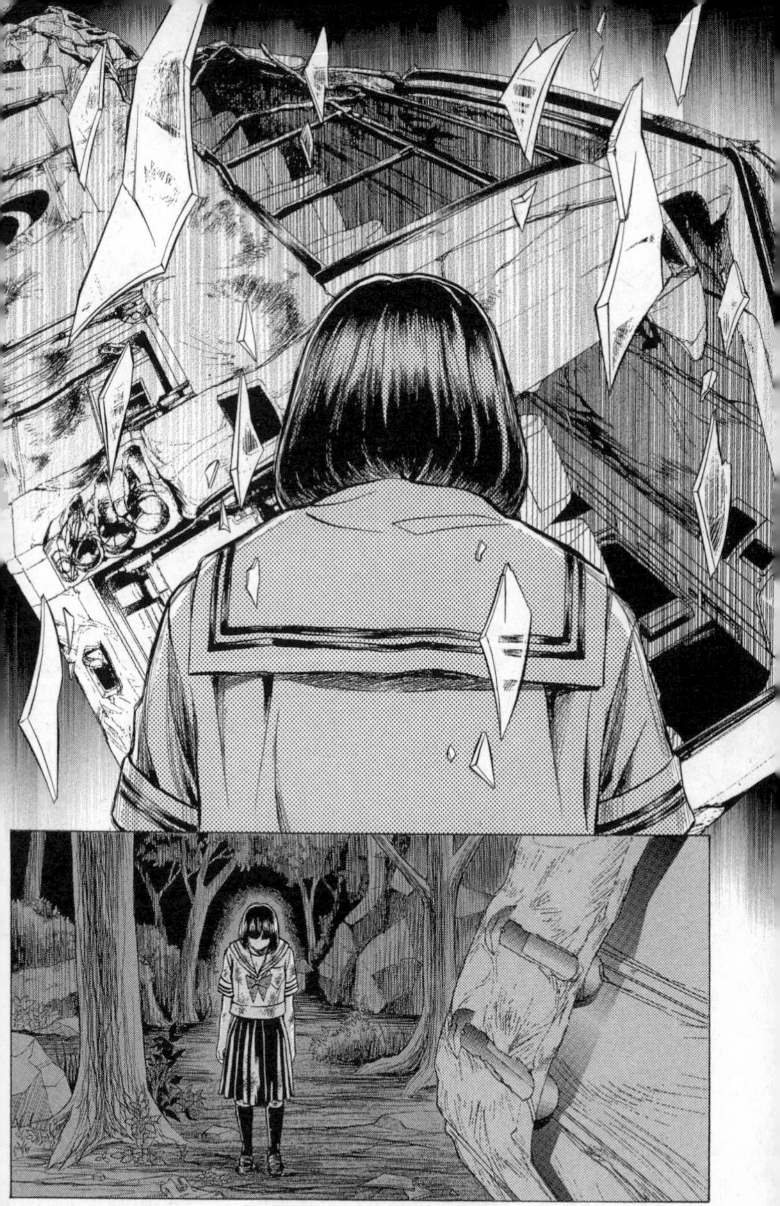

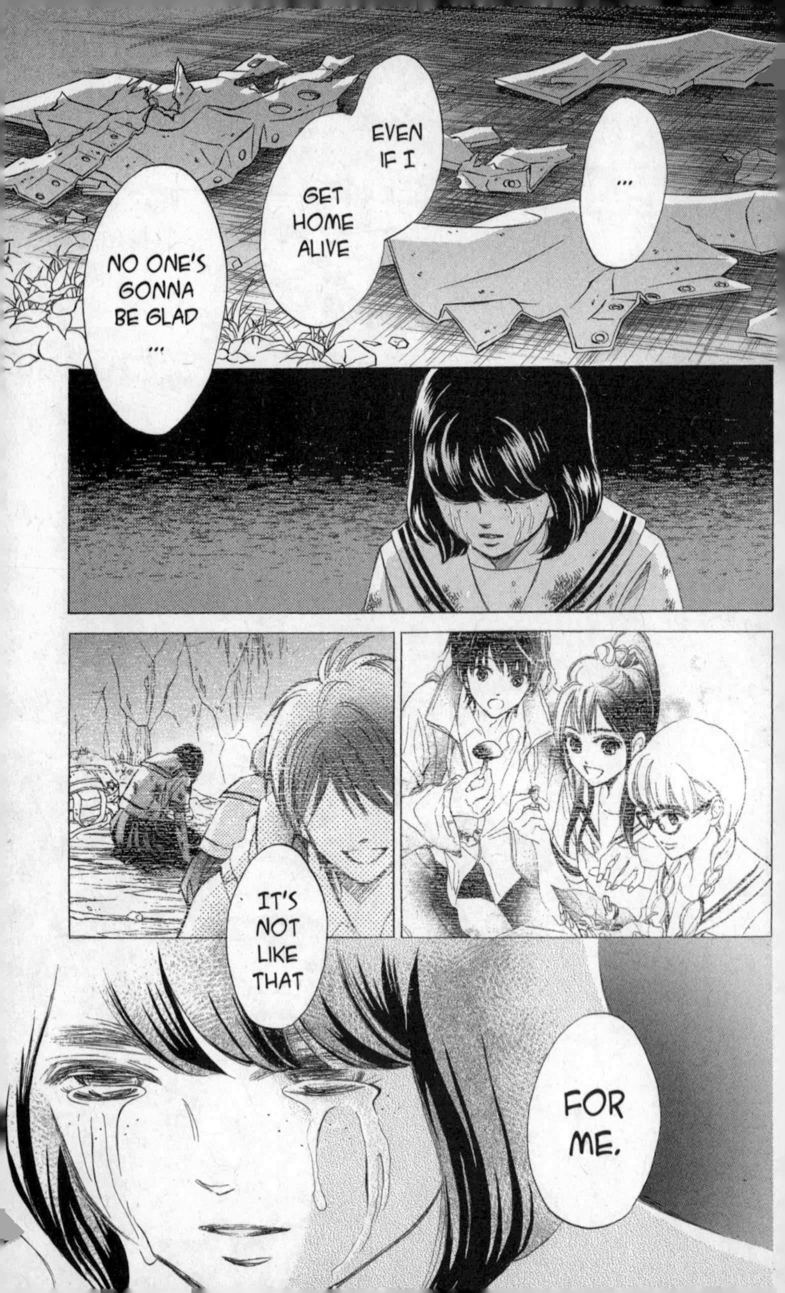
...
EVEN IF I GET HOME ALIVE
NO ONE'S GONNA BE GLAD ...
IT'S NOT LIKE THAT
FOR ME.

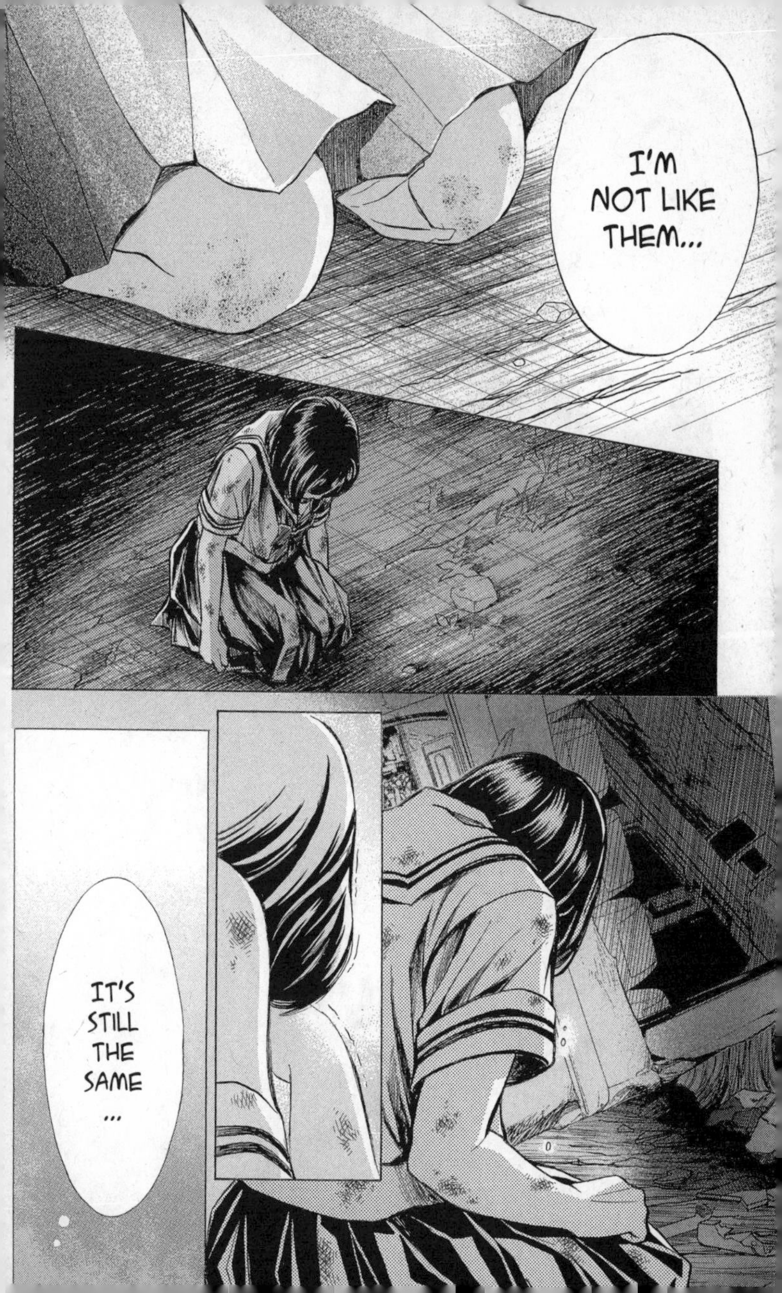
I'M NOT LIKE THEM...
IT'S STILL THE SAME ...

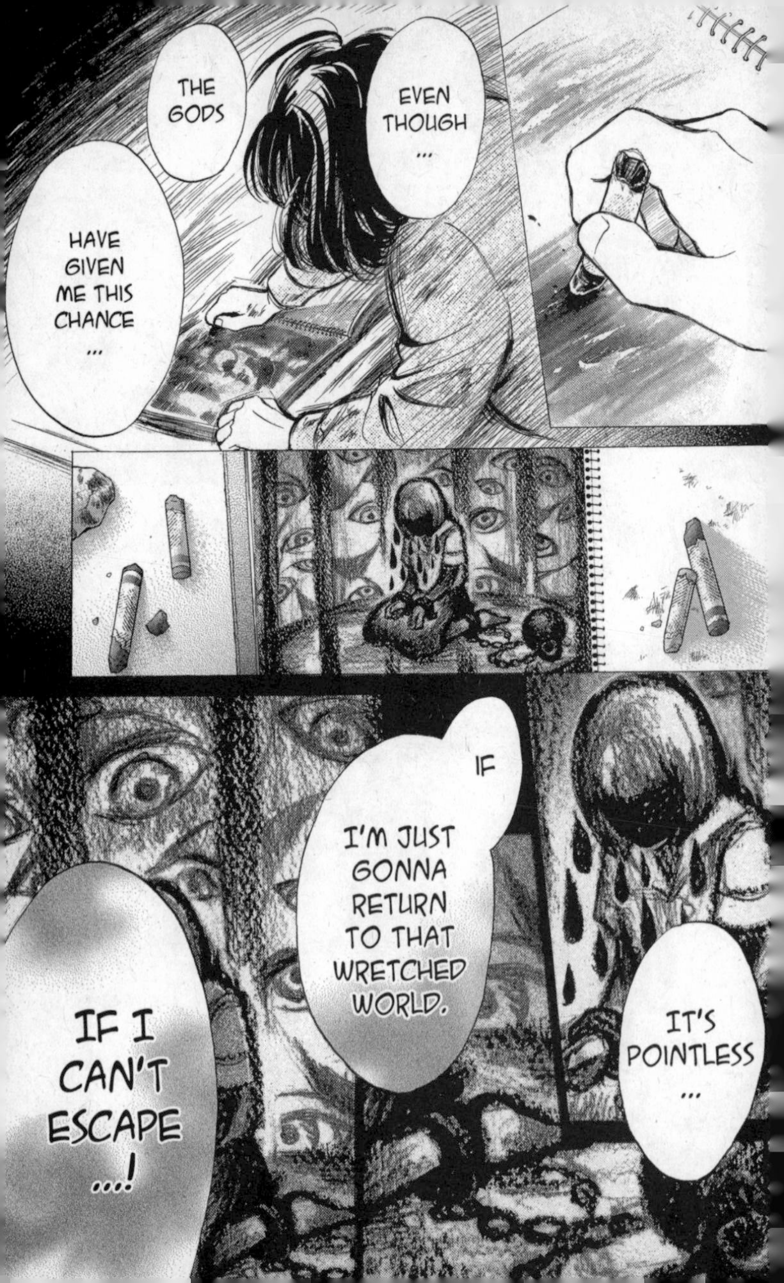
EVEN THOUGH ...
THE GODS
HAVE GIVEN ME THIS CHANCE ...
IT'S POINTLESS ...
IF I'M JUST GONNA RETURN TO THAT WRETCHED WORLD.
IF I CAN'T ESCAPE ...!

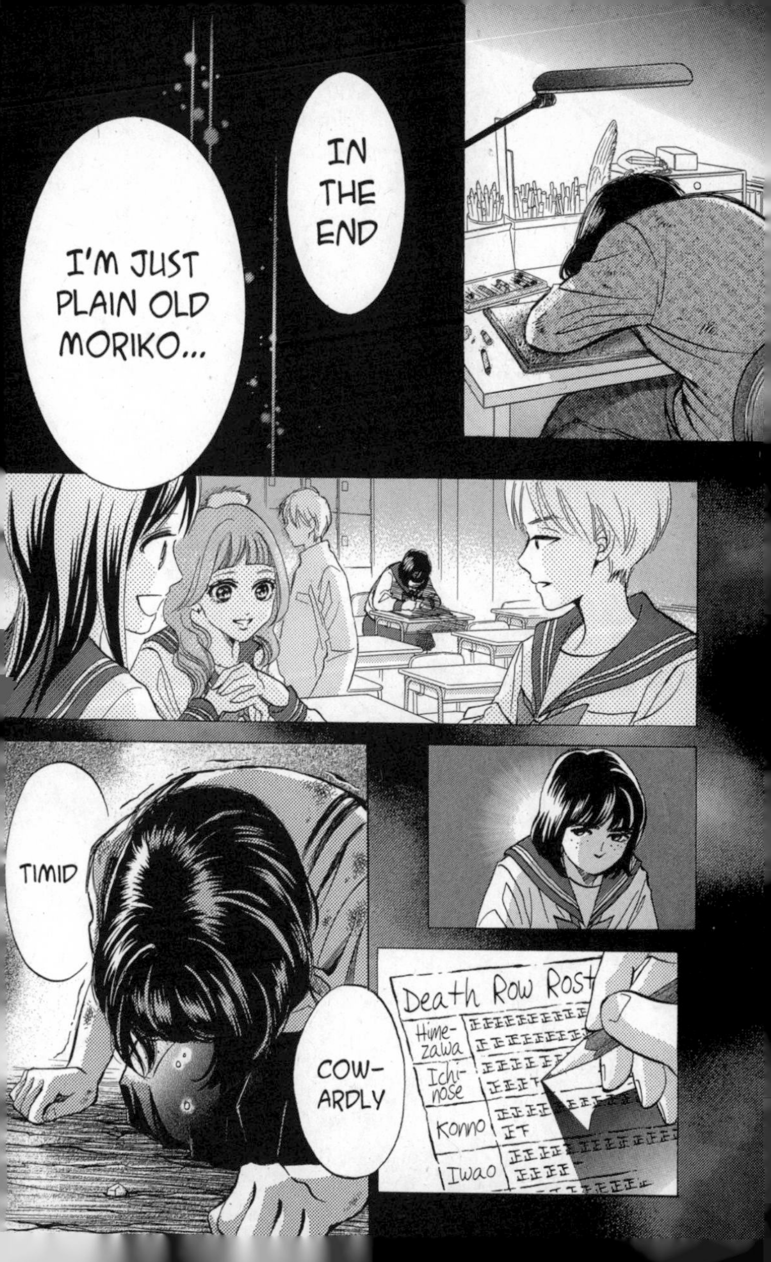
IN THE END
I'M JUST PLAIN OLD MORIKO...
Death Row Rost
Hime-zawa
Ichi-nose
Konno
Iwao
COW-ARDLY
TIMID

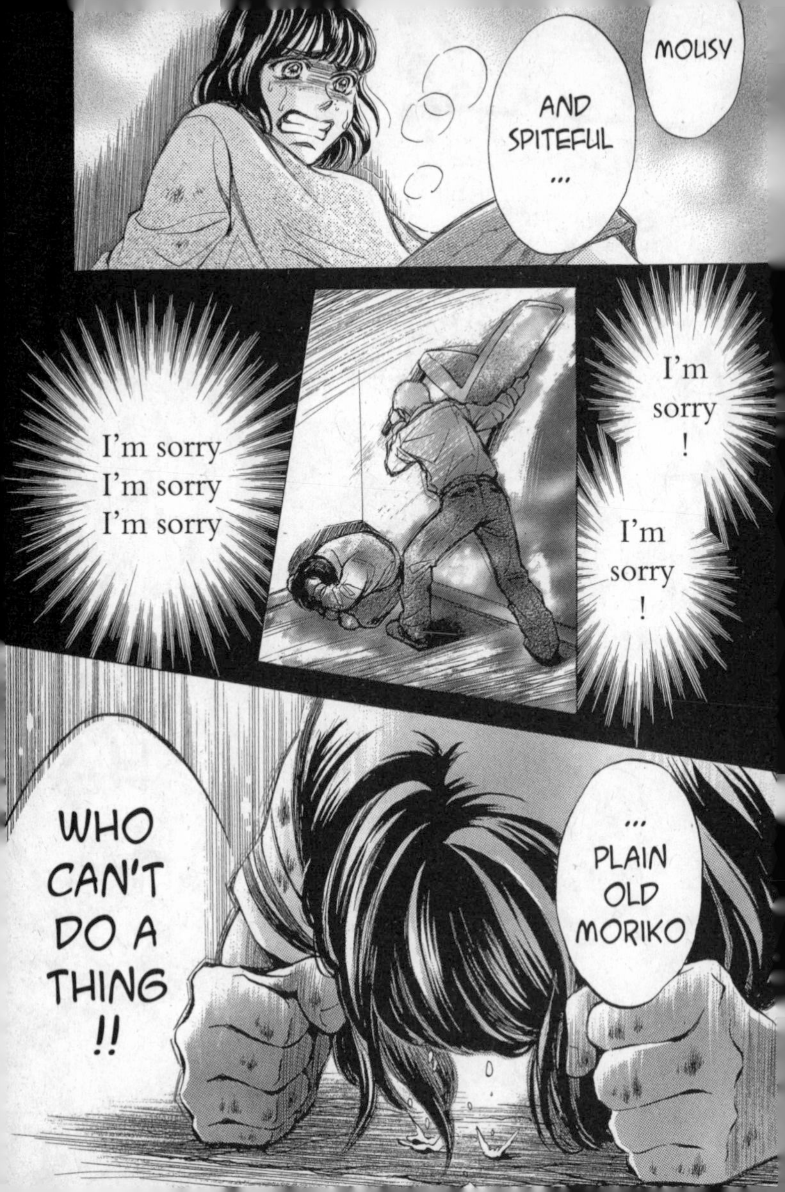
MOUSY
AND SPITEFUL ...
I'm sorry!
I'm sorry!
I'm sorry I'm sorry I'm sorry
... PLAIN OLD MORIKO
WHO CAN'T DO A THING !!

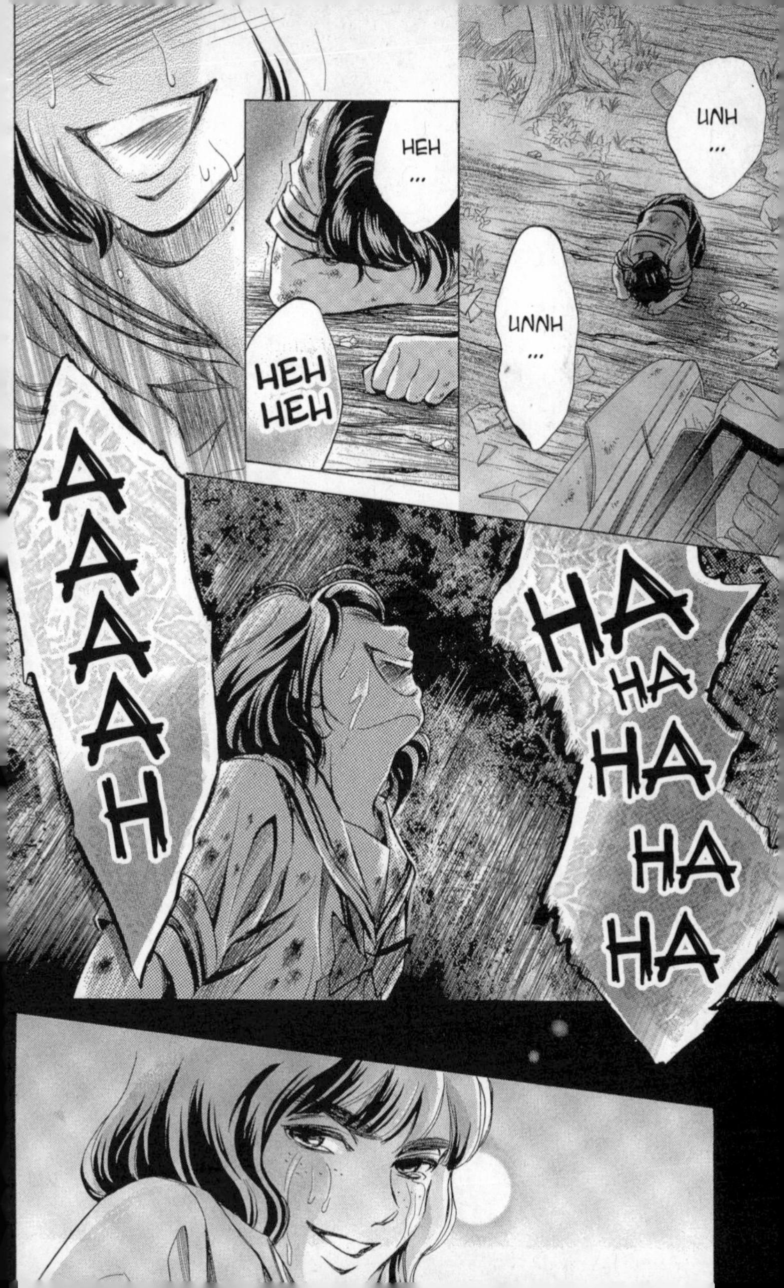
UNH ...
UNNH ...
HEH ...
HEH HEH
AAAAH
HA HA HA HA HA

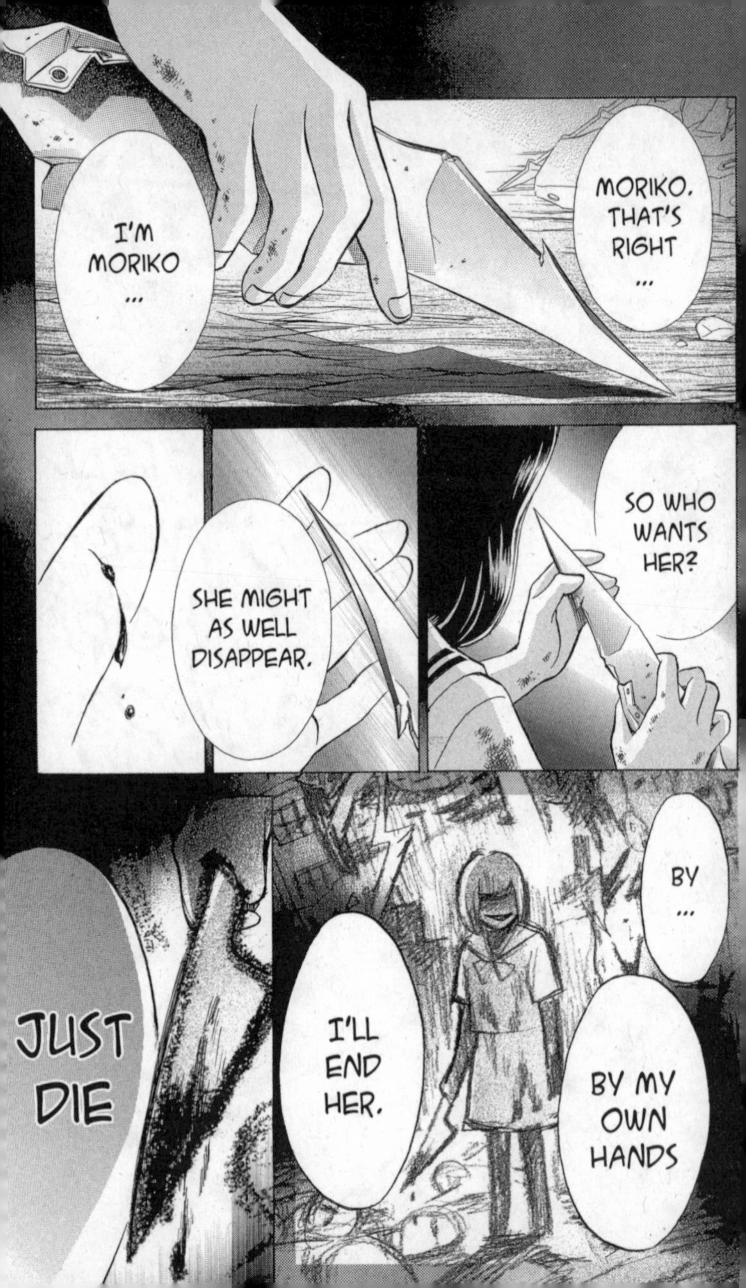
MORIKO. THAT'S RIGHT ...
I'M MORIKO ...
SO WHO WANTS HER?
SHE MIGHT AS WELL DISAPPEAR.
BY ...
BY MY OWN HANDS
I'LL END HER.
JUST DIE

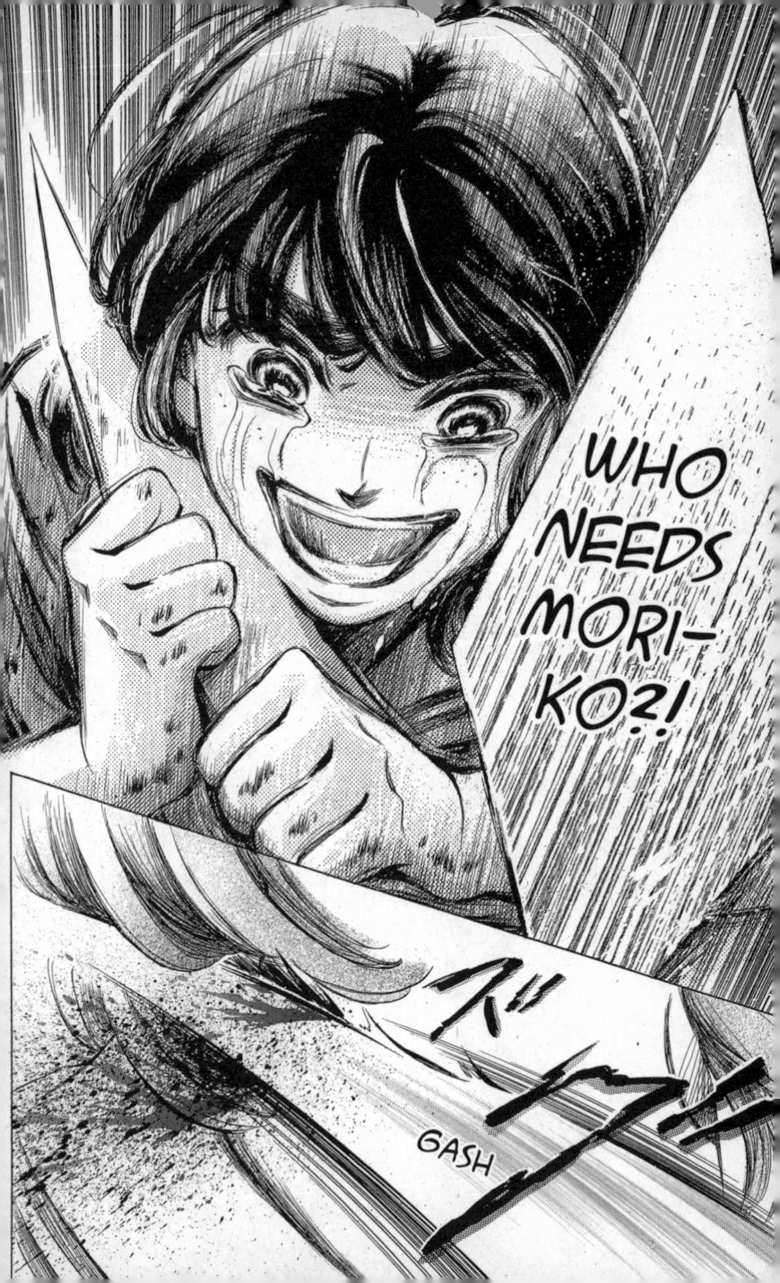
WHO NEEDS MORI-KO?!
GASH

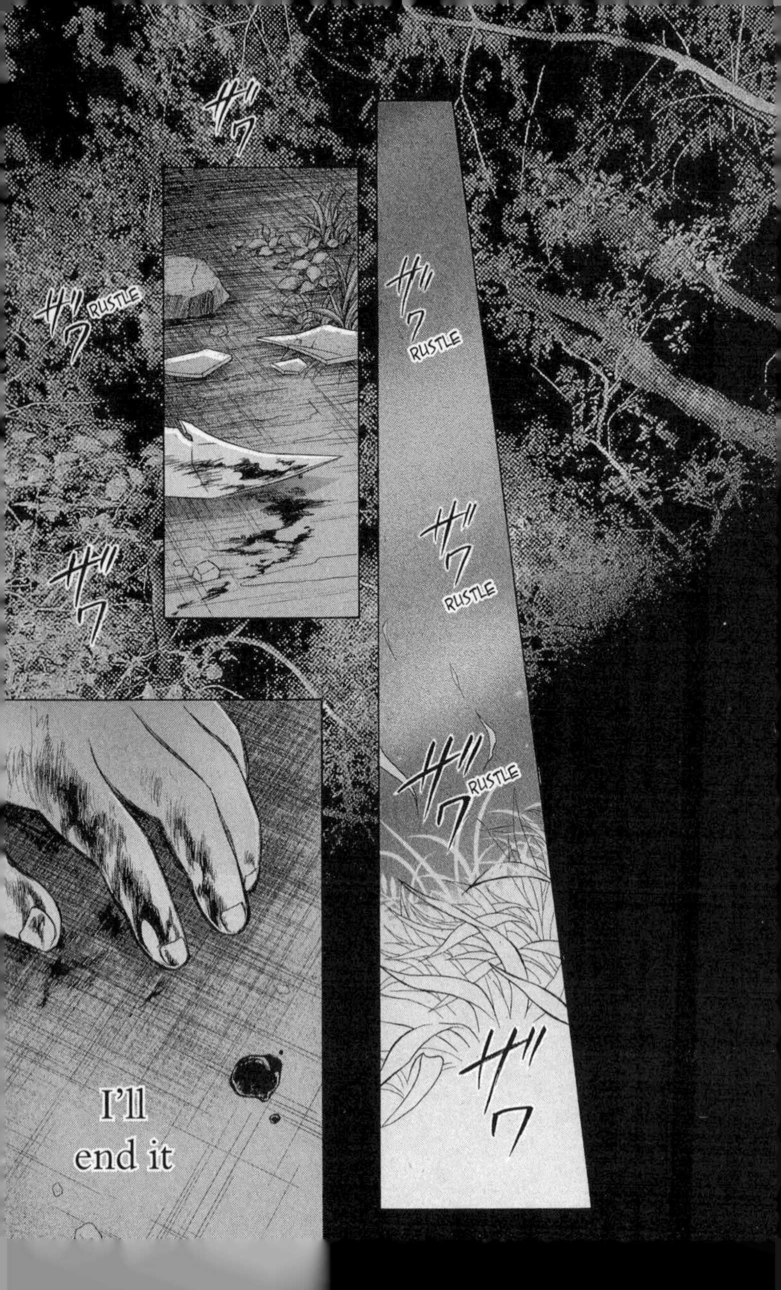
ザワ
RUSTLE
ザワ
RUSTLE
ザワ
RUSTLE
ザワ
ザワ
ザワ
RUSTLE
ザワ
I'll end it

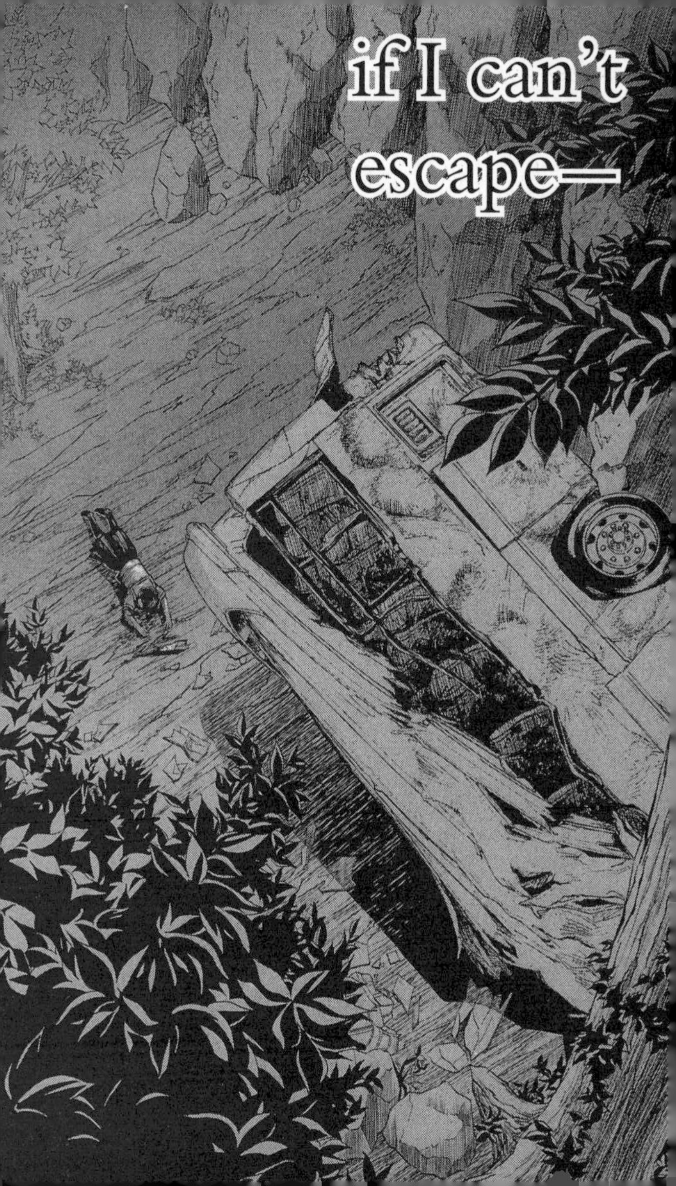
if I can't
escape—

L
I
M
I
T

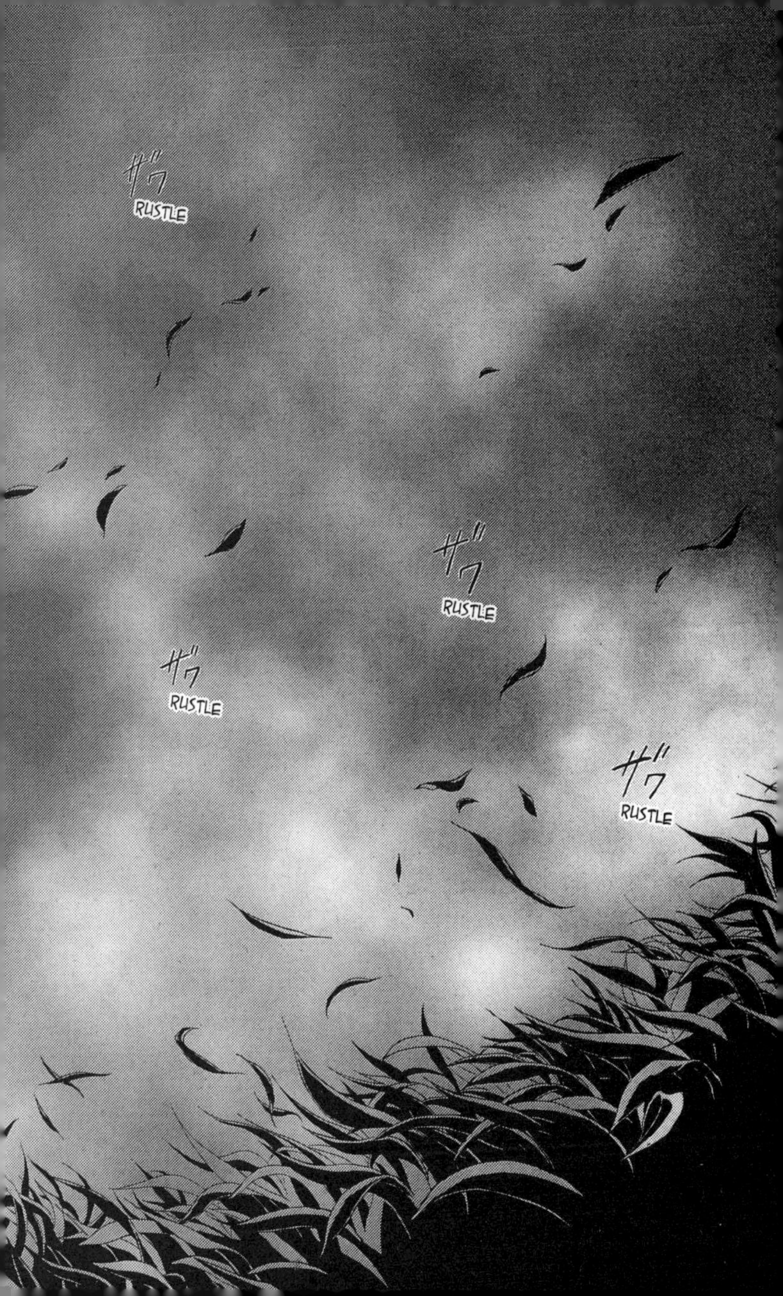
ザワ
RUSTLE
ザワ
RUSTLE
ザワ
RUSTLE
ザワ
RUSTLE

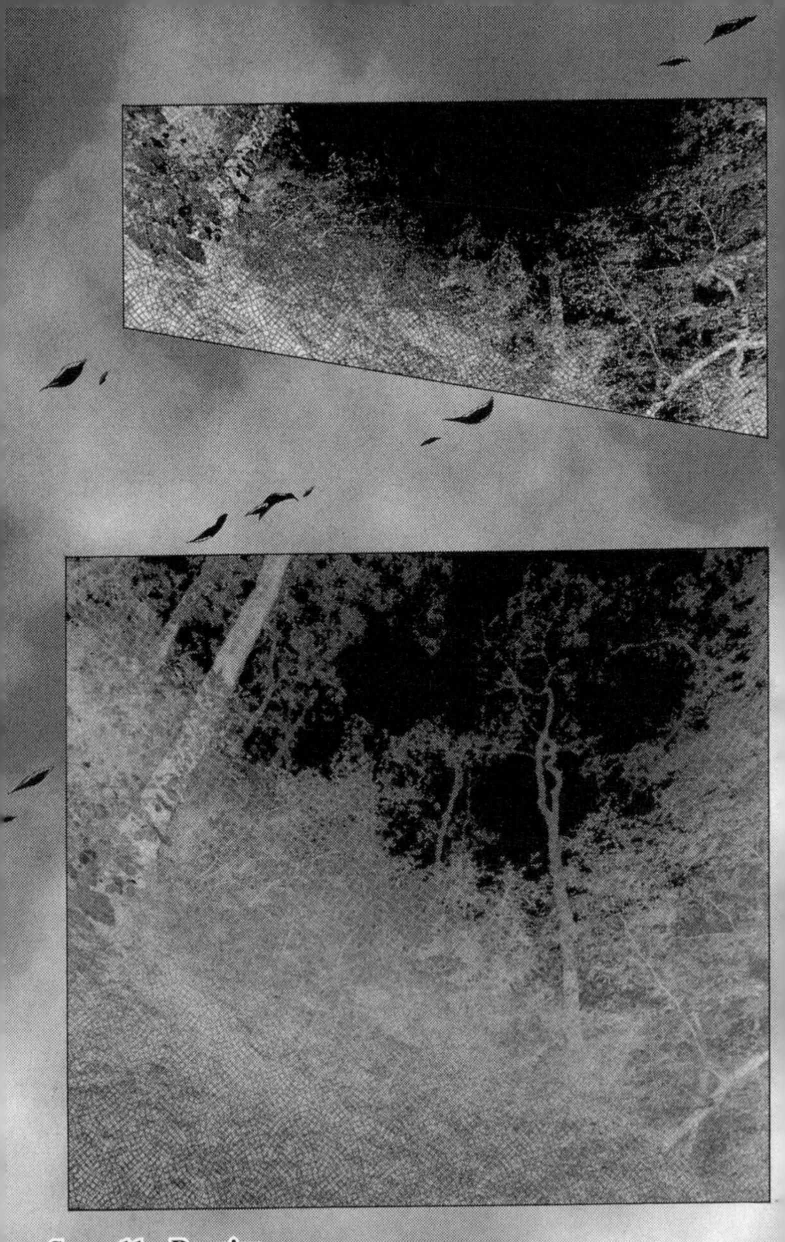

Scene.11 – Reunion

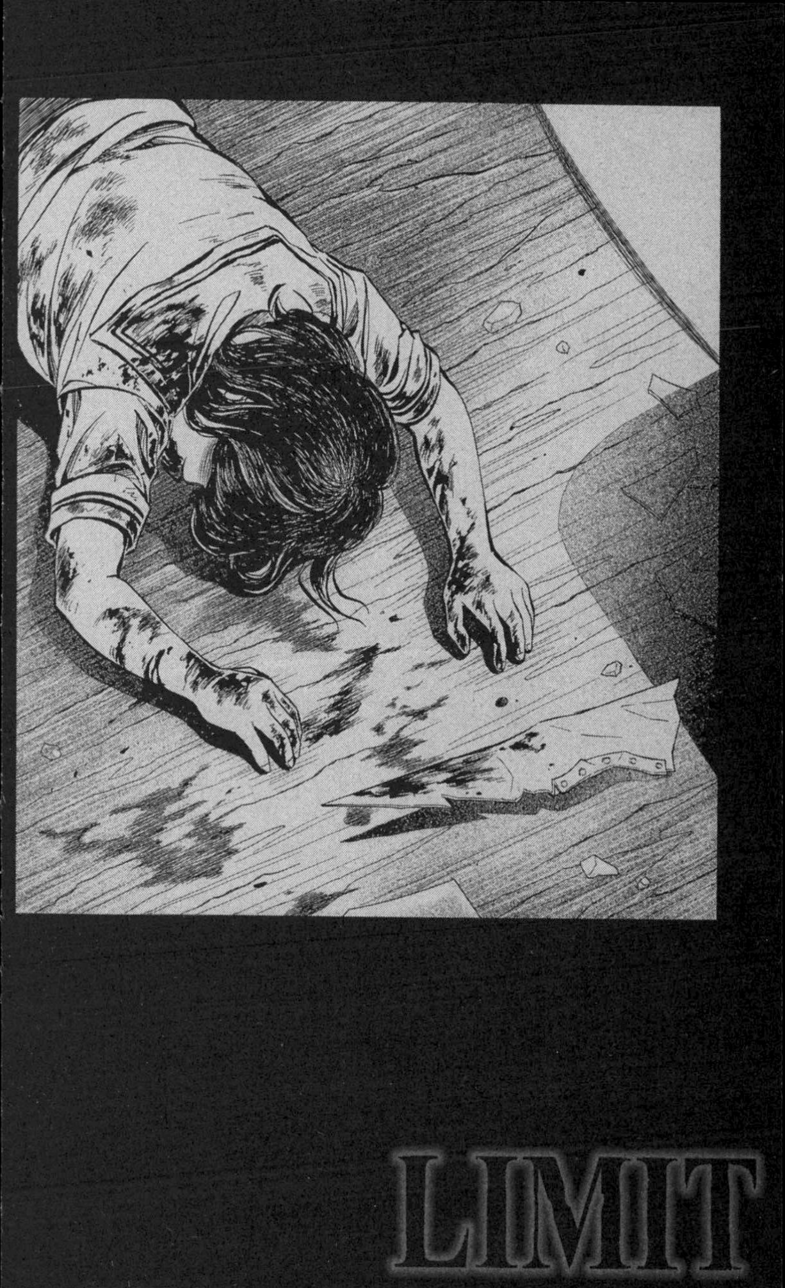

LIMIT

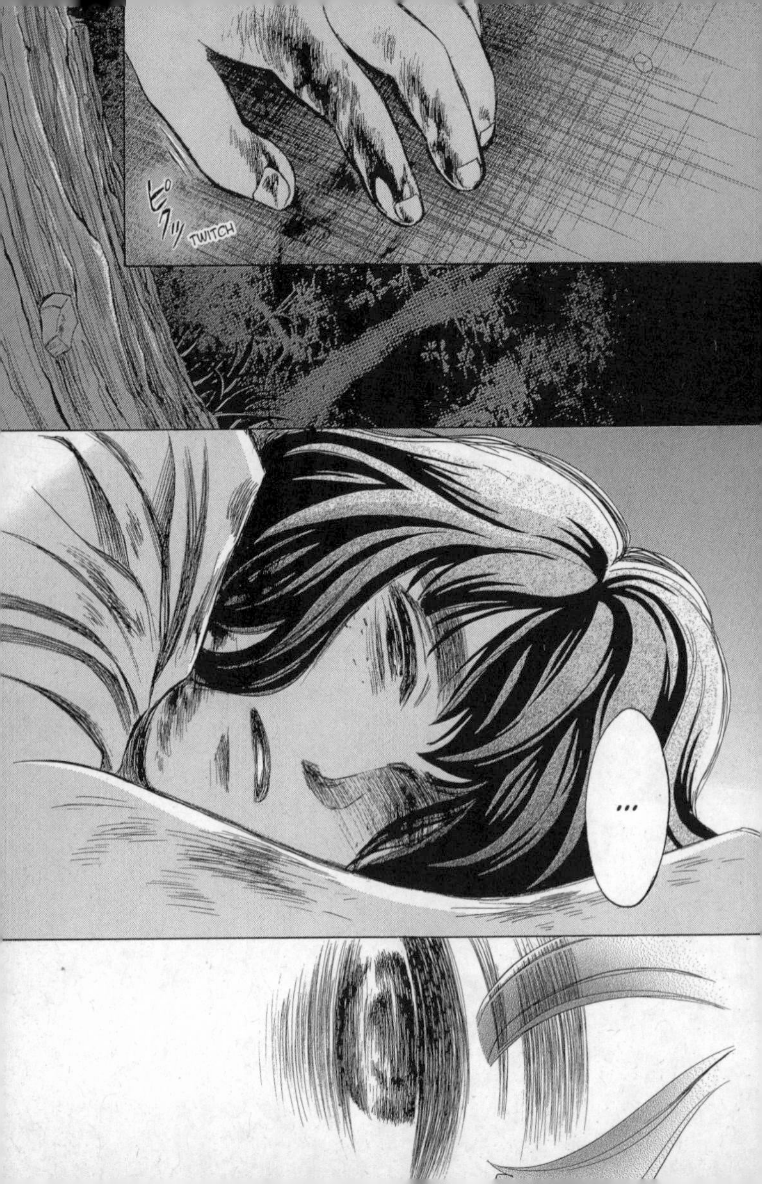
ピクッ
TWITCH
...

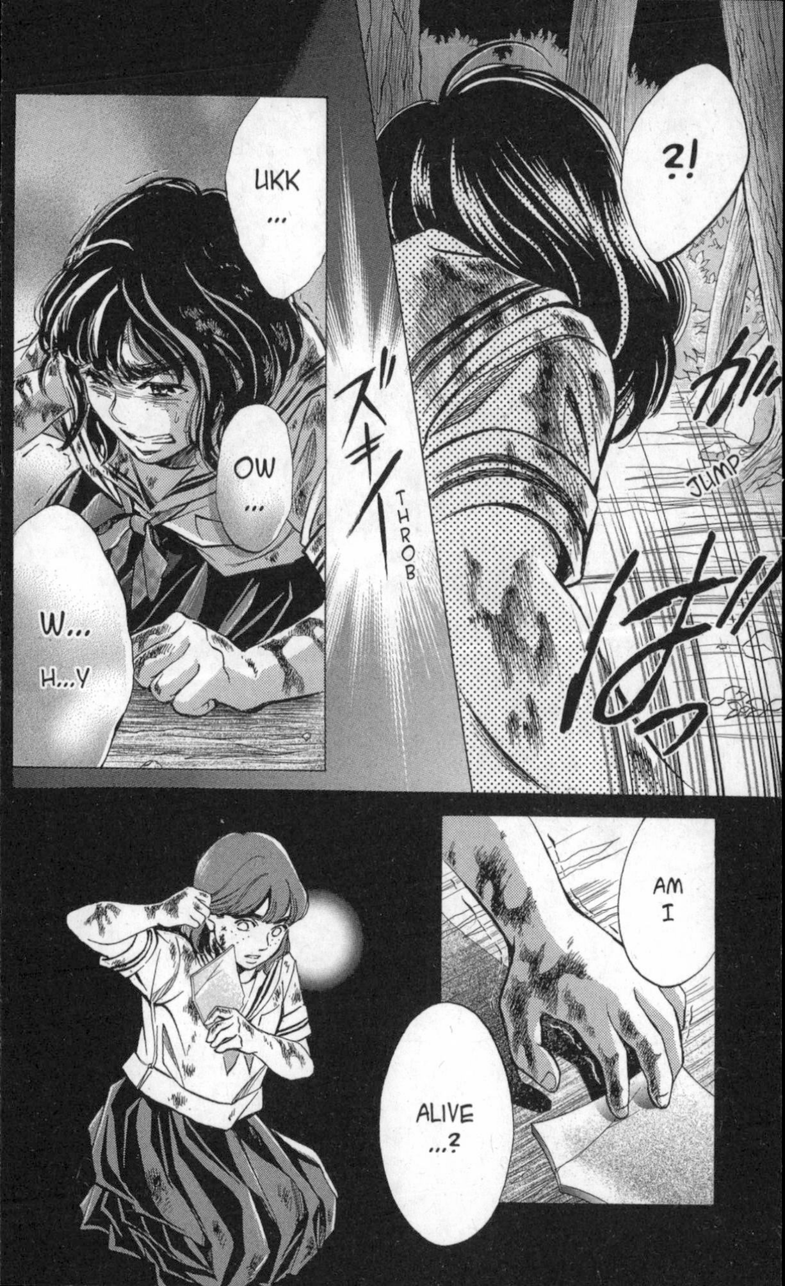
?!
JUMP
UKK ...
OW ...
W... H...Y
THROB
AM I
ALIVE ...?

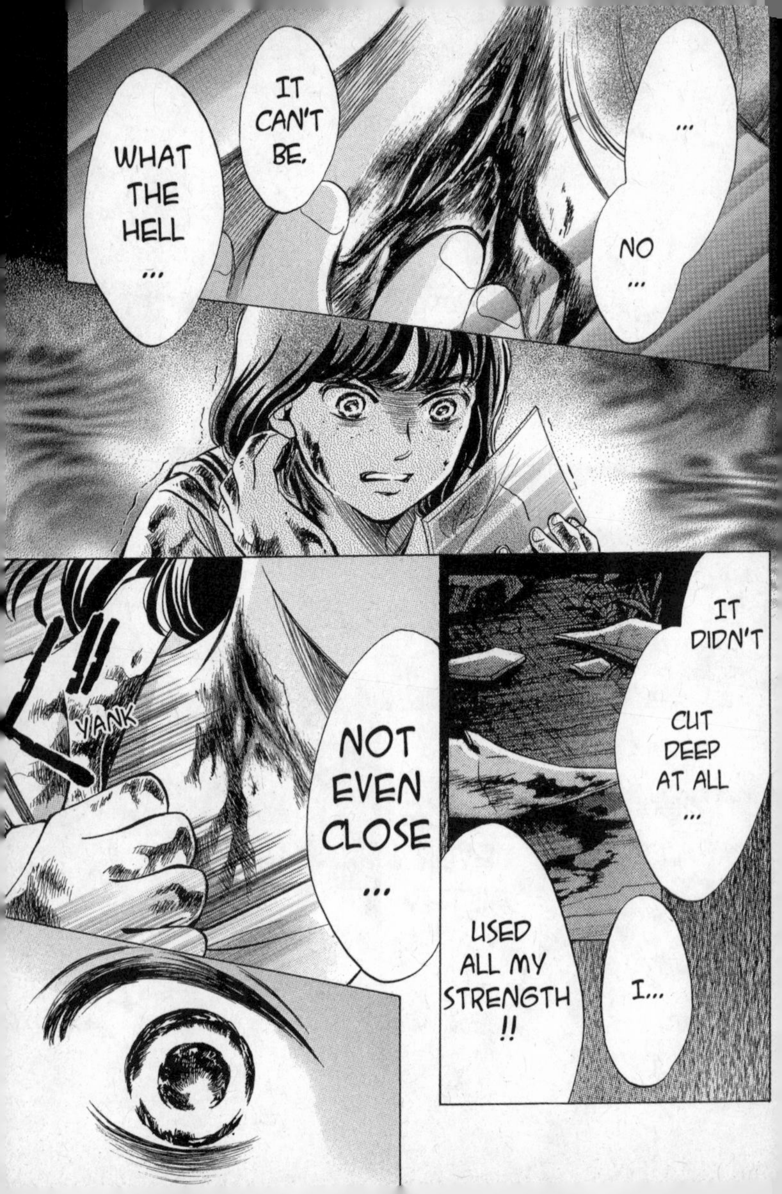
... NO ...
IT CAN'T BE.
WHAT THE HELL ...
IT DIDN'T CUT DEEP AT ALL ...
I...
USED ALL MY STRENGTH !!
YANK
NOT EVEN CLOSE ...

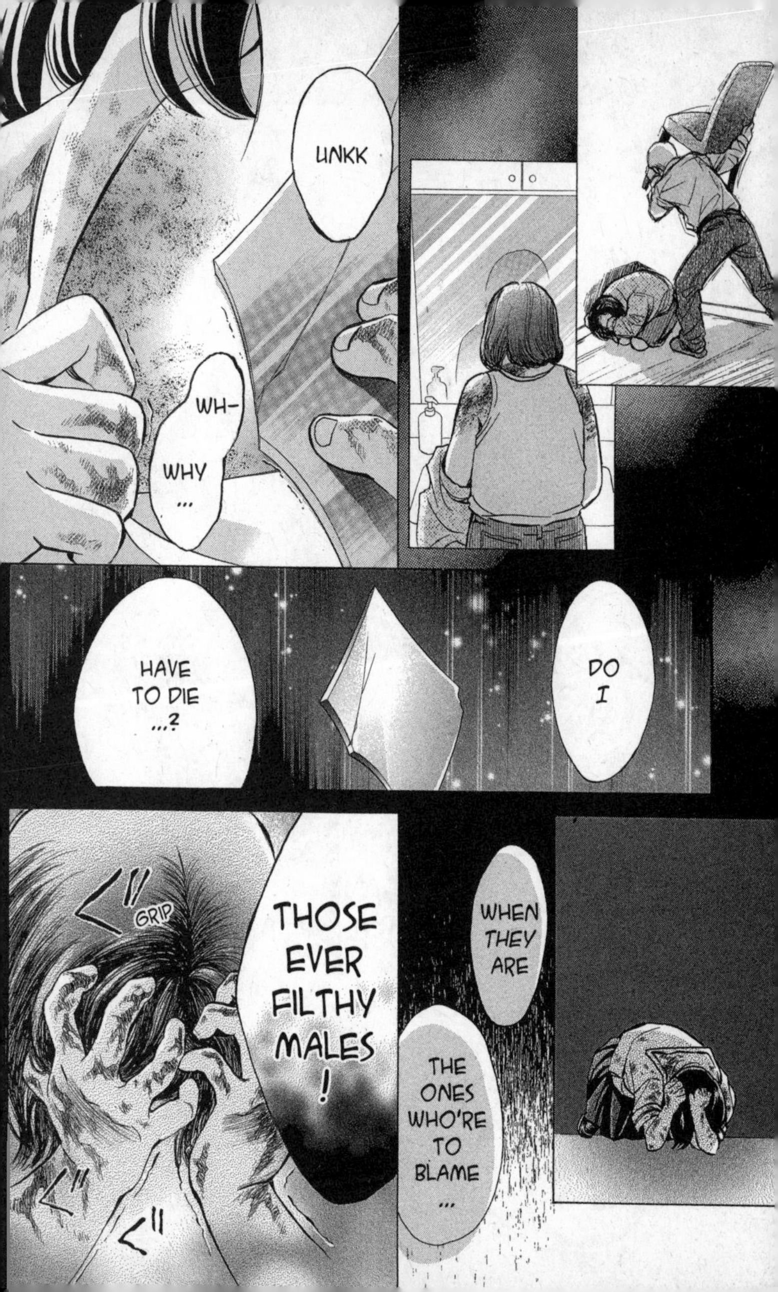
UNKK
WH- WHY ...
DO I
HAVE TO DIE ...?
WHEN THEY ARE
THE ONES WHO'RE TO BLAME ...
THOSE EVER FILTHY MALES !
GRIP

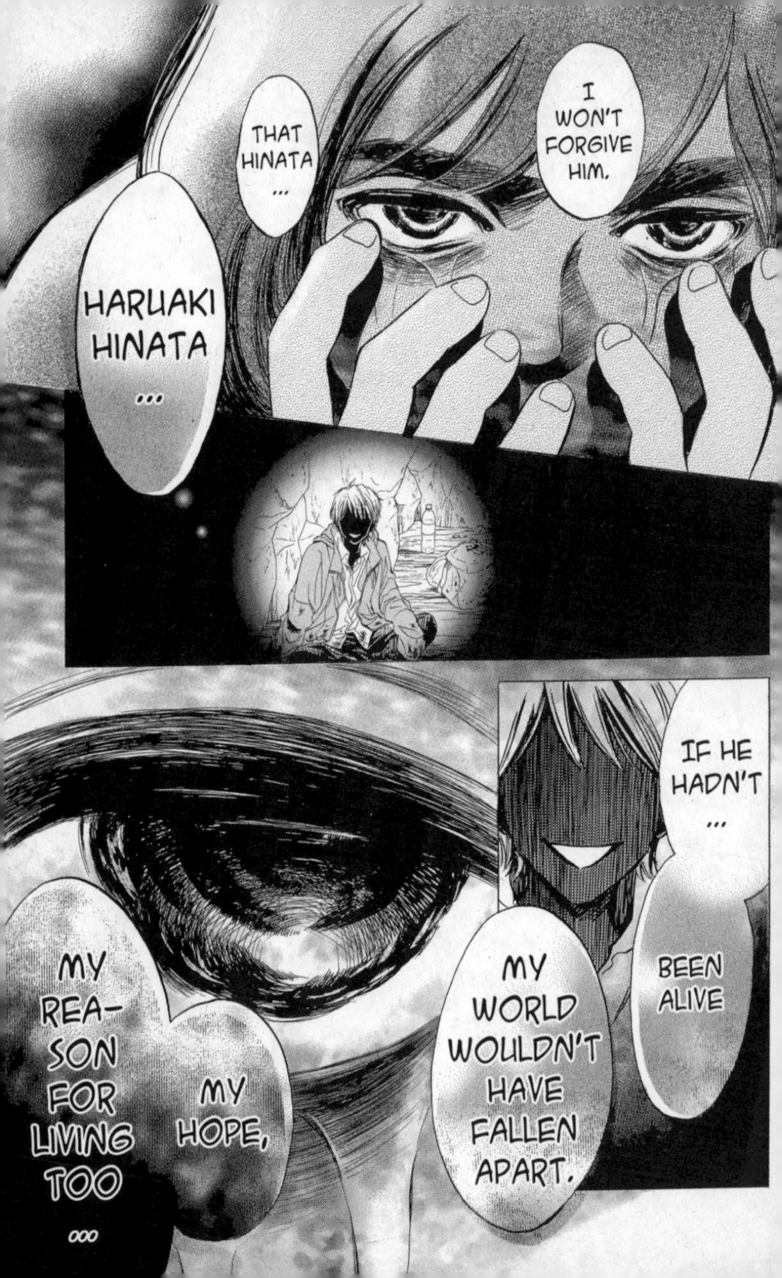
I WON'T FORGIVE HIM.
THAT HINATA ...
HARUAKI HINATA ...
IF HE HADN'T ...
BEEN ALIVE
MY WORLD WOULDN'T HAVE FALLEN APART.
MY HOPE,
MY REA-SON FOR LIVING TOO ...

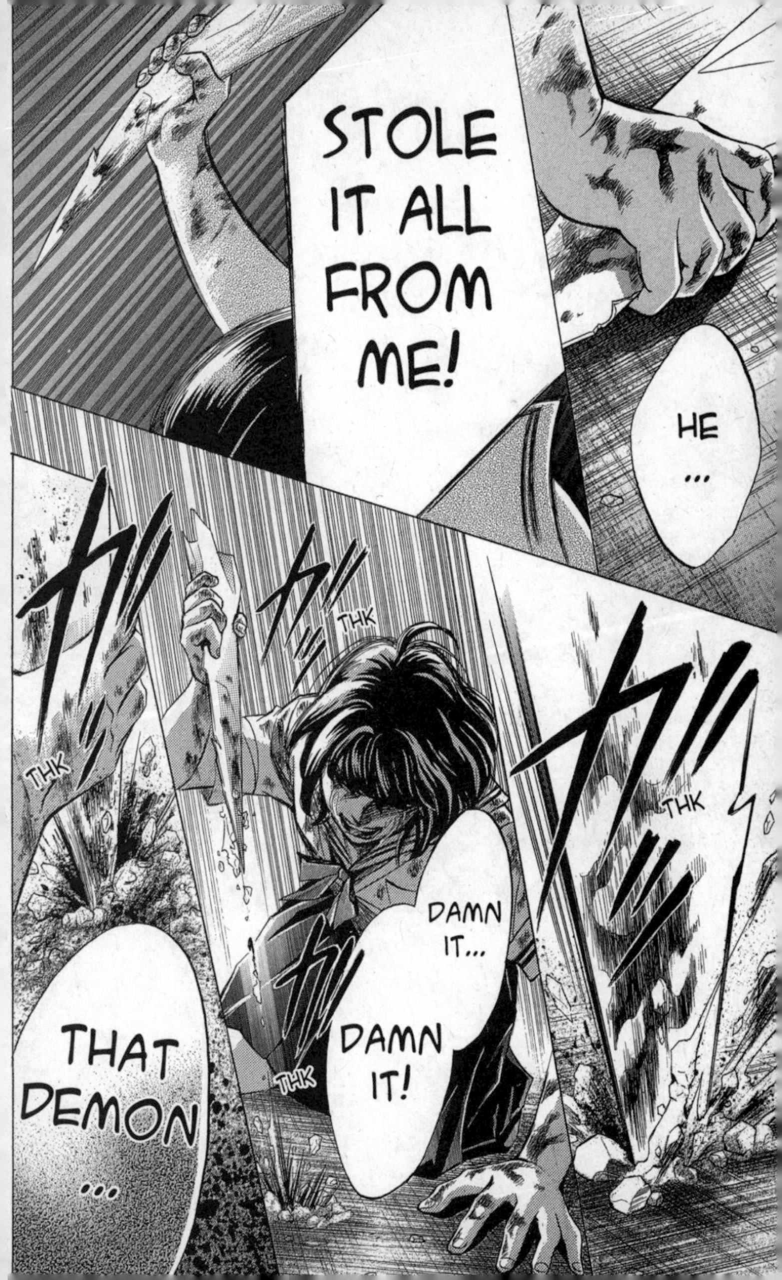
HE ...
STOLE IT ALL FROM ME!
THK
THK
DAMN IT...
DAMN IT!
THK
THK
THAT DEMON ...

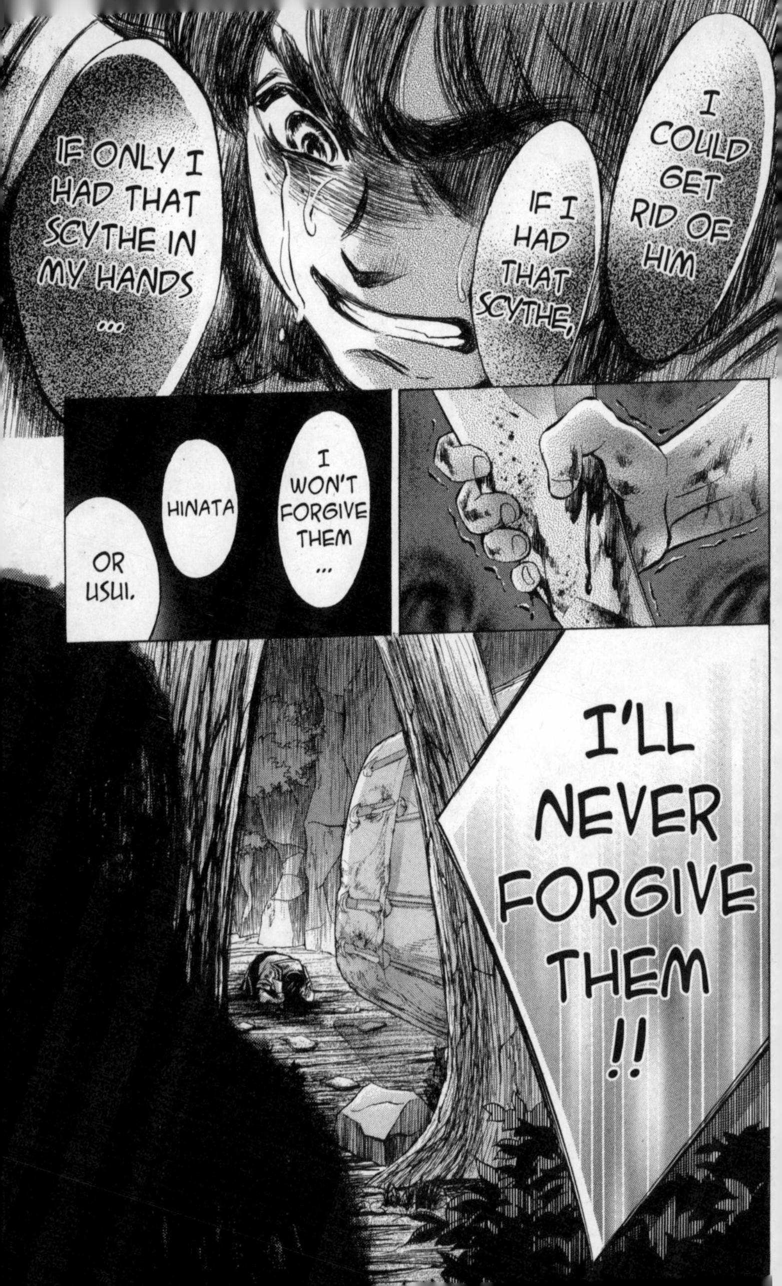

I COULD GET RID OF HIM
IF I HAD THAT SCYTHE,
IF ONLY I HAD THAT SCYTHE IN MY HANDS ...
I WON'T FORGIVE THEM ...
HINATA
OR USUI.
I'LL NEVER FORGIVE THEM !!

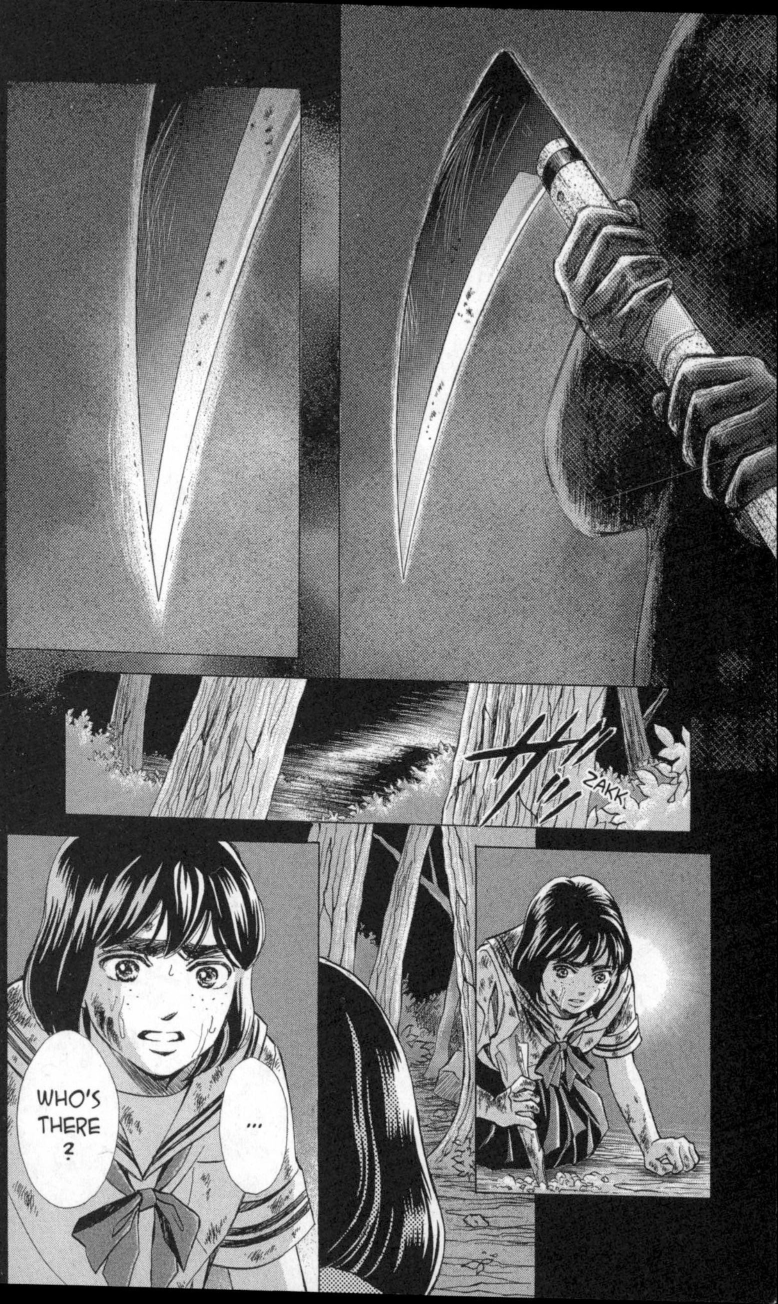
ZAKK
...
WHO'S THERE ?

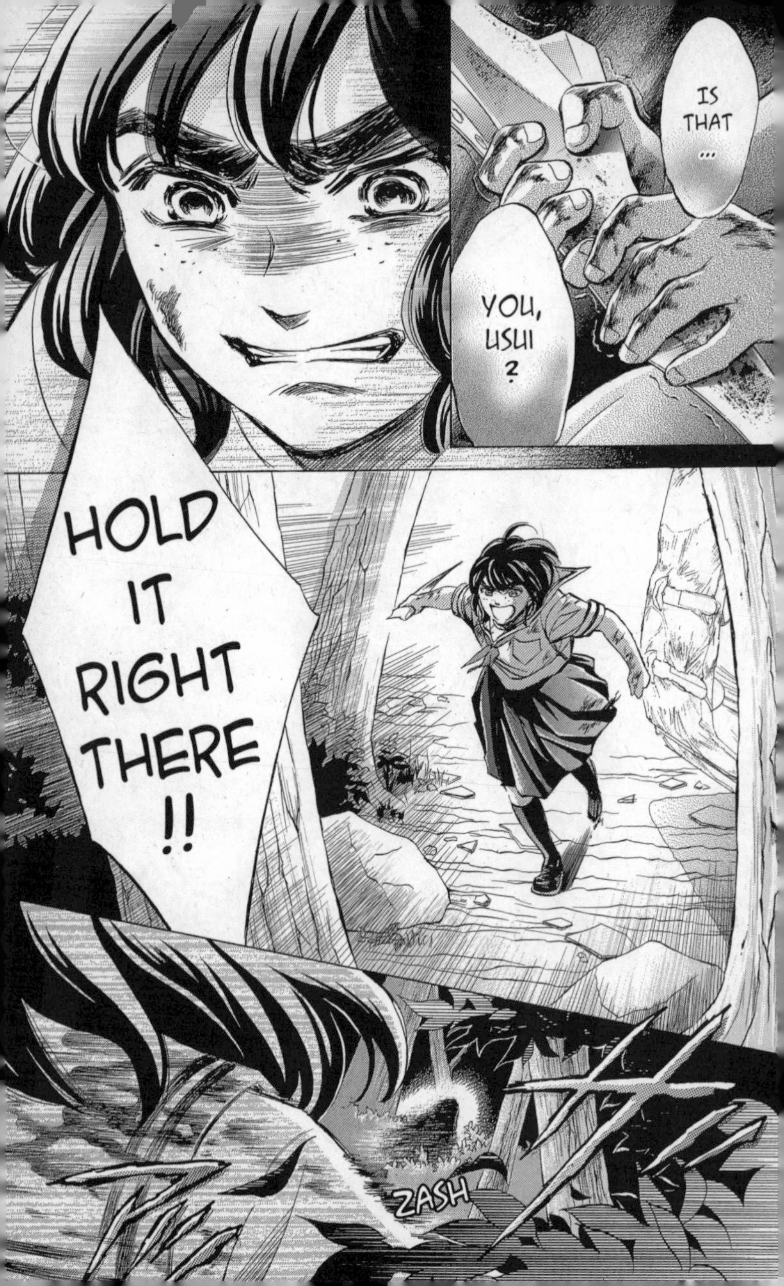
IS THAT ...
YOU, USUI ?
HOLD IT RIGHT THERE !!
ZASH

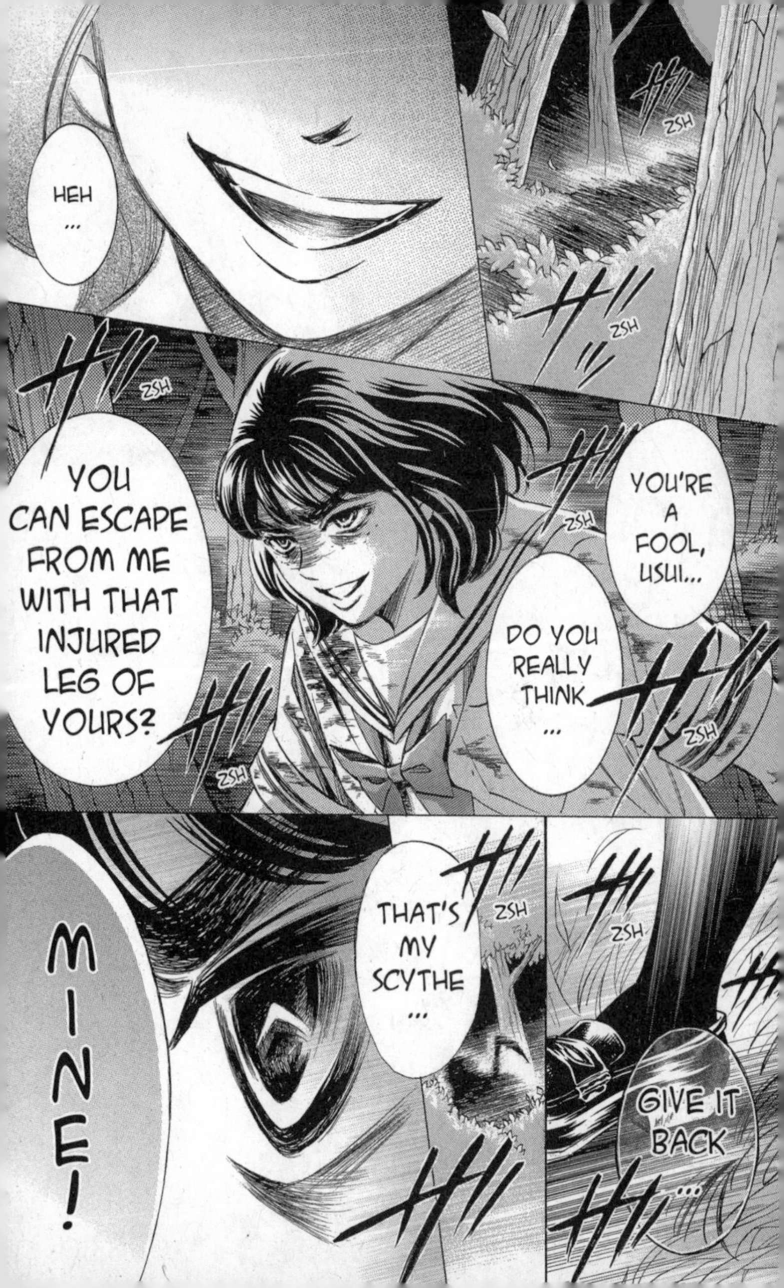
ZSH
ZSH
HEH ...
ZSH
YOU'RE A FOOL, USUI...
ZSH
DO YOU REALLY THINK ...
ZSH
YOU CAN ESCAPE FROM ME WITH THAT INJURED LEG OF YOURS?
ZSH
ZSH
GIVE IT BACK ...
ZSH
THAT'S MY SCYTHE ...
MINE!

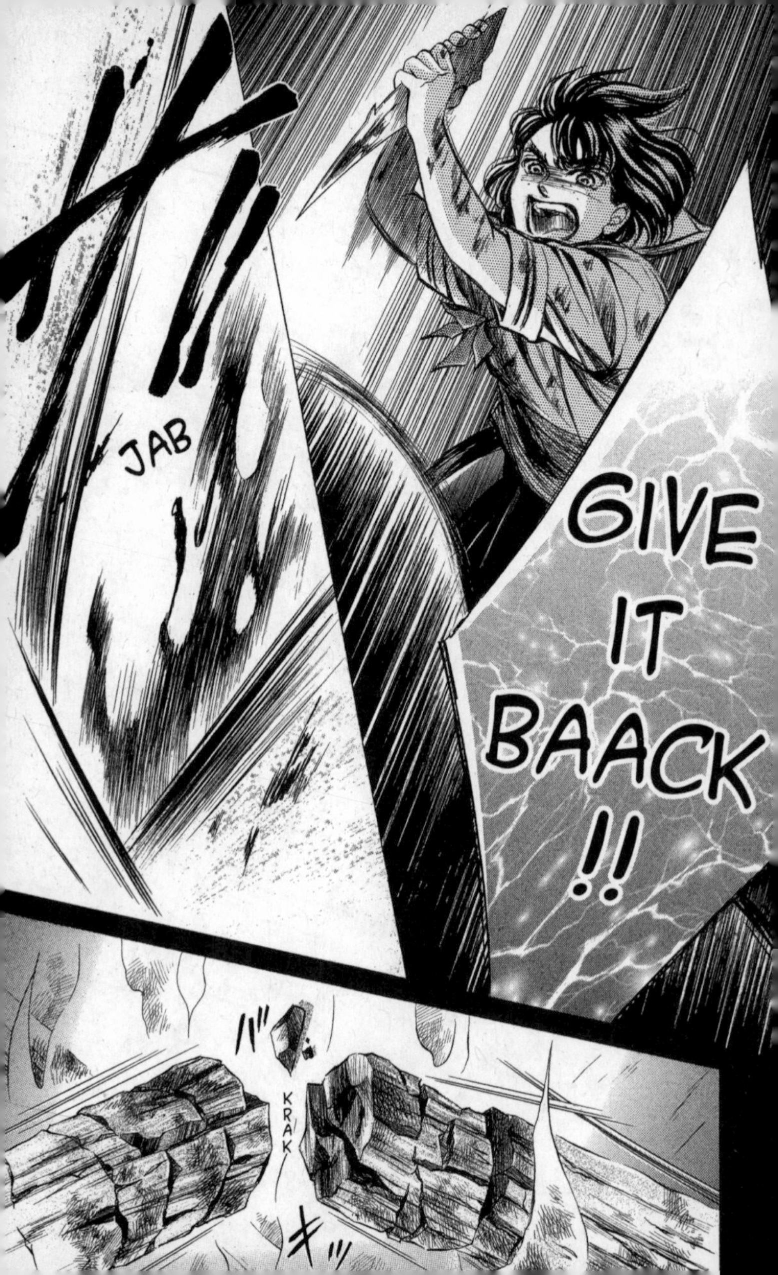
GIVE IT BAACK!!
JAB
KRAK

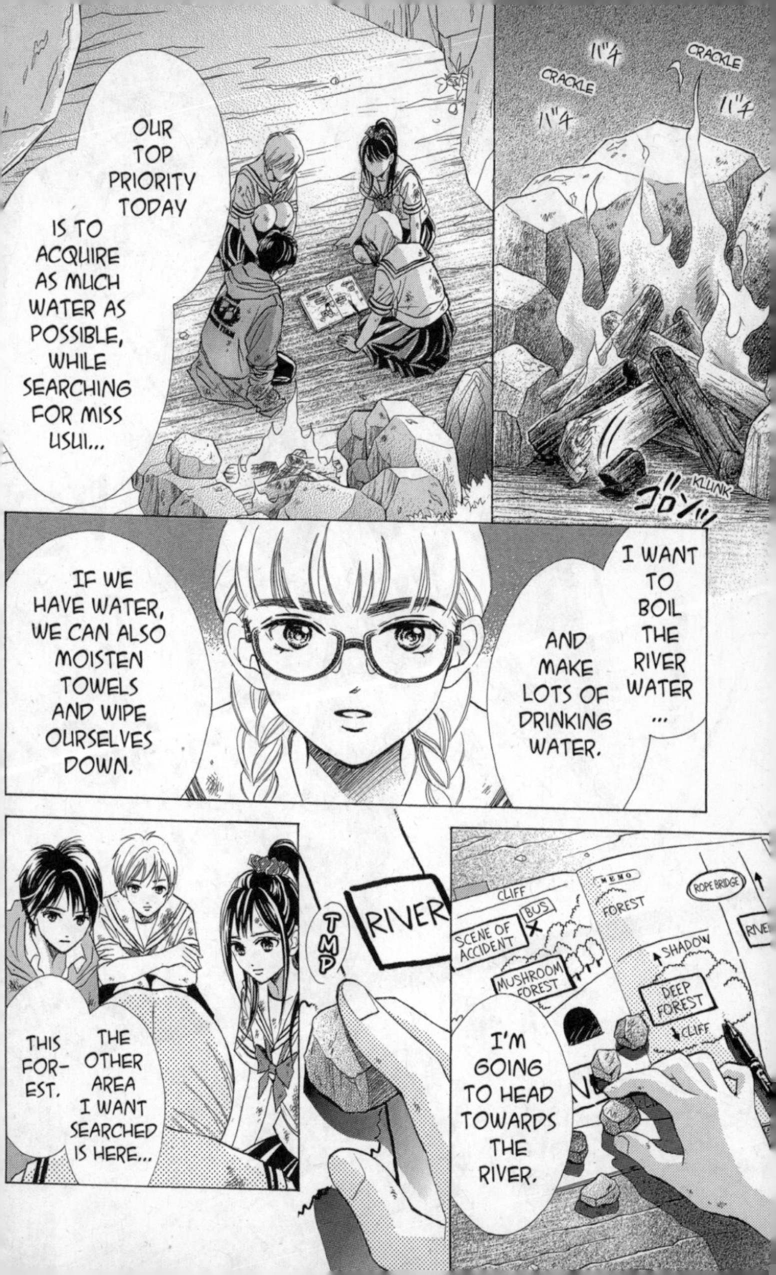

バチ
CRACKLE
CRACKLE
バチ
KLUNK
ゴロン
OUR TOP PRIORITY TODAY IS TO ACQUIRE AS MUCH WATER AS POSSIBLE, WHILE SEARCHING FOR MISS USUI...
I WANT TO BOIL THE RIVER WATER...
AND MAKE LOTS OF DRINKING WATER.
IF WE HAVE WATER, WE CAN ALSO MOISTEN TOWELS AND WIPE OURSELVES DOWN.
ROPE BRIDGE
MEMO
FOREST
CLIFF
BUS
SCENE OF ACCIDENT
MUSHROOM FOREST
SHADOW
DEEP FOREST
CLIFF
I'M GOING TO HEAD TOWARDS THE RIVER.
RIVER
TMP
THE OTHER AREA I WANT SEARCHED IS HERE...
THIS FOREST.

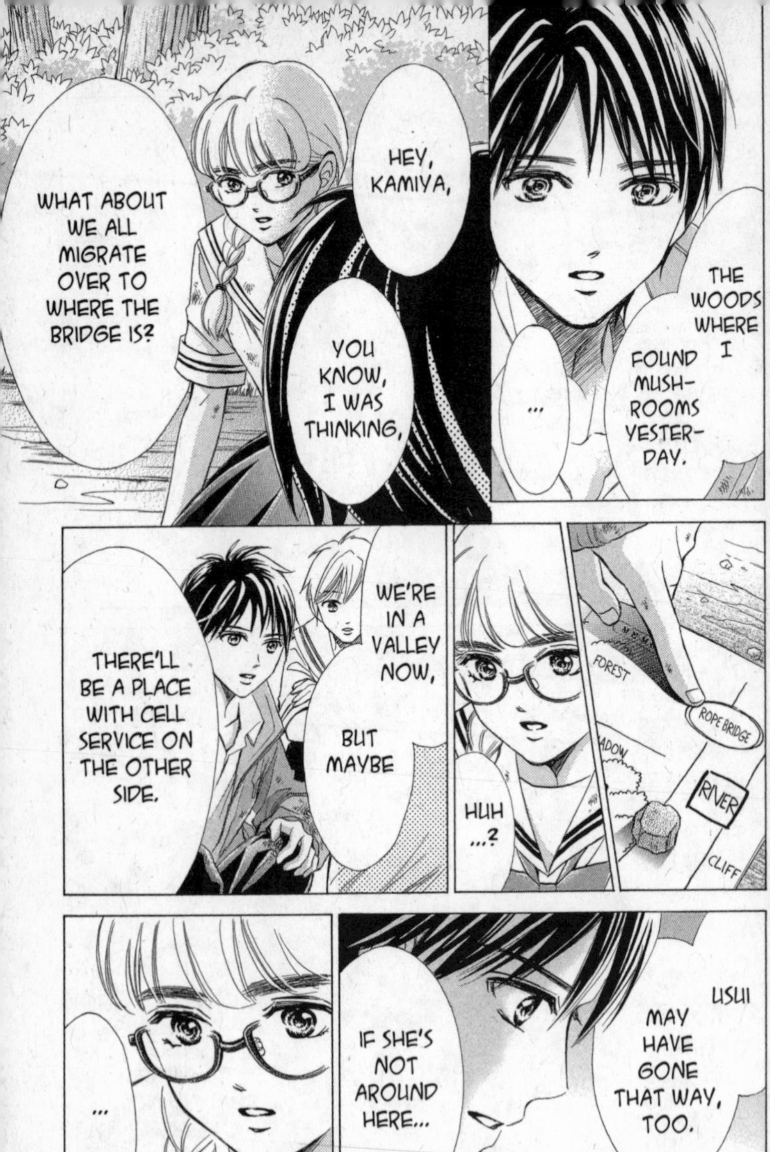
THE WOODS WHERE I FOUND MUSH-ROOMS YESTER-DAY.
...
HEY, KAMIYA,
YOU KNOW, I WAS THINKING,
WHAT ABOUT WE ALL MIGRATE OVER TO WHERE THE BRIDGE IS?
FOREST
ROPE BRIDGE
ADOW
RIVER
CLIFF
HUH ...?
WE'RE IN A VALLEY NOW,
BUT MAYBE
THERE'LL BE A PLACE WITH CELL SERVICE ON THE OTHER SIDE.
USUI MAY HAVE GONE THAT WAY, TOO.
IF SHE'S NOT AROUND HERE...
...

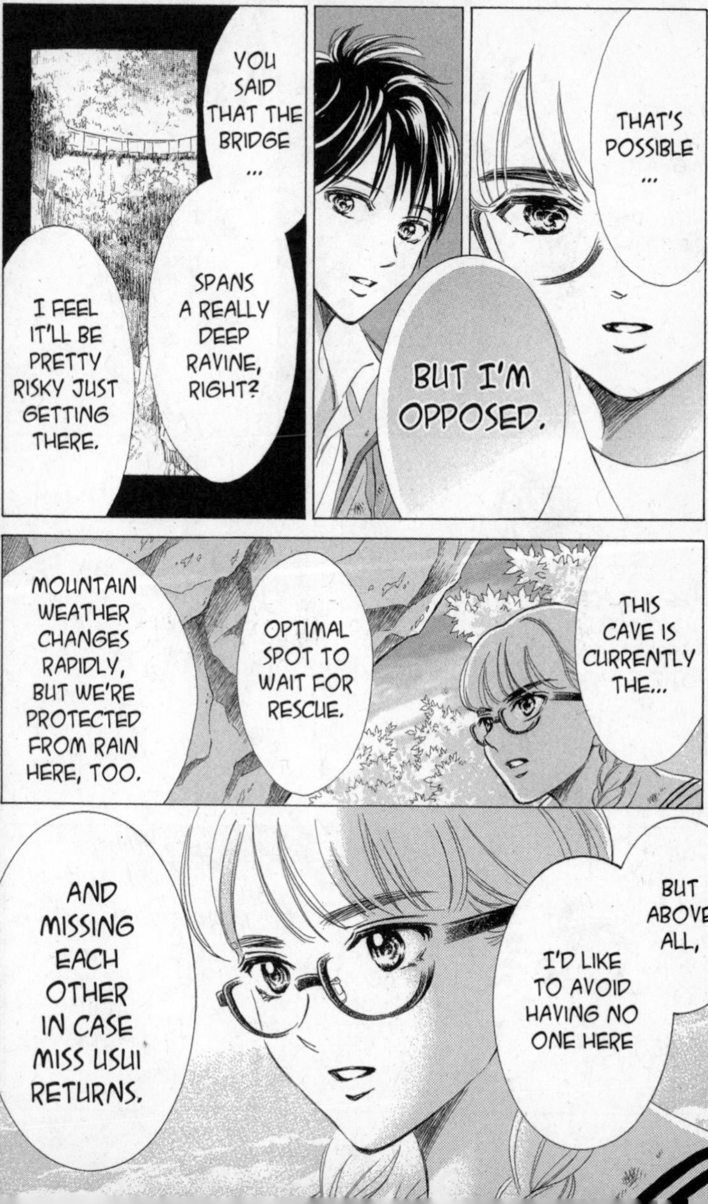
THAT'S POSSIBLE ...
BUT I'M OPPOSED.
YOU SAID THAT THE BRIDGE ...
SPANS A REALLY DEEP RAVINE, RIGHT?
I FEEL IT'LL BE PRETTY RISKY JUST GETTING THERE.
THIS CAVE IS CURRENTLY THE...
OPTIMAL SPOT TO WAIT FOR RESCUE.
MOUNTAIN WEATHER CHANGES RAPIDLY, BUT WE'RE PROTECTED FROM RAIN HERE, TOO.
BUT ABOVE ALL,
I'D LIKE TO AVOID HAVING NO ONE HERE
AND MISSING EACH OTHER IN CASE MISS USUI RETURNS.

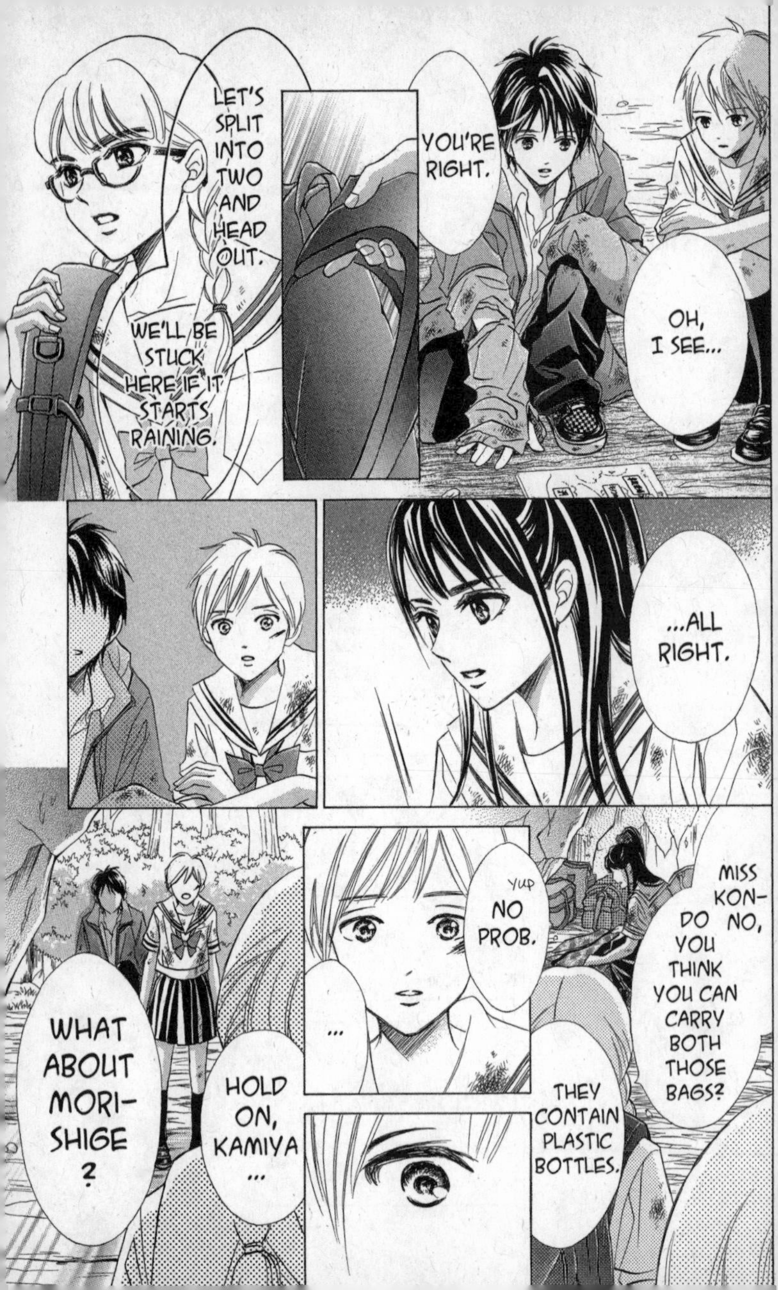
YOU'RE RIGHT.
OH, I SEE...
LET'S SPLIT INTO TWO AND HEAD OUT.
WE'LL BE STUCK HERE IF IT STARTS RAINING.
...ALL RIGHT.
MISS KONNO, DO YOU THINK YOU CAN CARRY BOTH THOSE BAGS?
THEY CONTAIN PLASTIC BOTTLES.
YUP
NO PROB.
...
HOLD ON, KAMIYA...
WHAT ABOUT MORISHIGE?

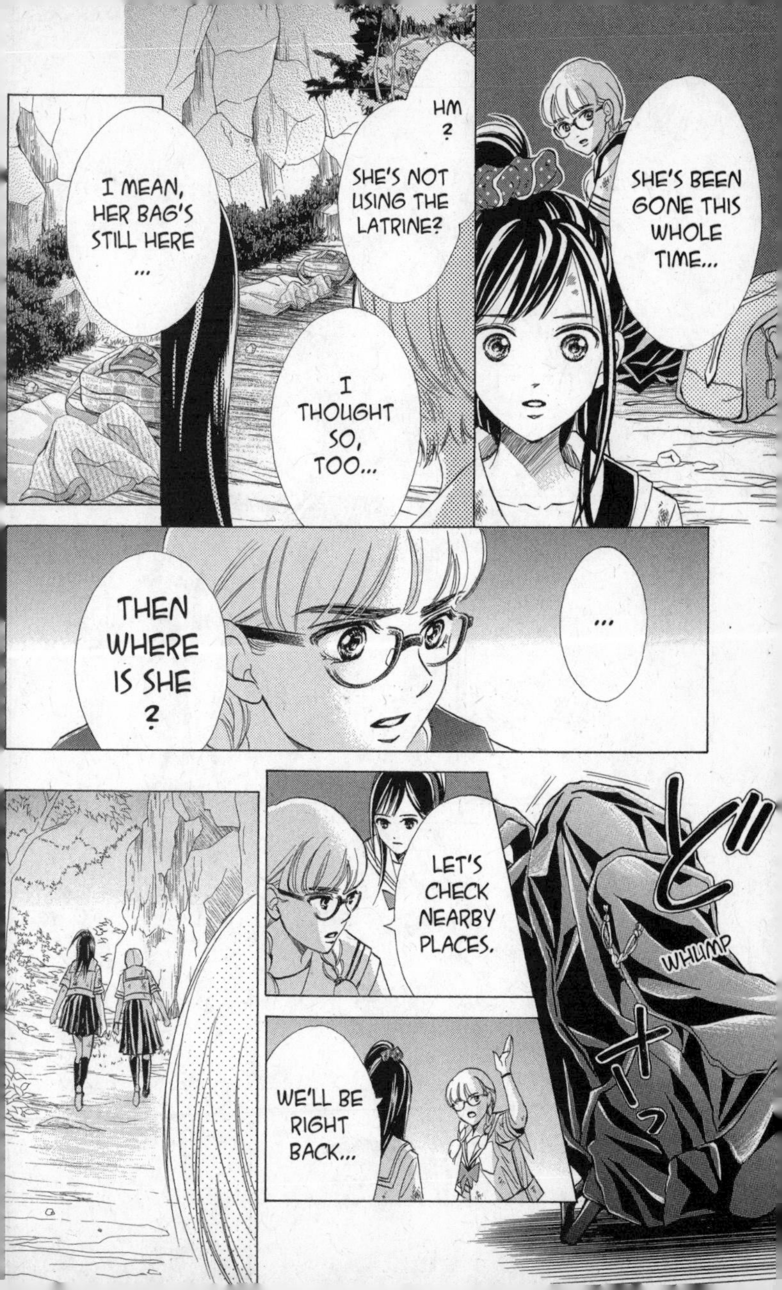

SHE'S BEEN GONE THIS WHOLE TIME...
HM? SHE'S NOT USING THE LATRINE?
I THOUGHT SO, TOO...
I MEAN, HER BAG'S STILL HERE ...
...
THEN WHERE IS SHE?
WHUMP
LET'S CHECK NEARBY PLACES.
WE'LL BE RIGHT BACK...

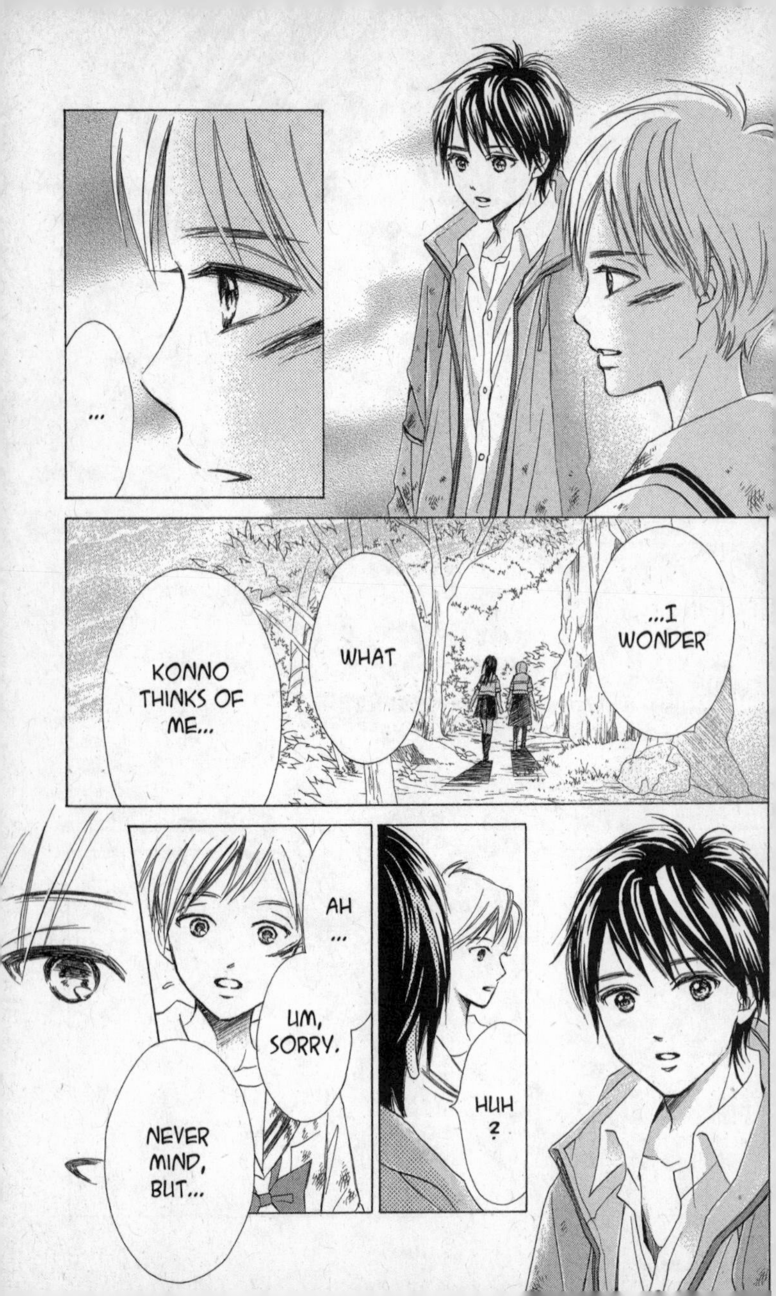
...
...I WONDER
WHAT
KONNO THINKS OF ME...
HUH ?
AH ...
UM, SORRY.
NEVER MIND, BUT...

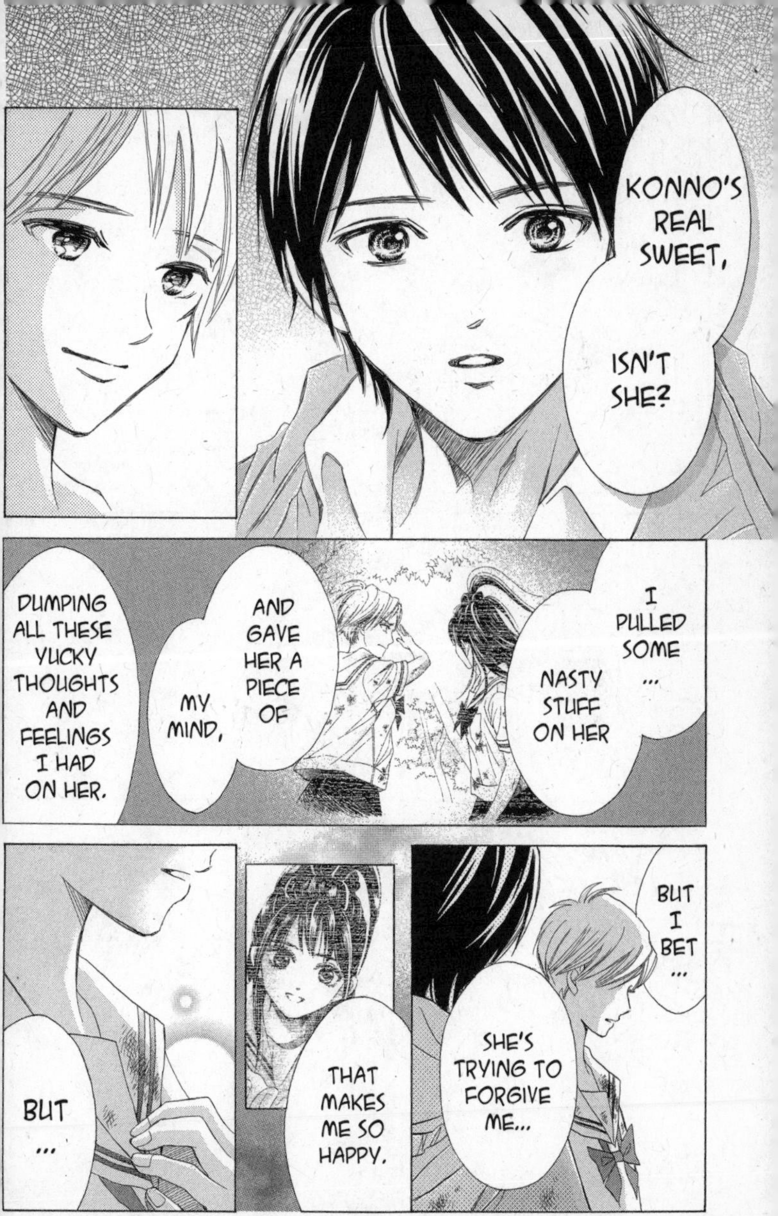
KONNO'S REAL SWEET,
ISN'T SHE?
I PULLED SOME ...
NASTY STUFF ON HER
AND GAVE HER A PIECE OF
MY MIND,
DUMPING ALL THESE YUCKY THOUGHTS AND FEELINGS I HAD ON HER.
BUT I BET ...
SHE'S TRYING TO FORGIVE ME...
THAT MAKES ME SO HAPPY.
BUT ...

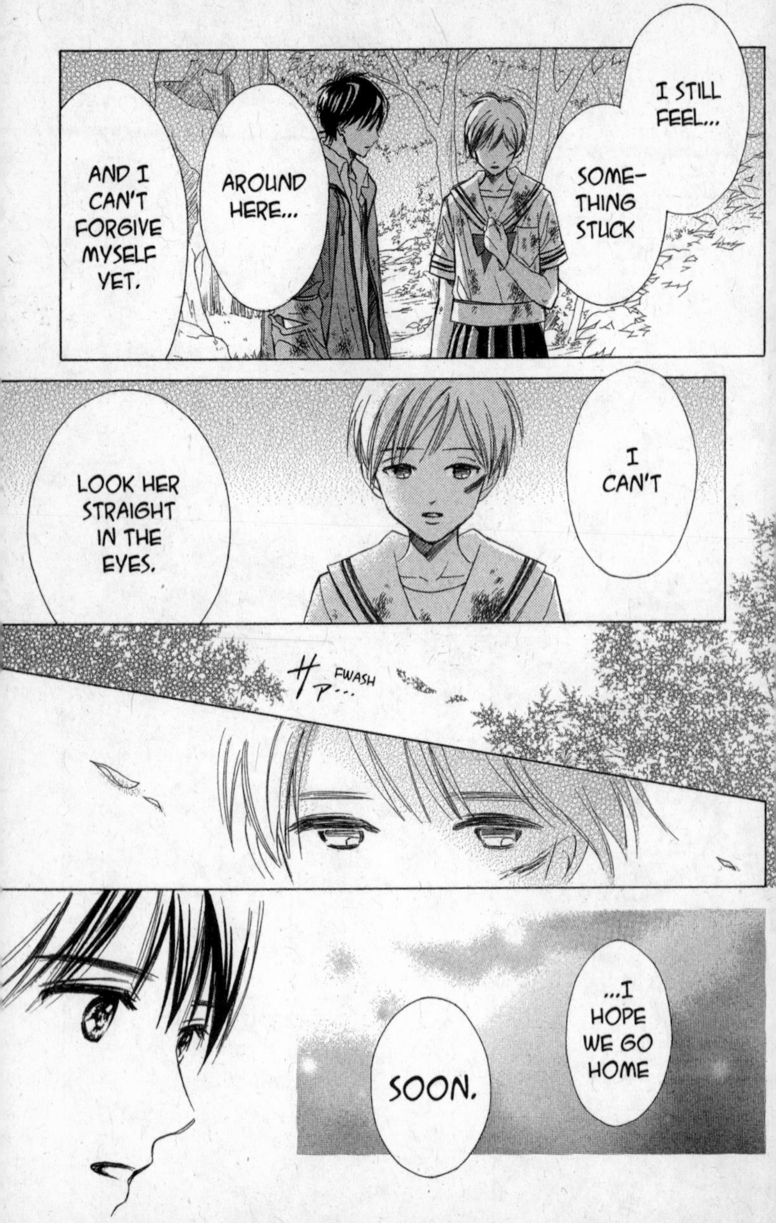
I STILL FEEL...
SOME-THING STUCK
AROUND HERE...
AND I CAN'T FORGIVE MYSELF YET.
I CAN'T
LOOK HER STRAIGHT IN THE EYES.
サァ… FWASH
...I HOPE WE GO HOME
SOON.

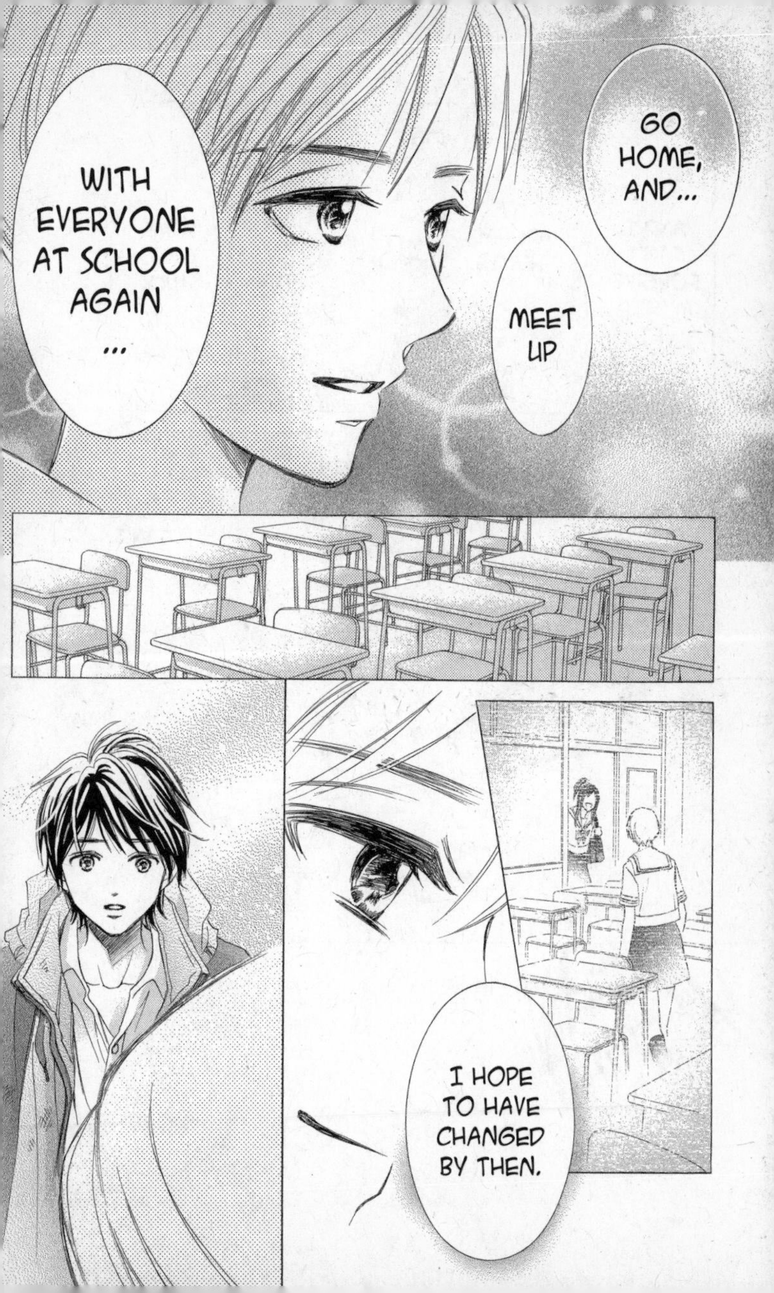
GO HOME, AND...
MEET UP
WITH EVERYONE AT SCHOOL AGAIN ...
I HOPE TO HAVE CHANGED BY THEN.

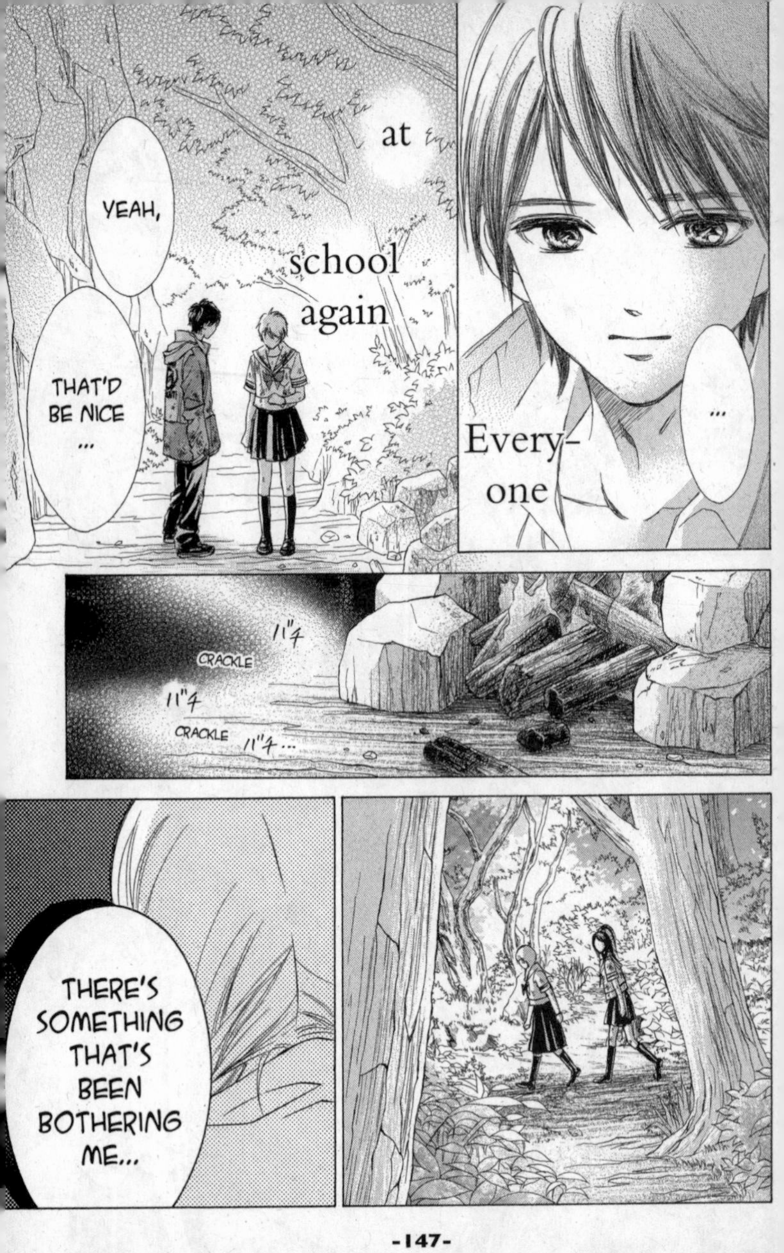
...
Every-
one
at
school
again
YEAH,
THAT'D BE NICE ...
バチ
CRACKLE
バチ
CRACKLE
バチ...
THERE'S SOMETHING THAT'S BEEN BOTHERING ME...

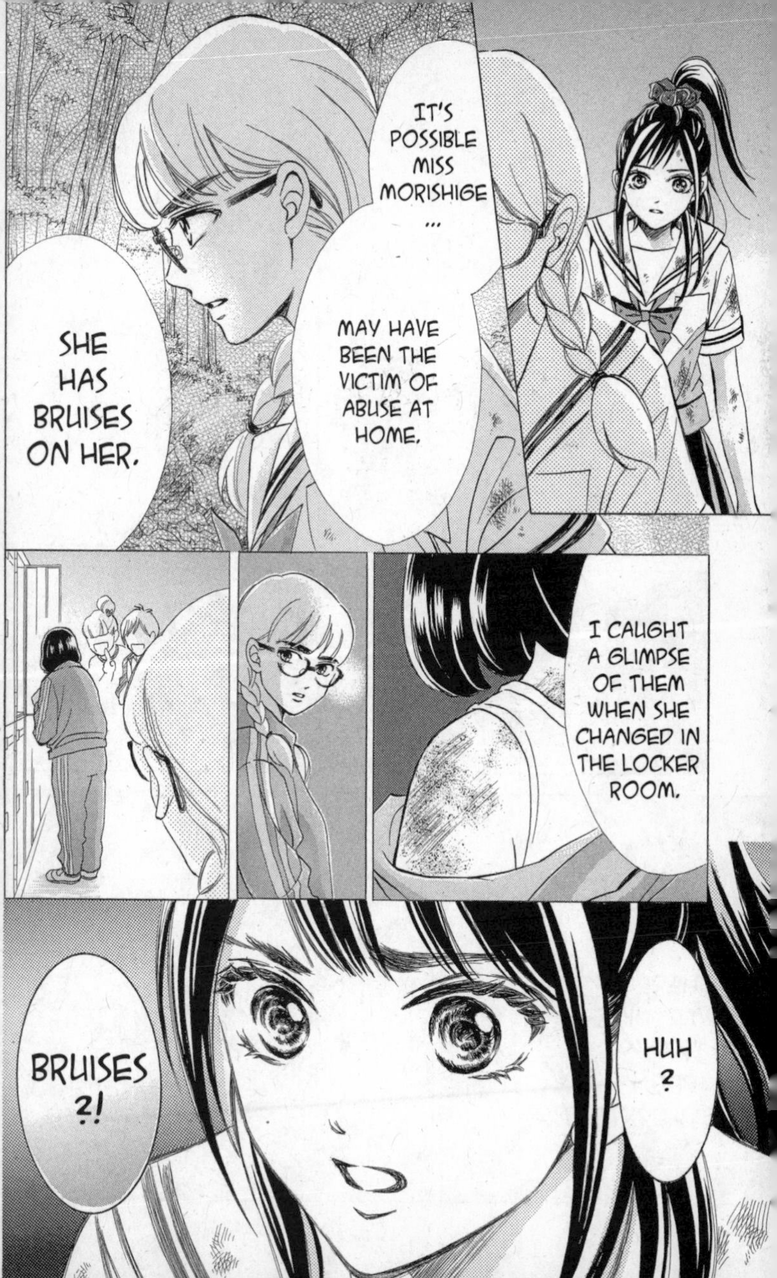
IT'S POSSIBLE MISS MORISHIGE ...
MAY HAVE BEEN THE VICTIM OF ABUSE AT HOME.
SHE HAS BRUISES ON HER.
I CAUGHT A GLIMPSE OF THEM WHEN SHE CHANGED IN THE LOCKER ROOM.
HUH?
BRUISES?!

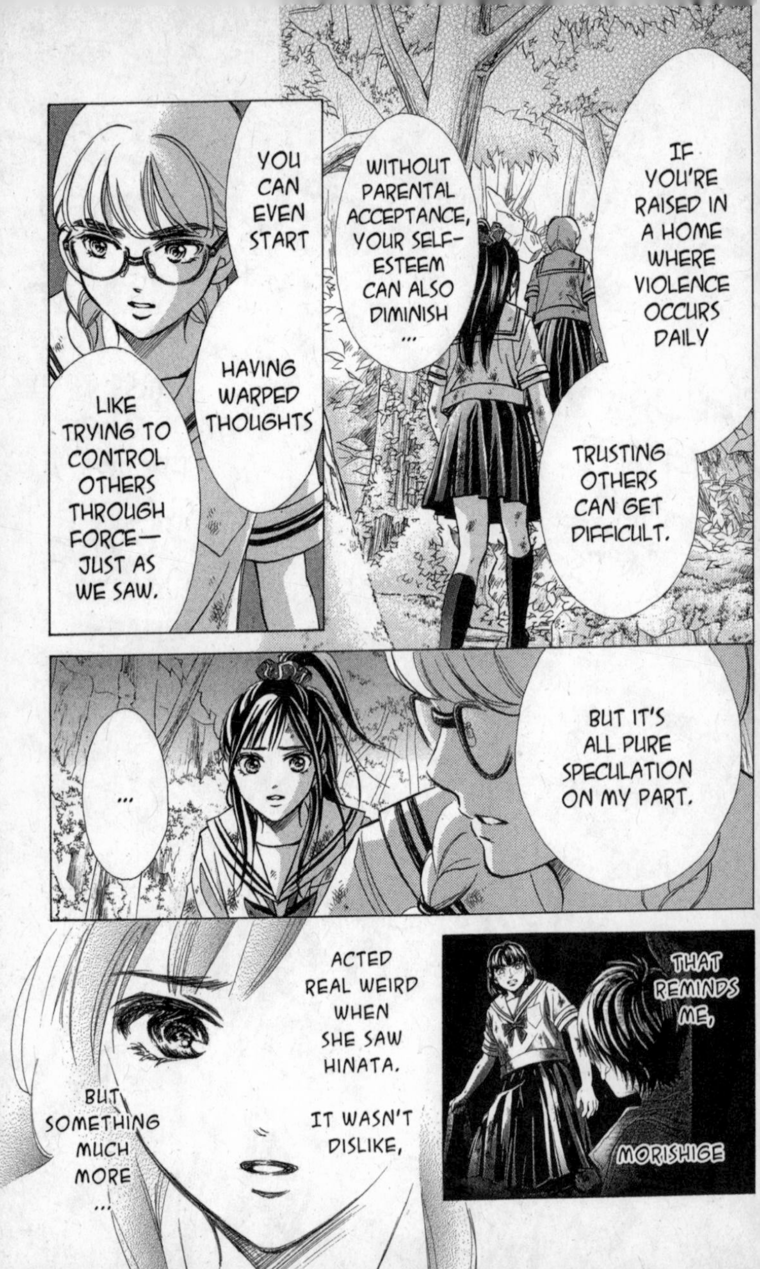
IF YOU'RE RAISED IN A HOME WHERE VIOLENCE OCCURS DAILY
WITHOUT PARENTAL ACCEPTANCE, YOUR SELF-ESTEEM CAN ALSO DIMINISH ...
TRUSTING OTHERS CAN GET DIFFICULT.
YOU CAN EVEN START
HAVING WARPED THOUGHTS
LIKE TRYING TO CONTROL OTHERS THROUGH FORCE—JUST AS WE SAW.
BUT IT'S ALL PURE SPECULATION ON MY PART.
...
THAT REMINDS ME,
MORISHIGE
ACTED REAL WEIRD WHEN SHE SAW HINATA.
IT WASN'T DISLIKE,
BUT SOMETHING MUCH MORE ...

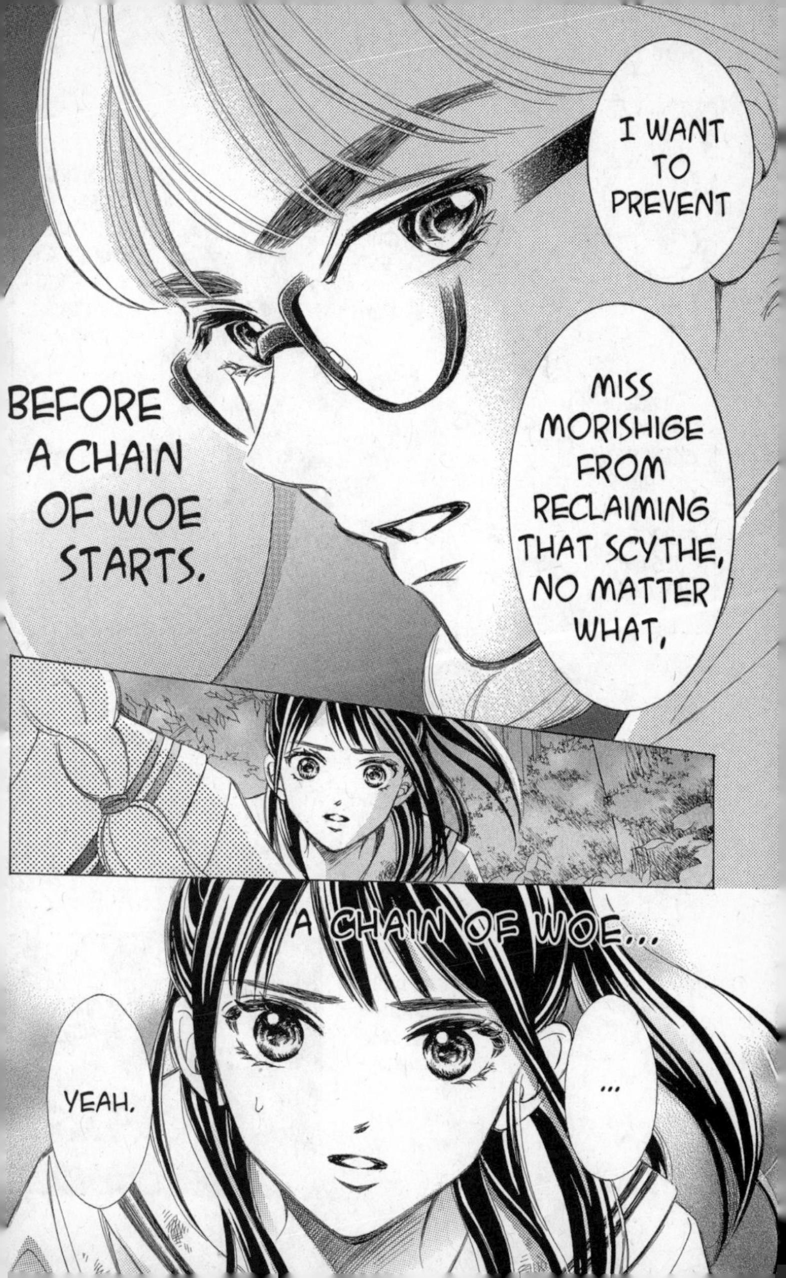
I WANT TO PREVENT
MISS MORISHIGE FROM RECLAIMING THAT SCYTHE, NO MATTER WHAT,
BEFORE A CHAIN OF WOE STARTS.
A CHAIN OF WOE...
...
YEAH.

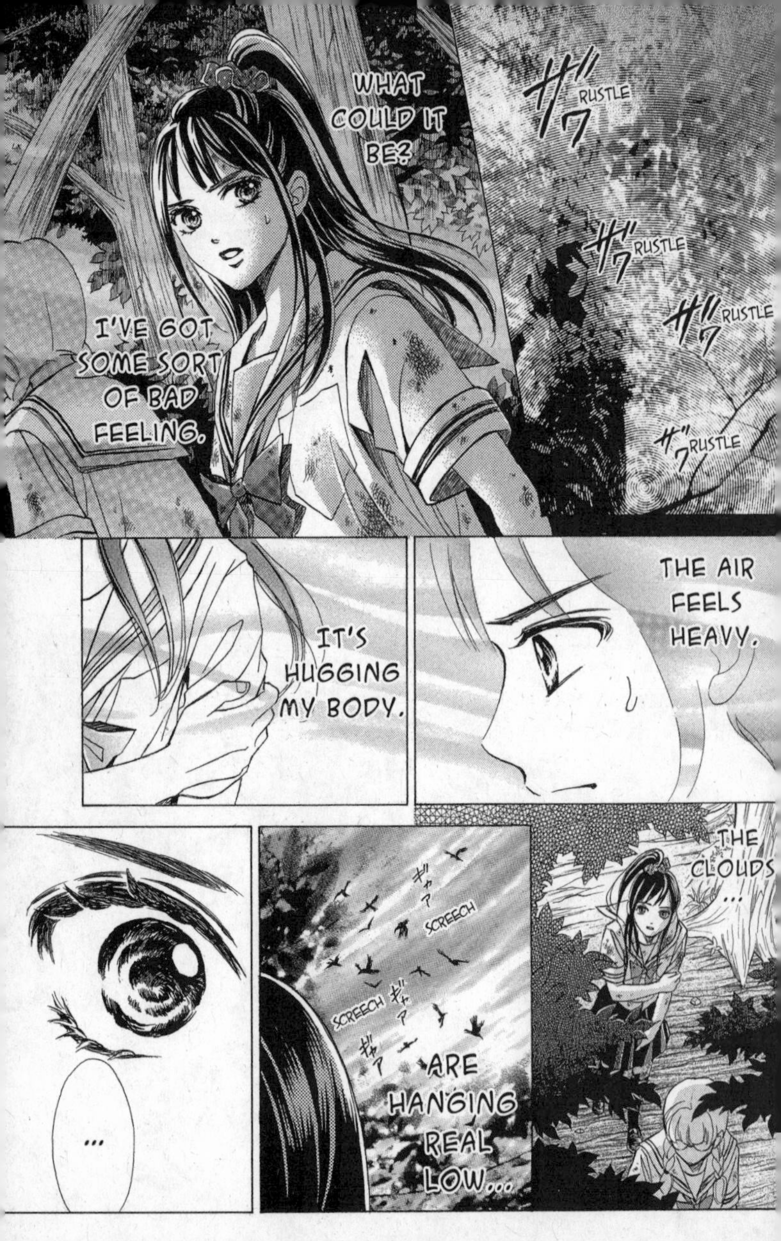
ザワ RUSTLE
ザワ RUSTLE
ザワ RUSTLE
ザワ RUSTLE
WHAT COULD IT BE?
I'VE GOT SOME SORT OF BAD FEELING.
THE AIR FEELS HEAVY.
IT'S HUGGING MY BODY.
THE CLOUDS...
ギャア SCREECH
ギャア SCREECH
ギャア
ARE HANGING REAL LOW...
...

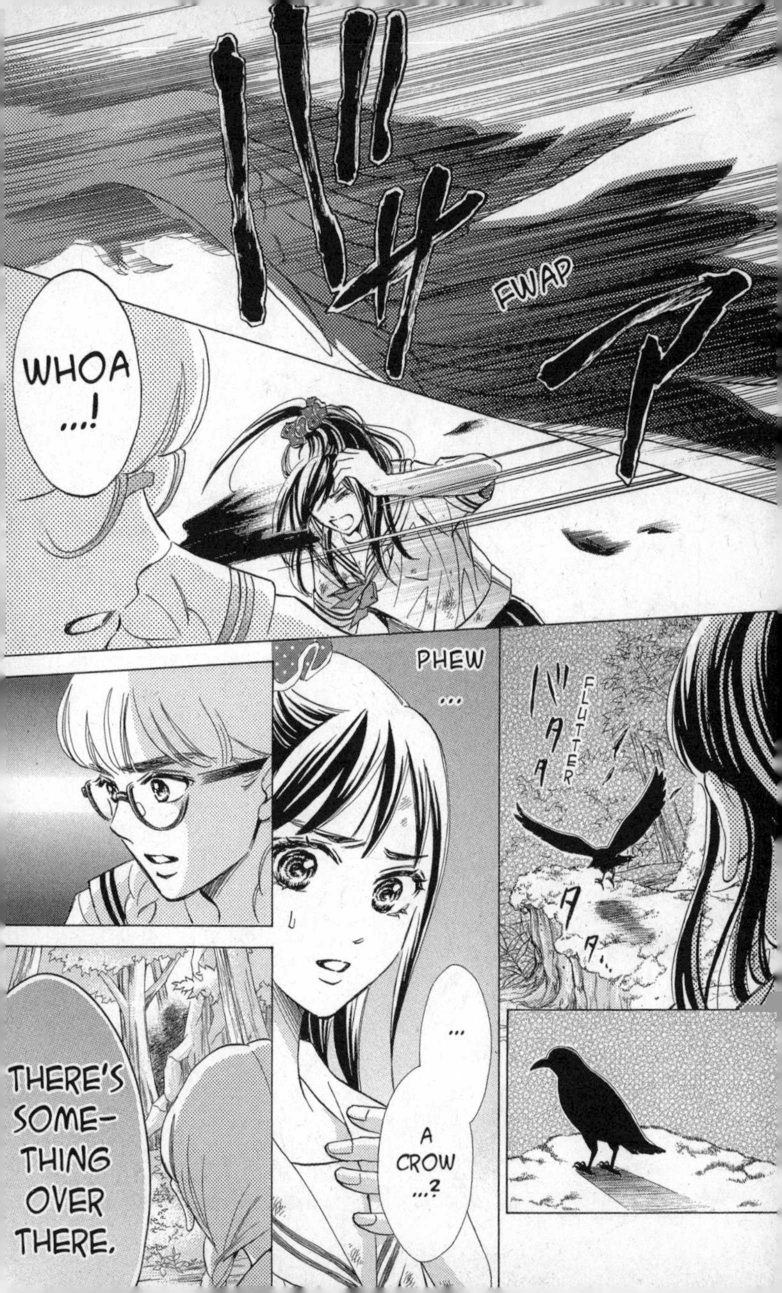
FWAP
WHOA ...!
FLUTTER
PHEW ...
...
A CROW ...?
THERE'S SOME-THING OVER THERE.

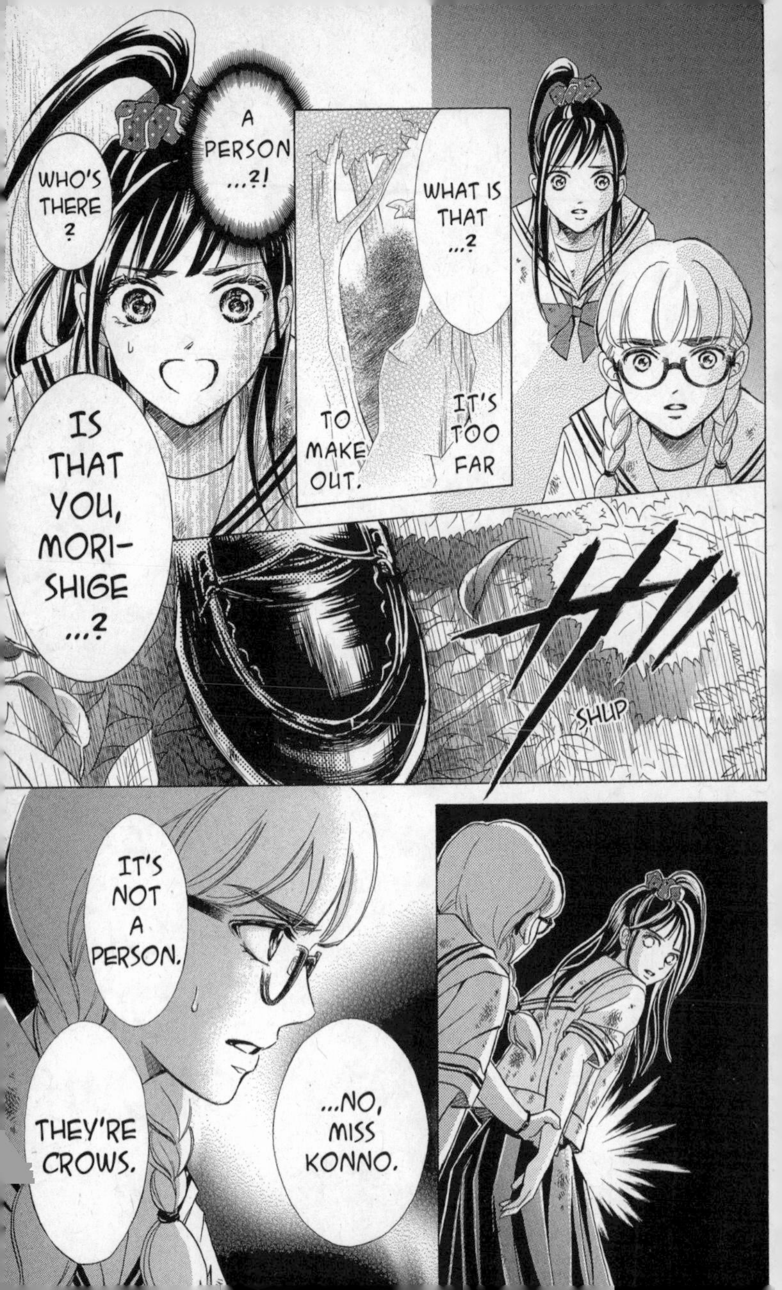
WHAT IS THAT ...?
IT'S TOO FAR
TO MAKE OUT.
A PERSON ...?!
WHO'S THERE?
IS THAT YOU, MORI-SHIGE ...?
SHUP
...NO, MISS KONNO.
IT'S NOT A PERSON.
THEY'RE CROWS.

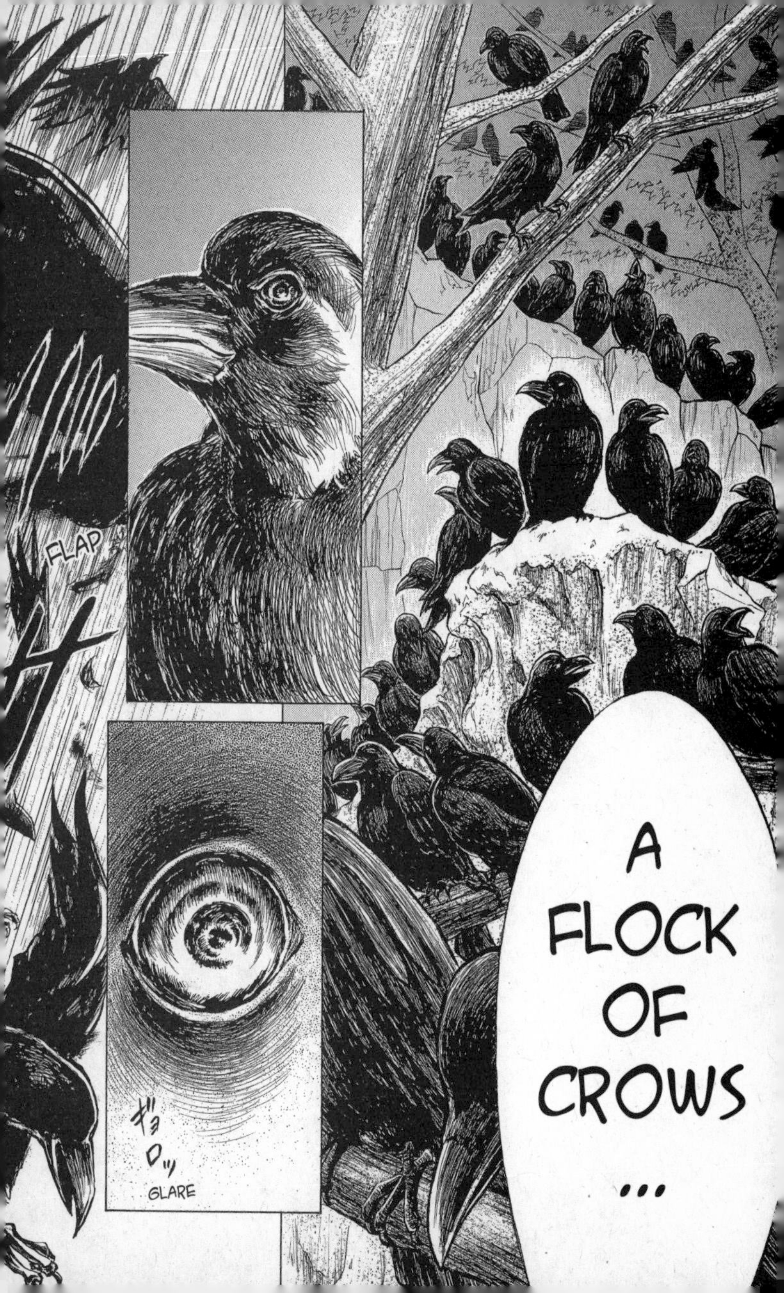
A FLOCK OF CROWS ...
FLAP
ギョロッ
GLARE

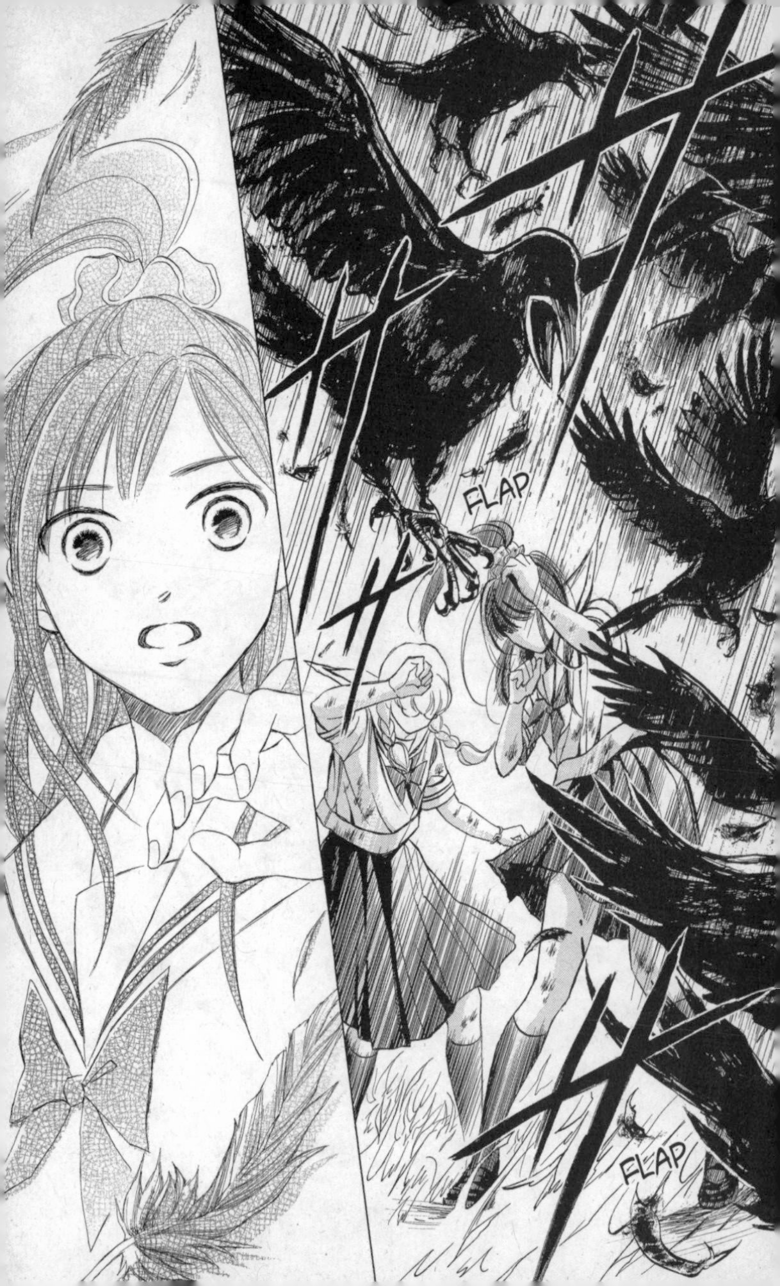
FLAP
FLAP

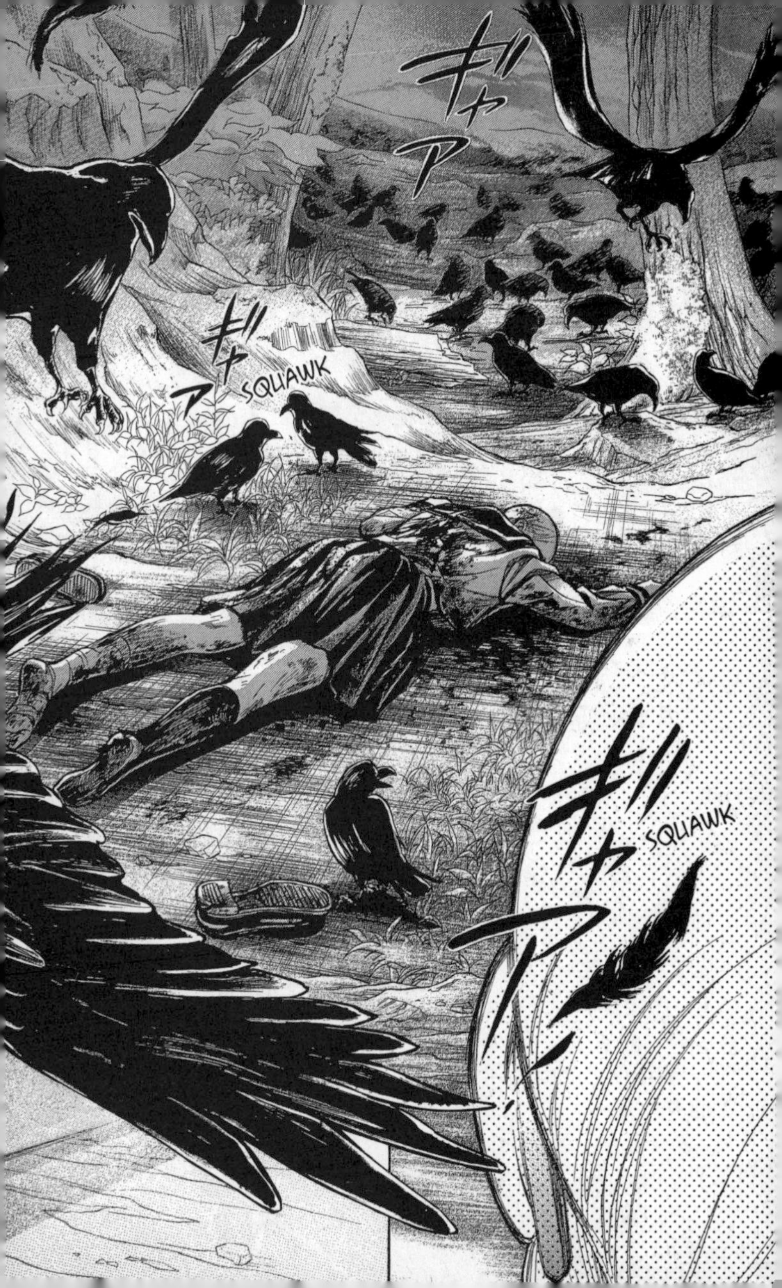
ギャア
ギャア
SQUAWK
ギャア
SQUAWK

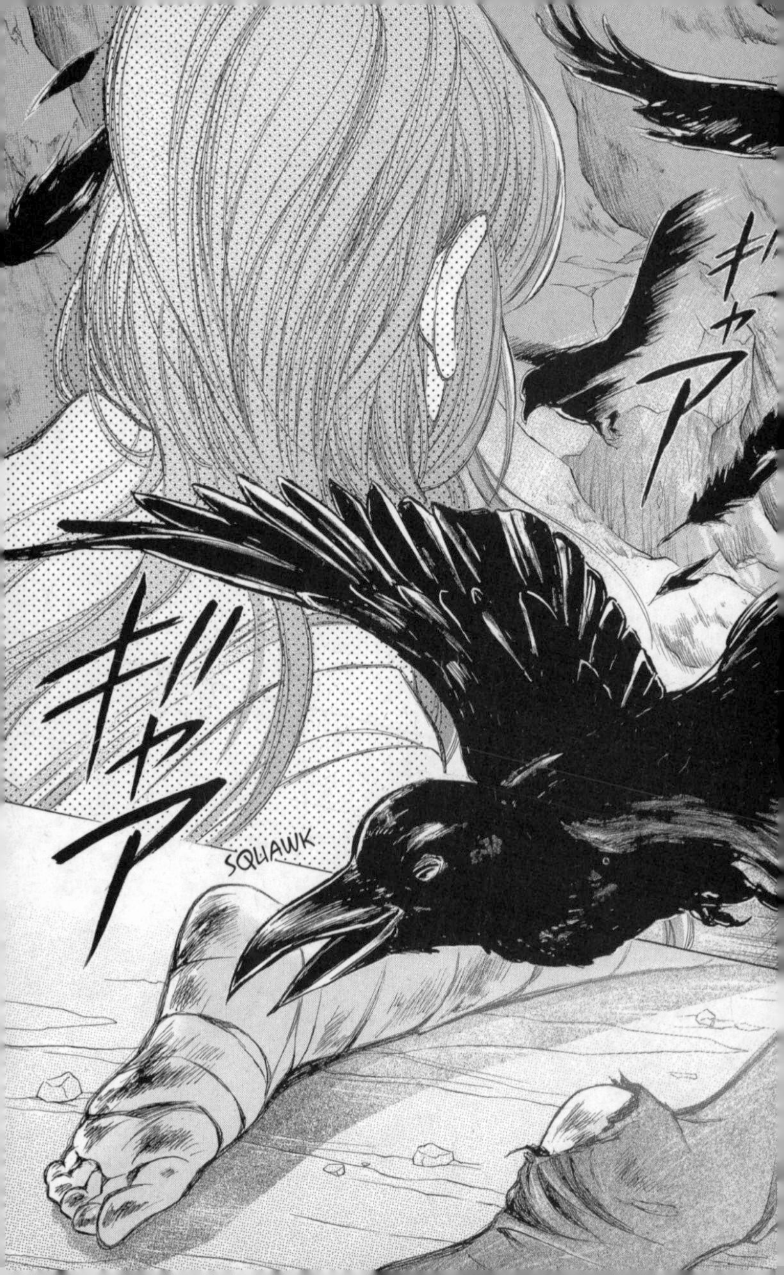
ギャァ
ギャァ
SQUAWK

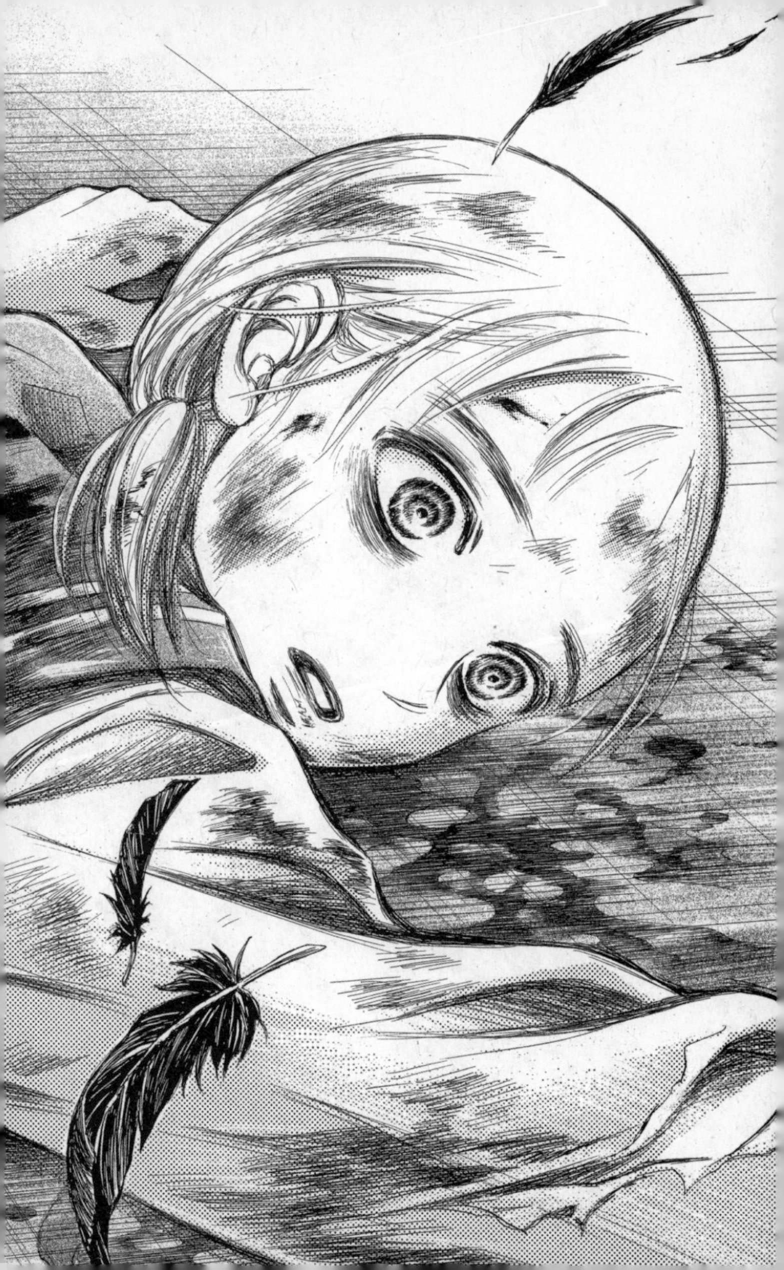

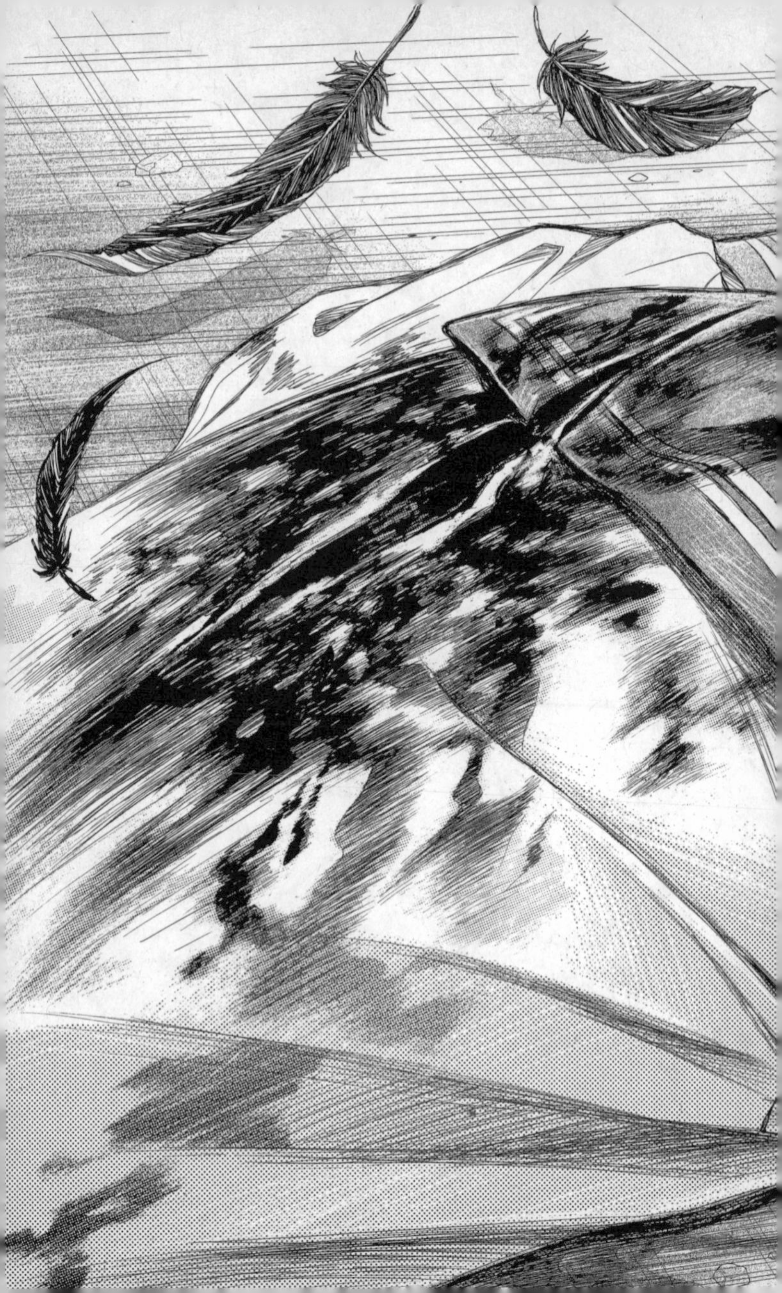

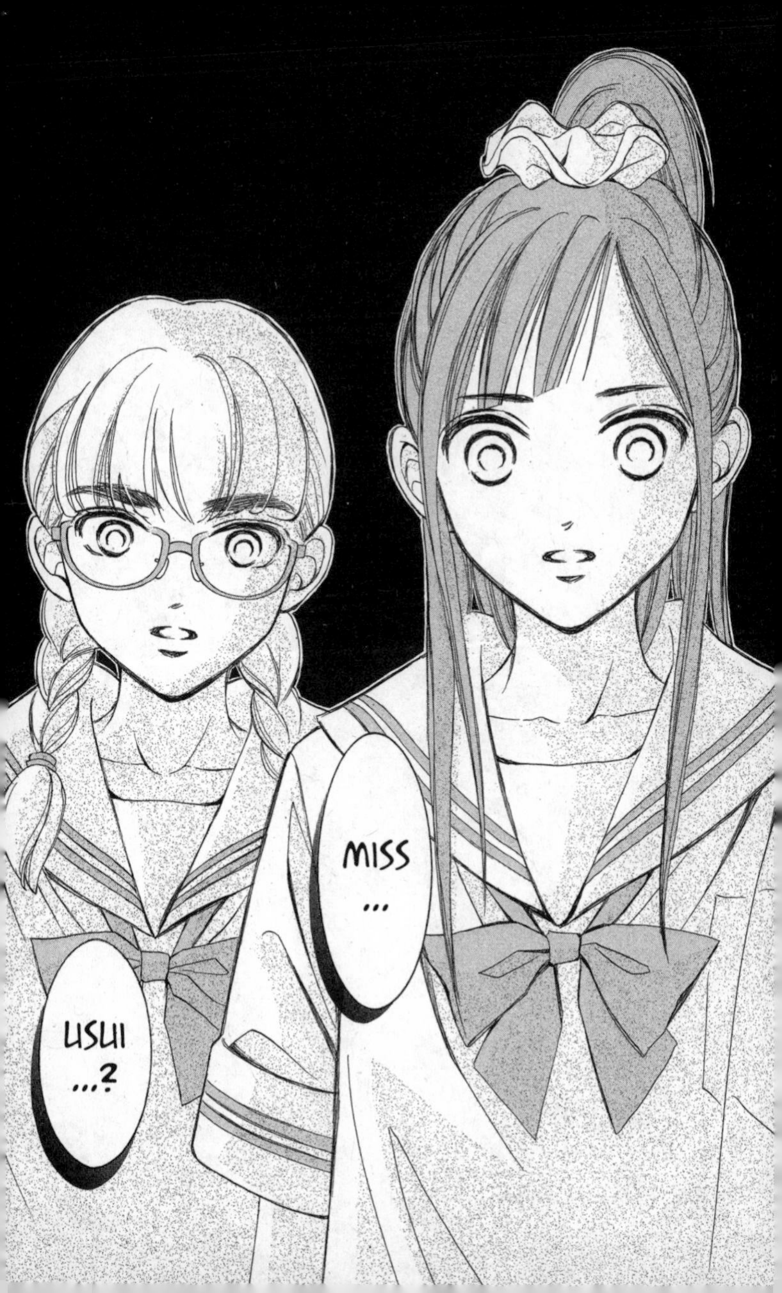
MISS ...
USUI ...?

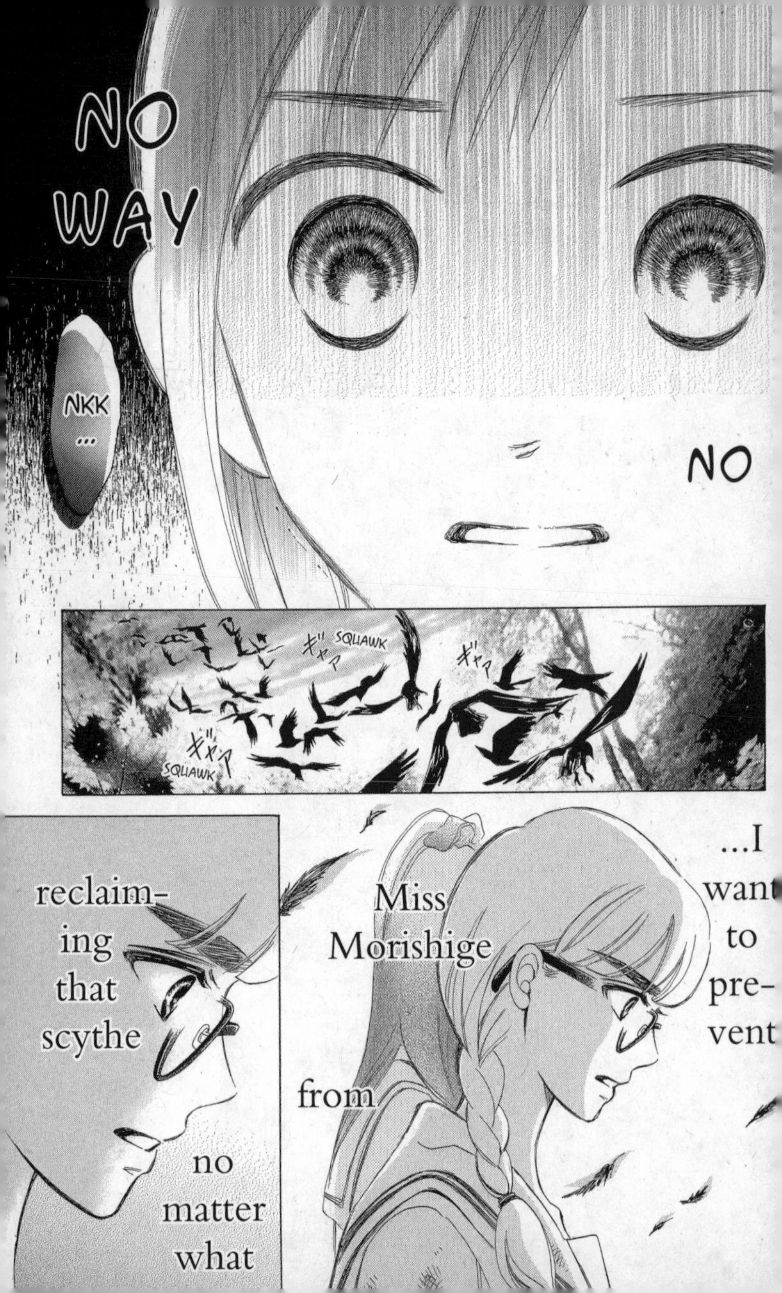
NO
NO WAY
NKK ...
SQUAWK
SQUAWK
...I want to prevent
Miss Morishige
from
reclaiming that scythe
no matter what

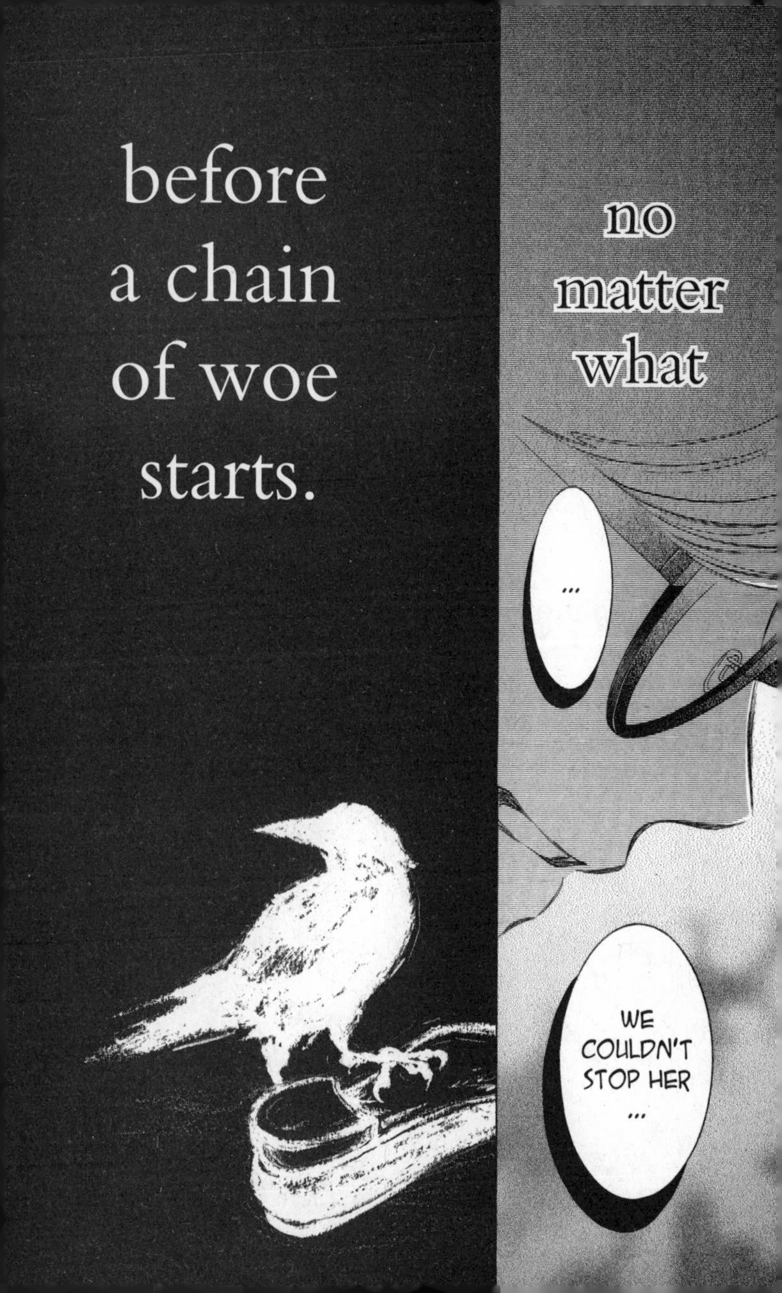

no matter what
...
WE COULDN'T STOP HER ...
before a chain of woe starts.

To be continued...

MY WORKROOM

Thank you very much to everyone who entered the

✧ Autographed Request-Shikishi Lottery ✧

I sketched shikishi for five people who were selected by lottery♥

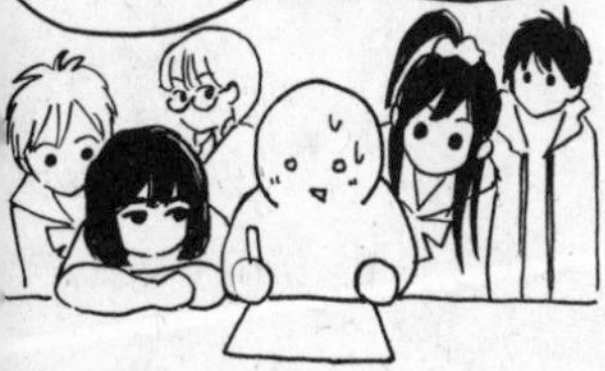

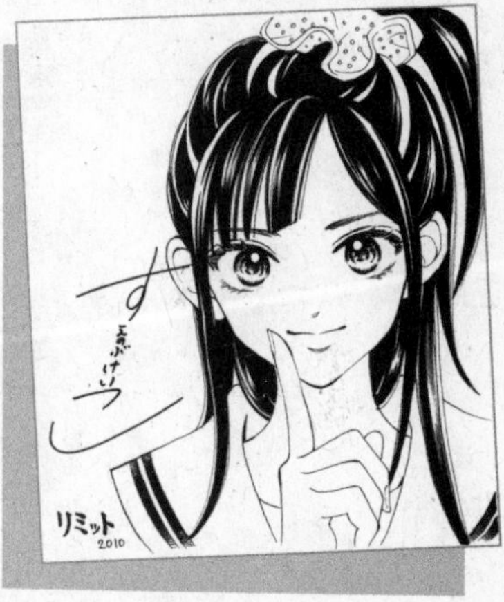
リミット
2010

Drawing on shikishi gives you a different feeling of tension than drawing manga, it made my heart pound.

I received so much encouragement from everyone's passionate messages. I pledge to keep working hard, and hope that there'll be a similar opportunity again some day...

Thank you!!

Please read LIMIT volume 4 as well!

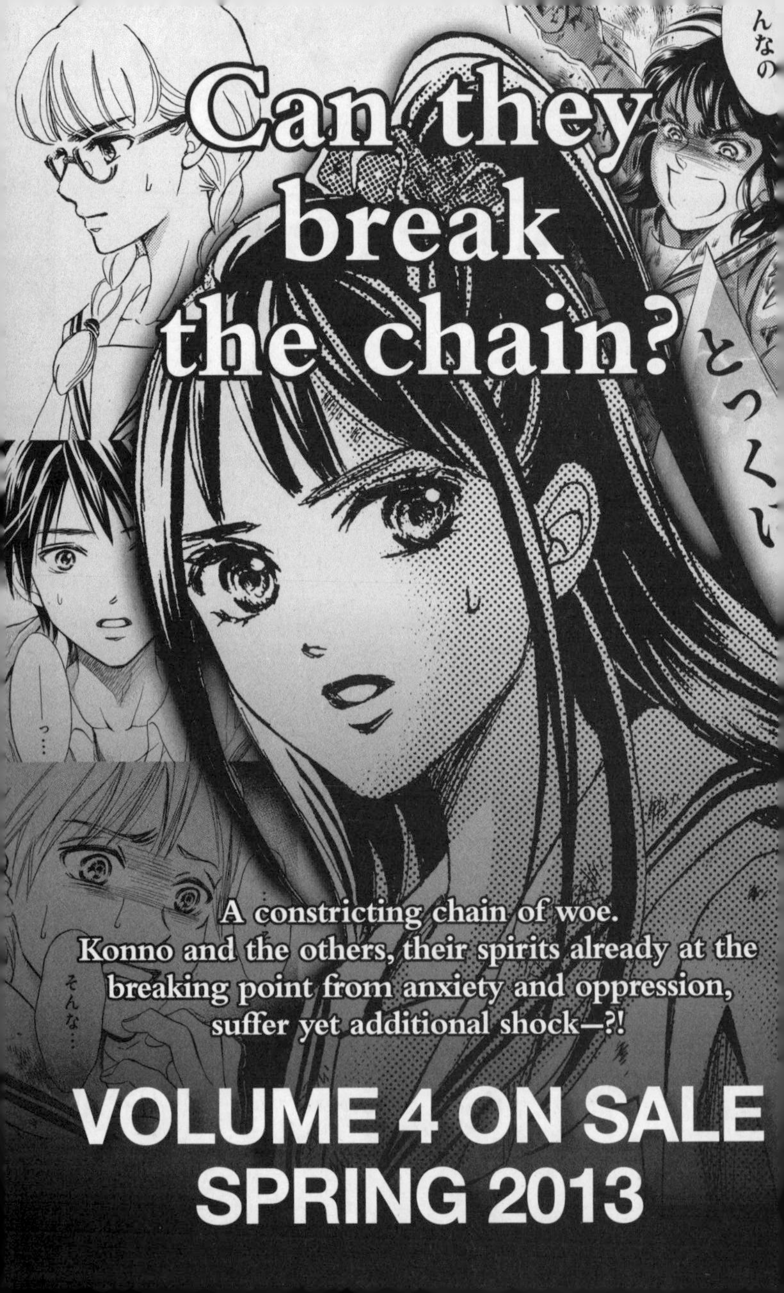
んなの
Can they break the chain?
とっくに
っ…
そんな…
A constricting chain of woe.
Konno and the others, their spirits already at the breaking point from anxiety and oppression, suffer yet additional shock—?!
VOLUME 4 ON SALE
SPRING 2013

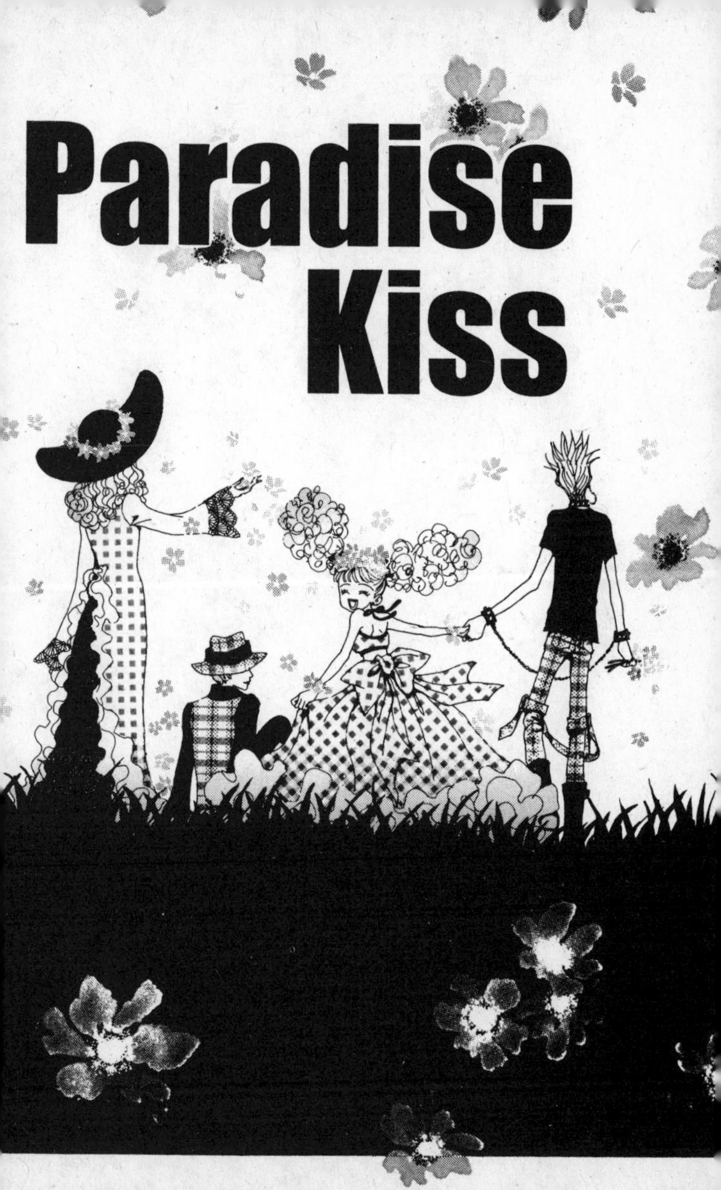
Paradise
Kiss

LIMIT

Limit: Volume 3

Translation: Mari Morimoto

Production: Hiroko Mizuno
           Taylor Esposito
           Nicole Dochych
           Daniela Yamada

First published in Japan in 2010 by Kodansha, Ltd., Tokyo
Publication for this English edition arranged through Kodansha, Ltd., Tokyo
English language version produced by Vertical, Inc.

Translation provided by Vertical, Inc., 2013
Published by Vertical, Inc., New York

Originally published in Japanese as *Limit 3* by Kodansha, Ltd.
Limit first serialized in *Bessatsu Friend*, Kodansha, Ltd., 2009-2011

This is a work of fiction.

ISBN: 978-1-935654-60-5

Manufactured in the United States of America

First Edition

Vertical, Inc.
451 Park Avenue South
7th Floor
New York, NY 10016
www.vertical-inc.com